STARLIGHT

Treasures Lost, Treasures Found

and

Local Hero

ANTHOLOGIES

From the Heart • *A Little Magic* • *A Little Fate*

Moon Shadows
(with Jill Gregory, Ruth Ryan Langan, and Marianne Willman)

The Once Upon Series
(with Jill Gregory, Ruth Ryan Langan, and Marianne Willman)
Once Upon a Castle • *Once Upon a Star* • *Once Upon a
Dream* • *Once Upon a Rose* • *Once Upon a Kiss* • *Once Upon
a Midnight*

Silent Night
(with Susan Plunkett, Dee Holmes, and Claire Cross)

Out of This World
(with Laurell K. Hamilton, Susan Krinard, and Maggie Shayne)

Bump in the Night
(with Mary Blayney, Ruth Ryan Langan, and Mary Kay McComas)

Dead of Night
(with Mary Blayney, Ruth Ryan Langan, and Mary Kay McComas)

Three in Death

Suite 606
(with Mary Blayney, Ruth Ryan Langan, and Mary Kay McComas)

In Death

The Lost
(with Patricia Gaffney, Ruth Ryan Langan, and Mary Blayney)

The Other Side
(with Mary Blayney, Patricia Gaffney, Ruth Ryan Langan,
and Mary Kay McComas)

Time of Death

The Unquiet
(with Mary Blayney, Patricia Gaffney, Ruth Ryan Langan,
and Mary Kay McComas)

Mirror, Mirror
(with Mary Blayney, Elaine Fox, Mary Kay McComas, and
R. C. Ryan)

Down the Rabbit Hole
(with Mary Blayney, Elaine Fox, Mary Kay McComas, and
R. C. Ryan)

ALSO AVAILABLE . . .

The Official Nora Roberts Companion
(edited by Denise Little and Laura Hayden)

STARLIGHT

Treasures Lost, Treasures Found

and

Local Hero

TWO NOVELS IN ONE

NORA ROBERTS

St. Martin's Paperbacks

Published in the United States by St. Martin's Paperbacks, an imprint of St. Martin's Publishing Group.

STARLIGHT: TREASURES LOST, TREASURES FOUND copyright © 1986 by Nora Roberts and LOCAL HERO copyright © 1987 by Nora Roberts.

For information, address St. Martin's Publishing Group, 120 Broadway, New York, NY 10271.

www.stmartins.com

ISBN: 978-1-250-89008-5

Our books may be purchased in bulk for promotional, educational, or business use. Please contact your local bookseller or the Macmillan Corporate and Premium Sales Department at 1-800-221-7945, ext. 5442, or by email at MacmillanSpecialMarkets@macmillan.com.

Printed in the United States of America

St. Martin's Paperbacks edition / July 2023

10 9 8 7 6 5 4 3 2 1

Treasures Lost, Treasures Found

CHAPTER 1

He had believed in it. Edwin J. Hardesty hadn't been the kind of man who had fantasies or followed dreams, but sometime during his quiet, literary life he had looked for a pot of gold. From the information in the reams of notes, the careful charts and the dog-eared research books, he thought he'd found it.

In the paneled study, a single light shot a beam across a durable oak desk. The light fell over a hand—narrow, slender, without the affectation of rings or polish. Yet even bare, it remained an essentially feminine hand, the kind that could be pictured holding a porcelain cup or waving a feather fan. It was a surprisingly elegant hand for a woman who didn't consider herself elegant, delicate or particularly feminine. Kathleen Hardesty was, as her father had been, and as he'd directed her to be, a dedicated educator.

Minds were her concern—the expanding and the fulfilling of them. This included her own as well as every one of her students'. For as long as she could remember, her father had impressed upon her the importance of education. He'd stressed the priority of it over every other aspect of life. Education was the cohesiveness that held civilization together.

She grew up surrounded by the dusty smell of books and the quiet, placid tone of patient instruction.

She'd been expected to excel in school, and she had. She'd been expected to follow her father's path into education. At twenty-eight, Kate was just finishing her first year at Yale as an assistant professor of English literature.

In the dim light of the quiet study, she looked the part. Her light brown hair was tidily secured at the nape of her neck with all the pins neatly tucked in. Her practical tortoiseshell reading glasses seemed dark against her milk-pale complexion. Her high cheekbones gave her face an almost haughty look that was often dispelled by her warm, doe-brown eyes.

Though her jacket was draped over the back of her chair, the white blouse she wore was still crisp. Her cuffs were turned back to reveal delicate wrists and a slim Swiss watch on her left arm. Her earrings were tasteful gold studs given to Kate by her father on her twenty-first birthday, the only truly personal gift she could ever remember receiving from him.

Seven long years later, one short week after her father's funeral, Kate sat at his desk. The room still carried the scent of his cologne and a hint of the pipe tobacco he'd only smoked in that room.

She'd finally found the courage to go through his papers.

She hadn't known he was ill. In his early sixties, Hardesty had looked robust and strong. He hadn't told his daughter about his visits to the doctor, his checkups, ECG results or the little pills he carried with him everywhere. She'd found his pills in his inside pocket after his fatal heart attack. Kate hadn't known his heart was weak because Hardesty never shared his shortcomings with anyone. She hadn't known about the charts and research papers in his desk; he'd never shared his dreams either.

Now that she was aware of both, Kate wasn't certain she

ever really knew the man who'd raised her. The memory of her mother was dim; that was to be expected after more than twenty years. Her father had been alive just a week before.

Leaning back for a moment, she pushed her glasses up and rubbed the bridge of her nose between her thumb and forefinger. She tried, with only the desk lamp between herself and the dark, to think of her father in precise terms.

Physically, he'd been a tall, big man with a full head of steel-gray hair and a patient face. He had favored dark suits and white shirts. The only vanity she could remember had been his weekly manicures. But it wasn't a physical picture Kate struggled with now. As a father . . .

He was never unkind. In all her memories, Kate couldn't remember her father ever raising his voice to her, ever striking her. He never had to, she thought with a sigh. All he had to do was express disappointment, disapproval, and that was enough.

He had been brilliant, tireless, dedicated. But all of that had been directed toward his vocation. As a father, Kate reflected . . . He'd never been unkind. That was all that would come to her, and because of it she felt a fresh wave of guilt and grief.

She hadn't disappointed him, that much she could cling to. He had told her so himself, in just those words, when she was accepted by the English Department at Yale. Nor had he expected her ever to disappoint him. Kate knew, though it had never been discussed, that her father wanted her to become head of the English Department within ten years. That had been the extent of his dream for her.

Had he ever realized just how much she'd loved him? She wondered as she shut her eyes, tired now from the hours of reading her father's handwriting. Had he ever known just how desperately she'd wanted to please him? If he'd just once said he was proud . . .

In the end, she hadn't had those few intense last moments with her father one reads about in books or sees in the movies. When she'd arrived at the hospital, he was already gone. There'd been no time for words. No time for tears.

Now she was on her own in the tidy Cape Cod house she'd shared with him for so long. The housekeeper would still come on Wednesday mornings, and the gardener would come on Saturdays to cut the grass. She alone would have to deal with the paperwork, the sorting, the shifting, the clearing out.

That could be done. Kate leaned back farther in her father's worn leather chair. It could be done because all of those things were practical matters. She dealt easily with the practical. But what about these papers she'd found? What would she do about the carefully drawn charts, the notebooks filled with information, directions, history, theory? In part, because she was raised to be logical, she considered filing them neatly away.

But there was another part, the part that enabled one to lose oneself in fantasies, in dreams, in the "perhapses" of life. This was the part that allowed Kate to lose herself totally in the possibilities of the written word, in the wonders of a book. The papers on her father's desk beckoned her.

He'd believed in it. She bent over the papers again. He'd believed in it or he never would have wasted his time documenting, searching, theorizing. She would never be able to discuss it with him. Yet, in a way, wasn't he telling her about it through his words?

Treasure. Sunken treasure. The stuff of fiction and Hollywood movies. Judging by the stack of papers and notebooks on his desk, Hardesty must have spent months, perhaps years, compiling information on the location of an English merchant ship lost off the coast of North Carolina two centuries before.

It brought Kate an immediate picture of Edward Teach— Blackbeard, the bloodthirsty pirate with the crazed superstitions and reign of terror. The stuff of romances, she thought. Of romance . . .

Ocracoke Island. The memory was sharp, sweet and painful. Kate had blocked out everything that had happened that summer four years before. Everything and everyone. Now, if she was to make a rational decision about what was to be done, she had to think of those long, lazy months on the remote Outer Banks of North Carolina.

She'd begun work on her doctorate. It had been a surprise when her father had announced that he planned to spend the summer on Ocracoke and invited her to accompany him. Of course, she'd gone, taking her portable typewriter, boxes of books, reams of paper. She hadn't expected to be seduced by white sand beaches and the call of gulls. She hadn't expected to fall desperately and insensibly in love.

Insensibly, Kate repeated to herself, as if in defense. She'd have to remember that was the most apt adjective. There'd been nothing sensible about her feelings for Ky Silver.

Even the name, she mused, was unique, unconventional, flashy. They'd been as suitable for each other as a peacock and a wren. Yet that hadn't stopped her from losing her head, her heart and her innocence during that balmy, magic summer.

She could still see him at the helm of the boat her father had rented, steering into the wind, laughing, dark hair flowing wildly. She could still remember that heady, weightless feeling when they'd gone scuba diving in the warm coastal waters. Kate had been too caught up in what was happening to herself to think about her father's sudden interest in boating and diving.

She'd been too swept away by her own feelings of astonishment that a man like Ky Silver should be attracted to someone like her to notice her father's preoccupation with currents and tides. There'd been too much excitement for her to realize that her father never bothered with fishing rods like the other vacationers.

But now her youthful fancies were behind her, Kate told herself. Now, she could clearly remember how many hours her father had closeted himself in his hotel room, reading book after book that he brought with him from the mainland library. He'd been researching even then. She was sure he'd continued that research in the following summers when she had refused to go back. Refused to go back, Kate remembered, because of Ky Silver.

Ky had asked her to believe in fairy tales. He asked her to give him the impossible. When she refused, frightened, he shrugged and walked away without a second look. She had never gone back to the white sand and gulls since then.

Kate looked down again at her father's papers. She had to go back now—go back and finish what her father had started. Perhaps, more than the house, the trust fund, the antique jewelry that had been her mother's, this was her father's legacy to her. If she filed those papers neatly away, they'd haunt her for the rest of her life.

She had to go back, Kate reaffirmed as she took off her glasses and folded them neatly on the blotter. And it was Ky Silver she'd have to go to. Her father's aspirations had drawn her away from Ky once; now, four years later, they were drawing her back.

But Dr. Kathleen Hardesty knew the difference between fairy tales and reality. Reaching in her father's desk drawer, she drew out a sheet of thick creamy stationery and began to write.

* * *

Ky let the wind buffet him as he opened the throttle. He liked speed in much the same way he liked a lazy afternoon in the hammock. They were two of the things that made life worthwhile. He was used to the smell of salt spray, but he still inhaled deeply. He was well accustomed to the vibration of the deck under his feet, but he still felt it. He wasn't a man to let anything go unnoticed or unappreciated.

He grew up in this quiet, remote little coastal town, and though he'd traveled and intended to travel more, he didn't plan to live anywhere else. It suited him—the freedom of the sea, and the coziness of a small community.

He didn't resent the tourists because he knew they helped keep the village alive, but he preferred the island in winter. Then the storms blew wild and cold, and only the hearty would brave the ferry across Hatteras Inlet.

He fished, but unlike the majority of his neighbors, he rarely sold what he caught. What he pulled out of the sea, he ate. He dove, occasionally collecting shells, but again, this was for his own pleasure. Often he took tourists out on his boat to fish or to scuba dive, because there were times he enjoyed the company. But there were afternoons, like this sparkling one, when he simply wanted the sea to himself.

He had always been restless. His mother had said that he came into the world two weeks early because he grew impatient waiting. Ky turned thirty-two that spring, but was far from settled. He knew what he wanted—to live as he chose. The trouble was that he wasn't certain just what he wanted to choose.

At the moment, he chose the open sky and the endless sea. There were other moments when he knew that that wouldn't be enough.

But the sun was hot, the breeze cool and the shoreline was drawing near. The boat's motor was purring smoothly and in the small cooler was a tidy catch of fish he'd cook up for his supper that night. On a crystal, sparkling afternoon, perhaps it was enough.

From the shore he looked like a pirate might if there were pirates in the twentieth century. His hair was long enough to curl over his ears and well over the collar of a shirt had he worn one. It was black, a rich, true black that might have come from his Arapaho or Sicilian blood. His eyes were the deep, dark green of the sea on a cloudy day. His skin was bronzed from years in the sun, taut from the years of swimming and pulling in nets. His bone structure was also part of his heritage, sculpted, hard, defined.

When he smiled as he did now, racing the wind to shore, his face took on that reckless freedom women found irresistible. When he didn't smile, his eyes could turn as cold as a lion's before a leap. He discovered long ago that women found that equally irresistible.

Ky drew back on the throttle so that the boat slowed, rocked, then glided into its slip in Silver Lake Harbor. With the quick, efficient movements of one born to the sea, he leaped onto the dock to secure the lines.

"Catch anything?"

Ky straightened and turned. He smiled, but absently, as one does at a brother seen almost every day of one's life. "Enough. Things slow at the Roost?"

Marsh smiled, and there was a brief flicker of family resemblance, but his eyes were a calm light brown and his hair was carefully styled. "Worried about your investment?"

Ky gave a half-shrug. "With you running things?"

Marsh didn't comment. They knew each other as intimately as men ever know each other. One was restless, the other calm. The opposition never seemed to matter. "Linda wants you to come up for dinner. She worries about you."

She would, Ky thought, amused. His sister-in-law loved to mother and fuss, even though she was five years younger than Ky. That was one of the reasons the restaurant she ran with Marsh was such a success—that, plus Marsh's business sense and the hefty investment and shrewd renovations Ky had made. Ky left the managing up to his brother and his sister-in-law. He didn't mind owning a restaurant, even keeping half an eye on the profit and loss, but he certainly had no interest in running one.

After the lines were secure, he wiped his palms down the hips of his cut-offs. "What's the special tonight?"

Marsh dipped his hands into his front pockets and rocked back on his heels. "Bluefish."

Grinning, Ky tossed back the lid of his cooler revealing his catch. "Tell Linda not to worry. I'll eat."

"That's not going to satisfy her." Marsh glanced at his brother as Ky looked out to sea. "She thinks you're alone too much."

"You're only alone too much if you don't like being alone." Ky glanced back over his shoulder. He didn't want to debate now, when the exhilaration of the speed and the sea were still upon him. But he'd never been a man to placate. "Maybe you two should think about having another baby, then Linda would be too busy to worry about big brothers."

"Give me a break. Hope's only eighteen months old."

"You've got to add nine to that," Ky reminded him carelessly. He was fond of his niece, despite—no, because she was a demon. "Anyway, it looks like the family lineage is in your hands."

"Yeah." Marsh shifted his feet, cleared his throat and fell silent. It was a habit he'd carried since childhood, one that could annoy or amuse Ky depending on his mood. At the moment, it was only mildly distracting.

Something was in the air. He could smell it, but he couldn't quite identify it. A storm brewing, he wondered? One of those hot, patient storms that seemed capable of brewing for weeks. He was certain he could smell it.

"Why don't you tell me what else is on your mind?" Ky suggested. "I want to get back to the house and clean these."

"You had a letter. It was put in our box by mistake."

It was a common enough occurrence, but by his brother's expression Ky knew there was more. His sense of an impending storm grew sharper. Saying nothing, he held out his hand.

"Ky . . ." Marsh began. There was nothing he could say, just as there'd been nothing to say four years before. Reaching in his back pocket, he drew out the letter.

The envelope was made from heavy cream-colored paper. Ky didn't have to look at the return address. The handwriting and the memories it brought leaped out at him. For a moment, he felt his breath catch in his lungs as it might if someone had caught him with a blow to the solar plexus. Deliberately, he expelled it. "Thanks," he said, as if it meant nothing. He stuck the letter in his pocket before he picked up his cooler and gear.

"Ky—" Again Marsh broke off. His brother had turned his head, and the cool, half-impatient stare said very clearly—back off. "If you change your mind about dinner," Marsh said.

"I'll let you know." Ky went down the length of the dock without looking back.

He was grateful he hadn't bothered to bring his car down to the harbor. He needed to walk. He needed the fresh air and the exercise to keep his mind clear while he remembered what he didn't want to remember. What he never really forgot.

Kate. Four years ago she'd walked out of his life with the same sort of cool precision with which she'd walked into it.

She had reminded him of a Victorian doll—a little prim, a little aloof. He'd never had much patience with neatly folded hands or haughty manners, yet almost from the first instant he'd wanted her.

At first, he thought it was the fact that she was so different. A challenge—something for Ky Silver to conquer. He enjoyed teaching her to dive, and watching the precise step-by-step way she learned. It hadn't been any hardship to look at her in a snug scuba suit, although she didn't have voluptuous curves. She had a trim, neat, almost boylike figure and what seemed like yards of thick, soft hair.

He could still remember the first time she took it down from its pristine knot. It left him breathless, hurting, fascinated. Ky would have touched it—touched her then and there if her father hadn't been standing beside her. But if a man was clever, if a man was determined, he could find a way to be alone with a woman.

Ky had found ways. Kate had taken to diving as though she'd been born to it. While her father had buried himself in his books, Ky had taken Kate out on the water—under the water, to the silent, dreamlike world that had attracted her just as it had always attracted him.

He could remember the first time he kissed her. They had been wet and cool from a dive, standing on the deck of his boat. He was able to see the lighthouse behind her and the vague line of the coast. Her hair had flowed down her back, sleek from the water, dripping with it. He'd reached out and gathered it in his hand.

"What are you doing?"

Four years later, he could hear that low, cultured, eastern voice, the curiosity in it. It took no effort for him to see the curiosity that had been in her eyes.

"I'm going to kiss you."

The curiosity had remained in her eyes, fascinating him. "Why?"

"Because I want to."

It was as simple as that for him. He wanted to. Her body had stiffened as he'd drawn her against him. When her lips parted in protest, he closed his over them. In the time it takes a heart to beat, the rigidity had melted from her body. She'd kissed him with all the young, stored-up passion that had been in her—passion mixed with innocence. He was experienced enough to recognize her innocence, and that too had fascinated him. Ky had, foolishly, youthfully and completely, fallen in love.

Kate had remained an enigma to him, though they shared impassioned hours of laughter and long, lazy talks. He admired her thirst for learning, and she had a predilection for putting knowledge into neat slots that baffled him. She was enthusiastic about diving, but it hadn't been enough for her simply to be able to swim freely underwater, taking her air from tanks. She had to know how the tanks worked, why they were fashioned a certain way. Ky watched her absorb what he told her, and knew she'd retain it.

They had taken walks along the shoreline at night and she had recited poetry from memory. Beautiful words, Byron, Shelley, Keats. And he, who'd never been overly impressed by such things, had eaten it up because her voice had made the words somehow personal. Then she'd begin to talk about syntax, iambic pentameters, and Ky would find new ways to divert her.

For three months, he did little but think of her. For the first time, Ky had considered changing his lifestyle. His little cottage near the beach needed work. It needed furniture. Kate would need more than milk crates and the hammock that had been his style. Because he'd been young and had never been in love before, Ky had taken his own plans for granted.

She'd walked out on him. She'd had her own plans, and he hadn't been part of them.

Her father came back to the island the following summer, and every summer thereafter. Kate never came back. Ky knew she had completed her doctorate and was teaching in a prestigious ivy league school where her father was all but a cornerstone. She had what she wanted. So, he told himself as he swung open the screen door of his cottage, did he. He went where he wanted, when he wanted. He called his own shots. His responsibilities extended only as far as he chose to extend them. To his way of thinking, that itself was a mark of success.

Setting the cooler on the kitchen floor, Ky opened the refrigerator. He twisted the top off a beer and drank half of it in one icy cold swallow. It washed some of the bitterness out of his mouth.

Calm now, and curious, he pulled the letter out of his pocket. Ripping it open, he drew out the single neatly written sheet.

Dear Ky,

You may or may not be aware that my father suffered a fatal heart attack two weeks ago. It was very sudden, and I'm currently trying to tie up the many details this involves.

In going through my father's papers, I find that he had again made arrangements to come to the island this summer, and engage your services. I now find it necessary to take his place. For reasons which I'd rather explain in person, I need your help. You have my father's deposit. When I arrive in Ocracoke on the fifteenth, we can discuss terms.

If possible, contact me at the hotel, or leave a message. I hope we'll be able to come to a mutually

agreeable arrangement. Please give my best to Marsh.
Perhaps I'll see him during my stay.

Best,
Kathleen Hardesty

* * *

So the old man was dead. Ky set down the letter and lifted
his beer again. He couldn't say he'd had any liking for Edwin Hardesty. Kate's father had been a stringent, humorless
man. Still, he hadn't disliked him. Ky had, in an odd way,
gotten used to his company over the past few summers. But
this summer, it would be Kate.

Ky glanced at the letter again, then jogged his memory
until he remembered the date. Two days, he mused. She'd
be there in two days . . . to discuss terms. A smile played
around the corners of his mouth but it didn't have anything
to do with humor. They'd discuss terms, he agreed silently as
he scanned Kate's letter again.

She wanted to take her father's place. Ky wondered if she'd
realized, when she wrote that, just how ironic it was. Kathleen Hardesty had been obediently dogging her father's foot-
steps all her life. Why should that change after his death?

Had she changed? Ky wondered briefly. Would that fascinating aura of innocence and aloofness still cling to
her? Or perhaps that had faded with the years. Would that
rather sweet primness have developed into a rigidity? He'd
see for himself in a couple of days, he realized, but tossed
the letter onto the counter rather than into the trash.

So, she wanted to engage his services, he mused. Leaning both hands on either side of the sink, he looked out the
window in the direction of the water he could smell, but not
quite see. She wanted a business arrangement—the rental of

his boat, his gear and his time. He felt the bitterness well up and swallowed it as cleanly as he had the beer. She'd have her business arrangement. And she'd pay. He'd see to that.

Ky left the kitchen with his catch still in the cooler. The appetite he'd worked up with salt spray and speed had vanished.

*   *   *

Kate pulled her car onto the ferry to Ocracoke and set the brake. The morning was cool and very clear. Even so, she was tempted to simply lean her head back and close her eyes. She wasn't certain what impulse had pushed her to drive from Connecticut rather than fly, but now that she'd all but reached her destination, she was too weary to analyze.

In the bucket seat beside her was her briefcase, and inside, all the papers she'd collected from her father's desk. Perhaps once she was in the hotel on the island, she could go through them again, understand them better. Perhaps the feeling that she was doing the right thing would come back. Over the past few days she'd lost that sense.

The closer she came to the island, the more she began to think she was making a mistake. Not to the island, Kate corrected ruthlessly—the closer she came to Ky. It was a fact, and Kate knew it was imperative to face facts so that they could be dealt with logically.

She had a little time left, a little time to calm the feelings that had somehow gotten stirred up during the drive south. It was foolish, and somehow it helped Kate to remind herself of that. She wasn't a woman returning to a lover, but a woman hoping to engage a diver in a very specific venture. Past personal feelings wouldn't enter into it because they were just that. Past.

The Kate Hardesty who'd arrived on Ocracoke four years

ago had little to do with the Dr. Kathleen Hardesty who was going there now. She wasn't young, inexperienced or impressionable. Those reckless, wild traits of Ky's wouldn't appeal to her now. They wouldn't frighten her. They would be, if Ky agreed to her terms, business partners.

Kate felt the ferry move beneath her as she stared through the windshield. Yes, she thought, unless Ky had changed a great deal, the prospect of diving for treasure would appeal to his sense of adventure.

She knew enough about diving in the technical sense to be sure she'd find no one better equipped for the job. It was always advisable to have the best. More relaxed and less weary, Kate stepped out of her car to stand at the rail. From there she could watch the gulls swoop and the tiny uninhabited islands pass by. She felt a sense of homecoming, but pushed it away. Connecticut was home. Once Kate did what she came for, she'd go back.

The water swirled behind the boat. She couldn't hear it over the motor, but looking down she could watch the wake. One island was nearly imperceptible under a flock of big, brown pelicans. It made her smile, pleased to see the odd, awkward-looking birds again. They passed the long spit of land, where fishermen parked trucks and tried their luck, near the point where bay met sea. She could watch the waves crash and foam where there was no shore, just a turbulent marriage of waters. That was something she hadn't forgotten, though she hadn't seen it since she left the island. Nor had she forgotten just how treacherous the current was along that verge.

Excitement. She breathed deeply before she turned back to her car. The treacherous was always exciting.

When the ferry docked, she had only a short wait before she could drive her car onto the narrow blacktop. The trip to town wouldn't take long, and it wasn't possible to lose your way if you stayed on the one long road. The sea battered on one side, the sound flowed smoothly on the other—both were deep blue in the late morning light.

Her nerves were gone, at least that's what she told herself. It had just been a case of last-minute jitters—very normal. She was prepared to see Ky again, speak to him, work with him if they could agree on the terms.

With the windows down, the soft, moist air blew around her. It was soothing. She'd almost forgotten just how soothing air could be, or the sound of water lapping constantly against sand. It was right to come. When she saw the first faded buildings of the village, she felt a wave of relief. She was here. There was no turning back now.

The hotel where she had stayed that summer with her father was on the sound side of the island. It was small and quiet. If the service was a bit slow by northern standards, the view made up for it.

Kate pulled up in front and turned off the ignition. Self-satisfaction made her sigh. She'd taken the first step and was completely prepared for the next.

Then as she stepped out of the car, she saw him. For an instant, the confident professor of English literature vanished. She was only a woman, vulnerable to her own emotions.

Oh God, he hasn't changed. Not at all. As Ky came closer, she could remember every kiss, every murmur, every crazed storm of their loving. The breeze blew his hair back from his face so that every familiar angle and plane was clear to her. With the sun warm on her skin, bright in her eyes, she felt the years spin back, then forward again. He hadn't changed.

He hadn't expected to see her yet. Somehow he thought she'd arrive that afternoon. Yet he found it necessary to go by the Roost that morning knowing the restaurant was directly across from the hotel where she'd be staying.

She was here, looking neat and a bit too thin in her tailored slacks and blouse. Her hair was pinned up so that the soft femininity of her neck and throat were revealed. Her eyes seemed too dark against her pale skin—skin Ky knew would turn golden slowly under the summer sun.

She looked the same. Soft, prim, calm. Lovely. He ignored the thud in the pit of his stomach as he stepped in front of her. He looked her up and down with the arrogance that was so much a part of him. Then he grinned because he had an overwhelming urge to strangle her.

"Kate. Looks like my timing's good."

She was almost certain she couldn't speak and was therefore determined to speak calmly. "Ky, it's nice to see you again."

"Is it?"

Ignoring the sarcasm, Kate walked around to her trunk and released it. "I'd like to get together with you as soon as possible. There are some things I want to show you, and some business I'd like to discuss."

"Sure, always open for business."

He watched her pull two cases from her trunk, but didn't offer to help. He saw there was no ring on her hand—but it wouldn't have mattered.

"Perhaps we can meet this afternoon then, after I've settled in." The sooner the better, she told herself. They would establish the purpose, the ground rules and the payment. "We could have lunch in the hotel."

"No, thanks," he said easily, leaning against the side of her car while she set her cases down. "You want me, you know where to find me. It's a small island."

With his hands in the pockets of his jeans, he walked away from her. Though she didn't want to, Kate remembered that the last time he'd walked away, they'd stood in almost the same spot.

Picking up her cases, she headed for the hotel, perhaps a bit too quickly.

CHAPTER 2

She knew where to find him. If the island had been double in size, she'd still have known where to find him. Kate acknowledged that Ky hadn't changed. That meant if he wasn't out on his boat, he would be at home, in the small, slightly dilapidated cottage he owned near the beach. Because she felt it would be a strategic error to go after him too soon, she dawdled over her unpacking.

But there were memories even here, where she'd spent one giddy, whirlwind night of love with Ky. It had been the only time they were able to sleep together through the night, embracing each other in the crisp hotel sheets until the first light of dawn crept around the edges of the window shades. She remembered how reckless she'd felt during those few stolen hours, and how dull the morning had seemed because it brought them to an end.

Now she could look out the same window she had stood by then, staring out in the same direction she'd stared out then when she watched Ky walk away. She remembered the sky had been streaked with a rose color before it had brightened to a pure, pale blue.

Then, with her skin still warm from her lover's touch and her mind glazed with lack of sleep and passion, Kate had believed such things could go on forever. But of course they couldn't. She had seen that only weeks later. Passion and reckless nights of loving had to give way to responsibilities, obligations.

Staring out the same window, in the same direction, Kate could feel the sense of loss she'd felt that long ago dawn without the underlying hope that they'd be together again. And again.

They wouldn't be together again, and there'd been no one else since that one heady summer. She had her career, her vocation, her books. She had had her taste of passion.

Turning away, she busied herself by rearranging everything she'd just arranged in her drawers and closet. When she decided she'd stalled in her hotel room long enough, Kate started out. She didn't take her car. She walked, just as she always walked to Ky's home.

She told herself she was over the shock of seeing him again. It was only natural that there be some strain, some discomfort. She was honest enough to admit that it would have been easier if there'd been only strain and discomfort, and not that one sharp quiver of pleasure. Kate acknowledged it, now that it had passed.

No, Ky Silver hadn't changed, she reminded herself. He was still arrogant, self-absorbed and cocky. Those traits might have appealed to her once, but she'd been very young. If she were wise, she could use those same traits to persuade Ky to help her. Yes, those traits, she thought, and the tempting offer of a treasure hunt. Even at her most pessimistic, she couldn't believe Ky would refuse. It was his nature to take chances.

This time she'd be in charge. Kate drew in a deep breath of warm air that tasted of sea. Somehow she felt it would steady her. Ky was going to find she was no longer naive, or susceptible to a few careless words of affection.

With her briefcase in hand, Kate walked through the village. This too was the same, she thought. She was glad of it. The simplicity and solitude still appealed to her. She enjoyed the dozens of little shops, the restaurants and small inns tucked here and there, all somehow using the harbor as a central point, the lighthouse as a landmark. The villagers still made the most of their notorious one-time resident and permanent ghost, Blackbeard. His name or face was lavishly displayed on store signs.

She passed the harbor, unconsciously scanning for Ky's boat. It was there, in the same slip he'd always used—clean lines, scrubbed deck, shining hardware. The flying bridge gleamed in the afternoon light and looked the same as she remembered. Reckless, challenging. The paint was fresh and there was no film of salt spray on the bridge windows. However careless Ky had been about his own appearance or his home, he'd always pampered his boat.

The *Vortex*. Kate studied the flamboyant lettering on the stern. He could pamper, she thought again, but he also expected a lot in return. She knew the speed he could urge out of the secondhand cabin cruiser he'd lovingly reconstructed himself. Nothing could block the image of the days she'd stood beside him at the helm. The wind had whipped her hair as he'd laughed and pushed for speed, and more speed. Her heart thudded, her pulse raced until she was certain nothing and no one could catch them. She'd been afraid, of him, of the rush of wind—but she'd stayed with both. In the end, she'd left both.

He enjoyed the demanding, the thrilling, the frightening. Kate gripped the handle of her briefcase tighter. Isn't that why she came to him? There were dozens of other experienced divers, many, many other experts on the coastal waters of the Outer Banks. There was only one Ky Silver.

"Kate? Kate Hardesty?"

At the sound of her name, Kate turned and felt the years tumble back again. "Linda!" This time there was no restraint. With an openness she showed to very few, Kate embraced the woman who dashed up to her. "It's wonderful to see you." With a laugh, she drew Linda away to study her. The same chestnut hair cut short and pert, the same frank, brown eyes. It seemed very little had changed on the island. "You look wonderful."

"When I looked out the window and saw you, I could hardly believe it. Kate, you've barely changed at all." With her usual candor and lack of pretension, Linda took a quick, thorough survey. It was quick only because she did things quickly, but it wasn't subtle. "You're too thin," she decided. "But that might be jealousy."

"You still look like a college freshman," Kate returned. "That is jealousy."

As swiftly as the laugh had come, Linda sobered. "I'm sorry about your father, Kate. These past weeks must've been difficult for you."

Kate heard the sincerity, but she'd already tied up her grief and stored it away. "Ky told you?"

"Ky never tells me anything," Linda said with a sniff. In an unconscious move, she glanced in the direction of his boat. It was in its slip and Kate had been walking north—in the direction of Ky's cottage. There could be only one place she could have been going. "Marsh did. How long are you going to stay?"

"I'm not sure yet." She felt the weight of her briefcase. Dreams held the same weight as responsibilities. "There are some things I have to do."

"One of the things you have to do is have dinner at the Roost tonight. It's the restaurant right across from your hotel."

Kate looked back at the rough wooden sign. "Yes, I noticed it. Is it new?"

Linda glanced over her shoulder with a self-satisfied nod. "By Ocracoke standards. We run it."

"We?"

"Marsh and I." With a beaming smile, Linda held out her left hand. "We've been married for three years." Then she rolled her eyes in a habit Kate remembered. "It only took me fifteen years to convince him he couldn't live without me."

"I'm happy for you." She was, and if she felt a pang, she ignored it. "Married and running a restaurant. My father never filled me in on island gossip."

"We have a daughter too. Hope. She's a year and a half old and a terror. For some reason, she takes after Ky." Linda sobered again, laying a hand lightly on Kate's arm. "You're going to see him now." It wasn't a question; she didn't bother to disguise it as one.

"Yes." *Keep it casual,* Kate ordered herself. Don't let the questions and concern in Linda's eyes weaken you. There were ties between Linda and Ky, not only newly formed family ones, but the older tie of the island. "My father was working on something. I need Ky's help with it."

Linda studied Kate's calm face. "You know what you're doing?"

"Yes." She didn't show a flicker of unease. Her stomach slowly wrapped itself in knots. "I know what I'm doing."

"Okay." Accepting Kate's answer, but not satisfied, Linda dropped her hand. "Please come by—the restaurant or the house. We live just down the road from Ky. Marsh'll want to see you, and I'd like to show off Hope—and our menu," she added with a grin. "Both are outstanding."

"Of course I'll come by." On impulse, she took both of Linda's hands. "It's really good to see you again. I know I didn't keep in touch, but—"

"I understand." Linda gave her hands a quick squeeze. "That was yesterday. I've got to get back, the lunch crowd's pretty heavy during the season." She let out a little sigh, wondering if Kate was as calm as she seemed. And if Ky were as big a fool as ever. "Good luck," she murmured, then dashed across the street again.

"Thanks," Kate said under her breath. She was going to need it.

The walk was as beautiful as she remembered. She passed the little shops with their display windows showing handmade crafts or antiques. She passed the blue-and-white clapboard houses and the neat little streets on the outskirts of town with their bleached green lawns and leafy trees.

A dog raced back and forth on the length of his chain as she wandered by, barking at her as if he knew he was supposed to but didn't have much interest in it. She could see the tower of the white lighthouse. There'd been a keeper there once, but those days were over. Then she was on the narrow path that led to Ky's cottage.

Her palms were damp. She cursed herself. If she had to remember, she'd remember later, when she was alone. When she was safe.

The path was as it had been, just wide enough for a car, sparsely graveled, lined with bushes that always grew out a bit too far. The bushes and trees had always had a wild, overgrown look that suited the spot. That suited him.

Ky had told her he didn't care much for visitors. If he wanted company, all he had to do was go into town where he knew everyone. That was typical of Ky Silver, Kate mused. If I want you, I'll let you know. Otherwise, back off.

He'd wanted her once . . . Nervous, Kate shifted the briefcase to her other hand. Whatever he wanted now, he'd have to hear her out. She needed him for what he was best at—diving and taking chances.

When the house came into view, she stopped, staring.

It was still small, still primitive. But it no longer looked as though it would keel over on its side in a brisk wind.

The roof had been redone. Obviously Ky wouldn't need to set out pots and pans during a rain any longer. The porch he'd once talked vaguely about building now ran the length of the front, sturdy and wide. The screen door that had once been patched in a half a dozen places had been replaced by a new one. Yet nothing looked new, she observed. It just looked right. The cedar had weathered to silver, the windows were untrimmed but gleaming. There was, much to her surprise, a spill of impatiens in a long wooden planter.

She'd been wrong, Kate decided as she walked closer. Ky Silver had changed. Precisely how, and precisely how much, she had yet to find out.

She was nearly to the first step when she heard sounds coming from the rear of the house. There was a shed back there, she remembered, full of boards and tools and salvage. Grateful that she didn't have to meet him in the house, Kate walked around the side to the tiny backyard. She could hear the sea and knew it was less than a two-minute walk through high grass and sand dunes.

Did he still go down there in the evenings? she wondered. Just to look, he'd said. Just to smell. Sometimes he'd pick up driftwood or shells or whatever small treasures the sea gave up to the sand. Once he'd given her a small smooth shell that fit into the palm of her hand—very white with a delicate pink center. A woman with her first gift of diamonds could not have been more thrilled.

Shaking the memories away, she went into the shed. It was as tall as the cottage and half as wide. The last time she'd been there, it'd been crowded with planks and boards and boxes of hardware. Now she saw the hull of a boat. At a worktable with his back to her, Ky sanded the mast.

"You've built it." The words came out before she could stop them, full of astonished pleasure. How many times had he told her about the boat he'd build one day? It had seemed to Kate it had been his only concrete ambition. Mahogany on oak, he'd said. A seventeen-foot sloop that would cut through the water like a dream. He'd have bronze fastenings and teak on the deck. One day he'd sail the inner coastal waters from Ocracoke to New England. He'd described the boat so minutely that she'd seen it then just as clearly as she saw it now.

"I told you I would." Ky turned away from the mast and faced her. She, in the doorway, had the sun at her back. He was half in shadow.

"Yes." Feeling foolish, Kate tightened her grip on the briefcase. "You did."

"But you didn't believe me." Ky tossed aside the sandpaper. Did she have to look so neat and cool, and impossibly lovely? A trickle of sweat ran down his back. "You always had a problem seeing beyond the moment."

Reckless, impatient, compelling. Would he always bring those words to her mind? "You always had a problem dealing with the moment," she said.

His brow lifted, whether in surprise or derision she couldn't be sure. "Then it might be said *we* always had a problem." He walked to her, so that the sun slanting through the small windows fell over him, then behind him. "But it didn't always seem to matter." To satisfy himself that he still could, Ky reached out and touched her face. She didn't move, and her skin was as soft and cool as he remembered. "You look tired, Kate."

The muscles in her stomach quivered, but not her voice. "It was a long trip."

His thumb brushed along her cheekbone. "You need some sun."

This time she backed away. "I intend to get some."

"So I gathered from your letter." Pleased that she'd retreated first, Ky leaned against the open door. "You wrote that you wanted to talk to me in person. You're here. Why don't you tell me what you want?"

The cocky grin might have made her melt once. Now it stiffened her spine. "My father was researching a project. I intend to finish it."

"So?"

"I need your help."

Ky laughed and stepped past her into the sunlight. He needed the air, the distance. He needed to touch her again. "From your tone, there's nothing you hate more than asking me for it."

"No." She stood firm, feeling suddenly strong and bitter. "Nothing."

There was no humor in his eyes as he faced her again. The expression in them was cold and flat. She'd seen it before. "Then let's understand each other before we start. You left the island and me, and took what I wanted."

He couldn't make her cringe now as he once had with only that look. "What happened four years ago has nothing to do with today."

"The hell it doesn't." He came toward her again so that she took an involuntary step backward. "Still afraid of me?" he asked softly.

As it had a moment ago, the question turned the fear to anger. "No," she told him, and meant it. "I'm not afraid of you, Ky. I've no intention of discussing the past, but I will agree that I left the island and you. I'm here now on business. I'd like you to hear me out. If you're interested, we'll discuss terms, nothing else."

"I'm not one of your students, professor." The drawl crept into his voice, as it did when he let it. "Don't instruct."

She curled her fingers tighter around the handle of her briefcase. "In business, there are always ground rules."

"Nobody agreed to let you make them."

"I made a mistake," Kate said quietly as she fought for control. "I'll find someone else."

She'd taken only two steps away when Ky grabbed her arm. "No, you won't." The stormy look in his eyes made her throat dry. She knew what he meant. She'd never find anyone else that could make her feel as he made her feel, or want as he made her want. Deliberately, Kate removed his hand from her arm.

"I came here on business. I've no intention of fighting with you over something that doesn't exist any longer."

"We'll see about that." How long could he hold on? Ky wondered. It hurt just to look at her and to feel her withdrawing with every second that went by. "But for now, why don't you tell me what you have in that businesslike briefcase, professor."

Kate took a deep breath. She should have known it wouldn't be easy. Nothing was ever easy with Ky. "Charts," she said precisely. "Notebooks full of research, maps, carefully documented facts and precise theories. In my opinion, my father was very close to pinpointing the exact location of the *Liberty,* an English merchant vessel that sank, stores intact, off the North Carolina coast two hundred and fifty years ago."

He listened without a comment or a change of expression from beginning to end. When she finished, Ky studied her face for one long moment. "Come inside," he said and turned toward the house. "Show me what you've got."

His arrogance made her want to turn away and go back to town exactly as she'd come. There were other divers, others who knew the coast and the waters as well as Ky did. Kate forced herself to calm down, forced herself to think. There were others, but if it was a choice between the devil she knew and the unknown, she had no choice. Kate followed him into the house.

This, too, had changed. The kitchen she remembered had had a paint splattered floor, with the only usable counter space being a tottering picnic table. The floor had been stripped and varnished, the cabinets redone, and scrubbed butcher block counters lined the sink. He had put in a skylight so that the sun spilled down over the picnic table, now re-worked and repainted, with benches along either side.

"Did you do all of this yourself?"

"Yeah. Surprised?"

So he didn't want to make polite conversation. Kate set her briefcase on the table. "Yes. You always seemed content that the walls were about to cave in on you."

"I was content with a lot of things, once. Want a beer?"

"No." Kate sat down and drew the first of her father's notebooks out of her briefcase. "You'll want to read these. It would be unnecessary and time-consuming for you to read every page, but if you'd look over the ones I've marked, I think you'll have enough to go by."

"All right." Ky turned from the refrigerator, beer in hand. He sat, watching her over the rim as he took the first swallow, then he opened the notebook.

Edwin Hardesty's handwriting was very clear and precise. He wrote down his facts in didactic, unromantic terms. What could have been exciting was as dry as a thesis, but it was accurate. Ky had no doubt of that.

The *Liberty* had been lost, with its stores of sugar, tea, silks, wine and other imports for the colonies. Hardesty had listed the manifest down to the last piece of hardtack. When it had left England, the ship had also been carrying gold. Twenty-five thousand in coins of the realm. Ky glanced up from the notebook to see Kate watching him.

"Interesting," he said simply, and turned to the next page she marked.

There'd been only three survivors who'd washed up on the

island. One of the crew had described the storm that had sunk the *Liberty,* giving details on the height of the waves, the splintering wood, the water gushing into the hole. It was a grim, grisly story which Hardesty had recounted in his pragmatic style, complete with footnotes. The crewman had also given the last known location of the ship before it had gone down. Ky didn't require Hardesty's calculations to figure the ship had sunk two-and-a-half miles off the coast of Ocracoke.

Going from one notebook to another, Ky read through Hardesty's well-drafted theories, his clear to-the-point documentations, corroborated and recorroborated. He scanned the charts, then studied them with more care. He remembered the man's avid interest in diving, which had always seemed inconsistent with his precise lifestyle.

So he'd been looking for gold, Ky mused. All these years the man had been digging in books and looking for gold. If it had been anyone else, Ky might have dismissed it as another fable. Little towns along the coast were full of stories about buried treasure. Edward Teach had used the shallow waters of the inlets to frustrate and outwit the crown until his last battle off the shores of Ocracoke. That alone kept the dreams of finding sunken treasures alive.

But it was Dr. Edwin J. Hardesty, Yale professor, an unimaginative, humorless man who didn't believe there was time to be wasted on the frivolous, who'd written these notebooks.

Ky might still have dismissed it, but Kate was sitting across from him. He had enough adventurous blood in him to believe in destinies.

Setting the last notebook aside, he picked up his beer again. "So, you want to treasure hunt."

She ignored the humor in his voice. With her hands folded

on the table, she leaned forward. "I intend to follow through with what my father was working on."

"Do you believe it?"

Did she? Kate opened her mouth and closed it again. She had no idea. "I don't believe that all of my father's time and research should go for nothing. I want to try. As it happens, I need you to help me do it. You'll be compensated."

"Will I?" He studied the liquid left in the beer bottle with a half smile. "Will I indeed?"

"I need you, your boat and your equipment for a month, maybe two. I can't dive alone because I just don't know the waters well enough to risk it, and I don't have the time to waste. I have to be back in Connecticut by the end of August."

"To get more chalk dust under your fingernails."

She sat back slowly. "You have no right to criticize my profession."

"I'm sure the chalk's very exclusive at Yale," Ky commented. "So you're giving yourself six weeks or so to find a pot of gold."

"If my father's calculations are viable, it won't take that long."

"If," Ky repeated. Setting down his bottle, he leaned forward. "I've got no timetable. You want six weeks of my time, you can have it. For a price."

"Which is?"

"A hundred dollars a day and fifty percent of whatever we find."

Kate gave him a cool look as she slipped the notebooks back into her briefcase. "Whatever I was four years ago, Ky, I'm not a fool now. A hundred dollars a day is outrageous when we're dealing with monthly rates. And fifty percent is out of the question." It gave her a certain satisfaction to bargain with him. This made it business, pure and simple. "I'll give you fifty dollars a day and ten percent."

With the maddening half grin on his face he swirled the beer in the bottle. "I don't turn my boat on for fifty a day."

She tilted her head a bit to study him. Something tore inside him. She'd often done that whenever he said something she wanted to think over. "You're more mercenary than you once were."

"We've all got to make a living, professor." Didn't she feel anything? he thought furiously. Wasn't she suffering just a little, being in the house where they'd made love their first and last time? "You want a service," he said quietly, "you pay for it. Nothing's free. Seventy-five a day and twenty-five percent. We'll say it's for old-times' sake."

"No, we'll say it's for business' sake." She made herself extend her hand, but when his closed over it, she regretted the gesture. It was callused, hard, strong. Kate knew how his hand felt skimming over her skin, driving her to desperation, soothing, teasing, seducing.

"We have a deal." Ky thought he could see a flash of remembrance in her eyes. He kept her hand in his knowing she didn't welcome his touch. Because she didn't. "There's no guarantee you'll find your treasure."

"That's understood."

"Fine. I'll deduct your father's deposit from the total."

"All right." With her free hand, she clutched at her briefcase. "When do we start?"

"Meet me at the harbor at eight tomorrow." Deliberately, he placed his other free hand over hers on the leather case. "Leave this with me. I want to look over the papers some more."

"There's no need for you to have them," Kate began, but his hands tightened on hers.

"If you don't trust me with them, you take them along."

His voice was very smooth and very quiet. At its most dangerous. "And find yourself another diver."

Their gazes locked. Her hands were trapped and so was she. Kate knew there would be sacrifices she'd have to make. "I'll meet you at eight."

"Fine." He released her hands and sat back. "Nice doing business with you, Kate."

Dismissed, she rose. Just how much had she sacrificed already? she wondered. "Goodbye."

He lifted and drained his half-finished beer when the screen shut behind her. Then he made himself sit there until he was certain that when he rose and walked to the window she'd be out of sight. He made himself sit there until the air flowing through the screens had carried her scent away.

Sunken ships and deep-sea treasure. It would have excited him, captured his imagination, enthusiasm and interest if he hadn't had an overwhelming urge to just get in his boat and head toward the horizon. He hadn't believed she could still affect him that way, that much, that completely. He'd forgotten that just being within touching distance of her tied his stomach in knots.

He'd never gotten over her. No matter what he filled his life with over the past four years, he'd never gotten over the slim, intellectual woman with the haughty face and doe's eyes.

Ky sat, staring at the briefcase with her initials stamped discreetly near the handle. He'd never expected her to come back, but he'd just discovered he'd never accepted the fact that she'd left him. Somehow, he'd managed to deceive himself through the years. Now, seeing her again, he knew it had just been a matter of pure survival and nothing to do with truth. He'd had to go on, to pretend that that part of his life was behind him, or he would have gone mad.

She was back now, but she hadn't come back to him. A business arrangement. Ky ran his hand over the smooth leather of the case. She simply wanted the best diver she knew and was willing to pay for him. Fee for services, nothing more, nothing less. The past meant little or nothing to her.

Fury grew until his knuckles whitened around the bottle. He'd give her what she paid for, he promised himself. And maybe a bit extra.

This time when she went away, he wouldn't be left feeling like an inadequate fool. She'd be the one who would have to go on pretending for the rest of her life. This time when she went away, he'd be done with her. God, he'd have to be.

Rising quickly, he went out to the shed. If he stayed inside, he'd give in to the need to get very, very drunk.

CHAPTER 3

Kate had the water in the tub so hot that the mirror over the white pedestal sink was fogged. Oil floated on the surface, subtly fragrant and soothing. She'd lost track of how long she lay there—soaking, recharging. The next irrevocable step had been taken. She'd survived. Somehow during her discussion with Ky in his kitchen she had fought back the memories of laughter and passion. She couldn't count how many meals they'd shared there, cooking their catch, sipping wine.

Somehow during the walk back to her hotel, she'd overcome the need to weep. Tomorrow would be just a little easier. Tomorrow, and every day that followed. She had to believe it.

His animosity would help. His derision toward her kept Kate from romanticizing what she had to tell herself had never been more than a youthful summer fling. Perspective. She'd always been able to stand back and align everything in its proper perspective.

Perhaps her feelings for Ky weren't as dead as she had hoped or pretended they were. But her emotions were tinged with bitterness. Only a fool asked for more sorrow. Only a romantic believed that bitterness could ever be sweet. It had

been a long time since Kate had been a romantic fool. Even
so, they would work together because both had an interest in
what might be lying on the sea floor.

Think of it. Two hundred and fifty years. Kate closed
her eyes and let her mind drift. The silks and sugar would be
gone, but would they find brass fittings deep in corrosion after two-and-a-half centuries? The hull would be covered with
fungus and barnacles, but how much of the oak would still
be intact? Might the log have been secured in a waterproof
hold and still be legible? It could be donated to a museum
in her father's name. It would be something—the last something she could do for him. Perhaps then she'd be able to lay
all her ambiguous feelings to rest.

The gold, Kate thought as she rose from the tub, the gold
would survive. She wasn't immune to the lure of it. Yet she
knew it would be the hunt that would be exciting, and somehow fulfilling. If she found it . . .

What would she do? Kate wondered. She dropped the hotel towel over the rod before she wrapped herself in her robe.
Behind her, the mirror was still fogged with steam from the
water that drained slowly from the tub. Would she put her
share tidily in some conservative investments? Would she
take a leisurely trip to the Greek islands to see what Byron
had seen and fallen in love with there? With a laugh, Kate
walked through to the other room to pick up her brush.
Strange, she hadn't thought beyond the search yet. Perhaps
that was for the best, it wasn't wise to plan too far ahead.

You always had a problem seeing beyond the moment.

Damn him! With a sudden fury, Kate slammed the brush
onto the dresser. She'd seen beyond the moment. She'd seen
that he'd offered her no more than a tentative affair in a run-
down beach shack. No guarantees, no commitment, no future.
She only thanked God she'd had enough of her senses left to
understand it and to walk away from what was essentially

nothing at all. She'd never let Ky know just how horribly it had hurt to walk away from nothing at all.

Her father had been right to quietly point out the weaknesses in Ky, and her obligation to herself and her chosen profession. Ky's lack of ambition, his careless attitude toward the future weren't qualities, but flaws. She'd had a responsibility, and by accepting it had given herself independence and satisfaction.

Calmer, she picked up her brush again. She was dwelling on the past too much. It was time to stop. With the deft movements of habit, she secured her hair into a sleek twist. From this time on, she'd think only of what was to come, not what had, or might have been.

She needed to get out.

With panic just under the surface, Kate pulled a dress out of her closet. It no longer mattered that she was tired, that all she really wanted to do was to crawl into bed and let her mind and body rest. Nerves wouldn't permit it. She'd go across the street, have a drink with Linda and Marsh. She'd see their baby, have a long, extravagant dinner. When she came back to the hotel, alone, she'd make certain she'd be too tired for dreams.

Tomorrow, she had work to do.

Because she dressed quickly, Kate arrived at the Roost just past six. What she saw, she immediately approved of. It wasn't elegant, but it was comfortable. It didn't have the dimly lit, cathedral feel of so many of the restaurants she'd dined in with her father, with colleagues, back in Connecticut. It was relaxed, welcoming, cozy.

There were paintings of ships and boats along the stuccoed walls, of armadas and cutters. Throughout the dining room was other sailing paraphernalia—a ship's compass with its brass gleaming, a colorful spinnaker draped behind the bar with the stools in front of it shaped like wooden kegs. There

was a crow's nest spearing toward the ceiling with ferns spill-
ing out and down the mast.

The room was already half full of couples and families,
the bulk of whom Kate identified as tourists. She could
hear the comforting sound of cutlery scraping lightly over
plates. There was the smell of good food and the hum of
mixed conversations.

Comfortable, she thought again, but definitely well organized. Waiters and waitresses in sailor's denims moved
smoothly, making every second count without looking rushed.
The window opened out to a full evening view of Silver Lake
Harbor. Kate turned her back on it because she knew her gaze
would fall on the *Vortex* or its empty slip.

Tomorrow was soon enough for that. She wanted one night
without memories.

"Kate."

She felt the hands on her shoulders and recognized the
voice. There was a smile on her face when she turned around.
"Marsh, I'm so glad to see you."

In his quiet way, he studied her, measured her and saw both
the strain and the relief. In the same way, he'd had a crush on
her that had faded into admiration and respect before the end
of that one summer. "Beautiful as ever. Linda said you were,
but it's nice to see for myself."

She laughed, because he'd always been able to make her
feel as though life could be honed down to the most simple
of terms. She'd never questioned why that trait had made her
relax with Marsh and tingle with Ky.

"Several congratulations are in order, I hear. On your marriage, your daughter and your business."

"I'll take them all. How about the best table in the house?"

"No less than I expected." She linked her arm through his.
"Your life agrees with you," she decided as he led her to a
table by the window. "You look happy."

"Look and am." He lifted a hand to brush hers. "We were sorry to hear about your father, Kate."

"I know. Thank you."

Marsh sat across from her and fixed her with eyes so much calmer, so much softer than his brother's. She'd always wondered why the man with the dreamer's eyes had been so practical while Ky had been the real dreamer. "It's tragic, but I can't say I'm sorry it brought you back to the island. We've missed you." He paused, just long enough for effect. "All of us."

Kate picked up the square carmine-colored napkin and ran it through her hands. "Things change," she said deliberately. "You and Linda are certainly proof of that. When I left, you thought she was a bit of a nuisance."

"That hasn't changed," he claimed and grinned. He glanced up at the young, ponytailed waitress. "This is Cindy, she'll take good care of you, Miss Hardesty—" He looked back at Kate with a grin. "I guess I should say Dr. Hardesty."

"Miss'll do," Kate told him. "I've taken the summer off."

"Miss Hardesty's a guest, a special one," he added, giving the waitress a smile. "How about a drink before you order? Or a bottle of wine?"

"Piesporter," the reply came from a deep, masculine voice.

Kate's fingers tightened on the linen, but she forced herself to look up calmly to meet Ky's amused eyes.

"The professor has a fondness for it."

"Yes, Mr. Silver."

Before Kate could agree or disagree, the waitress had dashed off.

"Well, Ky," Marsh commented easily. "You have a way of making the help come to attention."

With a shrug, Ky leaned against his brother's chair. If the three of them felt the air was suddenly tighter, each concealed it in their own way. "I had an urge for scampi."

"I can recommend it," Marsh told Kate. "Linda and the chef debated the recipe, then babied it until they reached perfection."

Kate smiled at Marsh as though there were no dark, brooding man looking down at her. "I'll try it. Are you going to join me?"

"I wish I could. Linda had to run home and deal with some crisis—Hope has a way of creating them and browbeating the babysitter—but I'll try to get back for coffee. Enjoy your dinner." Rising, he sent his brother a cool, knowing look, then walked away.

"Marsh never completely got over that first case of adulation," Ky commented, then took his brother's seat without invitation.

"Marsh has always been a good friend." Kate draped the napkin over her lap with great care. "Though I realize this is your brother's restaurant, Ky, I'm sure you don't want my company for dinner any more than I want yours."

"That's where you're wrong." He sent a quick, dashing smile at the waitress as she brought the wine. He didn't bother to correct Kate's assumption on the Roost's ownership. Kate sat stone-faced, her manners too good to allow her to argue, while Cindy opened the bottle and poured the first sip for Ky to taste.

"It's fine," he told her. "I'll pour." Taking the bottle, he filled Kate's glass to within half an inch of the rim. "Since we've both chosen the Roost tonight, why don't we have a little test?"

Kate lifted her glass and sipped. The wine was cool and dry. She remembered the first bottle they'd shared—sitting on the floor of his cottage the night she gave him her innocence. Deliberately, she took another swallow. "What kind of test?"

"We can see if the two of us can share a civilized meal in public. That was something we never got around to before."

Kate frowned as he lifted his glass. She'd never seen Ky drink from a wineglass. The few times they had indulged in wine, it had been drunk out of one of the half a dozen water glasses he'd owned. The stemware seemed too delicate for his hand, the wine too mellow for the look in his eye.

No, they'd never eaten dinner in public before. Her father would have exuded disapproval for socializing with someone he'd considered an employee. Kate had known it, and hadn't risked it.

Things were different now, she told herself as she lifted her own glass. In a sense, Ky was now her employee. She could make her own judgments. Recklessly, she toasted him. "To a profitable arrangement then."

"I couldn't have said it better myself." He touched the rim of his glass to hers, but his gaze was direct and uncomfortable. "Blue suits you," he said, referring to her dress, but not taking his eyes off hers. "The deep midnight blue that makes your skin look like something that should be tasted very, very carefully."

She stared at him, stunned at how easily his voice could take on that low, intimate tone that had always made the blood rush out of her brain. He'd always been able to make words seem something dark and secret. That had been one of his greatest skills, one she had never been prepared for. She was no more prepared for it now.

"Would you care to order now?" The waitress stopped beside the table, cheerful, eager to please.

Ky smiled when Kate remained silent. "We're having scampi. The house dressing on the salads will be fine." He leaned back, glass in hand, still smiling. But the smile on his lips didn't connect with his eyes. "You're not drinking your wine. Maybe I should've asked if your taste has changed over the years."

"It's fine." Deliberately she sipped, then kept the glass in her hand as though it would anchor her. "Marsh looks well," she commented. "I was happy to hear about him and Linda. I always pictured them together."

"Did you?" Ky lifted his glass toward the lowering evening light slanting through the window. He watched the colors spear through the wine and glass and onto Kate's hand. "He didn't. But then . . ." Shifting his gaze, he met her eyes again. "Marsh always took more time to make up his mind than me."

"Recklessness," she continued as she struggled just to breathe evenly, "was always more your style than your brother's."

"But you didn't come to my brother with your charts and notes, did you?"

"No." With an effort she kept her voice and her eyes level. "I didn't. Perhaps I decided a certain amount of recklessness had its uses."

"Find me useful, do you, Kate?"

The waitress served the salads but didn't speak this time. She saw the look in Ky's eyes.

So had Kate. "When I'm having a job done, I've found that it saves a considerable amount of time and trouble to find the most suitable person." With forced calm, she set down her wine and picked up her fork. "I wouldn't have come back to Ocracoke for any other reason." She tilted her head, surprised by the quick surge of challenge that rushed through her. "Things will be simpler for both of us if that's clear up front."

Anger moved through him, but he controlled it. If they were playing word games, he had to keep his wits. She'd always been clever, but now it appeared the cleverness was glossed over with sophistication. He remembered the innocent, curious Kate with a pang. "As I recall, you were always one for complicating rather than simplifying. I had to explain the purpose, history and mechanics of every piece of equipment before you'd take the first dive."

"That's called caution, not complication."

"You'd know more about caution than I would. Some people spend half their lives testing the wind." He drank deeply of the wine. "I'd rather ride with it."

"Yes." This time it was she who smiled with her lips only. "I remember very well. No plans, no ties, tomorrow the wind might change."

"If you're anchored in one spot too long, you can become like those trees out there." He gestured out the window where a line of sparse junipers bent away from the sea. "Stunted."

"Yet you're still here, where you were born, where you grew up."

Slowly Ky poured her more wine. "The island's too isolated, the life a bit too basic for some. I prefer it to those structured little communities with their parties and country clubs."

Kate looked like she belonged in such a place, Ky thought as he fought against the frustrated desire that ebbed and flowed inside him. She belonged in an elegant silk suit, holding a Dresden cup and discussing an obscure eighteenth-century English poet. Was that why she could still make him feel rough and awkward and too full of longings?

If they could be swept back in time, he'd have stolen her, taken her out to open sea and kept her there. They would have traveled from port to exotic port. If having her meant he could never go home again, then he'd have sailed until his time was up. But he would have had her. Ky's fingers tightened around his glass. By God, he would have had her.

The main course was slipped in front of him discreetly. Ky

brought himself back to the moment. It wasn't the eighteenth century, but today. Still, she had brought him the past with the papers and maps. Perhaps they'd both find more than they'd bargained for.

"I looked over the things you left with me."

"Oh?" She felt a quick tingle of excitement but speared the first delicate shrimp as though it were all that concerned her.

"Your father's research is very thorough."

"Of course."

Ky let out a quick laugh. "Of course," he repeated, toasting her. "In any case, I think he might have been on the right track. You do realize that the section he narrowed it down to goes into a dangerous area."

Her brows drew together, but she continued to eat. "Sharks?"

"Sharks are a little difficult to confine to an area," he said easily. "A lot of people forget that the war came this close in the forties. There are still mines all along the coast of the Outer Banks. If we're going down to the bottom, it'd be smart to keep that in mind."

"I've no intention of being careless."

"No, but sometimes people look so far ahead they don't see what's under their feet."

Though he'd eaten barely half of his meal, Ky picked up his wine again. How could he eat when his whole system was aware of her? He couldn't stop himself from wondering what it would be like to pull those confining pins out of her hair as he'd done so often in the past. He couldn't prevent the memory from springing up about what it had been like to bundle her into his arms and just hold her there with her body fitting so neatly against his. He could picture those long, serious looks she'd give him just before passion would start to take over, then the freedom he could feel racing through her in those last heady moments of lovemaking.

How could it have been so right once and so wrong now? Wouldn't her body still fit against his? Wouldn't her hair flow through his hands as it fell—that quiet brown that took on such fascinating lights in the sun. She'd always murmur his name after passion was spent, as if the sound alone sustained her. He wanted to hear her say it, just once more, soft and breathless while they were tangled together, bodies still warm and pulsing. He wasn't sure he could resist it.

Absently Ky signaled for coffee. Perhaps he didn't want to resist it. He needed her. He'd forgotten just how sharp and sure a need could be. Perhaps he'd take her. He didn't believe she was indifferent to him—certain things never fade completely. In his own time, in his own way, he'd take what he once had from her. And pray it would be enough this time.

When he looked back at her, Kate felt the warning signals shiver through her. Ky was a difficult man to understand. She knew only that he'd come to some decision and that it involved her. Grateful for the warming effects of the coffee, she drank. She was in charge this time, she reminded herself, every step of the way and she'd make him aware of it. There was no time like the present to begin.

"I'll be at the harbor at eight," she said briskly. "I'll require tanks, of course, but I brought my own wet suit. I'd appreciate it if you'd have my briefcase and its contents on board. I believe we'd be wise to spend between six and eight hours out a day."

"Have you kept up with your diving?"

"I know what to do."

"I'd be the last to argue that you had the best teacher." He tilted his cup back in a quick, impatient gesture Kate found typical of him. "But if you're rusty, we'll take it slow for a day or two."

"I'm a perfectly competent diver."

"I want more than competence in a partner."

He saw the flare in her eyes and his need sharpened. It was a rare and arousing thing to watch her controlled and reasonable temperament heat up. "We're not partners. You're working for me."

"A matter of viewpoint," Ky said easily. He rose, deliberately blocking her in. "We'll be putting in a full day tomorrow, so you'd better go catch up on all the sleep you've been missing lately."

"I don't need you to worry about my health, Ky."

"I worry about my own," he said curtly. "You don't go under with me unless you're rested and alert. You come to the harbor in the morning with shadows under your eyes, you won't make the first dive." Furiously she squashed the urge to argue with the reasonable. "If you're sluggish, you make mistakes," Ky said briefly. "A mistake you make can cost me. That logical enough for you, professor?"

"It's perfectly clear." Bracing herself for the brush of bodies, Kate rose. But bracing herself didn't stop the jolt, not for either of them.

"I'll walk you back."

"It's not necessary."

His hand curled over her wrist, strong and stubborn. "It's civilized," he said lazily. "You were always big on being civilized."

Until you'd touch me, she thought. No, she wouldn't remember that, not if she wanted to sleep tonight. Kate merely inclined her head in cool agreement. "I want to thank Marsh."

"You can thank him tomorrow." Ky dropped the waitress's tip on the table. "He's busy."

She started to protest, then saw Marsh disappear into what must have been the kitchen. "All right." Kate moved by him and out into the balmy evening air.

The sun was low, though it wouldn't set for nearly an hour. The clouds to the west were just touched with mauve and rose.

When she stepped outside, Kate decided there were more people in the restaurant than there were on the streets.

A charter fishing boat glided into the harbor. Some of the tourists would be staying on the island, others would be riding back across Hatteras Inlet on one of the last ferries of the day.

She'd like to go out on the water now, while the light was softening and the breeze was quiet. Now, she thought, while others were coming in and the sea would stretch for mile after endless empty mile.

Shaking off the mood, she headed for the hotel. What she needed wasn't a sunset sail but a good solid night's sleep. Daydreaming was foolish, and tomorrow too important.

The same hotel. Ky glanced up at her window. He already knew she had the same room. He'd walked her there before, but then she'd have had her arm through his in that sweet way she had of joining them together. She'd have looked up and laughed at him over something that had happened that day. And she'd have kissed him, warm, long and lingeringly before the door would close behind her.

Because her thoughts had run the same gamut, Kate turned to him while they were still outside the hotel. "Thank you, Ky." She made a business out of shifting her purse strap on her arm. "There's no need for you to go any further out of your way."

"No, there isn't." He'd have something to take home with him that night, he thought with sudden, fierce impatience. And he'd leave her something to take up to the room where they'd had one long, glorious night. "But then we've always looked at needs from different angles." He cupped his hand around the back of her neck, holding firm as he felt her stiffen.

"Don't." She didn't back away. Kate told herself she didn't back away because to do so would make her seem vulnerable.

And she was, feeling those long hard fingers play against her skin again.

"I think this is something you owe me," he told her in a voice so quiet it shivered on the air. "Maybe something I owe myself."

He wasn't gentle. That was deliberate. Somewhere inside him was a need to punish for what hadn't been—or perhaps what had. The mouth he crushed on hers hungered, the arms he wrapped around her demanded. If she'd forgotten, he thought grimly, this would remind her. And remind him.

With her arms trapped between them, he could feel her hands ball into tight fists. Let her hate him, loathe him. He'd rather that than cool politeness.

But God she was sweet. Sweet and as delicate as one of the frothy waves that lapped and spread along the shoreline. Dimly, distantly, he knew he could drown in her without a murmur or complaint.

She wanted it to be different. Oh, how she wanted it to be different so that she'd feel nothing. But she felt everything.

The hard, impatient mouth that had always thrilled and bemused her—it was the same. The lean restless body that fit so unerringly against her—no different. The scent that clung to him, sea and salt—hadn't changed. Always when he kissed her, there'd been the sounds of water or wind or gulls. That, too, remained constant. Behind them boats rocked gently in their slips, water against wood. A gull resting on pilings let out a long, lonely call. The light dimmed as the sun dropped closer to the sea. The flood of past feelings rose up to merge and mingle with the moment.

She didn't resist him. Kate had told herself she wouldn't give him the satisfaction of a struggle. But the command to her brain not to respond was lost in the thin clouds of dusk. She gave because she had to. She took because she had no choice.

His tongue played over hers, and her fists uncurled until Kate's palms rested against his chest. So warm, so hard, so familiar. He kissed as he always had, with complete concentration, no inhibitions and little patience.

Time tumbled back and she was young and in love and foolish. Why, she wondered while her head swam, should that make her want to weep?

He had to let her go or he'd beg. Ky could feel it rising in him. He wasn't fool enough to plead for what was already gone. He wasn't strong enough to accept that he had to let go again. The tug-of-war going on inside him was fierce enough to make him moan. On the sound he pulled away from her, frustrated, infuriated, bewitched.

Taking a moment, he stared down at her. Her look was the same, he realized—that half surprised, half speculative look she'd given him after their first kiss. It disoriented him. Whatever he'd sought to prove, Ky knew now he'd only proven that he was still as much enchanted with her as he'd ever been. He bit back an oath, instead, giving her a half salute as he walked away.

"Get eight hours of sleep," he ordered without turning around.

CHAPTER 4

Some mornings the sun seemed to rise more slowly than others, as if nature wanted to show off her particular majesty just a bit longer. When she'd gone to bed, Kate had left her shades up knowing that the morning light would awaken her before the travel alarm beside her bed rang.

She took the dawn as a gift to herself, something individual and personal. Standing at the window, she watched it bloom. The first quiet breeze of morning drifted through the screen to run over her hair and face, through the thin material of her nightshirt, cool and promising. While she stood, Kate absorbed the colors, the light and the silent thunder of day breaking over water.

The lazy contemplation was far different from her structured routine of the past months and years. Mornings had been a time to dress, a time to run over her schedule and notes for the day's classes over two cups of coffee and a quick breakfast. She never had time to give herself the dawn, so she took it now.

She slept better than she'd expected, lulled by the quiet, exhausted by the days of traveling and the strain on her emotions. There'd been no dreams to haunt her from the time she'd turned back the sheets until the first light had fallen over her face. Then she rose quickly. There'd be no dreams now.

Kate let the morning wash over her with all its new promises, its beginnings. Today was the start. Everything, from the moment she'd taken out her father's papers until she'd seen Ky again, had been a prelude. Even the brief, torrid embrace of the night before had been no more than a ghost of the past. Today was the real beginning.

She dressed and went out into the morning.

Breakfast was impossible. The excitement she'd so meticulously held off was beginning to strain for freedom. The feeling that what she was doing was right was back with her. Whatever it took, whatever it cost her, she'd look for the gold her father had dreamed of. She'd follow his directions. If she found nothing, she'd have looked anyway.

In looking, Kate had come to believe she'd lay all her personal ghosts to rest.

Ky's kiss. It had been aching, disturbing as it had always been. She'd been absorbed, just as she'd always been. Though she knew she had to face both Ky and the past, she hadn't known it would be so frighteningly easy to go back—back to that dark, dreamy world where only he had taken her.

Now that she knew, now that she'd faced even that, Kate had to prepare to fight the wind.

He'd never forgiven her, she realized, for saying no. For bruising his pride. She'd gone back to her world when he'd asked her to stay in his. Asked her to stay, Kate remembered, without offering anything, not even a promise. If he'd given her that, no matter how casual or airy the promise might have been, she wouldn't have gone. She wondered if he knew that.

Perhaps he thought if he could make her lose herself to him again, the scales would be even. She wouldn't lose. Kate stuck her hands into the pockets of her brief pleated shorts. No, she didn't intend to lose. If he had pressed her last night, if he'd known just how weakened she'd been by that one kiss . . .

But he wouldn't know, she told herself. She wouldn't weaken again. For the summer, she'd make the treasure her goal and her one ambition. She wouldn't leave the island empty-handed this time.

He was already on board the *Vortex*. Kate could see him stowing gear, his hair tousled by the breeze that flowed in from the sea. With only cut-offs and a sleeveless T-shirt between him and the sun she could see the muscles coil and relax, the skin gleam.

Magnificent. She felt the dull ache deep in her stomach and tried to rationalize it away. After all, a well-honed masculine build should make a woman respond. It was natural. One could even call it impersonal, Kate decided. As she started down the dock she wished she could believe it.

He didn't see her. A fishing boat already well out on the water had caught his attention. For a moment, she stopped, just watching him. Why was it she could always sense the restlessness in him? There was movement in him even when he was still, sound even when he was silent. What was it he saw when he looked out over the sea? Challenge? Romance?

He was a man who always seemed poised for action, for doing. Yet he could sit quietly and watch the waves as if there were nothing more important than that endless battle between earth and water.

Just now he stood on the deck of his boat, hands on hips, watching the tubby fishing vessel putt toward the horizon. It was something he'd seen countless times, yet he stopped to take it in again. Kate looked where Ky looked and wished she could see what he was seeing.

Quietly she went forward, her deck shoes making no sound, but he turned, eyes still intense. "You're early," he said, and with no more greeting reached out a hand to help her on board.

"I thought you might be as anxious to start as I am."

Palm met palm, rough against smooth. Both of them broke contact as soon as possible.

"It should be an easy ride." He looked back to sea, toward the boat, but this time he didn't focus on it. "The wind's coming in from the north, no more than ten knots."

"Good." Though it wouldn't have mattered to her nor, she thought, to him, if the wind had been twice as fast. This was the morning to begin.

She could sense the impatience in him, the desire to be gone and doing. Wanting to make things as simple as possible Kate helped Ky cast off, then walked to the stern. That would keep the maximum distance between them. They didn't speak. The engine roared to life, shattering the calm. Smoothly, Ky maneuvered the small cruiser out of the harbor, setting up a small wake that caused the water to lap against pilings. He kept the same steady even speed while they sailed through the shallows of Ocracoke Inlet. Looking back, Kate watched the distance between the boat and the village grow.

The dreamy quality remained. The last thing she saw was a child walking down a pier with a rod cocked rakishly over his shoulder. Then she turned her face to the sea.

Warm wind, glaring sun. Excitement. Kate hadn't been sure the feelings would be the same. But when she closed her eyes, letting the dull red light glow behind her lids, the salty mist touch her face, she knew this was a love that had remained constant, one that had waited for her.

Sitting perfectly still, she could feel Ky increase the speed until the boat was eating its way through the water as sleekly as a cat moves through the jungle. With her eyes closed, she enjoyed the movement, the speed, the sun. This was a thrill that had never faded. Tasting it again, she understood that it never would.

She'd been right, Kate realized, the hunt would be much more exciting than the final goal. The hunt, and no matter how cautious she was, the man at the helm.

He'd told himself he wouldn't look back at her. But he had to—just once. Eyes closed, a smile playing around her mouth, hair dancing around her face where the wind nudged it from the pins. It brought back a flash of memory—to the first time he'd seen her like that and realized he had to have her. She looked calm, totally at peace. He felt there was a war raging inside him that he had no control over.

Even when he turned back to sea again Ky could see her, leaning back against the stern, absorbing what wind and water offered. In defense, he tried to picture her in a classroom, patiently explaining the intricacies of *Don Juan* or *Henry IV*. It didn't help. He could only imagine her sitting behind him, soaking up sun and wind as if she'd been starved for it.

Perhaps she had been. Though she didn't know what direction Ky's thoughts had taken, Kate realized she'd never been further away from the classroom or the demands she placed on herself there than she was at this moment. She was part teacher, there was no question of that, but she was also, no matter how she'd tried to banish it, part dreamer.

With the sun and the wind on her skin, she was too exhilarated to be frightened by the knowledge, too content to worry. It was a wild, free sensation to experience again something known, loved, then lost.

Perhaps . . . Perhaps it was too much like the one frenzied kiss she'd shared with Ky the night before, but she needed it. It might be a foolish need, even a dangerous one. Just once, only this once, she told herself, she wouldn't question it.

Steady, strong, she opened her eyes again. Now she could

watch the sun toss its diamonds on the surface of the water. They rippled, enticing, enchanting. The fishing boat Ky had watched move away from the island before them was anchored, casting its nets. A purse seiner, she remembered. Ky had explained the wide, weighted net to her once and how it was often used to haul in menhaden.

She wondered why he'd never chosen that life, where he could work and live on the water day after day. But not alone, she recalled with a ghost of a smile. Fishermen were their own community, on the sea and off it. It wasn't often Ky chose to share himself or his time with anyone. There were times, like this one, when she understood that perfectly.

Whether it was the freedom or the strength that was in her, Kate approached him without nerves. "It's as beautiful as I remember."

He dreaded having her stand beside him again. Now, however, he discovered the tension at the base of his neck had eased. "It doesn't change much." Together they watched the gulls swoop around the fishing boat, hoping for easy pickings. "Fishing's been good this year."

"Have you been doing much?"

"Off and on."

"Clamming?"

He had to smile when he remembered how she'd looked, jeans rolled up to her knees, bare feet full of sand as he'd taught her how to dig. "Yeah."

She, too, remembered, but her only memories were of warm days, warm nights. "I've often wondered what it's like on the island in winter."

"Quiet."

She took the single careless answer with a nod. "I've often wondered why you preferred that."

He turned to her, measuring. "Have you?"

Perhaps that had been a mistake. Since it had already been

made, Kate shrugged. "It would be foolish of me to say I hadn't thought of the island or you at all during the last four years. You've always made me curious."

He laughed. It was so typical of her to put things that way. "Because all your tidy questions weren't answered. You think too much like a teacher, Kate."

"Isn't life a multiple choice?" she countered. "Maybe two or three answers would fit, but only one's ultimately right."

"No, only one's ultimately wrong." He saw her eyes take on that thoughtful, considering expression. She was, he knew, weighing the pros and cons of his statement. Whether she agreed or not, she'd consider all the angles. "You haven't changed either," he murmured.

"I thought the same of you. We're both wrong. Neither of us have stayed the same. That's as it should be." Kate looked away from him, further east, then gave a quick cry of pleasure. "Oh, look!" Without thinking, she put her hand on his arm, slender fingers gripping taut muscle. "Dolphins."

She watched them, a dozen, perhaps more, leap and dive in their musical pattern. Pleasure was touched with envy. To move like that, she thought, from water to air and back to water again. It was a freedom that might drive a man mad with the glory of it. But what a madness . . .

"Fantastic, isn't it?" she murmured. "To be part of the air and the sea. I'd nearly forgotten."

"How much?" Ky studied her profile until he could have etched the shape of it on the wind. "How much have you nearly forgotten?"

Kate turned her head, only then realizing just how close they stood. Unconsciously, she'd moved nearer to him when she'd seen the dolphins. Now she could see nothing but his face, inches from hers, feel nothing but the warm skin beneath her hand. His question, the depth of it, seemed to echo off the surface of the water to haunt her.

She stepped back. The drop before her was very deep and torn with riptides. "All that was necessary," she said simply. "I'd like to look over my father's charts. Did you bring them on board?"

"Your briefcase is in the cabin." His hands gripped the wheel tightly, as though he were fighting against a storm. Perhaps he was. "You should be able to find your way below."

Without answering, Kate walked around him to the short steep steps that led belowdecks.

There were two narrow bunks with the spreads taut enough to bounce a coin if one was dropped. The galley just beyond would have all the essentials, she knew, in small, efficient scale. Everything would be in its place, as tidy as a monk's cell.

Kate could remember lying with Ky on one of the pristine bunks, flushed with passion while the boat swayed gently in the current and the music from his radio played jazz.

She gripped the leather of her case as if the pain in her fingers would help fight off the memories. To fight everything off entirely was too much to expect, but the intensity eased. Carefully she unfolded one of her father's charts and spread it on the bunk.

Like everything her father had done, the chart was precise and without frills. Though it had certainly not been his field, Hardesty had drawn a chart any sailor would have trusted.

It showed the coast of North Carolina, Pamlico Sound and the Outer Banks, from Manteo to Cape Lookout. As well as the lines of latitude and longitude, the chart also had the thin crisscrossing lines that marked depth.

Seventy-six degrees north by thirty-five degrees east. From the markings, that was the area her father had decided the *Liberty* had gone down. That was southeast of Ocracoke by no more than a few miles. And the depth . . . Yes, she decided as she frowned over the chart, the depth would still be considered shallow diving. She and Ky would have the relative freedom of wet suits and tanks rather than the leaded boots and helmets required for deep-sea explorations.

X marks the spot, she thought, a bit giddy, but made herself fold the chart with the same care she'd used to open it. She felt the boat slow then heard the resounding silence when the engines shut off. A fresh tremor of anticipation went through her as she climbed the steps into the sunlight again.

Ky was already checking the tanks though she knew he would have gone over all the equipment thoroughly before setting out. "We'll go down here," he said as he rose from his crouched position. "We're about half a mile from the last place your father went in last summer."

In one easy motion he pulled off his shirt. Kate knew he was self-aware, but he'd never been self-conscious. Ky had already stripped down to brief bikini trunks before she turned away for her own gear.

If her heart was pounding, it was possible to tell herself it was in anticipation of the dive. If her throat was dry, she could almost believe it was nerves at the thought of giving herself to the sea again. His body was hard and brown and lean, but she was only concerned with his skill and his knowledge. And he, she told herself, was only concerned with his fee and his twenty-five percent of the find.

She wore a snug tank suit under her shorts that clung to subtle curves and revealed long, slender legs that Ky knew were soft as water, strong as a runner's. He began to pull on the thin rubber wet suit. They were here to look for gold, to find a treasure that had been lost. Some treasures, he knew, could never be recovered.

As he thought of it, Ky glanced up to see Kate draw the pins from her hair. It fell, soft and slow, over, then past her shoulders. If she'd shot a dart into his chest, she couldn't have pierced his heart more accurately. Swearing under his breath, Ky lifted the first set of tanks.

"We'll go down for an hour today."

"But—"

"An hour's more than enough," he interrupted without sparing her a glance. "You haven't worn tanks in four years."

Kate slipped into the set he offered her, securing the straps until they were snug, but not tight. "I didn't tell you that."

"No, but you'd sure as hell have told me if you had." The corner of his mouth lifted when she remained silent. After attaching his own tanks, Ky climbed over the side onto the ladder. She could either argue, he figured, or she could follow.

To clear his mask, he spat into it, rubbed, then reached down to rinse it in salt water. Pulling it over his eyes and nose, Ky dropped into the sea. It took less than ten seconds before Kate plunged into the water beside him. He paused a moment, to make certain she didn't flounder or forget to breathe, then he headed for greater depth.

No, she wouldn't forget to breathe, but the first breath was almost a sigh as her body submerged. It was as thrilling to her as it had been the first time, this incredible ability to stay beneath the ocean's surface and breathe air.

Kate looked up to see the sun spearing through the water, and held out a hand to watch the watery light play on her skin. She could have stayed there, she realized, just reveling in it. But with a curl of her body and a kick, she followed Ky into depth and dimness.

Ky saw a school of menhaden and wondered if they'd end up in the net of the fishing boat he'd watched that morning. When the fish swerved in a mass and rushed past him, he turned to Kate again. She'd been right when she'd told him she knew what to do. She swam as cleanly and as competently as ever.

He expected her to ask him how he intended to look for the *Liberty,* what plan he'd outlined. When she hadn't, Ky had figured it was for one of two reasons. Either she didn't want to have any in-depth conversation with him at the moment, or she'd already reasoned it out for herself. It seemed more likely to be the latter, as her mind was also as clean and competent as ever.

The most logical method of searching seemed to be a semicircular route around Hardesty's previous dives. Slowly and methodically, they would widen the circle. If Hardesty had been right, they'd find the *Liberty* eventually. If he'd been wrong . . . they'd have spent the summer treasure hunting.

Though the tanks on her back reminded Kate not to take the weightless freedom for granted, she thought she could stay down forever. She wanted to touch—the water, the sea grass, the soft, sandy bottom. Reaching out toward a school of bluefish she watched them scatter defensively then regroup. She knew there were times when, as a diver moved through the dim, liquid world, he could forget the need for the sun. Perhaps Ky had been right in limiting the dive. She had to be careful not to take what she found again for granted.

The flattened disklike shape caught Ky's attention. Automatically, he reached for Kate's arm to stop her forward progress. The stingray that scuttled along the bottom looking for tasty crustaceans might be amusing to watch, but it was deadly. He gauged this one to be as long as he was tall with a tail as sharp and cruel as a razor. They'd give it a wide berth.

Seeing the ray reminded Kate that the sea wasn't all beauty and dreams. It was also pain and death. Even as she watched, the stingray struck out with its whiplike tail and caught a small, hapless bluefish. Once, then twice. It was nature, it was life. But she turned away. Through the protective masks, her eyes met Ky's.

She expected to see derision for an obvious weakness, or

worse, amusement. She saw neither. His eyes were gentle, as they were very rarely. Lifting a hand, he ran his knuckles down her cheek, as he'd done years before when he'd chosen to offer comfort or affection. She felt the warmth, it reflected in her eyes. Then, as quickly as the moment had come, it was over. Turning, Ky swam away, gesturing for her to follow.

He couldn't afford to be distracted by those glimpses of vulnerability, those flashes of sweetness. They had already done him in once. Top priority was the job they'd set out to do. Whatever other plans he had, Ky intended to be in full control. When the time was right, he'd have his fill of Kate. That he promised himself. He'd take exactly what he felt she owed him. But she wouldn't touch his emotions again. When he took her to bed, it would be with cold calculation.

That was something else he promised himself.

Though they found no sign of the *Liberty,* Ky saw wreckage from other ships—pieces of metal, rusted, covered with barnacles. They might have been from a sub or a battleship from World War II. The sea absorbed what remained in her.

He was tempted to swim farther out, but knew it would take twenty minutes to return to the boat. Circling around, he headed back, overlapping, double-checking the area they'd just covered.

Not quite a needle in a haystack, Ky mused, but close. Two centuries of storms and currents and sea quakes. Even if they had the exact location where the *Liberty* had sunk, rather than the last known location, it took calculation and guesswork, then luck to narrow the field down to a radius of twenty miles.

Ky believed in luck much the same way he imagined Hardesty had believed in calculation. Perhaps with a mixture of the two, he and Kate would find what was left of the *Liberty.*

Glancing over, he watched Kate gliding beside him. She was looking everywhere at once, but Ky didn't think her mind was on treasure or sunken ships. She was, as she'd been that summer before, completely enchanted with the sea and the life it held. He wondered if she still remembered all the information she'd demanded of him before the first dive. What about the physiological adjustments to the body? How was the CO_2 absorbed? What about the change in external pressure?

Ky felt a flash of humor as they started to ascend. He was dead sure Kate remembered every answer he'd given her, right down to the decimal point in pounds of pressure per square inch.

The sun caught her as she rose toward the surface, slowly. It shone around and through her hair, giving her an ethereal appearance as she swam straight up, legs kicking gently, face tilted toward sun and surface. If there were mermaids, Ky knew they'd look as she did—slim, long, with pale loose hair free in the water. A man could only hold on to a mermaid if he accepted the world she lived in as his own. Reaching out, he caught the tip of her hair in his fingers just before they broke the surface together.

Kate came up laughing, letting her mouthpiece fall and pushing her mask up. "Oh, it's wonderful! Just as I remembered." Treading water, she laughed again and Ky realized it was a sound he hadn't heard in four years. But he remembered it exactly.

"You looked like you wanted to play more than you wanted to look for sunken ships." He grinned at her, enjoying her pleasure and the ease of a smile he'd never expected to see again.

"I did." Almost reluctant, she reached out for the ladder to climb on board. "I never expected to find anything the first time down, and it was so wonderful just to dive again." She stripped off her tanks then checked the valves herself before she set them down. "Whenever I go down, I begin to believe I don't need the sun anymore. Then when I come up, it's warmer and brighter than I remember."

With the adrenaline still flowing, she peeled off her flippers, then her mask, to stand, face lifted toward the sun. "There's nothing else exactly like it."

"Skin diving." Ky tugged down the zipper of his wet suit. "I tried some in Tahiti last year. It's incredible being in that clear water with no equipment but a mask and flippers, and your own lungs."

"Tahiti?" Surprised and interested, Kate looked back as Ky stripped off the wet suit. "You went there?"

"Couple of weeks late last year." He dropped the wet suit in the big plastic can he used for storing equipment before rinsing.

"Because of your affection for islands?"

"And grass skirts."

The laughter bubbled out again. "I'm sure you'd look great in one."

He'd forgotten just how quick she could be when she relaxed. Because the gesture appealed, Ky reached over and gave her hair a quick tug. "I wish I'd taken snapshots," Turning, he jogged down the steps into the cabin.

"Too busy ogling the natives to put them on film for posterity?" Kate called out as she dropped down on the narrow bench on the starboard side.

"Something like that. And, of course, trying to pretend I didn't notice the natives ogling me."

She grinned. "People in grass skirts," she began then let out a muffled shout as he tossed a peach in her direction. Catching it cleanly, Kate smiled at him before she bit into the fruit.

"Still have good reflexes," Ky commented as he came up the last step.

"Especially when I'm hungry." She touched her tongue to her palm where juice dribbled. "I couldn't eat this morning, I was too keyed up."

He held out one of two bottles of cold soda he'd taken from the refrigerator. "About the dive?"

"That and . . ." Kate broke off, surprised that she was talking to him as if it had been four years before.

"And?" Ky prompted. Though his tone was casual, his gaze had sharpened.

Aware of it, Kate rose, turning away to look back over the stern. She saw nothing there but sky and water. "It was the morning," she murmured. "The way the sun came up over the water. All that color." She shook her head and water dripped from the ends of her hair onto the deck. "I haven't watched a sunrise in a very long time."

Making himself relax again, Ky leaned back, biting into his own peach as he watched her. "Why?"

"No time. No need."

"Do they both mean the same thing to you?"

Restless, she moved her shoulders. "When your life revolves around schedules and classes, I suppose one equals the other."

"That's what you want? A daily timetable?"

Kate looked back over her shoulder, meeting his eyes levelly. How could they ever understand each other? she wondered. Her world was as foreign to him as his to her. "It's what I've chosen."

"One of your multiple choices of life?" Ky countered, giving a short laugh before he tilted his bottle back again.

"Maybe, or maybe some parts of life only have one choice." She turned completely around, determined not to lose the euphoria that had come to her with the dive. "Tell me about Tahiti, Ky. What's it like?"

"Soft air, soft water. Blue, green, white. Those are the colors that come to mind, then outrageous splashes of red and orange and yellow."

"Like a Gauguin painting."

The length of the deck separated them. Perhaps that made it easier for him to smile. "I suppose, but I don't think he'd have appreciated all the hotels and resorts. It isn't an island that's been left to itself."

"Things rarely are."

"Whether they should be or not."

Something in the way he said it, in the way he looked at her, made Kate think he wasn't speaking of an island now, but of something more personal. She drank, cooling her throat, moistening her lips. "Did you scuba?"

"Some. Shells and coral so thick I could've filled a boat with them if I'd wanted. Fish that looked like they should've been in an aquarium. And sharks." He remembered one that had nearly caught him half a mile out. Remembering made him grin. "The waters off Tahiti are anything but boring."

Kate recognized the look, the recklessness that would always surface just under his skill. Perhaps he didn't look for trouble, but she thought he'd rarely side-step it. No, she doubted they'd ever fully understand each other, if they had a lifetime.

"Did you bring back a shark's tooth necklace?"

"I gave it to Hope." He grinned again. "Linda won't let her have it yet."

"I should think not. Does it feel odd, being an uncle?"

"No. She looks like me."

"Ah, the male ego."

Ky shrugged, aware that he had a healthy share and was comfortable with it. "I get a kick out of watching her run Marsh and Linda in circles. There's not much entertainment on the island."

She tried to imagine Ky being entertained by something as tame as a baby girl. She failed. "It's strange," Kate said after a moment. "Coming back to find Marsh and Linda married and parents. When I left Marsh treated Linda like his little sister."

"Didn't your father keep you up on progress on the island?"

The smile left her eyes. "No."

Ky lifted a brow. "Did you ask?"

"No."

He tossed his empty bottle into a small barrel. "He hadn't told you anything about the ship either, about why he kept coming back to the island year after year."

She tossed her drying hair back from her face. It hadn't been put in the tone of a question. Still, she answered because it was simpler that way. "No, he never mentioned the *Liberty* to me."

"That doesn't bother you?"

The ache came, but she pushed it aside. "Why should it?" she countered. "He was entitled to his own life, his privacy."

"But you weren't."

She felt the chill come and go. Crossing the deck, Kate dropped her bottle beside Ky's before reaching for her shirt. "I don't know what you mean."

"You know exactly what I mean." He closed his hand over hers before she could pull the shirt on. Because it would've been cowardly to do otherwise, she lifted her head and faced him. "You know," he said again, quietly. "You just aren't ready to say it out loud yet."

"Leave it alone, Ky." Her voice trembled, and though it infuriated her, she couldn't prevent it. "Just leave it."

He wanted to shake her, to make her admit, so that he could hear, that she'd left him because her father had preferred it. He wanted her to say, perhaps sob, that she hadn't had the strength to stand up to the man who had shaped and molded her life to suit his values and wants.

With an effort, he relaxed his fingers. As he had before,

Ky turned away with something like a shrug. "For now," he said easily as he went back to the helm. "Summer's just beginning." He started the engine before turning around for one last look. "We both know what can happen during a summer."

CHAPTER 5

"The first thing you have to understand about Hope," Linda began, steadying a vase the toddler had jostled, "is that she has a mind of her own."

Kate watched the chubby black-haired Hope climb onto a wing-backed chair to examine herself in an ornamental mirror. In the fifteen minutes Kate had been in Linda's home, Hope hadn't been still a moment. She was quick, surprisingly agile, with a look in her eyes that made Kate believe she knew exactly what she wanted and intended to get it, one way or the other. Ky had been right. His niece looked like him, in more ways than one.

"I can see that. Where do you find the energy to run a restaurant, keep a home and manage a fireball?"

"Vitamins." Linda sighed. "Lots and lots of vitamins. Hope, don't put your fingers on the glass."

"Hope!" the toddler cried out, making faces at herself in the mirror. "Pretty, pretty, pretty."

"The Silver ego," Linda commented. "It never tarnishes."

With a chuckle, Kate watched Hope crawl backward out of the chair, land on her diaper-padded bottom and begin to systematically destroy the tower of blocks she'd built a short time before. "Well, she is pretty. It only shows she's smart enough to know it."

"It's hard for me to argue that point, except when she's spread toothpaste all over the bathroom floor." With a contented sigh, Linda sat back on the couch. She enjoyed having Monday afternoons off to play with Hope and catch up on the dozens of things that went by the wayside when the restaurant demanded her time. "You've been here over a week now, and this is the first time we've been able to talk."

Kate bent over to ruffle Hope's hair. "You're a busy woman."

"So are you."

Kate heard the question, not so subtly submerged in the statement, and smiled. "You know I didn't come back to the island to fish and wade, Linda."

"All right, all right, the heck with being tactful." With a mother's skill, she kept her antenna honed on her active toddler and leaned toward Kate. "What *are* you and Ky doing out on his boat every day?"

With Linda, evasions were neither necessary nor advisable. "Looking for treasure," Kate said simply.

"Oh." Expressing only mild surprise, Linda saved a budding African violet from her daughter's curious fingers. "Blackbeard's treasure." She handed Hope a rubber duck in lieu of the plant. "My grandfather still tells stories about it. Pieces of eight, a king's ransom and bottles of rum. I always figured that it was buried on land."

Amused at the way Linda could handle the toddler without breaking rhythm, Kate shook her head. "No, not Blackbeard's."

There were dozens of theories and myths about where the infamous pirate had hidden his booty, and fantastic speculation on just how rich the trove was. Kate had never considered

them any more than stories. Yet, she supposed, in her own
way, she was following a similar fantasy.

"My father'd been researching the whereabouts of an English merchant ship that sank off the coast here in the eighteenth century."

"Your father?" Instantly Linda's attention sharpened. She
couldn't conceive of the Edwin Hardesty she remembered
from summers past as a treasure searcher. "That's why he
kept coming to the island every summer? I could never figure out why . . ." She broke off, grimaced, then plunged
ahead. "I'm sorry, Kate, but he never seemed the type to take
up scuba diving as a hobby, and I never once saw him with
a fish. He certainly managed to keep what he was doing a
secret."

"Yes, even from me."

"You didn't know?" Linda glanced over idly as Hope began to beat on a plastic bucket with a wooden puzzle piece.

"Not until I went through his papers a few weeks ago. I
decided to follow through on what he'd started."

"And you came to Ky."

"I came to Ky." Kate smoothed the material of her thin
summer skirt over her knees. "I needed a boat, a diver, preferably an islander. He's the best."

Linda's attention shifted from her daughter to Kate. There
was simple understanding there, but it didn't completely mask
impatience. "Is that the only reason you came to Ky?"

Needs rose up to taunt her. Memories washed up in one
warm wave. "Yes, that's the only reason."

Linda wondered why Kate should want her to believe what
Kate didn't believe herself. "What if I told you he's never forgotten you?"

Kate shook her head quickly, almost frantically. "Don't."

"I love him." Linda rose to distract Hope who'd discovered tossing blocks was more interesting than stacking them.

"Even though he's a frustrating, difficult man. He's Marsh's brother." She set Hope in front of a small army of stuffed animals before she turned and smiled. "He's my brother. And you were the first mainlander I was ever really close to. It's hard for me to be objective."

It was tempting to pour out her heart, her doubts. Too tempting. "I appreciate that, Linda. Believe me, what was between Ky and me was over a long time ago. Lives change."

Making a neutral sound, Linda sat again. There were some people you didn't press. Ky and Kate were both the same in that area, however diverse they were otherwise. "All right. You know what I've been doing the past four years." She sent a long-suffering look in Hope's direction. "Tell me what your life's been like."

"Quieter."

Linda laughed. "A small border war would be quieter than life in this house."

"Earning my doctorate as early as I did took a lot of concentrated effort." She'd needed that one goal to keep herself level, to keep herself . . . calm. "When you're teaching as well it doesn't leave much time for anything else." Shrugging, she rose. It sounded so staid, she realized. So dull. She'd wanted to learn, she'd wanted to teach, but in and of itself, it sounded hollow.

There were toys spread all over the living room, tiny pieces of childhood. A tie was tossed carelessly over the back of a chair next to a table where Linda had dropped her purse. Small pieces of a marriage. Family. She wondered, with a panic that came and went quickly, how she would ever survive the empty house back in Connecticut.

"This past year at Yale has been fascinating and difficult." Was she defending or explaining? Kate wondered impatiently. "Strange, even though my father taught, I didn't realize that being a teacher is just as hard and demanding as being a student."

"Harder," Linda declared after a moment. "You have to have the answers."

"Yes." Kate crouched down to look at Hope's collection of stuffed animals. "I suppose that's part of the appeal, though. The challenge of either knowing the answer or reasoning it out, then watching it sink in."

"Hoping it sinks in?" Linda ventured.

Kate laughed again. "Yes, I suppose that's it. When it does, that's the most rewarding aspect. Being a mother can't be that much different. You're teaching every day."

"Or trying to," Linda said dryly.

"The same thing."

"You're happy?"

Hope squeezed a bright pink dragon then held it out for Kate. Was she happy? Kate wondered as she obliged by cuddling the dragon in turn. She'd been aiming for achievement, she supposed, not happiness. Her father had never asked that very simple, very basic question. She'd never taken the time to ask herself. "I want to teach," she answered at length. "I'd be unhappy if I couldn't."

"That's a roundabout way of answering without answering at all."

"Sometimes there isn't any yes or no."

"Ky!" Hope shouted so that Kate jolted, whipping her head around to the front door.

"No." Linda noted the reaction, but said nothing. "She means the dragon. He gave it to her, so it's Ky."

"Oh." She wanted to swear but managed to smile as she handed the baby back her treasured dragon. It wasn't reasonable that just his name should make her hands unsteady, her pulse unsteady, her thoughts unsteady. "He wouldn't pick the usual, would he?" she asked carelessly as she rose.

"No." She gave Kate a very direct, very level look. "His tastes have always run to the unique."

Amusement helped to relax her. Kate's brow rose as she met the look. "You don't give up, do you?"

"Not on something I believe in." A trace of stubbornness came through. The stubbornness, Kate mused, that had kept her determinedly waiting for Marsh to fall in love with her. "I believe in you and Ky," Linda continued. "You two can make a mess of it for as long as you want, but I'll still believe in you."

"You haven't changed," Kate said on a sigh. "I came back to find you a wife, a mother and the owner of a restaurant, but you haven't changed at all."

"Being a wife and mother only makes me more certain that what I believe is right." She had her share of arrogance, too, and used it. "We don't own the restaurant," she added as an afterthought.

"No?" Surprised, Kate looked up again. "But I thought you said the Roost was yours and Marsh's."

"We run it," Linda corrected. "And we do have a twenty percent interest." Sitting back, she gave Kate a pleased smile. There was nothing she liked better than to drop small bombs in calm water and watch the ripples. "Ky owns the Roost."

"Ky?" Kate couldn't have disguised the astonishment if she'd tried. The Ky Silver she thought she knew hadn't owned anything but a boat and a shaky beach cottage. He hadn't wanted to. Buying a restaurant, even a small one on a remote island took more than capital. It took ambition.

"Apparently he didn't bother to mention it."

"No." He'd had several opportunities, Kate recalled, the night they'd had dinner. "No, he didn't. It doesn't seem characteristic," she murmured. "I can picture him buying another boat, a bigger boat or a faster boat, but I can't imagine him buying a restaurant."

"I guess it surprised everyone except Marsh—but then Marsh knows Ky better than anyone. A couple of weeks before we were married, Ky told us he'd bought the place and intended to remodel. Marsh was ferrying over to Hatteras every day to work, I was helping out in my aunt's craft shop during the season. When Ky asked if we wanted to buy in for twenty percent and take over as managers, we jumped at it." She smiled, pleased, and perhaps relieved. "It wasn't a mistake for any of us."

Kate remembered the homey atmosphere, the excellent seafood, the fast service. No, it hadn't been a mistake, but Ky . . . "I just can't picture Ky in business, not on land anyway."

"Ky knows the island," Linda said simply. "And he knows what he wants. To my way of thinking, he just doesn't always know how to get it."

Kate was going to avoid that area of speculation. "I'm going to take a walk down to the beach," she decided. "Would you like to come?"

"I'd love to, but—" With a gesture of her hand Linda indicated why Hope had been quiet for the last few minutes. With her arm hooked around her dragon, she was sprawled over the rest of the animals, sound asleep.

"It's either stop or go with her, isn't it?" Kate observed with a laugh.

"The nice thing is that when she stops, so can I." Expertly Linda gathered up Hope, cradling her daughter on her shoulder. "Have a nice walk, and stop into the Roost tonight if you have the chance."

"I will." Kate touched Hope's head, the thick, dark, disordered hair that was so much like her uncle's. "She's beautiful, Linda. You're very lucky."

"I know. It's something I don't ever forget."

Kate let herself out of the house and walked along the quiet street. Clouds were low, making the light gloomy, but the rain held off. She could taste it in the breeze, the clean freshness of it, mixed with the faintest hint of the sea. It was in that direction she walked.

On an island, she'd discovered, you were much more drawn to the water than to the land. It was the one thing she'd understood completely about Ky, the one thing she'd never questioned.

It had been easier to avoid going to the beach in Connecticut, though she'd always loved the rocky, windy New England coast. She'd been able to resist it, knowing what memories it would bring back. Pain. Kate had learned there were ways of avoiding pain. But here, knowing you could reach the edge of land by walking in any direction, she couldn't resist. It might have been wiser to walk to the sound, or the inlet. She walked to the sea.

It was warm enough that she needed no more than the sheer skirt and blouse, breezy enough so that the material fluttered around her. She saw two men, caps low over foreheads, their rods secured in the sand, talking together while they sat on buckets and waited for a strike. Their voices didn't carry above the roar and thunder of surf, but she knew their conversation would deal with bait and lures and yesterday's catch. She wouldn't disturb them, nor they her. It was the way of the islander to be friendly enough, but not intrusive.

The water was as gray as the sky, but she didn't mind. Kate had learned not just to accept its moods but to appreciate the contrasts of each one. When the sea was like this, brooding, with threats of violence on the surface, that meant a storm. She found it appealed to a restlessness in herself she rarely acknowledged.

Whitecaps tossed with systematic fever. The spray rose high and wide. The cry of gulls didn't seem lonely or plaintive now, but challenging. No, a gray gloomy sky meeting a gray sea was anything but dull. It teamed with energy. It boiled with life.

The wind tugged at her hair, loosening pins. She didn't notice. Standing just away from the edge of the surf, Kate faced wind and sea with her eyes wide. She had to think about what she'd just discovered about Ky. Perhaps what she had been determined not to discover about herself.

Thinking there, alone in the gray threatening light before a storm, was what Kate felt she needed. The constant wind blowing in from the east would keep her head clear. Maybe the smells and sounds of the sea would remind her of what she'd had and rejected, and what she'd chosen to have.

Once she'd had a powerful force that had held her swirling, breathless. That force was Ky, a man who could pull on your emotions, your senses, by simply being. The recklessness had attracted her once, the tough arrogance combined with unexpected gentleness. What she saw as his irresponsibility had disturbed her. Kate sensed that he was a man who would drift through life when she'd been taught from birth to seek out a goal and work for it to the exclusion of all else. It was that very different outlook on life that set them poles apart.

Perhaps he had decided to take on some responsibility in his life with the restaurant, Kate decided. If he had, she was glad of it. But it couldn't make any difference. They were still poles apart.

She chose the calm, the ordered. Success was satisfaction in itself when success came from something loved. Teaching was vital to her, not just a job, not even a profession. The giving of knowledge fed her. Perhaps for a moment in Linda's cozy, cluttered home it hadn't seemed like enough. Not quite enough. Still, Kate knew if you wished for too much, you often received nothing at all.

With the wind whipping at her face she watched the rain begin far out to sea in a dark curtain. If the past had been a treasure she'd lost, no chart could take her back. In her life, she'd been taught only one direction.

* * *

Ky never questioned his impulses to walk on the beach. He was a man who was comfortable with his own mood swings, so comfortable, he rarely noticed them. He hadn't deliberately decided to stop work on his boat at a certain time. He simply felt the temptation of sea and storm and surrendered to it.

Ky watched the seas as he made his way up and over the hill of sand. He could have found his way without faltering in the dark, with no moon. He'd stood on shore and watched the rain at sea before, but repetition didn't lessen the pleasure. The wind would bring it to the island, but there was still time to seek shelter if shelter were desired. More often than not, Ky would let the rain flow over him while the waves rose and fell wildly.

He'd seen his share of tropical storms and hurricanes. While he might find them exhilarating, he appreciated the relative peace of a summer rain. Today he was grateful for it. It had given him a day away from Kate.

They had somehow reached a shaky, tense coexistence that made it possible for them to be together day after day in a relatively small space. The tension was making him nervy; nervy enough to make a mistake when no diver could afford to make one.

Seeing her, being with her, knowing she'd withdrawn from him as a person was infinitely more difficult than being apart from her. To Kate, he was only a means to an end, a tool she used in the same way he imagined she used a textbook. If that was a bitter pill, he felt he had only himself to blame. He'd accepted her terms. Now all he had to do was live with them.

He hadn't heard her laugh again since the first dive. He missed that, Ky discovered, every bit as much as he missed the taste of her lips, the feel of her in his arms. She wouldn't give him any of it willingly, and he'd nearly convinced himself he didn't want her any other way.

But at night, alone, with the sound of the surf in his head, he wasn't sure he'd survive another hour. Yet he had to. It was the fierce drive for survival that had gotten him through the past years. Her rejection had eaten away at him, then it had pushed him to prove something to himself. Kate had been the reason for his risking every penny he'd had to buy the Roost. He'd needed something tangible. The Roost had given him that, in much the same way the charter boat he'd recently bought gave him a sense of worth he once thought was unnecessary.

So he owned a restaurant that made a profit, and a boat that was beginning to justify his investment. It had given his innate love of risk an outlet. It wasn't money that mattered, but the dealing, the speculation, the possibilities. A search for sunken treasure wasn't much different.

What was she looking for really? Ky wondered. Was the gold her objective? Was she simply looking for an unusual way to spend her holiday? Was she still trying to give her father the blind devotion he'd expected all her life? Was it the hunt? Watching the wall of rain move slowly closer, Ky found of all the possibilities he wanted it to be the last.

With perhaps a hundred yards between them, both Kate and Ky looked out to the sea and the rain without being aware of each other. He thought of her and she of him, but the rain crept closer and time slipped by. The wind grew bolder. Both of them could admit to the restlessness that churned inside them, but neither could acknowledge simple loneliness.

Then they turned to walk back up the dunes and saw each other.

Kate wondered how long he'd been there, and how, when she could feel the waves of tension and need, she hadn't known the moment he'd stepped onto the beach. Her mind, her body—always so calm and cooperative—sprang to fevered life when she saw him. Kate knew she couldn't fight that, only the outcome. Still, she wanted him. She told herself that just wanting was asking for disaster, but that didn't stop the need. If she ran from him now she'd admit defeat. Instead, Kate took the first step across the sand toward him.

The thin white cotton of her skirt flapped around her, billowing, then clinging to the slender body he already knew. Her skin seemed very pale, her eyes very dark. Again Ky thought of mermaids, of illusions and of foolish dreams.

"You always liked the beach before a storm," Kate said when she reached him. She couldn't smile though she told herself she would. She wanted, though she told herself she wouldn't.

"It won't be much longer." He hooked his thumbs into the front pockets of his jeans. "If you didn't bring your car, you're going to get wet."

"I was visiting Linda." Kate turned her head to look back at the rain. No, it wouldn't be much longer. "It doesn't matter," she murmured. "Storms like this are over just as quickly as they begin." Storms like this, she thought, and like others. "I met Hope. You were right."

"About what?"

"She looks like you." This time she did manage to smile, though the tension was balled at the base of her neck. "Did you know she named a doll after you?"

"A dragon's not a doll," Ky corrected. His lips curved. He could resist a great deal, be apathetic about a great deal more, but he found it virtually impossible to do either when it came to his niece. "She's a great kid. Hell of a sailor."

"You take her out on your boat?"

He heard the astonishment and shrugged it away. "Why not? She likes the water."

"I just can't picture you . . ." Breaking off, Kate turned back to the sea again. No, she couldn't picture him entertaining a child with toy dragons and boat rides, just as she couldn't picture him in the business world with ledgers and accountants. "You surprise me," she said a bit more casually. "About a lot of things."

He wanted to reach out and touch her hair, wrap those loose blowing ends around his finger. He kept his hands in his pockets. "Such as?"

"Linda told me you own the Roost."

He didn't have to see her face to know it would hold that thoughtful, considering expression. "That's right, or most of it anyway."

"You didn't mention it when we were having dinner there."

"Why should I?" She didn't have to see him to know he shrugged. "Most people don't care who owns a place as long as the food's good and the service is quick."

"I guess I'm not most people." She said it quietly, so quietly the words barely carried over the sound of the waves. Even so, Ky tensed.

"Why would it matter to you?"

Before she could think, she turned back, her eyes full of emotion. "Because it all matters. The whys, the hows. Because so much has changed and so much is the same. Because I want . . ." Breaking off, she took a step back. The look in her eyes turned to panic just before she started to dash away.

"What?" Ky demanded, grabbing her arm. "What do you want?"

"I don't know!" she shouted, unaware that it was the first

time she'd done so in years. "I don't know what I want. I don't understand why I don't."

"Forget about understanding." He pulled her closer, holding her tighter when she resisted—or tried to. "Forget everything that's not here and now." The nights of restlessness and frustration already had his mercurial temperament on edge. Seeing her when he hadn't expected to made his emotions teeter. "You walked away from me once, but I won't crawl for you again. And you," he added with his eyes suddenly dark, his face suddenly close, "you damn well won't walk away as easily this time, Kate. Not this time."

With his arms wrapped around her he held her against him. His lips hovered above hers, threatening, promising. She couldn't tell. She didn't care. It was their taste she wanted, their pressure, no matter how harsh, how demanding. No matter what the consequence. Intellect and emotion might battle, and the battle might be eternal. Yet as she stood there crushed against him, feeling the wind whip at both of them, she already knew what the inevitable outcome would be.

"Tell me what you want, Kate." His voice was low, but as demanding as a shout. "Tell me what you want—now."

Now, she thought. If there could only be just now. She started to shake her head, but his breath feathered over her skin. That alone made future and past fade into insignificance.

"You," she heard herself murmur. "Just you." Reaching up she drew his face down to hers.

A wild passionate wind, a thunderous surf, the threat of rain just moments away. She felt his body—hard and confident against hers. She tasted his lips—soft, urgent. Over the thunder in her head and the thunder to the east, she heard her own moan. She wanted, as long as the moment lasted.

His tongue tempted; she surrendered to it. He dove deep and took all, then more. It might never be enough. With no hesitation, Kate met demand with demand, heat with heat.

While mouth sought mouth, her hands roamed his face, teaching what she hadn't forgotten, reacquainting her with the familiar.

His skin was rough with a day's beard, the angle of cheek and jaw, hard and defined. As her fingers inched up she felt the soft brush of his hair blown by the wind. The contrast made her tremble before she dove her fingers deeper.

She could make him blind and deaf with needs. Knowing it, Ky couldn't stop it. The way she touched him, so sure, so sweet while her mouth was molten fire. Desire boiled in him, rising so quickly he was weak with it before his mind accepted what his body couldn't deny. He held her closer, hard against soft, rough against smooth, flame against flame.

Through the thin barrier of her blouse he felt her flesh warm to his touch. He knew the skin here would be delicate, as fragile as the underside of a rose. The scent would be as sweet, the taste as honeyed. Memories, the moment, the dream of more, all these combined to make him half mad. He knew what it would be like to have her, and knowing alone aroused. He felt her now, and feeling made him irrational.

He wanted to take her right there, next to the sea, while the sky opened up and poured over them.

"I want you." With his face buried against her neck he searched for all the places he remembered. "You know how much. You always knew."

"Yes." Her head was spinning. Every touch, every taste added speed to the whirl. Whatever doubts she'd had, Kate had never doubted the want. She hadn't always understood it, the intensity of it, but she'd never doubted it. It was pulling at her now—his, hers—the mutual, mindless passion they'd always been able to ignite in one another. She knew where it would lead—to dark, secret places full of sound and velocity. Not the eye of the hurricane, never the calm with him, but full fury from beginning to end. She knew where it would lead, and knew there'd be glory and freedom. But Ky had spoken no less than the truth when he'd said she wouldn't walk away so easily this time. It was that truth that made her reach for reason, when it would have been so simple to reach for madness.

"We can't." Breathless, she tried to turn in his arms. "Ky, I can't." This time when she took his face in her hands it was to draw it away from hers. "This isn't right for me."

Fury mixed with passion. It showed in his eyes, in the press of his fingers on her arms. "It's right for you. It's never been anything but right for you."

"No." She had to deny it, she had to mean it, because he was so persuasive. "No, it's not. I've always been attracted to you. It'd be ridiculous for me to try to pretend otherwise, but this isn't what I want for myself."

His fingers tightened. If they brought her pain neither of them acknowledged it. "I told you to tell me what you wanted. You did."

As he spoke the sky opened, just as he'd imagined. Rain swept in from the sea, tasting of salt, the damp wind and mystery. Instantly drenched, they stood just as they were, close, distant, with his hands firm on her arms and hers light on his face. She felt the water wash over her body, watched it run over his. It stirred her. She couldn't say why, she wouldn't give in to it.

"At that moment I did want you, I can't deny it."

"And now?" he demanded.

"I'm going back to the village."

"Damn it, Kate, what else do you want?"

She stared at him through the rain. His eyes were dark, stormy as the sea that raged behind him. Somehow he was more difficult to resist when he was like this, volatile, on edge, not quite controlled. She felt desire knot in her stomach, and swim in her head. That was all, Kate told herself. That was all it had ever been. Desire without understanding. Passion without future. Emotion without reason.

"Nothing you can give me," she whispered, knowing she'd have to dig for the strength to walk away, dig for it even to take the first step. "Nothing we can give to each other." Dropping her hands she stepped back. "I'm going back."

"You'll come back to me," Ky said as she took the first steps from him. "And if you don't," he added in a tone that made her hesitate, "it won't make any difference. We'll finish what's been started again."

She shivered, but continued to walk. *Finish what's been started again.* That was what she most feared.

CHAPTER 6

The storm passed. In the morning the sea was calm and blue, sprinkled with diamonds of sunlight from a sky where all clouds had been whisked away. It was true that rain freshened things—the air, grass, even the wood and stone of buildings.

The day was perfect, the wind calm. Kate's nerves rolled and jumped.

She'd committed herself to the project. It was her agreement with Ky that forced her to go to the harbor as she'd been doing every other morning. It made her climb on deck when she wanted nothing more than to pack and leave the island the way she'd come. If Ky could complete the agreement after what had passed between them on the beach, so could she.

Perhaps he sensed the fatigue she was feeling, but he made no comment on it. They spoke only when necessary as he headed out to open sea. Ky stood at the helm, Kate at the stern. Still, even the roar of the engine didn't disguise the strained silence. Ky checked the boat's compass, then cut the engines. Silence continued, thunderously.

With the deck separating them, each began to don their equipment—wet suits, the weight belts that would give them neutral buoyancy in the water, headlamps to light the sea's dimness, masks for sight. Ky checked his depth gauge and compass on his right wrist, then the luminous dial of the watch on his left while Kate attached the scabbard for her diver's knife onto her leg just below the knee.

Without speaking, they checked the valves and gaskets on the tanks, then strapped them on, securing buckles. As was his habit, Ky went into the water first, waiting until Kate joined him. Together they jackknifed below the surface.

The familiar euphoria reached out for her. Each time she dived, Kate expected the underwater world to become more commonplace. Each time it was still magic. She acknowledged what made it possible for her to join creatures of the sea—the regulator with its mouthpiece and hose that brought her air from the tanks on her back, the mask that gave her visibility. She knew the importance of every gauge. She acknowledged the technology, then put it in the practical side of her brain while she simply enjoyed.

They swam deeper, keeping in constant visual contact. Kate knew Ky often dived alone, and that doing so was always a risk. She also knew that no matter how much anger and resentment he felt toward her, she could trust him with her life.

She relied on Ky's instincts as much as his ability. It was his expertise that guided her now, perhaps more than her father's careful research and calculations. They were combing the very edge of the territory her father had mapped out, but Kate felt no discouragement. If she hadn't trusted Ky's skill and instincts, she would never have come back to Ocracoke.

They were going deeper now than they had on their other dives. Kate equalized by letting a tiny bit of air into her suit. Feeling the "squeeze" on her eardrums at the change in pressure, she relieved it carefully. A damaged eardrum could mean weeks without being able to dive.

When Ky signaled for her to switch on her headlamp, she obeyed without question. Excitement began to rise.

The sunlight was fathoms above them. The world here never saw it. Sea grass swayed in the current. Now and then a fish, curious and brave enough, would swim along beside them only to vanish in the blink of an eye at a sudden movement.

Ky swam smoothly through the water, using his feet to propel him at a steady pace. Their lamps cut through the murk, surprising more fish, illuminating rock formations that had existed under the sea for centuries. Kate discovered shapes and faces in them.

No, she could never dive alone, Kate decided as Ky slowed his pace to keep rhythm with her more meandering one. It was so easy for her to lose her sense of time and direction. Air came into her lungs with a simple drawing of breath as long as the tanks held oxygen, but the gauges on her wrist only worked if she remembered to look at them.

Even mortality could be forgotten in enchantment. And enchantment could too easily lead to a mistake. It was a lesson she knew, but one that could slip away from her. The timelessness, the freedom was seductive. The feeling was somehow as sensual as the timeless freedom felt in a lover's arms. Kate knew this pleasure could be as dangerous as a lover, but found it as difficult to resist.

There was so much to see, to touch. Crustaceans of different shapes, sizes and hues. They were alive here in their own milieu, so different from when they washed up helplessly on the beach for children to collect in buckets. Fish swam in and out of waving grass that would be limp and lifeless on land. Unlike dolphins or man, some creatures would never know the thrill of both air and water.

Her beam passed over another formation, crusted with barnacles and sea life. She nearly passed it, but curiosity made

her turn back so that the light skimmed over it a second time.
Odd, she thought, how structured some of the shapes could
be. It almost looked like . . .

Hesitating, using her arms to reverse her progress, Kate
turned in the water to play her light over the shape from end
to end. Excitement rose so quickly she grabbed Ky's arm in
a grip strong enough to make him stop to search for a defect
in her equipment. With a shake of her head Kate warded him
off, then pointed.

When their twin lights illuminated the form on the ocean
floor, Kate nearly shouted with the discovery. It wasn't a shelf
of rock. The closer they swam toward it the more apparent
that became. Though it was heavily corroded and covered
with crustaceans, the shape of the cannon remained recog-
nizable.

Ky swam around the barrel. When he removed his knife
and struck the cannon with the hilt, the metallic sound rang
out strangely. Kate was certain she'd never heard anything
more musical. Her laughter came out in a string of bubbles
that made Ky look in her direction and grin.

They'd found a corroded cannon, he thought, and she was
as thrilled as if they'd found a chest full of doubloons. And
he understood it. They'd found something perhaps no one had
seen for two centuries. That in itself was a treasure.

With a movement of his hand he indicated for her to follow, then they began to swim slowly east. If they'd found a
cannon, it was likely they'd find more.

Reluctant to leave her initial discovery, Kate swam with
him, looking back as often as she looked ahead. She hadn't
realized the excitement would be this intense. How could she
explain what it felt like to discover something that had lain
untouched on the sea floor for more than two centuries? Who
would understand more clearly, she wondered, her colleagues

at Yale or Ky? Somehow she felt her colleagues would understand intellectually, but they would never understand the exhilaration. Intellectual pleasure didn't make you giddy enough to want to turn somersaults.

How would her father have felt if he'd found it? She wished she knew. She wished she could have given him that one instant of exultation, perhaps shared it with him as they'd so rarely shared anything. He'd only known the planning, the theorizing, the bookwork. With one long look at that ancient weapon, she'd known so much more.

When Ky stopped and touched her shoulders, her emotions were as mixed as her thoughts. If she could have spoken she'd have told him to hold her, though she wouldn't have known why. She was thrilled, yet running through the joy was a thin shaft of sorrow—for what was lost, she thought. For what she'd never be able to find again.

Perhaps he knew something of what moved her. They couldn't communicate with words, but he touched her cheek— just a brush of his finger over her skin. It was more comforting to her than a dozen soft speeches.

She understood then that she'd never stopped loving him. No matter how many years, how many miles had separated them, what life she had she'd left with him. The time in between had been little more than existence. It was possible to live with emptiness, even to be content with it until you had that heady taste of life again.

She might have panicked. She might have run if she hadn't been trapped there, fathoms deep in the midst of a discovery. Instead, she accepted the knowledge, hoping that time would tell her what to do.

He wanted to ask her what was going through her mind. Her eyes were full of so many emotions. Words would have to wait. Their time in the sea was almost up. He touched her face again and waited for the smile. When she gave it to him, Ky pointed at something behind her that he had just noticed moments before.

An oaken plank, old, splintered and bumpy with para- sites. For the second time Ky removed his knife and began to pry the board from its bed. Silt floated up thinly, cut- ting visibility before it settled again. Replacing his knife, Ky gave the thumbs-up signal that meant they'd surface. Kate shook her head indicating that they should continue to search, but Ky merely pointed to his watch, then again to the surface.

Frustrated with the technology that allowed her to dive, but also forced her to seek air again, Kate nodded.

They swam west, back toward the boat. When she passed the cannon again, Kate felt a quick thrill of pride. She'd found it. And the discoveries were only beginning.

The moment her head was above water, she started to laugh. "We found it!" She grabbed the ladder with one hand as Ky began to climb up, placing his find and his tanks on the deck first. "I can't believe it, after hardly more than a week. It's incredible, that cannon lying down there all these years." Water ran down her face but she didn't notice. "We have to find the hull, Ky." Impatient, she released her tanks and handed them up to him before she climbed aboard.

"The chances are good—eventually."

"Eventually?" Kate tossed her wet hair out of her eyes. "We found this in just over a week." She indicated the board on the deck. She crouched over it, just wanting to touch. "We found the *Liberty*."

"We found a wreck," he corrected. "It doesn't have to be the *Liberty*."

"It is," she said with a determination that caused his brow to lift. "We found the cannon and this just on the edge of the area my father had charted. It all fits too well."

"Regardless of what wreck it is, it's undocumented. You'll get your name in the books, professor."

Annoyed, she rose. They stood facing each other on either side of the plank they'd lifted out of the sea. "I don't care about having my name in the books."

"Your father's name then." He unzipped his wet suit to let his skin dry.

She remembered her feelings after spotting the cannon, how Ky had seemed to understand them. Could they only be kind to each other, only be close to each other, fathoms under the surface? "Is there something wrong with that?"

"Only if it's an obsession. You always had a problem with your father."

"Because he didn't approve of you?" she shot back.

His eyes took on that eerily calm, almost flat expression that meant his anger was lethal. "Because it mattered too much to you what he approved of."

That stung. The truth often did. "I came here to finish my father's project," she said evenly. "I made that clear from the beginning. You're still getting your fee."

"You're still following directions. His directions." Before she could retort, he turned toward the cabin. "We'll eat and rest before we go back under."

With an effort, she held on to her temper. She wanted to dive again, badly. She wanted to find more. Not for her father's approval, Kate thought fiercely. Certainly not for Ky's. She wanted this for herself. Pulling down the zipper of her wet suit, she went down the cabin steps.

She'd eat because strength and energy were vital to a diver. She'd rest for the same reason. Then, she determined, she'd go back to the wreck and find proof that it was the *Liberty*.

Calmer, she watched Ky go through a small cupboard. "Peanut butter?" she asked when she saw the jar he pulled out.

"Protein."

Her laugh helped her to relax again. "Do you still eat it with bananas?"

"It's still good for you."

Though she wrinkled her nose at the combination, she reminded herself that beggars couldn't be choosers. "When we find the treasure," she said recklessly, "I'll buy you a bottle of champagne."

Their fingers brushed as he handed her the first sandwich. "I'll hold you to it." He picked up his own sandwich and a quart of milk. "Let's eat on deck."

He wasn't certain if he wanted the sun or the space, but it wasn't any easier to be with her in that tiny cabin than it had been the first time, or the last. Taking her assent for granted, Ky went up the stairs again, without looking back. Kate followed.

"It might be good for you," Kate commented as she took the first bite, "but it still tastes like something you give five-year-olds when they scrape their knees."

"Five-year-olds require a lot of protein."

Giving up, Kate sat cross-legged on the deck. The sun was bright, the movement of the boat gentle. She wouldn't let his digs get to her, nor would she dig back. They were in this together, she reminded herself. Tension and sniping wouldn't help them find what they sought.

"It's the *Liberty,* Ky," she murmured, looking at the plank again. "I know it is."

"It's possible." He stretched out with his back against the port side. "But there are a lot of wrecks, unidentified and otherwise, all through these waters. Diamond Shoals is a graveyard."

"Diamond Shoals is fifty miles north."

"And the entire coastline along these barrier islands is full of littoral currents, rip currents and shifting sand ridges. Two hundred years ago they didn't have modern navigational devices. Hell, they didn't even have the lighthouses until the nineteenth century. I couldn't even give you an educated guess as to how many ships went down from the time Columbus set out until World War II."

Kate took another bite. "We're only concerned with one ship."

"Finding one's no big problem," he returned. "Finding a specific one's something else. Last year, after a couple of hurricanes breezed through, they found wrecks uncovered on the beach on Hatteras. There are plenty of houses on the island that were built from pieces of wreckage like that." He pointed to the plank with the remains of his sandwich.

Kate frowned at the board again. "It could be the *Liberty* just as easily as it couldn't."

"All right." Appreciating her stubbornness, Ky grinned. "But whatever it is, there might be treasure. Anything lost for more than two hundred years is pretty much finders keepers."

She didn't want to say that it wasn't any treasure she wanted. Just the *Liberty*'s. From what he said before, Kate was aware he already understood that. It was simply different for him. She took a long drink of cold milk. "What do you plan to do with your share?"

With his eyes half closed, he shrugged. He could do as he pleased now, a cache of gold wouldn't change that. "Buy another boat, I imagine."

"With what two-hundred-year-old gold would be worth today, you'd be able to buy a hell of a boat."

He grinned, but kept his eyes shaded. "I intend to. What about you?"

"I'm not sure." She wished she had some tangible goal for the money, something exciting, even fanciful. It just didn't seem possible to think beyond the hunt yet. "I thought I might travel a bit."

"Where?"

"Greece maybe. The islands."

"Alone?"

The food and the motion of the boat lulled her. She made a neutral sound as she shut her eyes.

"Isn't there some dedicated teacher you'd take with you? Someone you could discuss the Trojan War with?"

"Mmm, I don't want to go to Greece with a dedicated teacher."

"Someone else?"

"There's no one."

Sitting on the deck with her face lifted, her hair blowing, she looked like a finely crafted piece of porcelain. Something a man might look at, admire, but not touch. When her eyes were open, hot, her skin flushed with passion, he burned for her. When she was like this, calm, distant, he ached. He let the needs run through him because he knew there was no stopping them.

"Why?"

"Hmm?"

"Why isn't there anyone?"

Lazily she opened her eyes. "Anyone?"

"Why don't you have a lover?"

The sleepy haze cleared from her eyes instantly. He saw her fingers tense on the dark blue material that stretched snugly over her knees. "It's none of your business whether I do or not."

"You've just told me you don't."

"I told you there's no one I'd travel with," she corrected, but when she started to rise, he put a hand on her shoulder.

"It's the same thing."

"No, it's not, but it's still none of your business, Ky, any more than your personal life is mine."

"I've had women," he said easily. "But I haven't had a lover since you left the island."

She felt the pain and the pleasure sweep up through her. It was dangerous to dwell on the sensation. As dangerous as it was to lose yourself deep under the ocean. "Don't." She lifted her hand to remove his from her shoulder. "This isn't good for either of us."

"Why?" His fingers linked with hers. "We want each other. We both know the rules this time around."

Rules. No commitment, no promises. Yes, she understood them this time, but like mortality during a dive, they could easily be forgotten. Even now, with his eyes on hers, her fingers caught in his, the structure of those rules became dimmer and dimmer. He would hurt her again. There was never any question of that. Somehow, in the past twenty-four hours, it had become a matter of *how* she would deal with the pain, not *if.*

"Ky, I'm not ready." Her voice was low, not pleading, but plainly vulnerable. Though she wasn't aware of it, there was no defense she could put to better use.

He drew her up so that they were both standing, touching only hand to hand. Though she was tall, her slimness made her appear utterly fragile. It was that and the way she looked at him, with her head tilted back so their eyes could meet, that prevented him from taking what he was determined to have, without questions, without her willingness. Ruthlessly, that was how he told himself he wanted to take her, even though he knew he couldn't.

"I'm not a patient man."

"No."

He nodded, then released her hand while he still could. "Remember it," he warned before he turned to go to the helm. "We'll take the boat east, over the wreck and dive again."

An hour later they found a piece of rigging, broken and corroded, less than three yards from the cannon. By hand signals, Ky indicated that they'd start a stockpile of the salvage. Later they'd come back with the means of bringing it up. There were more planks, some too big for a man to carry up, some small enough for Kate to hold in one hand.

When she found a pottery bowl, miraculously unbroken, she realized just what an archaeologist must feel after hours of digging when he unearths a fragment of another era. Here it was, cupped in her hand, a simple bowl, covered with silt, covered with age. Someone had eaten from it once, a seaman, relaxing briefly below deck, perhaps on his first voyage across the Atlantic to the New World. His last journey in any event, Kate mused as she turned the bowl over in her hand.

The rigging, the cannon, the planks equaled ship. The bowl equaled man.

Though she put the bowl with the other pieces of their find, she intended to take it up with her on this dive. Whatever other artifacts they found could go to a museum, but the first, she'd keep.

They found pieces of glass that might have come from bottles that held whiskey, chunks of crockery that hadn't survived intact like the bowl. Bits of cups, bowls, plates littered the sea floor.

The galley, she decided. They must have found the galley. Over the years, the water pressure would have simply disintegrated the ship until it was all pieces spread on and under the floor of the ocean. It would, in essence, have become part of the sea, a home for the creatures and plant life that dwelt there.

But they'd found the galley. If they could find something, just one thing with the ship's name inscribed on it, they'd be certain.

Diligently, using her knife as a digging tool, Kate worked

at the floor of the sea. It wasn't a practical way to search, but she saw no harm in trying her luck. They'd found crockery, glass, the unbroken bowl. Even as she glanced up she saw Ky examining what might have been half a dinner plate.

When she unearthed a long wooden ladle, Kate found that her excitement increased. They *had* found the galley, and in time, she'd prove to Ky that they'd found the *Liberty*.

Engrossed in her find, she turned to signal to Ky and moved directly into the path of a stingray.

He saw it. Ky was no more than a yard from Kate when the movement of the ray unearthing itself from its layer of sand and silt had caught his eye. His movement was pure reflex, done without thought or plan. He was quick. But even as he grabbed Kate's hand to swing her back behind him, out of range, the wicked, saw-toothed tail lashed out.

Her scream was muffled by the water, but the sound went through Ky just as surely as the stingray's poison went through Kate. Her body went stiff against his, rigid in pain and shock. The ladle she'd found floated down, out of her grip, until it landed silently on the bottom.

He knew what to do. No rational diver goes down unless he has a knowledge of how to handle an emergency. Still, Ky felt a moment of panic. This wasn't just another diver, it was Kate. Before his mind could clear, her stiffened body went limp against him. Then he acted.

Cool, almost mechanically, he tilted her head back with the chin carry to keep her air passage open. He held her securely, pressing his chest into her tanks, keeping his hand against her rib cage. It ran through his mind that it was best she'd fainted. Unconscious she wouldn't struggle as she might had she been awake and in pain. It was best she'd fainted because he couldn't bear to think of her in pain. He kicked off for the surface.

On the rise he squeezed her, hard, forcing expanding air

out of her lungs. There was always the risk of embolism. They were going up faster than safety allowed. Even while he ventilated his own lungs, Ky kept a lookout. She would bleed, and blood brought sharks.

The minute they surfaced, Ky released her weight belt. Supporting her with his arm wrapped around her, his hand grasping the ladder, Ky unhooked his tanks, slipped them over the side of the boat, then removed Kate's. Her face was waxy, but as he pulled the mask from her face she moaned. With that slight sound of life some of the blood came back to his own body. With her draped limply over his shoulder, he climbed the ladder onto the *Vortex*.

He laid her down on the deck, and with hands that didn't hesitate, began to pull the wet suit from her. She moaned again when he drew the snug material over the wound just above her ankle, but she didn't reach the surface of consciousness. Grimly, Ky examined the laceration the ray had caused. Even through the protection of her suit, the tail had penetrated deep into her skin. If Ky had only been quicker . . .

Cursing himself, Ky hurried to the cabin for the first-aid kit.

As consciousness began to return, Kate felt the ache swimming up from her ankle to her head. Spears of pain shot through her, sharp enough to make her gasp and struggle, as if she could move away from it and find ease again.

"Try to lie still."

The voice was gentle and calm. Kate balled her hands into fists and obeyed it. Opening her eyes, she stared up at the pure blue sky. Her mind whirled with confusion, but she stared at the sky as though it were the only tangible thing in her life. If she concentrated, she could rise above the hurt. The ladle. Opening her hand she found it empty, she'd lost the ladle. For some reason it seemed vital that she have it.

"We found the galley." Her voice was hoarse with anguish,

but her one hand remained open and limp. "I found a ladle. They'd have used it for spooning soup into that bowl. The bowl—it wasn't even broken. Ky . . ." Her voice weakened with a new flood of sensation as memory began to return. "It was a stingray. I wasn't watching for it, it just seemed to be there. Am I going to die?"

"No!" His answer was sharp, almost angry. Bending over her, he placed both hands on her shoulders so that she'd look directly into his face. He had to be sure she understood everything he said. "It was a stingray," he confirmed, not adding that it had been a good ten feet long. "Part of the spine's broken off, lodged just above your ankle."

He watched her eyes cloud further, part pain, part fear. His hands tightened on her shoulders. "It's not in deep. I can get it out, but it'll hurt like hell."

She knew what he was saying. She could stay as she was until he got her back to the doctor on the island, or she could trust him to treat her now. Though her lips trembled, she kept her eyes on his and spoke clearly.

"Do it now."

"Okay." He continued to stare at her, into the eyes that were glazed with shock. "Hang on. Don't try to be brave. Scream as much as you want but try not to move. I'll be quick." Bending farther, he kissed her hard. "I promise."

Kate nodded, then concentrating on the feeling of his lips against hers, shut her eyes. He was quick. Within seconds she felt the hurt rip through her, over the threshold she thought she could bear and beyond . . . She pulled in air to scream, but went back under the surface into liquid dimness.

Ky let the blood flow freely onto the deck for a moment, knowing it would wash away some of the poison. His hands had been rock steady when he'd pulled the spine from her flesh. His mind had been cold. Now with her blood on his hands, they began to shake. Ignoring them, and the icy fear of seeing Kate's smooth skin ripped and raw, Ky washed the wound, cleansed it, bound it. Within the hour, he'd have her to a doctor.

With unsteady fingers, he checked the pulse at the base of her neck. It wasn't strong, but it was steady. Lifting an eyelid with his thumb, he checked her pupils. He didn't believe she was in shock, she'd simply escaped from the pain. He thanked God for that.

On a long breath he let his forehead rest against hers, only for a moment. He prayed that she'd remain unconscious until she was safely under a doctor's care.

He didn't take the time to wash her blood from his hands before he took the helm. Ky whipped the boat around in a quick circle and headed full throttle back to Ocracoke.

CHAPTER 7

As she started to float toward consciousness, Kate focused, drifted, then focused again. She saw the whirl of a white ceiling rather than the pure blue arc of sky. Even when the mist returned she remembered the hurt and thrashed out against it. She couldn't face it a second time. Yet she found as she rose closer to the surface that she didn't have the will to fight against it. That brought fear. If she'd had the strength, she might have wept.

Then she felt a cool hand on her cheek. Ky's voice pierced the last layers of fog, low and gentle. "Take it easy, Kate. You're all right now. It's all over."

Though her breath hitched as she inhaled, Kate opened her eyes. The pain didn't come. All she felt was his hand on her cheek, all she saw was his face. "Ky." When she said his name, Kate reached for his hand, the one solid thing she was sure of. Her own voice frightened her. It was hardly more than a wisp of air.

"You're going to be fine. The doctor took care of you." As he spoke, Ky rubbed his thumb over her knuckles, establishing a point of concentration, and kept his other hand lightly on her cheek, knowing that contact was important. He'd nearly gone mad waiting for her to open her eyes again. "Dr. Bailey, you remember. You met him before."

It seemed vital that she should remember so she forced her mind to search back. She had a vague picture of a tough, weathered old man who looked more suited to the sea than the examining room. "Yes. He likes . . . likes ale and flounder."

He might have laughed at her memory if her voice had been stronger. "You're going to be fine, but he wants you to rest for a few more days."

"I feel . . . strange." She lifted a hand to her own head as if to assure herself it was still there.

"You're on medication, that's why you're groggy. Understand?"

"Yes." Slowly she turned her head and focused on her surroundings. The walls were a warm ivory, not the sterile white of a hospital. The dark oak trim gleamed dully. On the hardwood floor lay a single rug, its muted Indian design fading with age. It was the only thing Kate recognized. The last time she'd been in Ky's bedroom only half the drywall had been in place and one of the windows had had a long, thin crack in the bottom pane. "Not the hospital," she managed.

"No." He stroked her head, needing to touch as much as to check for her fever that had finally broken near dawn. "It was easier to bring you here after Bailey took care of you. You didn't need a hospital, but neither of us liked the idea of your being in a hotel right now."

"Your house," she murmured, struggling to concentrate her strength. "This is your bedroom, I remember the rug."

They'd made love on it once. That's what Ky remembered. With an effort, he kept his hands light. "Are you hungry?"

"I don't know." Basically, she felt nothing. When she tried to sit up, the drug spun in her head, making both the room and reality reel away. That would have to stop, Kate decided while she waited for the dizziness to pass. She'd rather have some pain than that helpless, weighted sensation.

Without fuss, Ky moved the pillows and shifted her to a sitting position. "The doctor said you should eat when you woke up. Just some soup." Rising he looked down on her, in much the same way, Kate thought, as he'd looked at a cracked mast he was considering mending. "I'll fix it. Don't get up," he added as he walked to the door. "You're not strong enough yet."

As he went into the hall he began to swear in a low, steady stream.

Of course she wasn't strong enough, he thought with a last vicious curse. She was pale enough to fade into the sheets she lay on. No resistance, that's what Bailey had said. Not enough food, not enough sleep, too much strain. If he could do nothing else, Ky determined as he pulled open a kitchen cupboard, he could do something about that. She was going to eat, and lie flat on her back until the doctor said otherwise.

He'd known she was weak, that was the worst of it. Ky dumped the contents of a can into a pot then hurled the empty container into the trash. He'd seen the strain on her face, the shadows under her eyes, he'd heard the traces of fatigue come and go in her voice, but he'd been too wrapped up in his own needs to do anything about it.

With a flick of the wrist, he turned on the burner under the soup, then the burner under the coffee. God, he needed coffee. For a moment he simply stood with his fingers pressed against his eyes waiting for his system to settle.

He couldn't remember ever spending a more frantic twenty-four hours. Even after the doctor had checked and treated her, even when Ky had brought her home and she'd been fathoms deep under the drug, his nerves hadn't eased. He'd been terrified to leave the room for more than five minutes at a time. The fever had raged through her, though she'd been unaware.

Most of the night he'd sat beside her, bathing away the sweat and talking to her, though she couldn't hear.

Through the night he'd existed on coffee and nerves. With a half laugh he reached for a cup. It looked like that wasn't going to change for a while yet.

He knew he still wanted her, knew he still felt something for her, under the bitterness and anger. But until he'd seen her lying unconscious on the deck of his boat, with her blood on his hands, he hadn't realized that he still loved her.

He'd known what to do about the want, even the bitterness, but now, faced with love, Ky hadn't a clue. It didn't seem possible for him to love someone so frail, so calm, so . . . different than he. Yet the emotion he'd once felt for her had grown and ripened into something so solid he couldn't see any way around it. For now, he'd concentrate on getting her on her feet again. He poured the soup into a bowl and carried it upstairs.

It would have been an easy matter to close her eyes and slide under again. Too easy. Willing herself to stay awake, Kate concentrated on Ky's room. There were a number of changes here as well, she mused. He'd trimmed the windows in oak, giving them a wide sill where he'd scattered the best of his shells. A piece of satiny driftwood stood, beautiful as a piece of sculpture. There was a paneled closet door with a faceted glass knob where there'd once been a rod, a round-backed rattan chair where there'd been packing crates.

Only the bed was the same, she mused. The wide four-poster had been his mother's. She knew he'd given the rest of his family's furniture to Marsh. Ky had told her once he'd felt no need or desire for it, but he kept the bed. He was born there, unexpectedly, during a night in which the island had been racked by a storm.

And they'd made love there, Kate remembered as she ran her fingers over the sheets. The first time, and the last.

Stopping the movement of her fingers, she looked over as

Ky came back into the room. Memories had to be pushed aside. "You've done a lot of work in here."

"A bit." He set the tray over her lap as he sat on the edge of the bed.

As the scent of the soup reached her, Kate shut her eyes. Just the aroma seemed to be enough. "It smells wonderful."

"The smell won't put any meat on you."

She smiled, and opened her eyes again. Then before she'd realized it, Ky had spoon-fed her the first bite. "It tastes wonderful too." Though she reached for the spoon, he dipped it into the bowl himself then held it to her lips. "I can do it," she began, then was forced to swallow more broth.

"Just eat." Fighting off waves of emotion he spoke briskly. "You look like hell."

"I'm sure I do," she said easily. "Most people don't look their best a couple of hours after being stung by a stingray."

"Twenty-four," Ky corrected as he fed her another spoon of soup.

"Twenty-four what?"

"Hours." Ky slipped in another spoonful when her eyes widened.

"I've been unconscious for twenty-four hours?" She looked to the window and the sunlight as if she could find some means of disproving it.

"You slipped in and out quite a bit before Bailey gave you the shot. He said you probably wouldn't remember." *Thank God,* Ky added silently. Whenever she'd fought her way back to consciousness, she'd been in agony. He could still hear her moans, feel the way she'd clutched him. He never knew a person could suffer physically for another's pain the way he'd suffered for hers. Even now it made his muscles clench.

"That must've been some shot he gave me."

"He gave you what you needed." His eyes met hers. For the first time Kate saw the fatigue in them, and the anger.

"You've been up all night," she murmured. "Haven't you had any rest at all?"

"You needed to be watched," he said briefly. "Bailey wanted you to stay under, so you'd sleep through the worst of the pain, and so you'd just sleep period." His voice changed as he lost control over the anger. He couldn't prevent the edge of accusation from showing, partly for her, partly for himself. "The wound wasn't that bad, do you understand? But you weren't in any shape to handle it. Bailey said you've been well on the way to working yourself into exhaustion."

"That's ridiculous. I don't—"

Ky swore at her, filling her mouth with more soup. "Don't tell me it's ridiculous. I had to listen to him. I had to look at you. You don't eat, you don't sleep, you're going to fall down on your face."

There was too much of the drug in her system to allow her temper to bite. Instead of annoyance, her words came out like a sigh. "I didn't fall on my face."

"Only a matter of time." Fury was coming too quickly. Though his fingers tightened on the spoon, Ky held it back. "I don't care how much you want to find the treasure, you can't enjoy it if you're flat on your back."

The soup was warming her. As much as her pride urged her to refuse, her system craved the food. "I won't be," she told him, not even aware that her words were beginning to slur. "We'll dive again tomorrow, and I'll prove it's the *Liberty*."

He started to swear at her, but one look at the heavy eyes and the pale cheeks had him swallowing the words. "Sure." He spooned in more soup knowing she'd be asleep again within moments.

"I'll give the ladle and the rigging and the rest to a museum." Her eyes closed. "For my father."

Ky set the tray on the floor. "Yes, I know."

"It was important to him. I need . . . I just need to give him something." Her eyes fluttered open briefly. "I didn't know he was ill. He never told me about his heart, about the pills. If I'd known . . ."

"You couldn't have done any more than you did." His voice was gentle again as he shifted the pillows down.

"I loved him."

"I know you did."

"I could never seem to make the people I love understand what I need. I don't know why."

"Rest now. When you're well, we'll find the treasure."

She felt herself sinking into warmth, softness, the dark. "Ky." Kate reached out and felt his fingers wrap around hers. With her eyes closed, it was all the reality she needed.

"I'll stay," he murmured, brushing the hair from her cheek. "Just rest."

"All those years . . ." He could feel her fingers relaxing in his as she slipped deeper. "I never forgot you. I never stopped wanting you. Not ever . . ."

He stared down at her as she slept. Her face was utterly peaceful, pale as marble, soft as silk. Unable to resist, he lifted her fingers to his own cheek, just to feel her flesh against his. He wouldn't think about what she'd said now. He couldn't. The strain of the last day had taken a toll on him as well. If he didn't get some rest, he wouldn't be able to care for her when she woke again.

Rising, Ky pulled down the shades, and took off his shirt. Then he lay down next to Kate in the big four-poster bed and slept for the first time in thirty-six hours.

* * *

The pain was a dull, consistent throb, not the silvery sharp flash she remembered, but a gnawing ache that wouldn't pass. When it woke her, Kate lay still, trying to orient herself. Her mind was clearer now. She was grateful for that, even though with the drug out of her system she was well aware of the wound. It was dark, but the moonlight slipped around the edges of the shades Ky had drawn. She was grateful for that too. It seemed she'd been a prisoner of the dark for too long.

It was night. She prayed it was only hours after she'd last awoken, not another full day later. She didn't want that quick panic at the thought of losing time again. Because she needed to be certain she was in control this time, she went over everything she remembered.

The pottery bowl, the ladle, then the stingray. She closed her eyes a moment, knowing it would be a very long time before she forgot what it had felt like to be struck with that whiplike tail. She remembered waking up on the deck of the *Vortex,* the pure blue sky overhead, and the strong, calm way Ky had spoken to her before he'd pulled out the spine. That pain, the horror of that one instant was very clear. Then, there was nothing else.

She remembered nothing of the journey back to the island, or of Dr. Bailey's ministrations or of being transported to Ky's home. Her next clear image was of waking in his bedroom, of dark oak trim on the windows, wide sills with shells set on them.

He'd fed her soup—yes, that was clear, but then things started to become hazy again. She knew he'd been angry, though she couldn't remember why. At the moment, it was more important to her that she could put events in some sort of sequence.

As she lay in the dark, fully awake and finally aware, she heard the sound of quiet, steady breathing beside her. Turning her head, Kate saw Ky beside her, hardly more than a silhouette with the moonlight just touching the skin of his chest so that she could see it rise and fall.

He'd said he would stay, she remembered. And he'd been tired. Abruptly Kate remembered there'd been fatigue in his eyes as well as temper. He'd been caring for her.

A mellow warmth moved through her, one she hadn't felt in a very long time. He had taken care of her, and though it had made him angry, he'd done it. And he'd stayed. Reaching out, she touched his cheek.

Though the gesture was whisper light, Ky awoke immediately. His sleep had been little more than a half doze so that he could recharge his system yet be aware of any sign that Kate needed attention. Sitting up, he shook his head to clear it.

He looked like a boy caught napping. For some reason the gesture moved Kate unbearably. "I didn't mean to wake you," she murmured.

He reached for the lamp beside the bed and turned it on low. Though his body revolted against the interruption, his mind was fully awake. "Pain?"

"No."

He studied her face carefully. The glazed look from the drug had left her eyes, but the color hadn't returned. "Kate."

"All right. Some."

"Bailey left some pills."

As he started to rise, Kate reached for him again. "No, I don't want anything. It makes me groggy."

"It takes away the pain."

"Not now, Ky, please. I promise I'll tell you if it gets bad."

Because her voice was close to desperate he made himself content with that. At the moment, she looked too fragile to argue with. "Are you hungry?"

She smiled, shaking her head. "No. It must be the middle

of the night. I was only trying to orient myself." She touched him again, in gratitude, in comfort. "You should sleep."

"I've had enough. Anyway, you're the patient."

Automatically, he put his hand to her forehead to check for fever. Touched, Kate laid hers over it. She felt the quick reflexive tensing of his fingers.

"Thank you." When he would have removed his hand, she linked her fingers with his. "You've been taking good care of me."

"You needed it," he said simply and much too swiftly. He couldn't allow her to stir him now, not when they were in that big, soft bed surrounded by memories.

"You haven't left me since it happened."

"I had no place to go."

His answer made her smile. Kate reached up her free hand to touch his cheek. There had been changes, she thought, many changes. But so many things had stayed the same. "You were angry with me."

"You haven't been taking care of yourself." He told himself he should move away from the bed, from Kate, from everything that weakened him there.

He stayed, leaning over her, one hand caught in hers. Her eyes were dark, soft in the dim light, full of the sweetness and innocence he remembered. He wanted to hold her until there was no more pain for either of them, but he knew, if he pressed his body against hers now, he wouldn't stop. Again he started to move, pulling away the hand that held hers. Again Kate stopped him.

"I would've died if you hadn't gotten me up."

"That's why it's smarter to dive with a partner."

"I might still have died if you hadn't done everything you did."

He shrugged this off, too aware that the fingers on his face were stroking lightly, something she had done in the past.

Sometimes before they'd made love, and often afterward, when they'd talked in quiet voices, she'd stroke his face, tracing the shape of it as though she'd needed to memorize it. Perhaps she, too, sometimes awoke in the middle of the night and remembered too much.

Unable to bear it, Ky put his hand around her wrist and drew it away. "The wound wasn't that bad," he said simply.

"I've never seen a stingray that large." She shivered and his hand tightened on her wrist.

"Don't think about it now. It's over."

Was it? she wondered as she lifted her head and looked into his eyes. Was anything ever really over? For four years she'd told herself there were joys and pains that could be forgotten, absorbed into the routine that was life as it had to be lived. Now, she was no longer sure. She needed to be. More than anything else, she needed to be sure.

"Hold me," she murmured.

Was she trying to make him crazy? Ky wondered. Did she want him to cross the border, that edge he was trying so desperately to avoid? It took most of the strength he had left just to keep his voice even. "Kate, you need to sleep now. In the morning—"

"I don't want to think about the morning," she murmured. "Only now. And now I need you to hold me." Before he could refuse, she slipped her arms around his waist and rested her head on his shoulder.

She felt his hesitation, but not his one vivid flash of longing before his arms came around her. On a long breath Kate closed her eyes. Too much time had passed since she'd had this, the gentleness, the sweetness she'd experienced only with Ky. No one else had ever held her with such kindness, such simple compassion. Somehow, she never found it odd that a man could be so reckless and arrogant, yet kind and compassionate at the same time.

Perhaps she'd been attracted to the recklessness, but it had been the kindness she had fallen in love with. Until now, in the quiet of the deep night, she hadn't understood. Until now, in the security of his arms, she hadn't accepted what she wanted.

Life as it had to be lived, she thought again. Was taking what she so desperately needed part of that?

She was so slender, so soft beneath the thin nightshirt. Her hair lay over his skin, loose and free, its color muted in the dim light. He could feel her palms against his back, those elegant hands that had always made him think more of an artist than a teacher. Her breathing was quiet, serene, as he knew it was when she slept. The light scent of woman clung to the material of the nightshirt.

Holding her didn't bring the pain he'd expected but a contentment he'd been aching for without realizing it. The tension in his muscles eased, the knot in his stomach vanished. With his eyes closed, he rested his cheek on her hair. It seemed like a lifetime since he'd known the pleasure of quiet satisfaction. She'd asked him to hold her, but had she known he needed to be held just as badly?

Kate felt him relax degree by degree and wondered if it had been she who'd caused the tension in him, and she who'd ultimately released it. Had she hurt him more than she'd realized? Had he cared more than she'd dared to believe? Or was it simply that the physical need never completely faded? It didn't matter, not tonight.

Ky was right. She knew the rules this time around. She wouldn't expect more than he offered. Whatever he offered was much, much more than she'd had in the long, dry years without him. In turn, she could give what she ached to give. Her love.

"It's the same for me as it always was," she murmured.

Then, tilting her head back, she looked at him. Her hair streamed down her back, her eyes were wide and honest. He felt the need slam into him like a fist.

"Kate—"

"I never expected to feel the same way when I came back," she interrupted. "I don't think I'd have come. I wouldn't have had the courage."

"Kate, you're not well." He said it very slowly, as if he had to explain to them both. "You've lost blood, had a fever. It's taken a lot out of you. It'd be best, I think, if you tried to sleep now."

She felt no fever now. She felt cool and light and full of needs. "That day on the beach during the storm, you said I'd come to you." Kate brought her hands up his back until they reached his shoulders. "Even then I knew you were right. I'm coming to you now. Make love with me, Ky, here, in the bed where you loved me that first time."

And the last, he remembered, fighting back a torrent of desire. "You're not well," he managed a second time.

"Well enough to know what I want." She brushed her lips over his chin where his beard grew rough with neglect. So long . . . that was all that would come clearly to her. It had been so long. Too long. "Well enough to know what I need. It's always been you." Her fingers tightened on his shoulders, her lips inches from his. "It's only been you."

Perhaps moving away from her was the answer. But some answers were impossible. "Tomorrow you may be sorry."

She smiled in her calm, quiet way that always moved him. "Then we'll have tonight."

He couldn't resist her. The warmth. He didn't want to hurt her. The softness. The need building inside him threatened to send them both raging even though he knew she was still weak, still fragile. He remembered how it had been the first time, when she'd been innocent. He'd been so careful, though he had never felt the need to care before, and hadn't since. Remembering that, he laid her back.

"We'll have tonight," he repeated and touched his lips to hers.

Sweet, fresh, clean. Those words went through his head, those sensations went through his system as her lips parted for his. So he lingered over her kiss, enjoying with tenderness what he'd once promised himself to take ruthlessly. His mouth caressed, without haste, without pressure. Tasting, just tasting, while the hunger grew.

Her hands reached for his face, fingers stroking, the rough, the smooth. She could hear her own heart beat in her head, feel the slow, easy pleasure that came in liquid waves. He murmured to her, lovely, quiet words that made her thrill when she felt them formed against her mouth. With his tongue he teased hers in long, lazy sweeps until she felt her mind cloud as it had under the drug. Then when she felt the first twinge of desperation, he kissed her with an absorbed patience that left her weak.

He felt it—that initial change from equality to submission that had always excited him. The aggression would come later, knocking the breath from him, taking him to the edge. He knew that too. But for the moment, she was soft, yielding.

He slid his hands over the nightshirt, stroking, lingering. The material between his flesh and hers teased them both. She moved to his rhythm, glorying in the steady loss of control. He took her deeper with a touch, still deeper with a taste. She dove, knowing the full pleasure of ultimate trust. Wherever he took her, she wanted to go.

With a whispering movement he took his hand over the slender curve of her breast. She was soft, the material smooth, making her hardening nipple a sensuous contrast. He loitered there while her breathing grew unsteady, reveling in the changes of her body. Lingering over each separate button of her nightshirt, Ky unfastened them, then slowly parted the material, as if he were unveiling a priceless treasure.

He'd never forgotten how lovely she was, how exciting delicacy could be. Now that he had her again, he allowed himself the time to look, to touch carefully, all the while watching the contact of his lean, tanned hand against her pale skin. With tenderness he felt seldom and demonstrated rarely, he lowered his mouth, letting his lips follow the progress his fingers had already begun.

She was coming to life under him. Kate felt her blood begin to boil as though it had lain dormant in her veins for years. She felt her heart begin to thump as though it had been frozen in ice until that moment. She heard her name as only he said it. As only he could.

Sensations? Could there be so many of them? Could she have known them all once, experienced them all once, then lived without them? A whisper, a sigh, the brush of a fingertip along her skin. The scent of a man touched by the sea, the taste of her lover lingering on her lips. The glow of soft lights against closed lids. Time faded. No yesterday. No tomorrow.

She could feel the slick material of the nightshirt slide away, then the warm, smooth sheets beneath her back. The skim of his tongue along her rib cage incited a thrill that began in her core and exploded inside her head.

She remembered the dawn breaking slowly over the sea. Now she knew the same magnificence inside her own body. Light and warmth spread through her, gradually, patiently, until she was glowing with a new beginning.

He hadn't known he could hold such raging desire in check and still feel such complete pleasure, such whirling excitement. He was aware of every heightening degree of passion that worked through her. He understood the changing, rippling thrill she felt if he used more pressure here, a longer taste there. It brought him a wild sense of power, made only more acute by the knowledge that he must harness it. She was fluid. She was silk. And then with a suddenness that sent him reeling, she was fire.

Her body arched on the first tumultuous crest. It ripped through her like a madness. Greedy, ravenous for more, she began to demand what he'd only hinted at. Her hands ran over him, nearly destroying his control in a matter of seconds. Her mouth was hot, hungry, and sought his with an urgency he couldn't resist. Then she rained kisses over his face, down his throat until he gripped the sheets with his hands for fear of crushing her too tightly and bruising her skin.

She touched him with those slender, elegant fingers so that the blood rushed fast and furious into his head. "You make me crazy," he murmured.

"Yes." She could do no more than whisper, but her eyes opened. "Yes."

"I want to watch you go up," he said softly as he slid into her. "I want to see what making love with me does to you."

She arched again, the moan inching out of her as she experienced a second wild peak. He saw her eyes darken, cloud as he took her slowly, steadily toward the verge between passion and madness. He watched the color come into her cheeks, saw her lips tremble as she spoke his name. Her hands gripped his shoulders, but neither of them knew her short, tapered nails dug into his skin.

They moved together, neither able to lead, both able to follow. As pleasure built, he never took his eyes from her face.

All sensation focused into one. They were only one. With a freedom that reaches perfection only rarely, they gave perfection to each other.

CHAPTER 8

She was sleeping soundly when Ky woke. Ky observed a hint of color in her cheeks and was determined to see that it stayed there. The touch of his hand to her hair was gentle but proprietary. Her skin was cool and dry, her breathing quiet but steady.

What she'd given him the night before had been offered with complete freedom, without shadows of the past, with none of the bitter taste of regret. It was something else he intended to keep constant.

No, he wasn't going to allow her to withdraw from him again. Not an inch. He'd lost her four years ago, or perhaps he'd never really had her—not in the way he'd believed, not in the way he'd taken for granted. But this time, Ky determined, it would be different.

In his own way, he needed to take care of her. Her fragility drew that from him. In another way, he needed a partner on equal terms. Her strength offered him that. For reasons he never completely understood, Kate was exactly what he'd always wanted.

Clumsiness, arrogance, inexperience, or perhaps a combination of all three made him lose her once. Now that he had a second chance, he was going to make sure it worked. With a little more time, he might figure out how.

Rising, he dressed in the shaded light of the bedroom, then left her to sleep.

When she woke slowly, Kate was reluctant to surface from the simple pleasure of a dream. The room was dim, her mind was hazy with sleep and fantasy. The throb in her leg came as a surprise. How could there be pain when everything was so perfect? With a sigh, she reached for Ky and found the bed empty.

The haze vanished immediately, as did all traces of sleep and the pretty edge of fantasy. Kate sat up, and though the movement jolted the pain in her leg, she stared at the empty space beside her.

Had that been a dream as well? she wondered. Tentatively, she reached out and found the sheets cool. All a fantasy brought on by medication and confusion? Unsure, unsteady, she pushed the hair away from her face. Was it possible that she'd imagined it all—the gentleness, the sweetness, the passion?

She'd needed Ky. That hadn't been a dream. Even now she could feel the dull ache in her stomach that came from need. Had the need caused her to fantasize all that strange, stirring beauty during the night? The bed beside her was empty, the sheets cool. She was alone.

The pleasure she awoke with drained, leaving her empty, leaving her grateful for the pain that was her only grip on reality. She wanted to weep, but found she hadn't the energy for tears.

"So you're up."

Ky's voice made her whip her head around. Her nerves were strung tight. He walked into the bedroom carrying a tray, wearing an easy smile.

"That saves me from having to wake you up to get some

food into you." Before he approached the bed, he went to both windows and drew up the shades. Light poured into the room and the warm breeze that had been trapped behind the shades rushed in to ruffle the sheets. Feeling it, she had to control a shudder. "How'd you sleep?"

"Fine." The awkwardness was unexpected. Kate folded her hands and sat perfectly still. "I want to thank you for everything you've done."

"You've already thanked me once. It wasn't necessary then or now." Because her tone had put him on guard, Ky stopped next to the bed to take a good long look at her. "You're hurting."

"It's not bad."

"This time you take a pill." After setting the tray on her lap, he walked to the dresser and picked up a small bottle. "No arguments," he said, anticipating her refusal.

"Ky, it's really not bad." When had he offered her a pill before? The struggle to remember brought only more frustration. "There's barely any pain."

"Any pain's too much." He sat on the bed, and putting the pill into her palm curled her hand over it with his own. "When it's you."

With her fingers curled warmly under his, she knew. Elation came so quietly she was afraid to move and chase it away. "I didn't dream it, did I?" she whispered.

"Dream what?" He kissed the back of her hand before he handed her the glass of juice.

"Last night. When I woke up, I was afraid it had all been a dream."

He smiled and, bending, touched his lips to hers. "If it was, I had the same dream." He kissed her again, with humor in his eyes. "It was wonderful."

"Then it doesn't matter whether it was a dream or not."

"Oh, no, I prefer reality."

With a laugh, she started to drop the pill on the tray, but he stopped her. "Ky—"

"You're hurting," he said again. "I can see it in your eyes. Your medication wore off hours ago, Kate."

"And kept me unconscious for an entire day."

"This is mild, just to take the edge off. Listen—" His hand tightened on hers. "I had to watch you in agony."

"Ky, don't."

"No, you'll do it for me if not for yourself. I had to watch you bleed and faint and drift in and out of consciousness." He ran his hand down her hair, then cupped her face so she'd look directly into his eyes. "I can't tell you what it did to me because I don't know how to describe it. I know I can't watch you in pain anymore."

In silence, she took the pill and drained the glass of juice. For him, as he said, not for herself. When she swallowed the medication, Ky tugged at her hair. "It hardly has more punch than an aspirin, Kate. Bailey said he'd give you something stronger if you needed it, but he'd rather you go with this."

"It'll be fine. It's really more uncomfortable than painful." It wasn't quite the truth, nor did he believe her, but they both let it lie for the moment. Each of them moved cautiously, afraid to spoil what might have begun to bloom again. Kate glanced down at the empty juice glass. The cold, fresh flavor still lingered on her tongue. "Did Dr. Bailey say when I could dive again?"

"Dive?" Ky's brows rose as he uncovered the plate of bacon, eggs and toast. "Kate, you're not even getting up out of bed for the rest of the week."

"Out of bed?" she repeated. "A week?" She ignored the overloaded plate of food as she gaped at him. "Ky, I was stung by a stingray, not attacked by a shark."

"You were stung by a stingray," he agreed. "And your system was so depleted Bailey almost sent you to a hospital. I realize things might've been rough on you since your father died, but you haven't helped anything by not taking care of yourself."

It was the first time he'd mentioned her father's death, and Kate noted he still expressed no sympathy. "Doctors tend to fuss," she began.

"Bailey doesn't," he interrupted. The anger came back and ran along the edge of his words. "He's a tough, cynical old goat, but he knows his business. He told me that you'd apparently worked yourself right to the edge of exhaustion, that your resistance was nil and that you were a good ten pounds underweight." He held out the fork. "We're going to do something about that, professor. Starting now."

Kate looked down at what had to be four large eggs, scrambled, six slices of bacon and four pieces of toast. "I can see you intend to," she murmured.

"I'm not having you sick." He took her hand again and his grip was firm. "I'm going to take care of you, Kate, whether you like it or not."

She looked back at him in her calm, considering way. "I don't know if I do like it," she decided. "But I suppose we'll both find out."

Ky dipped the fork into the eggs. "Eat."

A smile played at the corners of her mouth. She'd never been pampered in her life and thought it might be entirely too easy to get used to it. "All right, but this time I'll feed myself."

She already knew she'd never finish the entire meal, but for his sake, and the sake of peace, she was determined to deal with half of it. That had been precisely his strategy. If he'd have brought her a smaller portion, she'd have eaten half of that, and have eaten less. He knew her better than either one of them fully realized.

"You're still a wonderful cook," she commented, breaking a piece of bacon in half. "Much better than I."

"If you're good, I might broil up some flounder tonight."

She remembered just how exquisitely he prepared fish. "How good?"

"As good as it takes." He accepted the slice of toast she offered him but dumped on a generous slab of jam. "Maybe I'll beg some of the hot fudge cake from the Roost."

"Looks like I'll have to be on my best behavior."

"That's the idea."

"Ky . . ." She was already beginning to poke at her eggs. Had eating always been quite such an effort? "About last night, what happened—"

"Should never have stopped," he finished.

Her lashes swept up, and her eyes were quiet and candid. "I'm not sure."

"I am," he countered. Taking her face in his hands, he kissed her, softly, with only a hint of passion. But the hint was a promise of much more. "Let it be enough for now, Kate. If it has to get complicated, let's wait until other things are a little more settled."

Complicated. Were commitments complicated, the future, promises? She looked down at her plate knowing she simply didn't have the strength to ask or to answer. Not now. "In a way I feel as though I'm slipping back—to that summer four years ago. And yet . . ."

"It's like a step forward."

Kate looked at him again, but this time reached out. He'd always understood. Though he said little, though his way was sometimes rough, he'd always understood. "Yes. Either way it's a little unnerving."

"I've never liked smooth water. You get a better ride with a few waves."

"Perhaps." She shook her head. Slipping back, stepping forward, it hardly mattered. Either way, she was moving toward him. "Ky, I can't eat any more."

"I figured." Easily, he picked up an extra fork from the tray and began eating the cooling eggs himself. "It's still probably more than you eat for breakfast in a week."

"Probably," she agreed in a murmur, realizing just how well he'd maneuvered her. Kate lay back against the propped-up pillows, annoyed that she was growing sleepy again. No more medication, she decided silently as Ky polished off their joint breakfast. If she could just avoid that, and go out for a little while, she'd be fine. The trick would be to convince Ky.

Kate looked toward the window, and the sunshine. "I don't want to lose a week's time going over the wreck."

He didn't have to follow the direction of her gaze to follow the direction of her thoughts. "I'll be going down," he said easily. "Tomorrow, the next day anyway." Sooner, he thought to himself, depending on how Kate mended.

"Alone?"

He caught the tone as he bit into the last piece of bacon. "I've gone down alone before."

She would have protested, stating how dangerous it was, if she'd believed it would have done any good. Ky did a great deal alone because that was how he preferred it. Instead, Kate chose another route.

"We're looking for the *Liberty* together, Ky. It isn't a one-man operation."

He sent her a long, quiet look before he picked up the coffee she hadn't touched. "Afraid I'll take off with the treasure?"

"Of course not." She wouldn't allow her emotions to get in the way. "If I hadn't trusted your integrity," she said evenly, "I wouldn't have shown you the chart in the first place."

"Fair enough," he allowed with a nod. "So if I continue to dive while you're recuperating, we won't lose time."

"I don't want to lose you either." It was out before she could stop it. Swearing lightly, Kate looked toward the window again. The sky was the pale blue sometimes seen on summer mornings.

Ky merely sat for a moment while the pleasure of her words rippled through him. "You'd worry about me?"

Angry, Kate turned back. He looked so smug, so infuriatingly content. "No, I wouldn't worry. God usually makes a point of looking after fools."

Grinning, he set the tray on the floor beside the bed. "Maybe I'd like you to worry, a little."

"Sorry I can't oblige you."

"Your voice gets very prim when you're annoyed," he commented. "I like it."

"I'm not prim."

He ran a hand down her loosened hair. No, she looked anything but prim at the moment. Soft and feminine, but not prim. "Your voice is. Like one of those pretty, lacy ladies who used to sit in parlors eating finger sandwiches."

She pushed his hand aside. He wouldn't get around her with charm. "Perhaps I should shout instead."

"Like that too, but more . . ." He kissed one cheek, then the other. "I like to see you smile at me. The way you smile at nobody else."

Her skin was already beginning to warm. No, he might not get around her with charm, but . . . he'd distract her from her point if she wasn't careful. "I'd be bored, that's all. If I have to sit here, hour after hour with nothing to do."

"I've got lots of books." He slipped her nightshirt down her shoulder then kissed her bare skin with the lightest of touches. "Probably lay my hands on some crossword puzzles, too."

"Thanks a lot."

"There's a copy of Byron downstairs."

Despite her determination not to, Kate looked toward him again. "Byron?"

"I bought it after you left. The words are wonderful." He had the three buttons undone with such quick expertise, she never noticed. "But I could always hear the way you'd say them. I remember one night on the beach, when the moon was full on the water. I don't remember the name of the poem, but I remember how it started, and how it sounded when you said it. 'It is the hour'," he began, then smiled at her.

"'It is the hour'," Kate continued, "'when from the boughs the nightingale is heard/It is the hour when lovers' vows seem sweet in every whisper'd word/And gentle winds, and waters near make music to the lonely ear' . . ." She trailed off, remembering even the scent of that night. "You were never very interested in Byron's technique."

"No matter how hard you tried to explain it to me."

Yes, he was distracting her. Kate was already finding it difficult to remember what point she'd been trying to make. "He was one of the leading poets of his day."

"Hmm." Ky caught the lobe of her ear between his teeth.

"He had a fascination for war and conflict, and yet he had more love affairs in his poems than Shelley or Keats."

"How about out of his poems?"

"There too." She closed her eyes as his tongue began to do outrageous things to her nervous system. "He used humor, satire as well as a pure lyrical style. If he'd ever completed *Don Juan* . . ." She trailed off with a sigh that edged toward a moan.

"Did I interrupt you?" Ky brushed his fingers down her thigh. "I really love to hear you lecture."

"Yes."

"Good." He traced her lips with his tongue. "I just thought maybe I could give you something to do for a while." He skimmed his hand over her hip then up to the side of her breast. "So you won't be bored by staying in bed. Want to tell me more about Byron?"

With a long quiet breath, she wound her arms around his neck. The point she'd been trying to make didn't seem important any longer. "No, but I might like staying in bed after all, even without the crossword puzzles."

"You'll relax." He said it softly, but the command was unmistakable. She might have argued, but the kiss was long and lingering, leaving her slow and helplessly yielding.

"I don't have a choice," she murmured. "Between the medication and you."

"That's the idea." He'd love her, Ky thought, but so gently she'd have nothing to do but feel. Then she'd sleep. "There are things I want from you." He lifted his head until their eyes met. "Things I need from you."

"You never tell me what they are."

"Maybe not." He laid his forehead on hers. Maybe he just didn't know how to tell her. Or how to ask. "For now, what I want is to see you well." Again he lifted his head, and his eyes focused on hers. "I'm not an unselfish man, Kate. I want that just as much for myself as I want it for you. I fully intended to have you back in my bed, but I didn't want it for you. I fully intended to have you back in my bed, but I didn't care to have you unconscious here first."

"Whatever you intended, I make my own choices." Her hands slid up his shoulders to touch his face. "I chose to make love with you then. I choose to make love with you now."

He laughed and pressed her palm to his lips. "Professor, you think I'd have given you a choice? Maybe we don't know each other as well as we should at this point, but you should know that much."

Thoughtfully, she ran her thumb down his cheekbone. It was hard, elegantly defined. Somehow it suited him in the same way the unshaven face suited him. But did she? Kate wondered. Were they, despite all their differences, right for each other?

It seemed when they were like this, there was no question of suitability, no question of what was right or wrong. Each completed the other. Yet there had to be more. No matter how much each of them denied it on the surface, there had to be more. And ultimately, there had to be a choice.

"When you take what isn't offered freely, you have nothing." She felt the rough scrape of his unshaven face on her palm and the thrill went through her system. "If I give, you have whatever you need without asking."

"Do I?" he murmured before he touched his lips to hers again. "And you? What do you have?"

She closed her eyes as her body drifted on a calm, quiet plane of pleasure. "What I need."

For how long? The question ran through his mind, prodding against his contentment. But he didn't ask. There'd be a time, he knew, for more questions, for the hundreds of demands he wanted to make. For ultimatums. Now she was sleepy, relaxed in the way he wanted her to be.

With no more words he let her body drift, stroking gently, letting her system steep in the pleasure he could give. With no one else could he remember asking so little for himself and receiving so much. She was the hinge that could open or close the door on the better part of him.

He listened to her sigh as he touched her. The second was a kind of pure contentment that mirrored his own feelings. It seemed neither of them required any more.

Kate knew it shouldn't be so simple. It had never been simple with anyone else, so that in the end she'd never given herself to anyone else. Only with Ky had she ever known that full excitement that left her free. Only with Ky had she ever known the pure ease that felt so right.

They'd been apart four years, yet if it had been forty, she would have recognized his touch in an instant. That touch was all she needed to make her want him.

She remembered the demands and fire that had always been threaded through their lovemaking before. It had been the excitement she'd craved even while it had baffled her. Now there was patience touched with a consideration she didn't know he was capable of.

Perhaps if she hadn't loved him already, she would have fallen in love at that moment when the sun filtered through the windows and his hands were on her skin. She wanted to give him the fire, but his hands kept it banked. She wanted to meet any demands, but he made none. Instead, she floated on the clouds he brought to her.

Though the heat smoldered inside him, she kept him sane. Just by her pliancy. Though passion began to take over, she kept him calm. Just by her serenity. He'd never looked for serenity in his life. It had simply come to him, as Kate had. He'd never understood what it meant to be calm, but he had known the emptiness and the chaos of living without it.

Without urgency or force, he slipped inside her. Slowly, with a sweetness that made her weak, he gave her the ultimate gift. Passion, fulfillment, with the softer emotions covering a need that seemed insatiable.

Then she slept, and he left her to her dreams.

* * *

When she awoke again, Kate wasn't groggy, but weak. Even as sleep cleared, a sense of helpless annoyance went though her. It was midafternoon. She didn't need a clock, the angle of the sunlight that slanted through the window across from the bed told her what time it was. More hours had been lost without her knowledge. And where was Ky?

Kate groped for her nightshirt and slipped into it. If he followed his pattern, he'd be popping through the door with a loaded lunch tray and a pill. Not this time, Kate determined as she eased herself out of bed. Nothing else was going into her system that made her lose time.

But as she stood, the dregs of the medication swam in her head. Reflexively, she nearly sat again before she stopped herself. Infuriated, she gripped the bedpost, breathed deeply then put her weight on her injured foot. It took the pain to clear her head.

Pain had its uses, she thought grimly. After she'd given the hurt a moment to subside, it eased into a throb. That could be tolerated, she told herself and walked to the mirror over Ky's dresser.

She didn't like what she saw. Her hair was listless, her face washed-out and her eyes dull. Swearing, she put her hands to her cheeks and rubbed as though she could force color into them. What she needed, Kate decided, was a hot shower, a shampoo and some fresh air. Regardless of what Ky thought, she was going to have them.

Taking a deep breath, she headed for the door. Even as she reached for the knob, it opened.

"What're you doing up?"

Though they were precisely the words she'd expected, Kate had expected them from Ky, not Linda. "I was just—"

"Do you want Ky to skin me alive?" Linda demanded, backing Kate toward the bed with a tray of steaming soup in her hand. "Listen, you're supposed to rest and eat, then eat and rest. Orders."

Realizing abruptly that she was retreating, Kate held her ground. "Whose?"

"Ky's. And," she continued before Kate could retort, "Dr. Bailey's."

"I don't have to take orders from either of them."

"Maybe you don't," Linda agreed dryly. "But I don't argue with a man who's protecting his woman, or with the man who poked a needle into my bottom when I was three. Both of them can be nasty. Now lie down."

"Linda . . ." Though she knew the sigh sounded long suffering, Kate couldn't prevent it. "I've a cut on my leg. I've been in bed for something like forty-eight hours straight. If I don't have a shower and a breath of air soon, I'm going to go crazy."

A smile tugged at Linda's mouth that she partially concealed by nibbling on her lower lip. "A bit grumpy, are we?"

"I can be more than a bit." This time the sigh was simply bad tempered. "Look at me!" Kate demanded, tugging on her hair. "I feel as though I've just crawled out from under a rock."

"Okay. I know how I felt after I'd delivered Hope. After I'd had my cuddle with her I wanted a shower and shampoo so bad I was close to tears." She set the tray on the table beside the bed. "You can have ten minutes in the shower, then you can eat while I change your bandage. But Ky made me swear I'd make you eat every bite." She put her hands on her hips. "So that's the deal."

"He's overreacting," Kate began. "It's absurd. I don't need to be babied this way."

"Tell me that when you don't look like I could blow you over. Now come on, I'll give you a hand in the shower."

"No, damn it, I'm perfectly capable of taking a shower by myself." Ignoring the pain in her leg, she stormed out of the room, slamming the door at her back. Linda swallowed a laugh and sat down on the bed to wait.

Fifteen minutes later, refreshed and thoroughly ashamed of herself, Kate came back in. Wrapped in Ky's robe, she rubbed a towel over her hair. "Linda—"

"Don't apologize. If I'd been stuck in bed for two days, I'd snap at the first person who gave me trouble. Besides—"

Linda knew how to play her cards "—if you're really sorry, you'll eat all your soup, so Ky won't yell at me."

"All right." Resigned, Kate sat back in the bed and took the tray on her lap. She swallowed the first bite of soup and stifled her objection as Linda began to fiddle with her bandage. "It's wonderful."

"The seafood chowder's one of our specialties. Oh, honey." Linda's eyes darkened with concern after she removed the gauze. "This must've hurt like hell. No wonder Ky's been frantic."

Drumming up her courage, Kate leaned over enough to look at the wound. There was no inflammation as she'd feared, no puffiness. Though the slice was six inches in length, it was clean. Her stomach muscles unknotted. "It's not so bad," she murmured. "There's no infection."

"Look, I've been caught by a stingray, a small one. I probably had a cut half an inch across and I cried like a baby. Don't tell me it's not so bad."

"Well, I slept through most of it." She winced, then deliberately relaxed her muscles.

Linda narrowed her eyes as she studied Kate's face. "Ky said you should have a pill if there was any pain when you woke."

"If you want to do me a favor, you can dump them out." Calmly, Kate ate another spoonful of soup. "I really hate to argue with him, or with you, but I'm not taking any more pills and losing any more time. I appreciate the fact that he wants to pamper me. It's unexpectedly sweet, but I can only take it so far."

"He's worried about you. He feels responsible."

"For my carelessness?" With a shake of her head, Kate concentrated on finishing the soup. "It was an accident, and if there's blame, it's mine. I was so wrapped up in looking for salvage I didn't take basic precautions. I practically bumped into the ray." With an effort, she controlled a shudder. "Ky acted much more quickly than I. He'd already started to pull me out of range. If he hadn't, things would have been much more serious."

"He loves you."

Kate's fingers tightened on the spoon. With exaggerated care, she set it back on the tray. "Linda, there's a vast difference between concern, attraction, even affection and love."

Linda simply nodded in agreement. "Yes. I said Ky loves you."

She managed to smile and pick up the tea that had been cooling beside the soup. "*You* said," Kate returned simply. "*Ky* hasn't."

"Well neither did Marsh until I was ready to strangle him, but that didn't stop me."

"I'm not you." Kate lay back against the pillows, grateful that most of the weakness and the weariness had passed. "And Ky isn't Marsh."

Impatient, Linda rose and swirled around the room. "People who complicate simple things make me so mad!"

Smiling, Kate sipped her tea. "Others simplify the complicated."

With a sniff, Linda turned back. "I've known Ky Silver all my life. I watched him bounce around from one cute girl to the next, then one attractive woman to another until I lost count. Then you came along." Stopping, she leaned against the bedpost. "It was as if someone had hit him over the head with a blunt instrument. You dazed him, Kate, almost from the first minute. You fascinated him."

"Dazing, fascinating." Kate shrugged while she tried to ignore the ache in her heart. "Flattering, I suppose, but neither of those things equals love."

The stubborn line came and went between Linda's brows.

"I don't believe love comes in an instant, it grows. If you could have seen the way Ky was after you left four years ago, you'd know—"

"Don't tell me about four years ago," Kate interrupted. "What happened four years ago is over. Ky and I are two different people today, with different expectations. This time . . ." She took a deep breath. "This time when it ends, I won't be hurt because I know the limits."

"You've just gotten back together and you're already talking about endings and limitations!" Dragging a hand through her hair, Linda came forward to sit on the edge of the bed. "What's wrong with you? Don't you know how to wish anymore? How to dream?"

"I was never very good at either. Linda . . ." She hesitated, wanting to choose her phrasing carefully. "I don't want to expect any more from Ky than what he can easily give. After August, I know we'll each go back to our separate worlds—there's no bridge between them. Maybe I was meant to come back so we could make up for whatever pain we caused each other before. This time I want to leave still being friends. He's . . ." She hesitated again because this phrasing was even more important. "He's always been a very important part of my life."

Linda waited a moment, then narrowed her eyes. "That's about the dumbest thing I've ever heard."

Despite herself, Kate laughed. "Linda—"

Holding up her hands, she shook her head and cut Kate off. "No, I can't talk about it anymore, I get too mad and I'm supposed to be taking care of you." She let out her breath on a huff as she removed Kate's tray. "I just can't understand how anyone so smart could be so stupid, but the more I think about it the more I can see that you and Ky deserve each other."

"That sounds more like an insult than a compliment."

"It was."

Kate pushed her tongue against her teeth to hold back a smile. "I see."

"Don't look so smug just because you've made me so angry I don't want to talk about it anymore." She drew her shoulders back. "I might just give Ky a piece of my mind when he gets home."

"That's his problem," Kate said cheerfully. "Where'd he go?"

"Diving."

Amusement faded. "Alone?"

"There's no use worrying about it." Linda spoke briskly as she cursed herself for not thinking of a simple lie. "He dives alone ninety percent of the time."

"I know." But Kate folded her hands, preparing to worry until he returned.

CHAPTER 9

I'm going with you."

The sunlight was strong, the scent of the ocean pure. Through the screen the sound of gulls from a quarter of a mile away could be heard clearly. Ky turned from the stove where he poured the last cup of coffee and eyed Kate as she stood in the doorway.

She'd pinned her hair up and had dressed in thin cotton pants and a shirt, both of which were baggy and cool. It occured to him that she looked more like a student than a college professor.

He knew enough of women and their illusions to see that she'd added color to her cheeks. She hadn't needed blusher the evening before when he'd returned from the wreck. Then she had been angry, and passionate. He nearly smiled as he lifted his cup.

"You wasted your time getting dressed," he said easily. "You're going back to bed."

Kate disliked stubborn people, people who demanded their own way flatly and unreasonably. At that moment, she decided they were *both* stubborn. "No." On the surface she remained as calm as he was while she walked into the kitchen. "I'm going with you."

Unlike Kate, Ky never minded a good argument. Preparing for one, he leaned back against the stove. "I don't take down a diver against doctor's orders."

She'd expected that. With a shrug, she opened the refrigerator and took out a bottle of juice. She knew she was being bad tempered, and though it was completely out of character, she was enjoying the experience. The simple truth was that she had to do something or go mad.

As far as she could remember, she'd never spent two more listless days. She had to move, think, feel the sun. It might have been satisfying to stomp her feet and demand, but, she thought, fruitless. If she had to compromise to get her way, then compromise she would.

"I can rent a boat and equipment and go down on my own." With the glass in hand, she turned, challenging. "You can't stop me."

"Try me."

It was said simply, quietly, but she'd seen the flare of anger in his eyes. *Better,* she thought. *Much better.* "I've a right to do precisely as I choose. We both know it." Perhaps her leg was uncomfortable, but as to the rest of her body, it was charged up and ready to move. Nor was there anything wrong with her mind. Kate had plotted her strategy very well. After all, she thought grimly, there'd certainly been enough time to think it through.

"We both know you're not in any shape to dive." His first urge was to carry her back to bed, his second to shake her until she rattled. Ky did neither, only drank his coffee and watched her over the rim. A power struggle wasn't something he'd expected, but he wouldn't back away from it. "You're not stupid, Kate. You know you can't go down yet, and you know I won't let you."

"I've rested for two days. I feel fine." As she walked toward him she was pleased to see him frown. He understood she had a mind of her own, and that he had to deal with it. The truth was, she was stronger than either of them had expected her to be. "As far as diving goes, I'm willing to leave that to you for the next couple of days, but . . ." She paused, wanting to be certain he knew she was negotiating, not conceding. "I'm going out on the *Vortex* with you. And I'm going out this morning."

He lifted a brow. She'd never intended to dive, but she'd used it as a pressure point to get what she wanted. He couldn't blame her. Ky remembered recovering from a broken leg when he was fourteen. The pain was vague in his mind now, but the boredom was still perfectly clear. "You'll lie down in the cabin when you're told."

She smiled and shook her head. "I'll lie down in the cabin if I need to."

He took her chin in his hand and squeezed. "Damn right you will. Okay, let's go. I want an early start."

Once he was resigned, Ky moved quickly. She could either keep up, or be left behind. Within minutes he parked his car near his slip at Silver Lake Harbor and was boarding the *Vortex*. Content, Kate took a seat beside him at the helm and prepared to enjoy the sun and the wind. Already she felt the energy begin to churn.

"I've done a chart of the wreck as of yesterday's dive," he told her as he maneuvered out of the harbor.

"A chart?" Automatically she pushed at her hair as she turned toward him. "You didn't show me."

"Because you were asleep when I finished it."

"I've been asleep ninety percent of the time," she mumbled.

As he headed out to sea, Ky laid a hand on her shoulder. "You look better, Kate, no shadows. No strain. That's more important."

For a moment, just a moment, she pressed her cheek

against his hand. Few women could resist such soft concern, and yet . . . she didn't want his concern to cloud their reason for being together. Concern could turn to pity. She needed him to see her as a partner, as equal. As long as she was his lover, it was vital that they meet on the same ground. Then when she left . . . When she left there'd be no regrets.

"I don't need to be pampered anymore, Ky."

His shoulders moved as he glanced at the compass. "I enjoyed it."

She was resisting being cared for. He understood it, appreciated it and regretted it. There had been something appealing about seeing to her needs, about having her depend on him. He didn't know how to tell her he wanted her to be well and strong just as much as he wanted her to turn to him in times of need.

Somehow, he felt their time together had been too short for him to speak. He didn't deal well with caution. As a diver, he knew its importance, but as a man . . . As a man he fretted to go with his instincts, with his impulses.

His fingers brushed her neck briefly before he turned to the wheel. He'd already decided he'd have to approach his relationship with Kate as he'd approach a very deep, very dangerous dive—with an eye on currents, pressure and the unexpected.

"That chart's in the cabin," he told her as he cut the engine. "You might want to look it over while I'm down."

She agreed with a nod, but the restlessness was already on her as Ky began to don his equipment. She didn't want to make an issue of his diving alone. He wouldn't listen to her in any case; if anything came of it, it would only be an argument. In silence she watched him check his tanks. He'd be down for an hour. Kate was already marking time.

"There are cold drinks in the galley." He adjusted the strap of his mask before climbing over the side. "Don't sit in the sun too long."

"Be careful," she blurted out before she could stop herself.

Ky grinned, then was gone with a quiet splash.

Though she ran over to the side, Kate was too late to watch him dive. For a long time after, she simply leaned over the boat, staring at the water's surface. She imagined Ky going deeper, deeper, adjusting his pressure, moving out with power until he'd reached the bottom and the wreck.

He'd brought back the bowl and ladle the evening before. They sat on the dresser in his bedroom while the broken rigging and pieces of crockery were stored downstairs. Thus far he'd done no more than gather what they'd already found together, but today, Kate thought with a twinge of impatience, he'd extend the search. Whatever he found, he'd find alone.

She turned away from the water, frustrated that she was excluded. It occurred to her that all her life she'd been an onlooker, someone who analyzed and explained the action rather than causing it. This search had been her first opportunity to change that, and now she was back to square one.

Stuffing her hands in her pockets, Kate looked up at the sky. There were clouds to the west, but they were thin and white. Harmless. She felt too much like that herself at the moment—something unsubstantial. Sighing, she went below deck. There was nothing to do now but wait.

Ky found two more cannons and sent up buoys to mark their position. It would be possible, if he didn't find something more concrete, to salvage the cannons and have them dated by an expert. Though he swam from end to end, searching carefully, he knew it was unlikely he'd find a date stamp through the layers of corrosion. But in time . . . Satisfied, he swam north.

If he accomplished nothing else on this dive, he wanted

to establish the size of the site. With luck it would be fairly small, perhaps no bigger than a football field. However, there was always the chance that the wreckage could be scattered over several square miles. Before they brought in a salvage ship, he wanted to take a great deal of care with the preliminary work.

They would need tools. A metal detector would be invaluable. Thus far, they'd done no more than find a wreck, no matter how certain Kate was that it was the *Liberty*. For the moment he had no way to determine the origin of the ship, he had to find cargo. Once he'd found that, perhaps treasure would follow.

Once he'd found the treasure . . . Would she leave? Would she take her share of the gold and the artifacts and drive home?

Not if he could help it, Ky determined as he shone his headlamp over the sea floor. When the search was over and they'd salvaged what could be salvaged from the sea, it would be time to salvage what they'd once had—what had perhaps never truly been lost. If they could find what had been buried for centuries, they could find what had been buried for four years.

He couldn't find much without tools. Most of the ship—or what remained of it—was buried under silt. On another dive, he'd use the prop-wash, the excavation device he'd constructed in his shop. With that he could blow away inches of sediment at a time—a slow but safe way to uncover artifacts. But someone would have to stay on board to run it.

He thought of Kate and rejected the idea immediately. Though he had no doubt she could handle the technical aspect—it would only have to be explained to her once—she'd never go for it. Ky began to think it was time they enlisted Marsh.

He knew his air time was almost up and he'd have to surface for fresh tanks. Still, he lingered near the bottom, searching, prodding. He wanted to take something up for Kate, something tangible that would put the enthusiasm back in her eyes.

It took him more than half of his allotted time to find it, but when Ky held the unbroken bottle in his hand, he knew Kate's reaction would be worth the effort. It was a common bottle, not priceless crystal, but he could see no mold marks, which meant it had been hand blown. Crust was weathered over it in layers, but Ky took the time to carefully chip some away, from the bottom only. If the date wasn't on the bottom, he'd need the crust to have the bottle dated. Already he was thinking of the Corning Glass Museum and their rate of success.

Then he saw the date, and with a satisfied grin placed the find in the goodie bag on his belt. With his air supply running short, he started toward the surface.

His hour was up. Or so nearly up, Kate thought, that he should have surfaced already if he'd allowed himself any safety factor. She paced from port to starboard and back again. Would he always risk his own welfare to the limit?

She'd long since given up sitting quietly in the cabin, going over the makeshift chart Ky had begun. She'd found a book on shipwrecks that Ky had obviously purchased recently, and though it had also been among her father's research books, she'd skimmed through it again.

It gave a detailed guide to identifying and excavating a wreck, listed common mistakes and hazards. She found it difficult to read about hazards while Ky was alone beneath the surface. Still, even the simple language of the book couldn't disguise the adventure. For perhaps half the time Ky had been gone, she'd lost herself in it. Spanish galleons, Dutch merchant ships, English frigates.

She'd found the list of wrecks off North Carolina alone extensive. But these, she'd thought, had already been located,

documented. The adventure there was over. One day, because
of the chain her father had started and she'd continued, the
Liberty would be among them.

Fretfully, Kate waited for Ky to surface. She thought of her
father. He'd pored over this same book as well—planning,
calculating. Yet his calculations hadn't taken him beyond
the initial stage. If he'd shared his goal with her, would he
have taken her on his summer quests? She'd never know, because she'd never been given the choice.

She was making her own choices now, Kate mused. Her
first had been to return to Ocracoke, accepting the consequences. Her next had been to give herself to Ky without
conditions. Her last, she thought as she stared down at the
quiet water, would be to leave him again. Yet, in reality,
perhaps she'd still been given no choice. It was all a matter of currents. She could only swim against them for so
long.

Relief washed over her when she spotted the flow of bubbles. Ky grabbed the bottom rung of the ladder as he pushed
up his mask. "Waiting for me?"

Relief mixed with annoyance for the time she'd spent worrying about him. "You cut it close."

"Yeah, a little." He passed up his tanks. "I had to stop and
get you a present."

"It's not a joke, Ky." Kate watched him come over the side,
agile, lean and energetic. "You'd be furious with me if I'd cut
my time that close."

"Leave it up to Linda to fuss," he advised as he pulled
down the zipper of his wet suit. "She was born that way." Then
he grabbed her, crushing her against him so that she felt the
excitement he'd brought up with him. His mouth closed over
hers, tasting of salt from the sea. Because he was wet, her
clothes clung to him, binding them together for the brief instant he held her. But when he would have released her, she

held fast, drawing the kiss out into something that warmed his cool skin.

"I worry about you, Ky." For one last moment, she held on fiercely. "Damn it, is that what you want to hear?"

"No." He took her face in his hands and shook his head. "No."

Kate broke away, afraid she'd say too much, afraid she'd say things neither of them were ready to hear. She knew the rules this time. She groped for something calm, something simple. "I suppose I got a bit frantic waiting up here. It's different when you're down."

"Yeah." What did she want from him? he wondered. Why was it that every time she started to show her concern for him, she clammed up? "I've got some more things to add to the chart."

"I saw the buoys you sent up." Kate moistened her lips and relaxed, muscle by muscle.

"Two more cannons. From the size of them, I'd say she was a fairly small ship. It's unlikely she was constructed for battle."

"She was a merchant ship."

"Maybe. I'm going to take the metal detector down and see what I come up with. From the stuff we've found, I don't think she's buried too deep."

Kate nodded. Delve into business, keep the personal aspect light. "I'd like to send off a piece of the planking and some of the glass to be analyzed. I think we'll have more luck with the glass, but it doesn't hurt to cover all the angles."

"No, it doesn't. Don't you want your present?"

At ease again, she smiled. "I thought you were joking. Did you bring me a shell?"

"I thought you'd like this better." Reaching into his bag, Ky brought out the bottle. "It's too bad it's not still corked. We could've had wine with peanut butter."

"Oh, Ky, it's not damaged!" Thrilled, she reached out for it, but he pulled it back out of reach and grinned.

"Bottoms up," he told her and turned the bottle upside down.

Kate stared at the smeared bottom of the bottle. "Oh, God," she whispered. "It's dated. 1749." Gingerly, she took the bottle in both hands. "The year before the *Liberty* sank."

"It's another ship, maybe," Ky reminded her. "But it does narrow down the time element."

"Over two hundred years," she murmured. "Glass, it's so breakable, so vulnerable, and yet it survived two centuries." Her eyes lit with enthusiasm as she looked back at him. "Ky, we should be able to find out where the bottle was made."

"Probably, but most glass bottles found on wrecks from the seventeenth and eighteenth century were manufactured in England anyway. It wouldn't prove the ship was English."

She let out a huff of breath, but her energy hadn't dimmed. "You've been doing your research."

"I don't go into any project until I know the angles." Ky knelt down to check the fresh tanks.

"You're going back down now?"

"I want to get as much mapped out as I can before we start dealing with too much equipment."

She'd done enough homework herself to know that the most common mistake of the modern-day salvor was in failing to map out a site. Yet she couldn't stem her impatience. It seemed so time-consuming when they could be concentrating on getting under the layers of silt.

It seemed to her that she and Ky had changed positions somehow. She'd always been the cautious one, proceeding step by logical step, while he'd taken the risks. Struggling with the impotence of having to wait and watch, she stood back while he strapped on the fresh tanks. As she watched, Ky picked up a brass rod.

"What's that for?"

"It's the base for this." He held out a device that resembled a compass. "It's called an azimuth circle. It's a cheap, effective way to map out the site. I drive this into the approximate center of the wreck so that it becomes the datum point, align the circle with the magnetic north, then I use a length of chain to measure the distance to the cannons, or whatever I need to map. After I get it set, I'll be back up for the metal detector."

Frustration built again. He was doing all the work while she simply stood still. "Ky, I feel fine. I could help if—"

"No." He didn't bother to argue or list reasons. He simply went over the side and under.

It was midafternoon when they started back. Ky spent the last hour at sea adding to the chart, putting in the information he'd gathered that day. He'd brought more up in his goodie bag —a tankard, spoons and forks that might have been made of iron. It seemed they had indeed found the galley. Kate decided she'd begin a detailed list of their finds that evening. If it was all she could do at the moment, she'd do it with pleasure.

Her mood had lifted a bit since she'd caught three good-size bluefish while Ky had been down at the wreck the second time. No matter how much Ky argued, she fully intended to cook them herself and eat them sitting at the table, not lying in bed.

"Pretty pleased with yourself, aren't you?"

She gave him a cool smile. They were cruising back toward Silver Lake Harbor and though she felt a weariness, it was a pleasant feeling, not the dragging fatigue of the past days. "Three bluefish in that amount of time's a very respectable haul."

"No argument there. Especially since I intend to eat half of them."

"I'm going to grill them."

"Are you?"

She met his lifted brow with a neutral look. "I caught, I cook."

Ky kept the boat at an even speed as he studied her. She looked a bit tired, but he thought he could convince her to take a nap if he claimed he wanted one himself. She was healing quickly. And she was right. He couldn't pamper her. "I could probably bring myself to start the charcoal for you."

"Fair enough. I'll even let you clean them."

He laughed at the bland tone and ruffled her hair until the pins fell out.

"Ky!" Automatically, Kate reached up to repair the damage.

"Wear it up in the school room," he advised, tossing some of the pins overboard. "I find it difficult to resist you when your hair's down and just a bit mussed."

"Is that so?" She debated being annoyed, then decided there were more productive ways to pass the time. Kate let the wind toss her hair as she moved closer to him so that their bodies touched. She smiled at the quick look of surprise in his eyes as she slipped both hands under his T-shirt. "Why don't you turn off the engine and show me what happens when you stop resisting?"

For all her generosity and freedom in lovemaking, she'd never been the initiator. Ky found himself both baffled and aroused as she smiled up at him, her hands stroking slowly over his chest. "You know what happens when I stop resisting," he murmured.

She gave a low, quiet laugh. "Refresh my memory." Without waiting for an answer, she drew back on the throttle herself until the boat was simply idling. "You didn't make love with me last night." Her hands slid around and up his back.

"You were sleeping." She was seducing him in the middle

of the afternoon, in the middle of the ocean. He found he wanted to savor the new experience as much as he wanted to bring it to fruition.

"I'm not sleeping now." Rising on her toes, she brushed her lips over his, lightly, temptingly. She felt his heartbeat race against her body and reveled in a sense of power she'd never explored. "Or perhaps you're in a hurry to get back, and uh, clean fish."

She was taunting him. Why had he never seen the witch in her before? Ky felt his stomach knot with need, but when he drew her closer, she resisted. Just slightly. Just enough to torment. "If I make love with you now, I won't be gentle."

She kept her lips inches from his. "Is that a warning?" she whispered. "Or a promise?"

He felt the first tremor move through him and was astonished. Not even for her had he ever trembled. Not even for her. The need grew, stretching restlessly, recklessly. "I'm not sure you know what you're doing, Kate."

Nor did she, but she smiled because it no longer mattered. Only the outcome mattered. "Come down to the cabin with me and we'll both find out." She slipped away from him and without a word disappeared below deck.

His hand wasn't steady when he reached for the key to turn off the engines. He needed a moment, perhaps a bit more, to regain the control he'd held so carefully since they'd become lovers again. Ever since he'd had her blood on his hands, he had a tremendous fear of hurting her. Since he'd had a taste of her again, he had an equal fear of driving her away. Caution was a strain, but he'd kept it in focus with sheer will. As Ky started down the steps, he told himself he'd continue to be cautious.

She'd unbuttoned her blouse but hadn't removed it. When he came into the narrow cabin with her, Kate smiled. She was afraid, though she hardly knew why. But over the fear was a heady sense of power and strength that fought for full release. She wanted to take him to the edge, to push him to the limits of passion. At that moment, she was certain she could.

When he came no closer to her, Kate stepped forward and pulled his shirt over his head. "Your skin's gold," she murmured. "It's always excited me." Taking her pleasure slowly, she ran her hands up his sides, feeling the quiver she caused. "You've always excited me."

Her hands were steady, her pulse throbbed as she unsnapped his cut-offs. With her eyes on his, she slowly, slowly, undressed him. "No one's ever made me want the way you make me want."

He had to stop her and take control again. She couldn't know the effect of those long, fragile fingers when they brushed easily over his skin, or how her calm eyes made him rage inside.

"Kate . . ." He took her hands in his and bent to kiss her. But she turned her head, meeting his neck with warm lips that sent a spear of fire up his spine.

Then her body was pressed against his, flesh meeting flesh where her blouse parted. Her mouth trailed over his chest, her hands down his back to his hips. He felt the fury of desire whip through him as though it had sharp, hungry teeth.

So he forgot control, gentleness, vulnerability. She drove him to forget. She intended to.

They were tangled on the narrow bunk, her blouse halfway down her back and parted so that her breasts pushed into his chest, driving him mad with their firm, subtle curves. She nipped at his lips, demanding, pushing for more, still more. Waves of passion overtook them.

His need was incendiary. She was like a flame, impossible to hold, searing here, singeing there until his body was burning with needs and fierce fantasies.

Her hands were swift, sending sharp gasping pleasure

everywhere at once until he wasn't sure he could take it anymore. Yet he no longer thought of stopping her. Less of stopping himself.

His hands gripped her with an urgency that made her moan from the sheer strength in them. She wanted his strength now—mindless strength that would carry them both to a place they'd never gone before. And she was leading. The knowledge made her laugh aloud as she tasted his skin, his lips, his tongue.

She slid down his body, feeling each jolt of pleasure as it shot through him. There could be no slow, lingering loving now. They'd pushed each other beyond reason. The air here was dark and thin and whirling with sound. Kate drank it in.

When he found her moist, hot and ready she let him take her over peak after shuddering peak, knowing as he drove her, she drove him. Her body was filled with sensations that came and went like comets, slipped away and burst on her again, and again. Through the thunder in her head she heard herself say his name, clear and quick.

On the sound, she took him into her and welcomed the madness.

CHAPTER 10

S he was wrong.

Kate had thought she'd be ready, even anxious to dive again. There hadn't been a day during her recuperation that she hadn't thought of going down. Every time Ky had brought back an artifact, she was thrilled with the discovery and frustrated with her own lack of participation. Like a schoolgirl approaching summer, she'd begun to count the days.

Now, a week after the accident, Kate stood on the deck of the *Vortex* with her mouth dry and her hands trembling as she pulled on her wet suit. She could only be grateful that Ky was already over the side, hooking up his home-rigged propwash to the boat's propeller. Drafted to the crew, Marsh stood at the stern watching his brother. With Linda's eager support, he'd agreed to give Ky a few hours a day of his precious free time while he was needed.

Kate took the moment she had alone to gather her thoughts and her nerve.

It was only natural to be anxious about diving after the experience she'd had. Kate told herself that was logical. But it didn't stop her hands from trembling as she zipped up her suit. She could equate it with falling off a horse and having to mount again. It was psychological. But it didn't ease the painful tension in her stomach.

Trembling hands and nerves. With or without them, she told herself as she hooked on her weight belt, she was going down. Nothing, not even her own fears, was going to stop her from finishing what she'd begun.

"He's got it," Marsh called out when Ky signaled him.

"I'll be ready." Kate picked up the cloth bag she'd use to bring up small artifacts. With luck, and if the prop-wash did its job, she knew they'd soon need more sophisticated methods to bring up the salvage.

"Kate."

She didn't look up, but continued to hook on the goodie bag. "Yes?"

"You know it's only natural that you'd be nervous going down." Marsh touched a hand to her shoulder, but she busied herself by strapping on her diving knife. "If you want a little more time, I'll work with Ky and you can run the wash."

"No." She said it too quickly, then cursed herself. "It's all right, Marsh." With forced calm she hung the underwater camera she'd purchased only the day before around her neck. "I have to take the first dive sometime."

"It doesn't have to be now."

She smiled at him again thinking how calm, how steady he appeared when compared to Ky. This was the sort of man it would have made sense for her to be attracted to. Confused emotions made no sense. "Yes, it does. Please." She put her hand on his arm before he could speak again. "Don't say anything to Ky."

Did she think he'd have to? Marsh wondered as he inclined his head in agreement. Unless he was way off the mark, Marsh was certain Ky knew every expression, every gesture, every intonation of her voice.

"Let's run it a couple of minutes at full throttle." Ky climbed over the side, dripping and eager. "With the depth and the size of the prop, we're going to have to test the effect. There might not be enough power to do us any good."

In agreement, Marsh went to the helm. "Are you thinking about using an air lift?"

Ky's only answer was a noncommittal grunt. He had thought of it. The metal tube with its stream of compressed air was a quick, efficient way to excavate on silty bottoms. They might get away with the use of a small air lift, if it became necessary. But perhaps the prop-wash would do the job well enough. Either way, he was thinking more seriously about a bigger ship, with more sophisticated equipment and more power. As he saw it, it all depended on what they found today.

He picked up one last piece of equipment—a small powerful spear gun. He'd take no more chances with Kate.

"Okay, slow it down to the minimum," he ordered. "And keep it there. Once Kate and I are down, we don't want the prop-wash shooting cannonballs around."

Kate stopped the deep breathing she was using to ease tension. Her voice was cool and steady. "Would it have that kind of power?"

"Not at this speed." Ky adjusted his mask then took her hand. "Ready?"

"Yes."

Then he kissed her, hard. "You've got guts, professor," he murmured. His eyes were dark, intense as they passed over her face. "It's one of the sexiest things about you." With this he was over the side.

He knew. Kate gave a quiet unsteady sigh as she started down the ladder. He knew she was afraid, and that had been his way of giving her support. She looked up once and saw Marsh. He lifted his hand in salute. Throat dry, nerves jumping, Kate let the sea take her.

She felt a moment's panic, a complete disorientation the moment she was submerged. It ran through her head that down here, she was helpless. The deeper she went, the more vulnerable she became. Choking for air, she kicked back toward the surface and the light.

Then Ky had her hands, holding her to him, holding her under. His grip was firm, stilling the first panic. Feeling the wild race of her pulse, he held on during her first resistance.

Then he touched her cheek, waiting until she'd calmed enough to look at him. In his eyes she saw strength and challenge. Pride alone forced her to fight her way beyond the fear and meet him, equal to equal.

When she'd regulated her breathing, accepting that her air came through the tanks on her back, he kissed the back of her hand. Kate felt the tension give. She wouldn't be helpless, she reminded herself. She'd be careful.

With a nod, she pointed down, indicating she was ready to dive. Keeping hands linked, they started toward the bottom.

The whirlpool action created by the wash of the prop had already blasted away some of the sediment. At first glance Ky could see that if the wreck was buried under more than a few feet, they'd need something stronger than his homemade apparatus and single prop engine. But for now, it would do. Patience, which came to him only with deliberate effort, was more important at this stage than speed. With the wreck, he thought, and—he glanced over at the woman beside him—with a great deal more. He had to take care not to hurry.

It was still working, blowing away some of the overburden at a rate Ky figured would equal an inch per minute. He and Kate alone couldn't deal with any more speed. He watched the swirl of water and sediment while she swam a few feet away to catalog one of the cannons on film. When she came closer, he grinned as she placed the camera in front of her face again. She was relaxed, her initial fear forgotten. He could see it simply in the way she moved. Then she let the camera fall so they could begin the search again.

Kate saw something solid wash away from the hole being created by the whirl of water. Grabbing it up, she found herself holding a candlestick. In her excitement, she turned it over and over in her hand.

Silver? she wondered with a rush of adrenaline. Had they found their first real treasure? It was black with oxidation, so it was impossible to be certain what it was made of. Still, it thrilled her. After days and days of only waiting, she was again pursuing the dream.

When she looked up, Ky was already gathering the uncovered items and laying them in the mesh basket. There were more candleholders, more tableware, but not the plain unglazed pottery they'd found before. Kate's pulse began to drum with excitement while she meticulously snapped pictures. They'd be able to find a hallmark, she was certain of it. Then they'd know if they had indeed found a British ship. Ordinary seamen didn't use silver, or even pewter table service. They'd uncovered more than the galley now. And they were just beginning.

When Ky found the first piece of porcelain he signaled to her. True, the vase—if that's what it once had been—had suffered under the water pressure and the years. It was broken so that only half of the shell remained, but so did the manufacturer's mark.

When Kate read it, she gripped Ky's arm. *Whieldon.* English. The master potter who'd trained the likes of Wedgwood. Kate cupped the broken fragment in her hands as though it were alive. When she lifted her eyes to Ky's, they were filled with triumph.

Fretting against her inability to speak, Kate pointed to

the mark again. Ky merely nodded and indicated the basket. Though she was loath to part with it, Kate found herself even more eager to discover more. She settled the porcelain in the mesh. When she swam back, Ky's hands were filled with other pieces. Some were hardly more than shards, others were identifiable as pieces left from bowls or lids.

No, it didn't prove it was a merchant ship, Kate told herself as she gathered what she could herself. So far, it only proved that the officers and perhaps some passengers had eaten elegantly on their way to the New World. English officers, she reminded herself. In her mind they'd taken the identification that far.

The force of the wash sent an object shooting up. Ky reached out for it and found a crusted, filthy pot he guessed would have been used for tea or coffee. Perhaps it was cracked under the layers, but it held together in his hands. He tapped on his tank to get Kate's attention.

She knew it was priceless the moment she saw it. Stemming impatience, she signaled for Ky to hold it out as she lifted the camera again. Obliging, he crossed his legs like a genie and posed.

It made her giggle. They'd perhaps just found something worth thousands of dollars, but he could still act silly. Nothing was too serious for Ky. As she brought him into frame, Kate felt the same foolish pleasure. She'd known the hunt would be exciting, perhaps rewarding, but she'd never known it would be fun. She swam forward and reached for the pot herself.

Running her fingers over it, she could detect some kind of design under the crust. Not ordinary pottery, she was sure. Not utility-ware. She held something elegant, something well crafted.

He understood its worth as well as she. Taking it from her, Ky indicated they would bring it and the rest of the morning's salvage to the surface. Pointing to his watch he showed her that their tanks were running low.

She didn't argue. They'd come back. The *Liberty* would wait for them. Each took a handle of the mesh basket and swam leisurely toward the surface.

"Do you know how I feel?" Kate demanded the moment she could speak.

"Yes." Ky gripped the ladder with one hand and waited for her to unstrap her tanks and slip them over onto the deck. "I know just how you feel."

"The teapot." Breathing fast, she hauled herself up the ladder. "Ky, it's priceless. It's like finding a perfectly formed rose inside a mass of briars." Before he could answer, she was laughing and calling out to Marsh. "It's fabulous! Absolutely fabulous."

Marsh cut the engine then walked over to help them. "You two work fast." Bending he touched a tentative finger to the pot. "God, it's all in one piece."

"We'll be able to date it as soon as it's cleaned. But look." Kate drew out the broken vase. "This is the mark of an English potter. English," she repeated, turning to Ky. "He trained Wedgwood, and Wedgwood didn't begin manufacturing until the 1760s, so—"

"So this piece more than likely came from the era we're looking for," Ky finished. "*Liberty* or not," he continued, crouching down beside her. "It looks like you've found yourself an eighteenth-century wreck that's probably of English origin and certainly hasn't been recorded before." He took one of her hands between both of his. "Your father would've been proud of you."

Stunned, she stared at him. Emotions raced through her with such velocity she had no way of controlling or channeling them. The hand holding the broken vase began to tremble. Quickly, she set it down in the basket again and rose.

"I'm going below," she managed and fled.

Proud of her. Kate put a hand over her mouth as she stumbled into the cabin. His pride, his love. Wasn't it all she'd really ever wanted from her father? Was it possible she could only gain it after his death?

She drank in deep gulps of air and struggled to level her emotions. No, she wanted to find the *Liberty,* she wanted to bring her father's dream to reality, have his name on a plaque in a museum with the artifacts they'd found. She owed him that. But she'd promised herself she'd find the *Liberty* for herself as well. For herself.

It was her choice, her first real decision to come in from the sidelines and act on her own. For herself, Kate thought again as she brought the first surge of emotion under control.

"Kate?"

She turned, and though she thought she was perfectly calm, Ky could see the turmoil in her eyes. Unsure how to handle it, he spoke practically.

"You'd better get out of that suit."

"But we're going back down."

"Not today." To prove his point he began to strip out of his own suit just as Marsh started the engines.

Automatically, she balanced herself as the boat turned. "Ky, we've got two more sets of tanks. There's no reason for us to go back when we're just getting started."

"Your first dive took most of the strength you've built up. If you want to dive tomorrow, you've got to take it slow today."

Her anger erupted so quickly, it left them both astonished. "The hell with that!" she exploded. "I'm sick to death of being treated as if I don't know my own limitations or my own mind and body."

Ky walked into the galley and picked up a can of beer. With a flick of his wrist, air hissed out. "I don't know what you're talking about."

"I lay in bed for the better part of a week because of pressure from you and Linda and anyone else who came around me. I'm not tolerating this any longer."

With one hand, he pushed dripping hair from his forehead as he lifted the can. "You're tolerating exactly what's necessary until I say differently."

"You say?" she tossed back. Cheeks flaming, she strode over to him. "I don't have to do what you say, or what anyone says. Not anymore. It's about time you remember just who's in charge of this salvage operation."

His eyes narrowed. "In charge?"

"I hired you. Seventy-five a day and twenty-five percent. Those were the terms. There was nothing in there about you running my life."

He abruptly went still. For a moment, all that could be heard over the engines was her angry breathing. *Dollars and percents,* he thought with a deadly sort of calm. *Just dollars and percents.* "So that's what it comes down to?"

Too overwrought to see beyond her own anger, she continued to lash out. "We made an agreement. I fully intend to see that you get everything we arranged, but I won't have you telling me when I can go down. I won't have you judging when I'm well and when I'm not. I'm sick to death of being dictated to. And I won't be—not by you, not by anyone. Not any longer."

The metal of the can gave under his fingers. "Fine. You do exactly what you want, professor. But while you're about it, get yourself another diver. I'll send you a bill." Ky went up the cabin steps the way he came down. Quickly and without a sound.

With her hands gripped together, Kate sat down on the bunk and waited until she heard the engines stop again. She refused to think. Thinking hurt. She refused to feel. There was too much to feel. When she was certain she was in control, she stood and went up on deck.

Everything was exactly as she'd left it—the wire basket filled with bits of porcelain and tableware, her nearly depleted tanks. Ky was gone. Marsh walked over from the stern where he'd been waiting for her.

"You're going to need a hand with these."

Kate nodded and pulled a thigh length T-shirt over her tank suit. "Yes. I want to take everything back to my room at the hotel. I have to arrange for shipping."

"Okay." But instead of reaching down for the basket, he took her arm. "Kate, I don't like to give advice."

"Good." Then she swore at her own rudeness. "I'm sorry, Marsh. I'm feeling a little rough at the moment."

"I can see that, and I know things aren't always smooth for you and Ky. Look, he has a habit of closing himself up, of not saying everything that's on his mind. Or worse," Marsh added. "Of saying the first thing that comes to mind."

"He's perfectly free to do so. I came here for the specific purpose of finding and excavating the *Liberty*. If Ky and I can't deal together on a business level, I have to do without his help."

"Listen, he has a few blind spots."

"Marsh, you're his brother. Your allegiance is with him as it should be."

"I care about both of you."

She took a deep breath, refusing to let the emotion surface and carry her with it. "I appreciate that. The best thing you can do for me now, perhaps for both of us, is to tell me where I can rent a boat and some equipment. I'm going back out this afternoon."

"Kate."

"I'm going back out this afternoon," she repeated. "With or without your help."

Resigned, Marsh picked up the mesh basket. "All right, you can use mine."

* * *

It took the rest of the morning for Kate to arrange everything, including the resolution of a lengthy argument with Marsh. She refused to let him come with her, ending by saying she'd simply rent a boat and do without his assistance altogether. In the end, she stood at the helm of his boat alone and headed out to sea.

She craved the solitude. Almost in defiance, she pushed the throttle forward. If it was defiance, she didn't care, any more than she cared whom she was defying. It was vital to do this one act for herself.

She refused to think about Ky, about why she'd exploded at him. If her words had been harsh, they'd also been necessary. She comforted herself with that. For too long, for a lifetime, she'd been influenced by someone else's opinion, someone else's expectations.

Mechanically, she stopped the engines and put on her equipment, checking and rechecking as she went. She'd never gone down alone before. Even that seemed suddenly a vital thing to do.

With a last look at her compass, she took the mesh basket over the side.

As she went deep, a thrill went through her. She was alone. In acres and acres of sea, she was alone. The water parted for her like silk. She was in control, and her destiny was her own.

She didn't rush. Kate found she wanted that euphoric feeling of being isolated under the sea where only curious fish bothered to give her a passing glance. Ultimately, her only responsibility here was to herself. Briefly, she closed her eyes and floated. At last, only to herself.

When she reached the site, she felt a new surge of pride. This was something she'd done without her father. She wouldn't think of the whys or the hows now, but simply the triumph. For two centuries, it had waited. And now, *she'd* found it. She circled the hole the prop-wash had created and began to fan using her hand.

Her first find was a dinner plate with a flamboyant floral pattern around the rim. She found one, then half a dozen, two of which were intact. On the back was the mark of an English potter. There were cups as well, dainty, exquisite English china that might have graced the table of a wealthy colonist, might have become a beloved heirloom, if nature hadn't interfered. Now they looked like something out of a horror show—crusted, misshapen with sea life. They couldn't have been more beautiful to her.

As she continued to fan, Kate nearly missed what appeared to be a dark sea shell. On closer examination she saw it was a silver coin. She couldn't make out the currency, but knew it didn't matter. It could just as easily be Spanish, as she'd read that Spanish currency had been used by all European nations with settlements in the New World.

The point was, it was a coin. The first coin. Though it was silver, not gold, and unidentifiable at the moment, she'd found it by herself.

Kate started to slip it into her goodie bag when her arm was jerked back.

The thrill of fear went wildly from her toes to her throat. The spear gun was on board the *Vortex.* She had no weapon. Before she could do more than turn in defense, she was caught by the shoulders with Ky's furious hands.

Terror died, but the anger in his eyes only incited her own.

Damn him for frightening her, for interfering. Shaking him away, Kate signaled for him to leave. With one arm, he encircled her waist and started for the surface.

Only once did she even come close to breaking away from him. Ky simply banded his arm around her again, more tightly, until she had a choice between submitting or cutting off her own air.

When they broke the surface, Kate drew in breath to shout, but even in this, she was out-maneuvered.

"Idiot!" he shouted at her, dragging her to the ladder. "One day off your back and you jump into forty feet of water by yourself. I don't know why in hell I ever thought you had any brains."

Breathless, she heaved her tanks over the side. When she was on solid ground again, she intended to have her say. For now, she'd let him have his.

"I take my eyes off you for a couple hours and you go off half-cocked. If I'd murdered Marsh, it would have been on your head."

To her further fury, Kate saw that she'd boarded the *Vortex*. Marsh's boat was nowhere in sight.

"Where's the *Gull?*" she demanded.

"Marsh had the sense to tell me what you were doing." The words came out like bullets as he stripped off his gear. "I didn't kill him because I needed him to come out with me and take the *Gull* back." He stood in front of her, dripping, and as furious as she'd ever seen him. "Don't you have any more sense than to dive out here alone?"

She tossed her head back. "Don't you?"

Infuriated, he grabbed her and started to peel the wet suit from her himself. "We're not talking about me, damn it. I've been diving since I was six. I know the currents."

"*I* know the currents."

"And I haven't been flat on my back for a week."

"I was flat on my back for a week because you were over-reacting." She struggled away from him, and because the wet suit was already down to her waist, peeled it off. "You've no right to tell me when and where I can dive, Ky. Superior strength gives you no right to drag me up when I'm in the middle of salvaging."

"The hell with what I have a right to do." Grabbing her again, he shook her with more violence than he'd ever shown her. A dozen things might have happened to her in the thirty minutes she'd been down. A dozen things he knew too well. "I make my own rights. You're not going down alone if I have to chain you up to stop it."

"You told me to get another diver," she said between her teeth. "Until I do, I dive alone."

"You threw that damn business arrangement in my face. Percentages. Lousy percentages and a daily rate. Do you know how that made me feel?"

"No!" she shouted, pushing him away. "No, I don't know how that made you feel. I don't know how anything makes you feel. You don't tell me." Dragging both hands through her dripping hair she walked away. "We agreed to the terms. That's all I know."

"That was before."

"Before what?" she demanded. Tears brimmed for no reason she could name, but she blinked them back again. "Before I slept with you?"

"Damn it, Kate." He was across the deck, backing her into the rail before she could take a breath. "Are you trying to get at me for something I did or didn't do four years ago? I don't even know what it is. I don't know what you want from me or what you don't want and I'm sick of trying to outguess you."

"I don't want to be pushed into a corner," she told him fiercely. "That's what I don't want. I don't want to be expected to fall in passively with someone else's plans for me. That's what I don't want. I don't want it assumed that I simply don't have any personal goals or wishes of my own. Or any basic competence of my own. *That's* what I don't want!"

"Fine." They were both losing control, but he no longer gave a damn. Ky ripped off his wet suit and tossed it aside. "You just remember something, lady. I don't expect anything of you and I don't assume. Once maybe, but not anymore. There was only one person who ever pushed you into a corner and it wasn't me." He hurled his mask across the deck where it bounced and smacked into the side. "I'm the one who let you go."

She stiffened. Even with the distance between them he could see her eyes frost over. "I won't discuss my father with you."

"You caught on real quick though, didn't you?"

"You resented him. You—"

"I?" Ky interrupted. "Maybe you better look at yourself, Kate."

"I loved him," she said passionately. "All my life I tried to show him. You don't understand."

"How do you know that I don't understand?" he exploded. "Don't you know I can see what you're feeling every time we find something down there? Do you think I'm so blind I don't see that you're hurting because *you* found it, not him? Don't you think it tears me apart to see that you punish yourself for not being what you think he wanted you to be? And I'm tired," he continued as her breath started to hitch. "Damn tired of being compared to and measured by a man you loved without ever being close to him."

"I don't." She covered her face, hating the weakness but powerless against it. "I don't do that. I only want . . ."

"What?" he demanded. "What do you want?"

"I didn't cry when he died," she said into her hands. "I

didn't cry, not even at the funeral. I owed him tears, Ky. I owed him something."

"You don't owe him anything you didn't already give him over and over again." Frustrated, he dragged a hand through his hair before he went to her. "Kate." Because words seemed useless, he simply gathered her close.

"I didn't cry."

"Cry now," he murmured. He pressed his lips to the top of her head. "Cry now."

So she did, desperately, for what she'd never been able to quite touch, for what she'd never been able to quite hold. She'd ached for love, for the simple companionship of understanding. She wept because it was too late for that now from her father. She wept because she wasn't certain she could ask for love again from anyone else.

Ky held her, lowering her onto the bench as he cradled her in his lap. He couldn't offer her words of comfort. They were the most difficult words for him to come by. He could only offer her a place to weep, and silence.

As the tears began to pass, she kept her face against his shoulder. There was such simplicity there, though it came from a man of complications. Such gentleness, though it sprang from a restless nature. "I couldn't mourn for him before," she murmured. "I'm not sure why."

"You don't have to cry to mourn."

"Maybe not," she said wearily. "I don't know. But it's true, what you said. I've wanted to do all this for him because he'll never have the chance to finish what he started. I don't know if you can understand, but I feel if I do this, I'll have done everything I could. For him, and for myself."

"Kate." Ky tipped back her head so he could see her face. Her eyes were puffy, rimmed with red. "I don't have to understand. I just have to love you."

He felt her stiffen in his arms and immediately cursed

himself. Why was it he never said things to her the way they should be said? Sweetly, calmly, softly. She was a woman who needed soft words, and he was a man who always struggled with them.

She didn't move, and for a long, long moment, they stayed precisely as they were.

"Do you?" she managed after a moment.

"Do I what?"

Would he make her drag it from him? "Love me?"

"Kate." Frustrated, he drew away from her. "I don't know how else to show you. You want bouquets of flowers, bottles of French champagne, poems? Damn it, I'm not made that way."

"I want a straight answer."

He let out a short breath. Sometimes her very calmness drove him to distraction. "I've always loved you. I've never stopped."

That went through her, sharp, hot, with a mixture of pain and pleasure she wasn't quite sure how to deal with. Slowly, she rose out of his arms, and walking across the deck, looked out to sea. The buoys that marked the site bobbed gently. Why were there no buoys in life to show you the way?

"You never told me."

"Look, I can't even count the number of women I've said it to." When she turned back with her brow raised, he rose, uncomfortable. "It was easy to say it to them because it didn't mean anything. It's a hell of a lot harder to get the words out when you mean them, and when you're afraid someone's going to back away from you the minute you do."

"I wouldn't have done that."

"You backed away, you went away for four years, when I asked you to stay."

"You asked me to stay," she reminded him. "You asked me not to go back to Connecticut, but to move in with you. Just like that. No promises, no commitment, no sign that you had any intention of building a life with me. I had responsibilities."

"To do what your father wanted you to do."

She swallowed that. It was true in its way. "All right, yes. But you never said you loved me."

He came closer. "I'm telling you now."

She nodded, but her heart was in her throat. "And I'm not backing away. I'm just not sure I can take the next step. I'm not sure you can either."

"You want a promise."

She shook her head, not certain what she'd do if indeed he gave her one. "I want time, for both of us. It seems we both have a lot of thinking to do."

"Kate." Impatient, he came to her, taking her hands. They trembled. "Some things you don't have to think about. Some things you can think about too much."

"You've lived your life a certain way a long time, and I mine," she said quickly. "Ky, I've just begun to change—to feel the change. I don't want to make a mistake, not with you. It's too important. With time—"

"We've lost four years," he interrupted. He needed to resolve something, he discovered, and quickly. "I can't wait any longer to hear it if it's inside you."

Kate let out the breath she'd been holding. If he could ask, she could give. It would be enough. "I love you, Ky. I never stopped either. I never told you when I should have."

He felt the weight drain from his body as he cupped her face. "You're telling me now."

It was enough.

CHAPTER 11

Love. Kate had read hundreds of poems about that one phenomenon. She'd read, analyzed and taught from countless novels where love was the catalyst to all action, all emotion. With her students, she'd dissected innumerable lines from books, plays and verse that all led back to that one word.

Now, for perhaps the first time in her life, it was offered to her. She found it had more power than could possibly be taught. She found she didn't understand it.

Ky hadn't Byron's way with words, or Keat's romantic phrasing. What he'd said, he'd said simply. It meant everything. She still didn't understand it.

She could, in her own way, understand her feelings. She'd loved Ky for years, since that first revelation one summer when she'd come to know what it meant to want to fully share oneself with another.

But what, she wondered, did Ky find in her to love? It wasn't modesty that caused her to ask herself this question, but the basic practicality she'd grown up with. Where there was an effect, there was a cause. Where there was reaction, there was action. The world ran on this principle. She'd won Ky's love—but how?

Kate had no insecurity about her own intelligence. Perhaps, if anything, she overrated her mind, and it was this that caused her to underrate her other attributes.

He was a man of action, of restless and mercurial nature. She, on the other hand, considered herself almost blandly level. While she thrived on routine, Ky thrived on the unexpected. Why should he love her? Yet he did.

If she accepted that, it was vital to come to a resolution. Love led to commitment. It was there that she found the wall solid, without footholds.

He lived on a remote island because he was basically a loner, because he preferred moving at his own pace, in his own time. She was a teacher who lived by a day-to-day schedule. Without the satisfaction of giving knowledge, she'd stagnate. In the structured routine of a college town, Ky would go mad.

Because she could find no compromise, Kate opted to do what she'd decided to do in the beginning. She'd ride with the current until the summer was over. Perhaps by then, an answer would come.

They spoke no more of percentages. Kate quietly dropped the notion of keeping her hotel room. These, she told herself, were small matters when so much more hung in the balance during her second summer with Ky.

The days went quickly with her and Ky working together with the prop-wash or by hand. Slowly, painstakingly, they uncovered more salvage. The candlesticks had turned out to be pewter, but the coin had been Spanish silver. Its date had been 1748.

In the next two-week period, they uncovered much more—a heavy intricately carved silver platter, more china and porcelain, and in another area dozens of nails and tools.

Kate documented each find on film, for practical and personal reasons. She needed the neat, orderly way of keeping track of the salvage. She wanted to be able to look back on those pictures and remember how she felt when Ky held up a crusted teacup or an oxidized tankard. She'd be able to look and remember how he'd played an outstaring game with a large lazy bluefish. And lost.

More than once Ky had suggested the use of a larger ship equipped for salvage. They discussed it, and its advantages, but they never acted on it. Somehow, they both felt they wanted to move slowly, working basically with their own hands until there came a time when they had to make a decision.

The cannons and the heavier pieces of ship's planking couldn't be brought up without help, so these they left to the sea for the time being. They continued to use tanks, rather than changing to a surface-supplied source of air, so they had to surface and change gear every hour or so. A diving rig would have saved time—but that wasn't their goal.

Their methods weren't efficient by professional salvor standards, but they had an unspoken agreement. Stretch time. Make it last.

The nights they spent together in the big four-poster, talking of the day's finds, or of tomorrow's, making love, marking time. They didn't speak of the future that loomed after the summer's end. They never talked of what they'd do the day after the treasure was found.

The treasure became their focus, something that kept them from reaching out when the other wasn't ready.

* * *

The day was fiercely hot as they prepared to dive. The sun was baking. It was mid-July. She'd been in Ocracoke for a month. For all her practicality, Kate told herself it was an omen. Today was the turning point of summer.

Even as she pulled the wet suit up to her waist, sweat beaded on her back. She could almost taste the cool freshness of the water. The sun glared on her tanks as she lifted them, bouncing off to spear her eyes.

"Here." Taking them from her, Ky strapped them onto her back, checking the gauges himself. "The water's going to feel like heaven."

"Yeah." Marsh tipped up a quart bottle of juice. "Think of me baking up here while you're having all the fun."

"Keep the throttle low, brother," Ky said with a grin as he climbed over the side. "We'll bring you a reward."

"Make it something round and shiny with a date stamped on it," Marsh called back, then winked at Kate as she started down the ladder. "Good luck."

She felt the excitement as the water lapped over her ankles. "Today, I don't think I need it."

The noise of the prop-wash disturbed the silence of the water, but not the mystery. Even with technology and equipment, the water remained an enigma, part beauty, part danger. They went deeper and deeper until they reached the site with the scoops in the silt caused by their earlier explorations.

They'd already found what they thought had been the officers' and passengers' quarters, identifying it by the discovery of a snuff box, a silver bedside candleholder and Ky's personal favorite—a decorated sword. The few pieces of jewelry they'd found indicated a personal cache rather than cargo.

Though they fully intended to excavate in the area of the cache, it was the cargo they sought. Using the passengers' quarters and the galley as points of reference, they concentrated on what should have been the stern of the ship.

There were ballast rocks to deal with. This entailed a slow, menial process that required moving them by hand to an area they'd already excavated. It was time consuming, unrewarding and necessary. Still, Kate found something peaceful in the mindless work, and something fascinating about the ability to do it under fathoms of water with basically little effort. She could move a ballast pile as easily as Ky, whereas on land, she would have tired quickly.

Reaching down to clear another area, Ky's fingers brushed something small and hard. Curious, he fanned aside a thin layer of silt and picked up what at first looked like a tab on a can of beer. As he brought it closer, he saw it was much more refined, and though there were layers of crust on the knob of the circle, he felt his heart give a quick jerk.

He'd heard of diamonds in the rough, but he'd never thought to find one by simply reaching for it. He was no expert, but as he painstakingly cleaned what he could from the stone, he judged it to be at least two carats. With a tap on Kate's shoulder, he got her attention.

It gave him a great deal of pleasure to see her eyes widen and to hear the muffled sound of her surprise. Together, they turned it over and over again. It was dull and dirty, but the gem was there.

They were finding bits and pieces of civilization. Perhaps a woman had worn the ring while dining with the captain on her way to America. Perhaps some British officer had carried it in his vest pocket, waiting to give it to the woman he'd hoped to marry. It might have belonged to an elderly widow, or a young bride. The mystery of it, and its tangibility, were more precious than the stone itself. It was . . . lasting.

Ky held it out to her, offering. Their routine had fallen into a finders-keepers arrangement, in that whoever found a particular piece carried it in their own bag to the surface where everything was carefully cataloged on film and paper. Kate looked at the small, water-dulled piece of the past in Ky's fingers.

Was he offering her the ring because it was a woman's fancy, or was he offering her something else? Unsure, she shook her head, pointing to the bag on his belt. If he were asking her something, she needed it to be done with words.

Ky dropped the ring into his bag, secured it, then went back to work.

He thought he understood her, in some ways. In other ways, Ky found she was as much a mystery as the sea. What did she want from him? If it was love, he'd given her that. If it was time, they were both running out of it. He wanted to demand, was accustomed to demanding, yet she blocked his ability with a look.

She said she'd changed—that she was just beginning to feel in control of her life. He thought he understood that, as well as her fierce need for independence. And yet . . . He'd never known anything but independence. He, too, had changed. He needed her to give him the boundaries and the borders that came with dependence. His for her, and hers for him. Was the timing wrong again? Would it ever be right?

Damn it, he wanted her, he thought as he heaved another rock out of his way. Not just for today, but for tomorrow. Not tied against him, but bound to him. Why couldn't she understand that?

She loved him. It was something she murmured in the night when she was sleepy and caught close against him. She wasn't a woman to use words unless they had meaning. Yet with the love he offered and the love she returned, she'd begun to hold something back from him, as though he could have only a portion of her, but not all. Edged with frustration, he cleared more ballast. He needed, and would have, all.

Marriage? Was he thinking of marriage? Kate found herself flustered and uneasy. She'd never expected Ky to look for that kind of commitment, that kind of permanency. Perhaps she'd misread him. After all, it was difficult to be certain of someone's intention, yet she knew just how clearly Ky and she had been able to communicate underwater.

There was so much to consider, so many things to weigh. He wouldn't understand that, Kate mused. Ky was a man who made decisions in an instant and took the consequences. He wouldn't think about all the variables, all the what-ifs, all the maybes. She had to think about them all. She simply knew no other way.

Kate watched the silt and sand blowing away, causing a cuplike indentation to form on the ocean floor. Outside influences, she mused. They could eat away at the layers and uncover the core, but sometimes what was beneath couldn't stand up to the pressure.

Is that what would happen between her and Ky? How would their relationship hold up under the pressure of variant lifestyles—the demands of her profession and the free-wheeling tone of his? Would it stay intact, or would it begin to sift away, layer by layer? How much of herself would he ask her to give? And in loving, how much of herself would she lose?

It was a possibility she couldn't ignore, a threat she needed to build a solid defense against. Time. Perhaps time was the answer. But summer was waning.

The force of the wash made a small object spin up, out of the layer of silt and into the water. Kate grabbed at it and the sharp edge scraped her palm. Curious, she turned it over for examination. A buckle? she wondered. The shape seemed to indicate it, and she could just make out a fastening. Even as she started to hold it out for Ky another, then another was pushed off the ocean bed.

Shoe buckles, Kate realized, astonished. Dozens of them. No, she realized as more and more began to twist up in the water's spin and reel away. Hundreds. With a quick frenzy, she began to gather what she could. More than hundreds, she discovered as her heart thudded. There were thousands of them, literally thousands.

She held a buckle in her hand and looked at Ky in triumph. They'd found the cargo. There'd been shoe buckles on the manifest of the *Liberty*. Five thousand of them. Nothing but a merchantman carried something like that in bulk.

Proof. She waved the buckle, her arm sweeping out in slow motion to take in the swarm of them swirling away from the wash and dropping again. Proof, her mind shouted out. The cargo-hold was beneath them. And the treasure. They had only to reach it.

Ky took her hands and nodded, knowing what was in her mind. Beneath his fingers he could feel the race of her pulse. He wanted that for her, the excitement, the thrill that came from discovering something only half believed in. She brought the back of his hand to her cheek, her eyes laughing, buckles spinning around them. Kate wanted to laugh until she was too weak to stand. Five thousand shoe buckles would guide them to a chest of gold.

Kate saw the humor in his eyes and knew Ky's thoughts ran along the same path as hers. He pointed to himself, then thumbs up. With a minimum of signaling, he told Kate that he would surface to tell Marsh to shut off the engines. It was time to work by hand.

Excited, she nodded. She wanted only to begin. Resting near the bottom, Kate watched Ky go up and out of sight. Oddly, she found she needed time alone. She'd shared the heady instant of discovery with Ky, and now she needed to absorb it.

The *Liberty* was beneath her, the ship her father had searched for. The dream he'd kept close, carefully researching, meticulously calculating, but never finding.

Joy and sorrow mixed as she gathered a handful of the buckles and placed them carefully in her bag. For him. In that moment she felt she'd given him everything she'd always needed to.

Carefully, and this time for personal reasons rather than the catalog, she began to shoot pictures. Years from now, she thought. Years and years from now, she'd look at a snapshot of swirling silt and drifting pieces of metal, and she'd remember. Nothing could ever take that moment of quiet satisfaction from her.

She glanced up at the sudden silence. The wash had stilled. Ky had reached the surface. Silt and the pieces of crusted, decorated metal began to settle again without the agitation of the wash. The sea was a world without sound, without movement.

Kate looked down at the scoop in the ocean floor. They were nearly there. For a moment she was tempted to begin to fan and search by herself, but she'd wait for Ky. They began together, and they'd finish together. Content, she watched for his return.

When Kate saw the movement above her, she started to signal. Her hand froze in place, then her arm, her shoulder and the rest of her body, degree by degree. It came smoothly through the water, sleek and silent. Deadly.

The noise of the prop-wash had kept the sea life away. Now the abrupt quiet brought out the curious. Among the schools of harmless fish glided the long bulletlike shape of a shark.

Kate was still, hardly daring to breathe as she feared even the trail of bubbles might attract him. He moved without haste, apparently not interested in her. Perhaps he'd already hunted successfully that day. But even with a full belly, a shark would attack what annoyed his uncertain temper.

She gauged him to be ten feet in length. Part of her mind registered that he was fairly small for what she recognized as a tiger shark. They could easily double that length. But she knew the jaws, those large sickle-shaped teeth, would be strong, merciless and fatal.

If she remained still, the chances were good that he would simply go in search of more interesting waters. Isn't that what she'd read sitting cozily under lamplight at her own desk? Isn't that what Ky had told her once when they'd shared a quiet lunch on his boat? All that seemed so remote, so unreal now, as she looked above and saw the predator between herself and the surface.

It was movement that attracted them, she reminded herself as she forced her mind to function. The movement a swimmer made with kicking feet and sweeping arms.

Don't panic. She forced herself to breathe slowly. No sudden moves. She forced her nervous hands to form tight, still fists.

He was no more than ten feet away. Kate could see the small black eyes and the gentle movement of his gills. Breathing shallowly, she never took her eyes from his. She had only to be perfectly still and wait for him to swim on.

But Ky. Kate's mouth went dry as she looked toward the direction where Ky had disappeared moments before. He'd be coming back, any minute, unaware of what was lurking near the bottom. Waiting. Cruising.

The shark would sense the disturbance in the water with the uncanny ability the hunter had. The kick of Ky's feet, the swing of his arms would attract the shark long before Kate would have a chance to warn him of any danger.

He'd be unaware, helpless, and then . . . Her blood seemed to freeze. She'd heard of the sensation but now she experienced it. Cold seemed to envelop her. Terror made her head light. Kate bit down on her lip until pain cleared her thoughts. She wouldn't stand by idly while Ky came blindly into a death trap.

Glancing down, she saw the spear gun. It was over five feet away and unloaded for safety. Safety, she thought hysterically. She'd never loaded one, much less shot one. And first, she'd have to get to it. There'd only be one chance. Knowing she'd have no time to settle her nerves, Kate made her move.

She kept her eyes on the shark as she inched slowly toward the gun. At the moment, he seemed to be merely cruising, not particularly interested in anything. He never even glanced her way. Perhaps he would move on before Ky came back, but she needed the weapon. Fingers shaking, she gripped the butt of the gun. Time seemed to crawl. Her movements were so slow, so measured, she hardly seemed to move at all. But her mind whirled.

Even as she gripped the spear she saw the shape that glided down from the surface. The shark turned lazily to the left. To Ky.

No! her mind screamed as she rammed the spear into position. Her only thought that of protecting what she loved. Kate swam forward without hesitation, taking a path between Ky and the shark. She had to get close.

Her mind was cold now, with fear, with purpose. For the second time, she saw those small, deadly eyes. This time, they focused on her. If she'd never seen true evil before, Kate knew she faced it now. This was cruelty, and a death that wouldn't come easily.

The shark moved toward her with a speed that made her heart stop. His jaws opened. There was a black, black cave behind them.

Ky dove quickly, wanting to get back to Kate, wanting to search for what had brought them back together. If it was the treasure she needed to settle her mind, he'd find it. With it, they could open whatever doors they needed to open, lock whatever needed to be locked. Excitement drummed through him as he dove deeper.

When he spotted the shark, he pulled up short. He'd felt that deep primitive fear before, but never so sharply. Though it was less than useless against such a predator, he reached for his diver's knife. He'd left Kate alone. Cold-bloodedly, he set for the attack.

Like a rocket, Kate shot up between himself and the shark. Terror such as he'd never known washed over him. Was she mad? Was she simply unaware? Giving no time to thought, Ky barreled through the water toward her.

He was too far away. He knew it even as the panic hammered into him. The shark would be on her before he was close enough to sink the knife in.

When he saw what she held in her hand, and realized her purpose he somehow doubled his speed. Everything was in slow motion, and yet it seemed to happen in the blink of an eye. He saw the gaping hole in the shark's mouth as it closed in on Kate. For the first time in his life, prayers ran through him like water.

The spear shot out, sinking deep through the shark's flesh. Instinctively, Kate let herself drop as the shark came forward full of anger and pain. He would follow her now, she knew. If the spear didn't work, he would be on her in moments.

Ky saw blood gush from the wound. It wouldn't be enough. The shark jerked as if to reject the spear, and slowed his pace. Just enough. Teeth bared, Ky fell on its back, hacking with the knife as quickly as the water would allow. The shark turned, furious. Using all his strength, Ky turned with it, forcing the knife into the underbelly and ripping down. It ran through his mind that he was holding death, and it was as cold as the poets said.

From a few feet away, Kate watched the battle. She was numb, body and mind. Blood spurted out to dissipate in the water. Letting the empty gun fall, she too reached for her knife and swam forward.

But it was over. One instant the fish and Ky were as one form, locked together. Then they were separate as the body of the shark sank lifelessly toward the bottom. She saw the eyes one last time.

Her arm was gripped painfully. Limp, Kate allowed herself to be dragged to the surface. Safe. It was the only clear thought her mind could form. He was safe.

Too breathless to speak, Ky pulled her toward the ladder, tanks and all. He saw her slip near the top and roll onto the deck. Even as he swung over himself, he saw two fins slice through the water and disappear below where the blood drew them.

"What the hell—" Jumping up from his seat, Marsh ran across the deck to where Kate still lay, gasping for air.

"Sharks." Ky cut off the word as he knelt beside her. "I had to bring her up fast. Kate." Ky reached a hand beneath her neck, lifting her up as he began to take off her tanks. "Are you dizzy? Do you have any pain—your knees, elbows?"

Though she was still gasping for air, she shook her head. "No, no, I'm all right." She knew he worried about decompression sickness and tried to steady herself to reassure him. "Ky, we weren't that deep after—when we came up."

He nodded, grimly acknowledging that she was winded, not incoherent. Standing, he pulled off his mask and heaved it across the deck. Temper helped alleviate the helpless shaking. Kate merely drew her knees up and rested her forehead on them.

"Somebody want to fill me in?" Marsh asked, glancing from one to the other. "I left off when Ky came up raving about shoe buckles."

"Cargo-hold," Kate murmured. "We found it."

"So Ky said." Marsh glanced at his brother whose knuckles were whitening against the rail as he looked out to sea. "Run into some company down there?"

"There was a shark. A tiger."

"She nearly got herself killed," Ky explained. Fury was a direct result of fear, and just as deadly. "She swam right in front of him." Before Marsh could make any comment, Ky turned on Kate. "Did you forget everything I taught you?" he demanded. "You manage to get a doctorate but you can't remember that you're supposed to minimize your movements when a shark's cruising? You know that arm and leg swings attract them, but you swim in front of him, flailing around as though you wanted to shake hands—holding a damn spear gun that's just as likely to annoy him as do any real damage. If I hadn't been coming down just then, he'd have torn you to pieces."

Kate lifted her head slowly. Whatever emotion she'd felt up to that moment was replaced by an anger so deep it overshadowed everything. Meticulously she removed her flippers, her mask and her weight belt before she rose. "If you hadn't been coming down just then," she said precisely, "there'd have been no reason for me to swim in front of him." Turning, she walked to the steps and down into the cabin.

For a full minute there was utter silence on deck. Above, a gull screeched, then swerved west. Knowing there'd be no more dives that day, Marsh went to the helm. As he glanced over he saw the deep stain of blood on the water's surface.

"It's customary," he began with his back to his brother, "to thank someone when they save your life." Without waiting for a comment, he switched on the engine.

Shaken, Ky ran a hand through his hair. Some of the shark's blood had stained his fingers. Standing still, he stared at it.

Not through carelessness, he thought with a jolt. It had been deliberate. Kate had deliberately put herself in the path of the shark. For him. She'd risked her life to save him. He ran both hands over his face before he started below deck.

He saw her sitting on a bunk with a glass in her hand. A bottle of brandy sat at her feet. When she lifted the glass to her lips her hand shook lightly. Beneath the tan the sun had given her, her face was drawn and pale. No one had ever put him first so completely, so unselfishly. It left him without any idea of what to say.

"Kate . . ."

"I'm not in the mood to be shouted at right now," she told him before she drank again. "If you need to vent your temper, you'll have to save it."

"I'm not going to shout." Because he felt every bit as unsteady as she did, he sat beside her and lifted the bottle, drinking straight from it. The brandy ran hot and strong through him. "You scared the hell out of me."

"I'm not going to apologize for what I did."

"I should thank you." He drank again and felt the nerves in his stomach ease. "The point is, you had no business doing what you did. Nothing but blind luck kept you from being torn up down there."

Turning her head, she stared at him. "I should've stayed safe and sound on the bottom while you dealt with the shark—with your diver's knife."

He met the look levelly. "Yes."

"And you'd have done that, if it'd been me?"

"That's different."

"Oh." Glass in hand, she rose. She took a moment to study him, that raw-boned, dark face, the dripping hair that needed a trim, the eyes that reflected the sea. "Would you care to explain that little piece of logic to me?"

"I don't have to explain it, it just is." He tipped the bottle back again. It helped to cloud his imagination which kept bringing images of what might have happened to her.

"No, it just isn't, and that's one of your major problems."

"Kate, have you any idea what could have happened if you hadn't lucked out and hit a vital spot with that spear?"

"Yes." She drained her glass and felt some of the edge dull. The fear might come back again unexpectedly, but she felt she was strong enough to deal with it. And the anger. No matter how it slashed at her, she would put herself between him and danger again. "I understand perfectly. Now, I'm going up with Marsh."

"Wait a minute." He stood to block her way. "Can't you see that I couldn't stand it if anything happened to you? I want to take care of you. I need to keep you safe."

"While you take all the risks?" she countered. "Is that supposed to be the balance of our relationship, Ky? You man, me woman? I bake bread, you hunt the meat?"

"Damn it, Kate, it's not as basic as that."

"It's just as basic as that," she tossed back. The color had come back to her face. Her legs were steady again. And she would be heard. "You want me to be quiet and content—and amenable to the way you choose to live. You want me to do as you say, bend to your will, and yet I know how you felt about my father."

It didn't seem she had the energy to be angry any longer. She was just weary, bone weary from slamming herself up against a wall that didn't seem ready to budge.

"I spent all my life doing what it pleased him to have me do," she continued in calmer tones. "No waves, no problems, no rebellion. He gave me a nod of approval, but no true respect and certainly no true affection. Now, you're asking me to do the same thing again with you." She felt no tears, only that weariness of spirit. "Why do you suppose the only two men I've ever loved should want me to be so utterly pliant to their will? Why do you suppose I lost both of them because I tried so hard to do just that?"

"No." He put his hands on her shoulders. "No, that's not true. It's not what I want from you or for you. I just want to take care of you."

She shook her head. "What's the difference, Ky?" she whispered. "What the hell's the difference?" Pushing past him, Kate went out on deck.

CHAPTER 12

Because in her quiet, immovable way Kate had demanded it, Ky left her alone. Perhaps it was for the best as it gave him time to think and to reassess what he wanted.

He realized that because of his fear for her, because of his need to care for her, he'd hurt her and damaged their already tenuous relationship.

On a certain level, she'd hit the mark in her accusations. He did want her to be safe and cared for while he sweated and took the risks. It was his nature to protect what he loved—in Kate's case, perhaps too much. It was also his nature to want other wills bent to his. He wanted Kate, and was honest enough to admit that he'd already outlined the terms in his own mind.

Her father's quiet manipulating had infuriated Ky and yet, he found himself doing the same thing. Not so quietly, he admitted, not nearly as subtly, but he was doing the same thing. Still, it wasn't for the same reasons. He wanted Kate to be with him, to align herself to him. It was as simple as that. He was certain, if she'd just let him, that he could make her happy.

But he never fully considered that she'd have demands or

terms of her own. Until now, Ky hadn't thought how he'd adjust to them.

* * *

The light of dawn was quiet as Ky added the finishing touches to the lettering on his sailboat. For most of the night, he'd worked in the shed, giving Kate her time alone, and himself the time to think. Now that the night was over, only one thing remained clear. He loved her. But it had come home to him that it might not be enough. Though impatience continued to push at him, he reined it in. Perhaps he had to leave it to her to show him what would be.

For the next few days, they would concentrate on excavating the cargo that had sunk two centuries before. The longer they searched, the more the treasure became a symbol for him. If he could give it to her, it would be the end of the quest for both of them. Once it was over, they'd both have what they wanted. She, the fulfillment of her father's dream, and he, the satisfaction of seeing her freed from it.

Ky closed the shed doors behind him and headed back for the house. In a few days, he thought with a glance over his shoulder, he'd have something else to give her. Something else to ask her.

He was still some feet away from the house when he smelled the morning scents of bacon and coffee drifting through the kitchen windows. When he entered, Kate was standing at the stove, a long T-shirt over her tank suit, her feet bare, her hair loose. He could see the light dusting of freckles over the bridge of her nose, and the pale soft curve of her lips.

His need to gather her close rammed into him with such power, he had to stop and catch his breath. "Kate—"

"I thought since we'd be putting in a long day we should

have a full breakfast." She'd heard him come in, sensed it. Because it made her knees weak, she spoke briskly. "I'd like to get an early start."

He watched her drop eggs into the skillet where the white began to sizzle and solidify around the edges. "Kate, I'd like to talk to you."

"I've been thinking we might consider renting a salvage ship after all," she interrupted, "and perhaps hiring another couple of divers. Excavating the cargo's going to be very slow work with just the two of us. It's certainly time we looked into lifting bags and lines."

Long days in the sun had lightened her hair. There were shades upon shades of variation so that as it flowed it reminded him of the smooth soft pelt of a deer. "I don't want to talk business now."

"It's not something we can put off too much longer." Efficiently, she scooped up the eggs and slid them onto plates. "I'm beginning to think we should expedite the excavation rather than dragging it out for what may very well be several more weeks. Then, of course, if we're talking about excavating the entire site, it would be months."

"Not now." Ky turned off the burner under the skillet. Taking both plates from Kate, he set them on the table. "Look, I have to do something, and I'm not sure I'll do it very well."

Turning, Kate took silverware from the drawer and went to the table. "What?"

"Apologize." When she looked back at him in her cool, quiet way, he swore. "No, I won't do it well."

"It isn't necessary."

"Yes, it's necessary. Sit down." He let out a long breath as she remained standing. "Please," he added, then took a chair himself. Without a word, Kate sat across from him. "You saved my life yesterday." Even saying it aloud, he felt uneasy about it. "It was no less than that. I never could have taken that shark with my diver's knife. The only reason I did was because you'd weakened and distracted him."

Kate lifted her coffee and drank as though they were discussing the weather. It was the only way she had of blocking out images of what might have been. "Yes."

With a frustrated laugh, Ky stabbed at his eggs. "Not going to make it easy on me, are you?"

"No, I don't think I am."

"I've never been that scared," he said quietly. "Not for myself, certainly not for anyone else. I thought he had you." He looked up and met her calm, patient eyes. "I was still too far away to do anything about it. If . . ."

"Sometimes it's best not to think about the ifs."

"All right." He nodded and reached for her hand. "Kate, realizing you put yourself in danger to protect me only made it worse somehow. The possibility of anything happening to you was bad enough, but the idea of it happening because of me was unbearable."

"You would've protected me."

"Yes, but—"

"There shouldn't be any buts, Ky."

"Maybe there shouldn't be," he agreed, "but I can't promise there won't be."

"I've changed." The fact filled her with an odd sense of power and unease. "For too many years I've channeled my own desires because I thought somehow that approval could be equated with love. I know better now."

"I'm not your father, Kate."

"No, but you also have a way of imposing your will on me. My fault to a point." Her voice was calm, level, as it was when she lectured her students. She hadn't slept while Ky had spent his hours in the shed. Like him, she'd spent her time in thought, in search for the right answers. "Four years ago,

I had to give to one of you and deny the other. It broke my heart. Today, I know I have to answer to myself first." With her breakfast hardly touched, she took her plate to the sink. "I love you, Ky," she murmured. "But I have to answer to myself first."

Rising, he went to her and laid his hands on her shoulders. Somehow the strength that suddenly seemed so powerful in her both attracted him yet left him uneasy. "Okay." When she turned into his arms, he felt the world settle a bit. "Just let me know what the answer is."

"When I can." She closed her eyes and held tight. "When I can."

* * *

For three long days they dove, working away the silt to find new discoveries. With a small air lift and their own hands, they found the practical, the beautiful and the ordinary. They came upon more than eight thousand of the ten thousand decorated pipes on the *Liberty*'s manifest. At least half of them, to Kate's delight, had their bowls intact. They were clay, long-stemmed pipes with the bowls decorated with oak leaves or bunches of grapes and flowers. In a heady moment of pleasure, she snapped Ky's picture as he held one up to his lips.

She knew that at auction, they would more than pay for the investment she'd made. And, with them, the donation she'd make to a museum in her father's name was steadily growing. But more than this, the discovery of so many pipes on a wreck added force to their claim that the ship was English.

There were also snuff boxes, again thousands, leaving literally no doubt in her mind that they'd found the merchantman *Liberty*. They found tableware, some of it elegant, some basic utility-ware, but again in quantity. Their list of salvage grew beyond anything Kate had imagined, but they found no chest of gold.

They took turns hauling their finds to the surface, using an inverted plastic trash can filled with air to help them lift. Even with this, they stored the bulk of it on the sea floor. They were working alone again, without a need for Marsh to man the prop-wash. As it had been in the beginning, the project became a personal chore for only the two of them. What they found became a personal triumph. What they didn't find, a personal disappointment.

Kate delegated herself to deal with the snuff boxes, transporting them to the mesh baskets. Already, she was planning to clean several of them herself as part of the discovery. Beneath the layers of time there might be something elegant, ornate or ugly. She didn't believe it mattered what she found, as long as she found it.

Tea, sugar and other perishables the merchant ship had carried were long since gone without a trace. What she and Ky found now were the solid pieces of civilization that had survived centuries in the sea. A pipe meant for an eighteenth-century man had never reached the New World. It should have made her sad but, because it had survived, because she could hold it in her hand more than two hundred years later, Kate felt a quiet triumph. Some things last, whatever the odds.

Reaching down, she disturbed something that lay among the jumbled snuff boxes. Automatically, she jerked her hand back. Memories of the stingray and other dangers were still very fresh. When the small round object clinked against the side of a box and lay still, her heart began to pound. Almost afraid to touch, Kate reached for it. Between her fingers, she held a gold coin from another era.

Though she had read it was likely, she hadn't expected it to be as bright and shiny as the day it was minted. The pieces of silver they'd found had blackened, and other metal pieces had corroded, some of them crystalized almost beyond recognition. Yet, the gold, the small coin she'd plucked from the sea floor, winked back at her.

Its origin was English. The long-dead king stared out at her. The date was 1750.

"Ky!" Foolishly, she said his name. Though the sound was muffled and indistinguishable, he turned. Unable to wait, Kate swam toward him, clutching the coin. When she reached him, she took his hand and pressed the gold into his palm.

He knew at the moment of contact. He had only to look into her eyes. Taking her hand, he brought it to his lips. She'd found what she wanted. For no reason he could name, he felt empty. He pressed the coin back into her hand, closing her fingers over it tightly. The gold was hers.

Swimming beside her, Ky moved to the spot where Kate had found the coin. Together, they fanned, using all the patience each of them had stored. In the twenty minutes of bottom time they had left, they uncovered only five more coins. As if they were as fragile as glass, Kate placed them in her bag. Each took a mesh basket filled with salvage and surfaced.

"It's there, Ky." Kate let her mouthpiece drop as Ky hauled the first basket over the rail. "It's the *Liberty,* we've proven it."

"It's the *Liberty,*" he agreed, taking the second basket from her. "You've finished what your father started."

"Yes." She unhooked her tanks, but it was more than their weight she felt lifted from her shoulders. "I've finished." Digging into her bag, she pulled out the six bright coins. "These were loose. We still haven't found the chest. If it still exists."

He'd already thought of that, but not how he'd tell her his own theory. "They might have taken the chest to another part of the boat when the storm hit." It was a possibility; it had given them hope that the chest was still there.

Kate looked down. The glittery metal seemed to mock her. "It's possible they put the gold in one of the lifeboats when they manned them. The survivor's story wasn't clear after the ship began to break up."

"A lot of things are possible." He touched her cheek briefly before he started to strip off his gear. "With a little luck and a little more time, we might find it all."

She smiled as she dropped the coins back into her bag. "Then you could buy your boat."

"And you could go to Greece." Stripped down to his bathing trunks, Ky went to the helm. "We need to give ourselves the full twelve hours before we dive again, Kate. We've been calling it close as it is."

"That's fine." She made a business of removing her own suit. She needed the twelve hours, she discovered, for more than the practical reason of residual nitrogen.

They spoke little on the trip back. They should've been ecstatic. Kate knew it, and though she tried, she couldn't recapture that quick boost she'd felt when she picked up the first coin.

She discovered that if she'd had a choice she would have gone back weeks, to the time when the gold was a distant goal and the search was everything.

It took the rest of the day to transport the salvage from the *Vortex* to Ky's house, to separate and catalog it. She'd already decided to contact the Park Service. Their advice in placing many of the artifacts would be invaluable. After taxes, she'd give her father his memorial. And, she mused, she'd give Ky whatever he wanted out of the salvage.

Their original agreement no longer mattered to her. If he wanted half, she'd give it. All she wanted, Kate realized, was the first bowl she'd found, the blackened silver coin and the gold one that had led her to the five other coins.

"We might think about investing in a small electrolytic reduction bath," Ky murmured as he turned what he guessed was a silver snuff box in his palm. "We could treat a lot of this salvage ourselves." Coming to a decision, he set the box down. "We're going to have to think about a bigger ship and equipment. It might be best to stop diving for the next couple of days while we arrange for it. It's been six weeks, and we've barely scratched the surface of what's down there."

She nodded, not entirely sure why she wanted to weep. He was right. It was time to move on, to expand. How could she explain to him, when she couldn't explain to herself, that she wanted nothing else from the sea? While the sun set, she watched him meticulously list the salvage.

"Ky . . ." She broke off because she couldn't find the words to tell him what moved through her. Sadness, emptiness, needs.

"What's wrong?"

"Nothing." But she took his hands as she rose. "Come upstairs now," she said quietly. "Make love with me before the sun goes down."

Questions ran through him, but he told himself they could wait. The need he felt from her touched off his own. He wanted to give her, and to take from her, what couldn't be found anywhere else.

When they entered the bedroom, it was washed with the warm, lingering light of the sun. The sky was slowly turning red as he lay beside her. Her arms reached out to gather him close. Her lips parted. Refusing to rush, they undressed each other. No boundaries. Flesh against flesh they lay. Mouth against mouth they touched.

Kisses—long and deep—took them both beyond the

ordinary world of place and time. Here, there were dozens of sensations to be felt, and no questions to be asked. Here, there was no past, no tomorrow, only the moment. Her body went limp under his, but her mouth hungered and sought.

No one else . . . No one else had ever taken her beyond herself so effortlessly. Never before had anyone made her so completely aware of her own body. A feathery touch along her skin drove pleasure through her with inescapable force.

The scent of sea still clung to both of them. As pleasure became liquid, they might have been fathoms under the ocean, moving freely without the strict rules of gravity. There were no rules here.

As his hands brought their emotions rising to the surface, so did hers for him. She explored the rippling muscles of his back, near the shoulders. Lingering there, she enjoyed just the feel of one of the subtle differences between them. His skin was smooth, but muscles bunched under it. His hands were gentle, but the palms were hard. He was lean, but there was no softness there.

Again and again she touched and tasted, needing to absorb him. Above all else, she needed to experience everything they'd ever had together this one time. They made love here, she remembered, that first time. The first time . . . and the last. Whenever she thought of him, she'd remember the quieting light of dusk and the distant sound of surf.

He didn't understand why he felt such restrained urgency from her, but he knew she needed everything he could give her. He loved her, perhaps not as gently as he could, but more thoroughly than ever before.

He touched. "Here," Ky murmured, using his fingertips to drive her up. As she gasped and arched, he watched her. "You're soft and hot."

He tasted. "And here . . ." With his tongue, he pushed her to the edge. As her hands gripped his, he groaned. Pleasure heaped upon pleasure. "You taste like temptation—sweet and forbidden. Tell me you want more."

"Yes." The word came out on a moan. "I want more."

So he gave her more.

Again and again, he took her up, watching the astonished pleasure on her face, feeling it in the arch of her body, hearing it in her quick breaths. She was helpless, mindless, his. He drove his tongue into her and felt her explode, wave after wave.

As she shuddered, he moved up her body, hands fast, mouth hot and open. Suddenly, on a surge of strength, she rolled on top of him. Within seconds, she'd devastated his claim to leadership. All fire, all speed, all woman, she took control.

Heedless, greedy, they moved over the bed. Murmurs were incoherent, care was forgotten. They took with only one goal in mind. Pleasure—sweet, forbidden pleasure.

Shaking, locked tight, they reached the goal together.

* * *

Dawn was breaking, clear and calm as Kate lay still, watching Ky sleep. She knew what she had to do for both of them, to both of them. Fate had brought them together a second time. It wouldn't bring them together again.

She'd bargained with Ky, offering him a share of gold for his skill. In the beginning, she'd believed that she wanted the treasure, needed it to give her all the options she'd never had before. That choice. Now, she knew she didn't want it at all. A hundred times more gold wouldn't change what was between her and Ky—what drew them to each other, and what kept them apart.

She loved him. She understood that, in his way, he loved her. Did that change the differences between them? Did that make her able and willing to give up her own life to suit his, or able and willing to demand that he do the same?

Their worlds were no closer together now than they'd been four years ago. Their desires no more in tune. With the gold she'd leave for him, he'd be able to do what he wanted with his life. She needed no treasure for that.

If she stayed . . . Unable to stop herself, Kate reached out to touch his cheek. If she stayed she'd bury herself for him. Eventually, she'd despise herself for it, and he'd resent her. Better that they take what they'd had for a few weeks than cover it with years of disappoinments.

The treasure was important to him. He'd taken risks for it, worked for it. She'd give her father his memorial. Ky would have the rest.

Quietly, still watching him sleep, she dressed.

It didn't take Kate long to gather what she'd come with. Taking her suitcase downstairs, she carefully packed what she'd take with her from the *Liberty*. In a box, she placed the pottery bowl wrapped in layers of newspaper. The coins, the blackened silver and the shiny gold, she zipped into a small pouch. With equal care, she packed the film she'd taken during their days under the ocean.

What she'd designated for the museum she'd already marked. Leaving the list on the table, she left the house.

She told herself it would be cleaner if she left no note, yet she found herself hesitating. How could she make him understand? After putting her suitcase in her car, she went back into the house. Quietly, she took the five gold coins upstairs and placed them on Ky's dresser. With a last look at him as he slept, she went back out again.

She'd have a final moment with the sea. In the quiet air of morning, Kate walked over the dunes.

She'd remember it this way—empty, endless and full of sound. Surf foamed against the sand, white on white. What was beneath the surface would always call her—the memories of peace, of excitement, of sharing both with Ky. Only a summer, she thought. Life was made of four seasons, not one.

Day was strengthening, and her time was up. Turning, she scanned the island until she saw the tip of the lighthouse. Some things lasted, she thought with a smile. She'd learned a great deal in a few short weeks. She was her own woman at last. She could make her own way. As a teacher, she told herself that knowledge was precious. But it made her ache with loneliness. She left the empty sea behind her.

Though she wanted to, Kate deliberately kept herself from looking at the house as she walked back to her car. She didn't need to see it again to remember it. If things had been different . . . Kate reached for the door handle of her car. Her fingers were still inches from it when she was spun around.

"What the hell're you doing?"

Facing Ky, she felt her resolve crumble, then rebuild. He was barely awake, and barely dressed. His eyes were heavy with sleep, his hair disheveled from it. All he wore was a pair of ragged cut-offs. She folded her hands in front of her and hoped her voice would be strong and clear.

"I had hoped to be gone before you woke."

"Gone?" His eyes locked on hers. "Where?"

"I'm going back to Connecticut."

"Oh?" He swore he wouldn't lose his temper. Not this time. This time, it might be fatal for both of them. "Why?"

Her nerves skipped. The question had been quiet enough, but she knew that cold, flat expression in his eyes. The wrong move, and he'd leap. "You said it yourself yesterday, Ky, when we came up from the last dive. I've done what I came for."

He opened his hand. Five coins shone in the morning sun. "What about this?"

"I left them for you." She swallowed, no longer certain how long she could speak without showing she was breaking in two. "The treasure isn't important to me. It's yours."

"Damn generous of you." Turning over his hand, he dropped the coins into the sand. "That's how much the gold means to me, professor."

She stared at the gold on the ground in front of her. "I don't understand you."

"*You* wanted the treasure," he tossed at her. "It never mattered to me."

"But you said," she began, then shook her head. "When I first came to you, you took the job because of the treasure."

"I took the job because of you. You wanted the gold, Kate."

"It wasn't the money." Dragging a hand through her hair, she turned away. "It was never the money."

"Maybe not. It was your father."

She nodded because it was true, but it no longer hurt. "I finished what he started, and I gave myself something. I don't want any more coins, Ky."

"Why are you running away from me again?"

Slowly, she turned back. "We're four years older than we were before, but we're the same people."

"So?"

"Ky, when I went away before, it was partially because of my father, because I felt I owed him my loyalty. But if I'd thought you'd wanted me. *Me,*" she repeated, placing her palm over her heart, "not what you wanted me to be. If I'd thought that, and if I'd thought you and I could make a future together, I wouldn't have gone. I wouldn't be leaving now."

"What the hell gives you the right to decide what I want, what I feel?" He whirled away from her, too furious to remain close. "Maybe I made mistakes, maybe I just assumed too much four years ago. Damn it, I paid for it, Kate, every day from the time you left until you came back. I've done everything I could to be careful this time around, not to push, not to assume. Then I wake up and find you leaving without a word."

"There aren't any words, Ky. I've always given you too many of them, and you've never given me enough."

"You're better with words than I am."

"All right, then I'll use them. I love you." She waited until he turned back to her. The restlessness was on him again. He was holding it off with sheer will. "I've always loved you, but I think I know my own limitations. Maybe I know yours too."

"No, you think too much about limitations, Kate, and not enough about possibilities. I let you walk away from me before. It's not going to be so easy this time."

"I have to be my own person, Ky. I won't live the rest of my life as I've lived it up to now."

"Who the hell wants you to?" he exploded. "Who the hell wants you to be anything but what you are? It's about time you stopped equating love with responsibility and started looking at the other side of it. It's sharing, giving and taking and laughing. If I ask you to give part of yourself to me, I'm going to give part of myself right back."

Unable to stop himself he took her arms in his hands, just holding, as if through the contact he could make his words sink in.

"I don't want your constant devotion. I don't want you to be obliged to me. I don't want to go through life thinking that whatever you do, you do because you want to please me. Damn it, I don't want that kind of responsibility."

Without words, she stared at him. He'd never said anything to her so simply, so free of half meanings. Hope rose in her. Yet still, he was telling her only what he didn't want. Once he gave her the flip side of that coin hope could vanish.

"Tell me what you do want."

He had only one answer. "Come with me a minute." Taking her hand, he drew her toward the shed. "When I started this, it was because I'd always promised myself I would.

Before long, the reasons changed." Turning the latch, he pulled the shed doors open.

For a moment, she saw nothing. Gradually, her eyes adjusted to the dimness and she stepped inside. The boat was nearly finished. The hull was sanded and sealed and painted, waiting for Ky to take it outside and attach the mast. It was lovely, clean and simple. Just looking at it, Kate could imagine the way it would flow with the wind. Free, light and clever.

"It's beautiful, Ky. I always wondered . . ." She broke off as she read the name printed boldly on the stern.

Second Chance.

"That's all I want from you," Ky told her, pointing to the two words. "The boat's yours. When I started it, I thought I was building it for me. But I built it for you, because I knew it was one dream you'd share with me. I only want what's printed on it, Kate. For both of us." Speechless, she watched him lean over the starboard side and open a small compartment. He drew out a tiny box.

"I had this cleaned. You wouldn't take it from me before." Opening the lid, he revealed the diamond he'd found, sparkling now in a simple gold setting. "It didn't cost me anything and it wasn't made especially for you. It's just something I found among a bunch of rocks."

When she started to speak, he held up a hand. "Hold on. You wanted words, I haven't finished with them yet. I know you have to teach, I'm not asking you to give it up. I am asking that you give me one year here on the island. There's a school here, not Yale, but people still have to be taught. A year, Kate. If it isn't what you want after that, I'll go back with you."

Her brows drew together. "Back? To Connecticut? You'd live in Connecticut?"

"If that's what it takes."

A compromise . . . she thought, baffled. Was he offering to adjust his life for hers? "And if that isn't right for you?"

"Then we'll try someplace else, damn it. We'll find someplace in between. Maybe we'll move half a dozen times in the next few years. What does it matter?"

What did it matter? she wondered as she studied him. He was offering her what she'd waited for all of her life. Love without chains.

"I want you to marry me." He wondered if that simple statement shook her as much as it did him. "Tomorrow isn't soon enough, but if you'll give me the year, I can wait."

She nearly smiled. He'd never wait. Once he had her promise of the year, he'd subtly and not so subtly work on her until she found herself at the altar. It was nearly tempting to make him go through the effort.

Limitations? Had she spoken of limitations? Love had none.

"No," she decided aloud. "You only get the year if I get the ring. And what goes with it."

"Deal." He took her hand quickly as though she might change her mind. "Once it's on, you're stuck, professor." Pulling the ring from the box he slipped it onto her finger. Swearing lightly, he shook his head. "It's too big."

"It's all right. I'll keep my hand closed for the next fifty years or so." With a laugh, she went into his arms. All doubts vanished. They'd make it, she told herself. South, north or anywhere in between.

"We'll have it sized," he murmured, nuzzling into her neck.

"Only if they can do it while it's on my finger." Kate closed her eyes. She'd just found everything. Did he know it? "Ky, about the *Liberty,* the rest of the treasure."

He tilted her face up to kiss her. "We've already found it."

Local Hero

For Dan, with thanks for the idea
and the tons of research material.
And for Jason, for keeping me in tune
with the ten-year-old mind.

CHAPTER 1

Zark drew a painful breath, knowing it could be his last. The ship was nearly out of oxygen, and he was nearly out of time. A life span could pass in front of the eyes in a matter of seconds. He was grateful that he was alone so no one else could witness his joys and mistakes

Leilah, it was always Leilah. With each ragged breath he could see her, the clear blue eyes and golden hair of his one and only beloved. As the warning siren inside the cockpit wailed, he could hear Leilah's laughter. Tender, sweet. Then mocking.

"By the red sun, how happy we were together!" The words shuddered out between gasps as he dragged himself over the floor toward the command console. "Lovers, partners, friends."

The pain in his lungs grew worse. It seared through him like dozens of hot knives tipped with poison from the pits of Argenham. He couldn't waste air on useless words. But his thoughts . . . his thoughts even now were on Leilah.

That she, the only woman he had ever loved, should be the cause of his ultimate destruction! His destruction, and the world's as they knew it. What fiendish twist of fate had caused the freak accident that had turned her from a devoted scientist to a force of evil and hate?

She was his enemy now, the woman who had once been his wife. Who was still his wife, Zark told himself as he painfully pulled himself up to the console. If he lived, and stopped her latest scheme to obliterate civilization on Perth, he would have to go after her. He would have to destroy her. If he had the strength.

Commander Zark, Defender of the Universe, Leader of Perth, hero and husband, pressed a trembling finger to the button.

CONTINUED IN THE NEXT EXCITING ISSUE!

* * *

Damn!" Radley Wallace mumbled the oath, then looked around quickly to be sure his mother hadn't heard. He'd started to swear, mostly in whispers, about six months ago, and wasn't anxious for her to find out. She'd get that look on her face.

But she was busy going through the first boxes the movers had delivered. He was supposed to be putting his books away but had decided it was time to take a break. He liked breaks best when they included Universal Comics and Commander Zark. His mother liked him to read real books, but they didn't have many pictures. As far as Radley was concerned, Zark had it all over Long John Silver or Huck Finn.

Rolling over on his back, Radley stared at the freshly painted ceiling of his new room. The new apartment was okay. Mostly he liked the view of the park, and having an elevator was cool. But he wasn't looking forward to starting a new school on Monday.

Mom had told him it would be fine, that he would make new friends and still be able to visit with some of the old ones.

She was real good about it, stroking his hair and smiling in
that way that made him feel everything was really okay. But
she wouldn't be there when all the kids gave him the once-
over. He wasn't going to wear that new sweater, either, even
if Mom said the color matched his eyes. He wanted to wear
one of his old sweatshirts so at least something would be familiar. He figured she'd understand, because Mom always
did.

She still looked sad sometimes, though. Radley squirmed
up to the pillow with the comic clutched in his hand. He
wished she wouldn't feel bad because his father had gone
away. It had been a long time now, and he had to think hard
to bring a picture of his father to his mind. He never visited
and only phoned a couple of times a year. That was okay.
Radley wished he could tell his mother it was okay, but he
was afraid she'd get upset and start crying.

He didn't really need a dad when he had her. He'd told
her that once, and she'd hugged him so hard he hadn't been
able to breathe. Then he'd heard her crying in her room that
night. So he hadn't told her that again.

Big people were funny, Radley thought with the wisdom
of his almost ten years. But his mom was the best. She hardly
ever yelled at him and was always sorry when she did. And
she was pretty. Radley smiled as he began to sleep. He
guessed his mom was just about as pretty as Princess Leilah.
Even though her hair was brown instead of golden and her
eyes were gray instead of cobalt blue.

She'd promised they could have pizza for dinner, too, to
celebrate their new apartment. He liked pizza best, next to
Commander Zark.

He drifted off to sleep so he, with the help of Zark, could
save the universe.

When Hester looked in a short time later, she saw her son,
her universe, dreaming with an issue of Universal Comics

in his hand. Most of his books, some of which he paged through from time to time, were still in the packing boxes. Another time she would have given him a mild lecture on responsibility when he woke, but she didn't have the heart for it now. He was taking the move so well. Another upheaval in his life.

"This one's going to be good for you, sweetie." Forgetting the mountain of her own unpacking, she sat on the edge of the bed to watch him.

He looked so much like his father. The dark blond hair, the dark eyes and sturdy chin. It was a rare thing now for her to look at her son and think of the man who had been her husband. But today was different. Today was another beginning for them, and beginnings made her think of endings.

Over six years now, she thought, a bit amazed at the passage of time. Radley had been just a toddler when Allan had walked out on them, tired of bills, tired of family, tired of her in particular. That pain had passed, though it had been a long, slow process. But she had never forgiven, and would never forgive, the man for leaving his son without a second glance.

Sometimes she worried that it seemed to mean so little to Radley. Selfishly she was relieved that he had never formed a strong, enduring bond with the man who would leave them behind, yet she often wondered, late at night when everything was quiet, if her little boy held something inside.

When she looked at him, it didn't seem possible. Hester stroked his hair now and turned to look at his view of Central Park. Radley was outgoing, happy and good-natured. She'd worked hard to help him be those things. She never spoke ill of his father, though there had been times, especially in the early years, when the bitterness and anger had simmered very close to the surface. She'd tried to be both mother and father, and most of the time thought she'd succeeded.

She'd read books on baseball so she would know how to

coach him. She'd raced beside him, clinging to the back of
the seat of his first two-wheeler. When it had been time to let
go, she'd forced back the urge to hang on and had cheered as
he'd made his wobbly way down the bike path.

She even knew about Commander Zark. With a smile, Hester eased the wrinkled comic book from his fist. Poor, heroic
Zark and his misguided wife, Leilah. Yes, Hester knew all
about Perth's politics and tribulations. Trying to wean Radley from Zark to Dickens or Twain wasn't easy, but neither
was raising a child on your own.

"There's time enough," she murmured as she stretched out
beside her son. Time enough for real books and for real life.
"Oh, Rad, I hope I've done the right thing." She closed her
eyes, wishing, as she'd learned to wish rarely, that she had
someone to talk to, someone who could advise her or make
decisions, right or wrong.

Then, with her arm hooked around her son's waist, she,
too, slept.

*   *   *

The room was dim with dusk when she awoke, groggy and
disoriented. The first thing Hester realized was that Radley was no longer curled beside her. Grogginess disappeared
in a quick flash of panic she knew was foolish. Radley could
be trusted not to leave the apartment without permission. He
wasn't a blindly obedient child, but her top ten rules were respected. Rising, she went to find him.

"Hi, Mom." He was in the kitchen, where her homing instinct had taken her first. He held a dripping peanut butter and
jelly sandwich in his hands.

"I thought you wanted pizza," she said, noting the good-
sized glop of jelly on the counter and the yet-to-be-resealed
loaf of bread.

"I do." He took a healthy bite, then grinned. "But I needed something now."

"Don't talk with your mouth full, Rad," she said automatically, even as she bent to kiss him. "You could have woken me if you were hungry."

"That's okay, but I couldn't find the glasses."

She glanced around, seeing that he'd emptied two boxes in his quest. Hester reminded herself that she should have made the kitchen arrangements her first priority. "Well, we can take care of that."

"It was snowing when I woke up."

"Was it?" Hester pushed the hair out of her eyes and straightened to see for herself. "Still is."

"Maybe it'll snow ten feet, and there won't be any school on Monday." Radley climbed onto a stool to sit at the kitchen counter.

Along with no first day on the new job, Hester thought, indulging in some wishful thinking of her own for a moment. No new pressures, new responsibilities. "I don't think there's much chance of that." As she washed out glasses, she looked over her shoulder. "Are you really worried about it, Rad?"

"Sort of." He shrugged his shoulders. Monday was still a day away. A lot could happen. Earthquakes, blizzards, an attack from outer space. He concentrated on the last.

He, Captain Radley Wallace of Earth's Special Forces, would protect and shield, would fight to the death, would—

"I could go in with you if you'd like."

"Aw, Mom, the kids would make fun of me." He bit into his sandwich. Grape jelly oozed out the sides. "It won't be so bad. At least that dumb Angela Wiseberry won't be at this school."

She didn't have the heart to tell him there was a dumb Angela Wiseberry at every school. "Tell you what. We'll both go to our new jobs Monday, then convene back here at 1600 for a full report."

His face brightened instantly. There was nothing Radley liked better than a military operation. "Aye, aye, sir."

"Good. Now I'll order the pizza, and while we're waiting, we'll put the rest of the dishes away."

"Let the prisoners do it."

"Escaped. All of them."

"Heads will roll," Radley mumbled as he stuffed the last of the sandwich into his mouth.

*　*　*

Mitchell Dempsey II sat at his drawing board without an idea in his head. He sipped cold coffee, hoping it would stimulate his imagination, but his mind remained as blank as the paper in front of him. Blocks happened, he knew, but they rarely happened to him. And not on deadline. Of course, he was going about it backward. Mitch cracked another peanut, then tossed the shell in the direction of the bowl. It hit the side and fell on the floor to join several others. Normally the story line would have come first, then the illustrations. Since he'd been having no luck that way, Mitch had switched in the hope that the change in routine would jog something loose.

It wasn't working, and neither was he.

Closing his eyes, Mitch tried for an out-of-body experience. The old Slim Whitman song on the radio cruised on, but he didn't hear it. He was traveling light-years away; a century was passing. The second millennium, he thought with a smile. He'd been born too soon. Though he didn't think he could blame his parents for having him a hundred years too early.

Nothing came. No solutions, no inspiration. Mitch opened his eyes again and stared at the blank white paper. With an editor like Rich Skinner, he couldn't afford to claim artistic temperament. Famine or plague would barely get you by. Disgusted, Mitch reached for another peanut.

What he needed was a change of scene, a distraction. His life was becoming too settled, too ordinary and, despite the temporary block, too easy. He needed challenge. Pitching the shells, he rose to pace.

He had a long, limber body made solid by the hours he spent each week with weights. As a boy he'd been preposterously skinny, though he'd always eaten like a horse. He hadn't minded the teasing too much until he'd discovered girls. Then, with the quiet determination he'd been born with, Mitch had changed what could be changed. It had taken him a couple of years and a lot of sweat to build himself, but he had. He still didn't take his body for granted and exercised it as regularly as he did his mind.

His office was littered with books, all read and reread. He was tempted to pull one out now and bury himself in it. But he was on deadline. The big brown mutt on the floor rolled over on his stomach and watched.

Mitch had named him Taz, after the Tasmanian Devil from the old Warner Brothers cartoons, but Taz was hardly a whirlwind of energy. He yawned now and rubbed his back lazily on the rug. He liked Mitch. Mitch never expected him to do anything that he didn't care to, and hardly ever complained about dog hair on the furniture or an occasional forage into the trash. Mitch had a nice voice, too, low and patient. Taz liked it best when Mitch sat on the floor with him and stroked his heavy brown fur, talking out one of his ideas. Taz could look up into the lean face as if he understood every word.

Taz liked Mitch's face, too. It was kind and strong, and the mouth rarely firmed into a disapproving line. His eyes were pale and dreamy. Mitch's wide, strong hands knew the right places to scratch. Taz was a very contented dog. He yawned and went back to sleep.

When the knock came to the door, the dog stirred enough to thump his tail and make a series of low noises in his throat.

"No, I'm not expecting anyone. You?" Mitch responded. "I'll go see." He stepped on peanut shells in his bare feet and swore, but didn't bother to stoop and pick them up. There was a pile of newspapers to be skirted around and a bag of clothes that hadn't made it to the laundry. Taz had left one of his bones on the Aubusson. Mitch simply kicked it into a corner before he opened the door.

"Pizza delivery."

A scrawny kid of about eighteen was holding a box that smelled like heaven. Mitch took one long, avaricious sniff. "I didn't order any."

"This 406?"

"Yeah, but I didn't order any pizza." He sniffed again. "Wish I had."

"Wallace?"

"Dempsey."

"Shoot."

Wallace, Mitch thought as the kid shifted from foot to foot. Wallace was taking over the Henley apartment, 604. He rubbed a hand over his chin and considered. If Wallace was that leggy brunette he'd seen hauling in boxes that morning, it might be worth investigating.

"I know the Wallaces," he said, and pulled crumpled bills out of his pocket. "I'll take it on up to them."

"I don't know. I shouldn't—"

"Worry about a thing," Mitch finished, and added another bill. Pizza and the new neighbor might be just the distraction he needed.

The boy counted his tip. "Okay, thanks." For all he knew, the Wallaces wouldn't be half as generous.

With the box balanced in his hand, Mitch started out. Then he remembered his keys. He took a moment to search through his worn jeans before he remembered he'd tossed them at the gateleg table when he'd come in the night before. He found them under it, stuck them in one pocket, found the hole in it and stuck them in the other. He hoped the pizza had some pepperoni.

"That should be the pizza," Hester announced, but caught Radley before he could dash to the door. "Let me open it. Remember the rules?"

"Don't open the door unless you know who it is," Radley recited, rolling his eyes behind his mother's back.

Hester put a hand on the knob but checked the peephole. She frowned a little at the face. She'd have sworn the man was looking straight back at her with amused and very clear blue eyes. His hair was dark and shaggy, as if it hadn't seen a barber or a comb in a little too long. But the face was fascinating, lean and bony and unshaven.

"Mom, are you going to open it?"

"What?" Hester stepped back when she realized she'd been staring at the delivery boy for a good deal longer than necessary.

"I'm starving," Radley reminded her.

"Sorry." Hester opened the door and discovered the fascinating face went with a long, athletic body. And bare feet.

"Did you order pizza?"

"Yes." But it was snowing outside. What was he doing barefoot?

"Good." Before Hester realized his intention, Mitch strolled inside.

"I'll take that," Hester said quickly. "Take this into the

kitchen, Radley." She shielded her son with her body and wondered if she'd need a weapon.

"Nice place." Mitch looked casually around at crates and open boxes.

"I'll get your money."

"It's on the house." Mitch smiled at her. Hester wondered if the self-defense course she'd taken two years before would come back to her.

"Radley, take that into the kitchen while I pay the delivery man."

"Neighbor," Mitch corrected. "I'm in 406—you know, two floors down. The pizza got delivered to my place by mistake."

"I see." But for some reason it didn't make her any less nervous. "I'm sorry for the trouble." Hester reached for her purse.

"I took care of it." He wasn't sure whether she looked more likely to lunge or to flee, but he'd been right about her being worth investigating. She was a tall one, he thought, model height, with that same kind of understated body. Her rich, warm brown hair was pulled back from a diamond-shaped face dominated by big gray eyes and a mouth just one size too large.

"Why don't you consider the pizza my version of the welcoming committee?"

"That's really very kind, but I couldn't—"

"Refuse such a neighborly offer?"

Because she was a bit too cool and reserved for his taste, Mitch looked past her to the boy. "Hi, I'm Mitch." This time his smile was answered.

"I'm Rad. We just moved in."

"So I see. From out of town?"

"Uh-uh. We just changed apartments because Mom got a

new job and the other was too small. I can see the park from my window."

"Me, too."

"Excuse me, Mr.—?"

"It's Mitch," he repeated with a glance at Hester.

"Yes, well, it's very kind of you to bring this up." As well as being very odd, she thought. "But I don't want to impose on your time."

"You can have a piece," Radley invited. "We never finish it all."

"Rad, I'm sure Mr.—Mitch has things to do."

"Not a thing." He knew his manners, had been taught them painstakingly. Another time, he might even have put them to use and bowed out, but something about the woman's reserve and the child's warmth made him obstinate. "Got a beer?"

"No, I'm sorry, I—"

"We've got soda," Radley piped up. "Mom lets me have one sometimes." There was nothing Radley liked more than company. He gave Mitch a totally ingenuous smile. "Want to see the kitchen?"

"Love to." With something close to a smirk for Hester, Mitch followed the boy.

She stood in the center of the room for a moment, hands on her hips, unsure whether to be exasperated or furious. The last thing she wanted after a day of lugging boxes was company. Especially a stranger's. The only thing to do now was to give him a piece of the damn pizza and blot out her obligation to him.

"We've got a garbage disposal. It makes great noises."

"I bet." Obligingly Mitch leaned over the sink while Radley flipped the switch.

"Rad, don't run that with nothing in it. As you can see, we're a bit disorganized yet." Hester went to the freshly lined cupboard for plates.

"I've been here for five years, and I'm still disorganized."

"We're going to get a kitten." Radley climbed up on a stool, then reached for the napkins his mother had already put in one of her little wicker baskets. "The other place wouldn't allow pets, but we can have one here, can't we, Mom?"

"As soon as we're settled, Rad. Diet or regular?" she asked Mitch.

"Regular's fine. Looks like you've gotten a lot accomplished in one day." The kitchen was neat as a pin. A thriving asparagus fern hung in a macrame holder in the single window. She had less space than he did, which he thought was too bad. She would probably make better use of the kitchen than he. He took another glance around before settling at the counter. Stuck to the refrigerator was a large crayon drawing of a spaceship. "You do that?" Mitch asked Rad.

"Yeah." He picked up the pizza his mother had set on his plate and bit in eagerly—peanut butter and jelly long since forgotten.

"It's good."

"It's supposed to be the *Second Millennium*, that's Commander Zark's ship."

"I know." Mitch took a healthy bite of his own slice. "You did a good job."

As he plowed through his pizza, Radley took it for granted that Mitch would recognize Zark's name and mode of transportation. As far as he was concerned, everybody did. "I've been trying to do the *Defiance*, Leilah's ship, but it's harder. Anyway, I think Commander Zark might blow it up in the next issue."

"Think so?" Mitch gave Hester an easy smile as she joined them at the counter.

"I don't know, he's in a pretty tough spot right now."

"He'll get out okay."

"Do you read comic books?" Hester asked. It wasn't until

she sat down that she noticed how large his hands were. He might have been dressed with disregard, but his hands were clean and had the look of easy competence.

"All the time."

"I've got the biggest collection of all my friends. Mom got me the very first issue with Commander Zark in it for Christmas. It's ten years old. He was only a captain then. Want to see?"

The boy was a gem, Mitch thought, sweet, bright and unaffected. He'd have to reserve judgment on the mother. "Yeah, I'd like that."

Before Hester could tell him to finish his dinner, Radley was off and running. She sat in silence a moment, wondering what sort of man actually read comic books. Oh, she paged through them from time to time to keep a handle on what her son was consuming, but to actually read them? An adult?

"Terrific kid."

"Yes, he is. It's nice of you to . . . listen to him talk about his comics."

"Comics are my life," Mitch said, straight-faced.

Her reserve broke down long enough for her to stare at him. Clearing her throat, Hester went back to her meal. "I see."

Mitch put his tongue in his cheek. She was some piece of work, all right, he decided. First meeting or not, he saw no reason to resist egging her on. "I take it you don't."

"Don't what?"

"Read comic books."

"No, I, ah, don't have a lot of time for light reading." She rolled her eyes, unaware that that was where Radley had picked up the habit. "Would you like another piece?"

"Yeah." He helped himself before she could serve him. "You ought to take some time, you know. Comics can be very educational. What's the new job?"

"Oh, I'm in banking. I'm the loan officer for National Trust."

Mitch gave an appreciative whistle. "Big job for someone your age."

Hester stiffened automatically. "I've been in banking since I was sixteen."

Touchy, too, he mused as he licked sauce from his thumb. "That was supposed to be a compliment. I have a feeling you don't take them well." Tough lady, he decided, then thought perhaps she'd had to be. There was no ring on her finger, not even the faintest white mark to show there had been one recently. "I've done some business with banks myself. You know, deposits, withdrawals, returned checks."

She shifted uncomfortably, wondering what was taking Radley so long. There was something unnerving about being alone with this man. Though she had always felt comfortable with eye contact, she was having a difficult time with Mitch. He never looked away for very long.

"I didn't mean to be abrupt."

"No, I don't suppose you did. If I wanted a loan at National Trust, who would I ask for?"

"Mrs. Wallace."

Definitely a tough one. "Mrs. is your first name?"

"Hester," she said, not understanding why she resented giving him that much.

"Hester, then." Mitch offered a hand. "Nice to meet you."

Her lips curved a bit. It was a cautious smile, Mitch thought, but better than none at all. "I'm sorry if I've been rude, but it's been a long day. A long week, really."

"I hate moving." He waited until she'd unbent enough to put her hand in his. Hers was cool and as slender as the rest of her. "Got anyone to help you?"

"No." She removed her hand, because his was as overwhelming as it looked. "We're doing fine."

"I can see that." *No Help Wanted*. The sign was up and posted in big letters. He'd known a few women like her, so fiercely independent, so suspicious of men in general that they had not only a defensive shield but an arsenal of poisonous darts behind it. A sensible man gave them a wide berth. Too bad, because she was a looker, and the kid was definitely a kick.

"I forgot where I'd packed it." Radley came back in, flushed with the effort. "It's a classic, the dealer even told Mom."

He'd also charged her an arm and a leg for it, Hester thought. But it had meant more to Radley than any of his other presents.

"Mint condition, too." Mitch turned the first page with the care of a jeweler cutting a diamond.

"I always make sure my hands are clean before I read it."

"Good idea." It was amazing that after all this time the pride would still be there. An enormous feeling it was, too, a huge burst of satisfaction.

It was there on the first page. Story and drawings by Mitch Dempsey. Commander Zark was his baby, and in ten years they'd become very close friends.

"It's a great story. It really explains why Commander Zark devoted his life to defending the universe against evil and corruption."

"Because his family had been wiped out by the evil Red Arrow in his search for power."

"Yeah." Radley's face lit up. "But he got even with Red Arrow."

"In issue 73."

Hester put her chin in her hand and stared at the two of them. The man was serious, she realized, not just humoring the child. He was as obsessed by comic books as her nine-year-old son.

Strange, he looked fairly normal; he even spoke well. In

fact, sitting next to him had been uncomfortable largely because he was so blatantly masculine, with that tough body, angular face and large hands. Hester shook off her thoughts quickly. She certainly didn't want to lean in that direction toward a neighbor, particularly not one whose mental level seemed to have gotten stuck in adolescence.

Mitch turned a couple of pages. His drawing had improved over a decade. It helped to remind himself of that. But he'd managed to maintain the same purity, the same straightforward images that had come to him ten years ago when he'd been struggling unhappily in commercial art.

"Is he your favorite?" Mitch pointed a blunt fingertip toward a drawing of Zark.

"Oh, sure. I like Three Faces, and the Black Diamond's pretty neat, but Commander Zark's my favorite."

"Mine, too." Mitch ruffled the boy's hair. He hadn't realized when he'd delivered a pizza that he would find the inspiration he'd been struggling for all afternoon.

"You can read this sometime. I'd lend it to you, but—"

"I understand." He closed the book carefully and handed it back. "You can't lend out a collector's item."

"I'd better put it away."

"Before you know it, you and Rad will be trading issues." Hester stood up to clear the plates.

"That amuses the hell out of you, doesn't it?"

His tone had her glancing over quickly. There wasn't precisely an edge to it, and his eyes were still clear and mild, but . . . something warned her to take care.

"I didn't mean to insult you. I just find it unusual for a grown man to read comic books as a habit." She stacked the plates in the dishwasher. "I've always thought it was something boys grew out of at a certain age, but I suppose one could consider it, what, a hobby?"

His brow lifted. She was facing him again, that half smile

on her lips. Obviously she was trying to make amends. He didn't think she should get off quite that easily. "Comic books are anything but a hobby with me, Mrs. Hester Wallace. I not only read them, I write them."

"Holy cow, really?" Radley stood staring at Mitch as though he'd just been crowned king. "Do you really? Honest? Oh, boy, are you Mitch Dempsey? The real Mitch Dempsey?"

"In the flesh." He tugged on Radley's ear while Hester looked at him as though he'd stepped in from another planet.

"Oh, boy, Mitch Dempsey right here! Mom, this is Commander Zark. None of the kids are going to believe it. Do you believe it, Mom, Commander Zark right here in our kitchen!"

"No," Hester murmured as she continued to stare. "I can't believe it."

CHAPTER 2

Hester wished she could afford to be a coward. It would be so easy to go back home, pull the covers over her head and hide out until Radley came home from school. No one who saw her would suspect that her stomach was in knots or that her palms were sweaty despite the frigid wind that whipped down the stairs as she emerged from the subway with a crowd of Manhattan's workforce.

If anyone had bothered to look, they would have seen a composed, slightly preoccupied woman in a long red wool coat and white scarf. Fortunately for Hester, the wind tunnel created by the skyscrapers whipped color into cheeks that would have been deadly pale. She had to concentrate on not chewing off her lipstick as she walked the half block to National Trust. And to her first day on the job.

It would only take her ten minutes to get back home, lock herself in and phone the office with some excuse. She was sick, there'd been a death in the family—preferably hers. She'd been robbed.

Hester clutched her briefcase tighter and kept walking. Big talk, she berated herself. She'd walked Radley to school that morning spouting off cheerful nonsense about how exciting new beginnings were, how much fun it was to start something new. Baloney, she thought, and hoped the little guy wasn't half as scared as she was.

She'd earned the position, Hester reminded herself. She was qualified and competent, with twelve years of experience under her belt. And she was scared right out of her shoes. Taking a deep breath, she walked into National Trust.

Laurence Rosen, the bank manager, checked his watch, gave a nod of approval and strode over to greet her. His dark blue suit was trim and conservative. A woman could have powdered her nose in the reflection from his shiny black shoes. "Right on time, Mrs. Wallace, an excellent beginning. I pride myself on having a staff that makes optimum use of time." He gestured toward the back of the bank, and her office.

"I'm looking forward to getting started, Mr. Rosen," she said, and felt a wave of relief that it was true. She'd always liked the feel of a bank before the doors opened to the public. The cathedral-like quiet, the pregame anticipation.

"Good, good, we'll do our best to keep you busy." He noted with a slight frown that two secretaries were not yet at their desks. In a habitual gesture, he passed a hand over his hair. "Your assistant will be in momentarily. Once you're settled, Mrs. Wallace, I'll expect you to keep close tabs on her comings and goings. Your efficiency depends largely on hers."

"Of course."

Her office was small and dull. She tried not to wish for something airier—or to notice that Rosen was as stuffy as they came. The increase this job would bring to her income would make things better for Radley. That, as always, was the bottom line. She'd make it work, Hester told herself as she took off her coat. She'd make it work well.

Rosen obviously approved of her trim black suit and understated jewelry. There was no room for flashy clothes or behavior in banking. "I trust you looked over the files I gave you."

"I familiarized myself with them over the weekend." She moved behind the desk, knowing it would establish her position. "I believe I understand National Trust's policy and procedure."

"Excellent, excellent. I'll leave you to get organized then. Your first appointment's at"—he turned pages over on her desk calendar—"9:15. If you have any problems, contact me. I'm always around somewhere."

She would have bet on it. "I'm sure everything will be fine, Mr. Rosen. Thank you."

With a final nod, Rosen strode out. The door closed behind him with a quiet click. Alone, Hester let herself slide bonelessly into her chair. She'd gotten past the first hurdle, she told herself. Rosen thought she was competent and suitable. Now all she had to do was be those things. She would be, because too much was riding on it. Not the least of those things was her pride. She hated making a fool of herself. She'd certainly done a good job of that the night before with the new neighbor.

Even hours later, remembering it, her cheeks warmed. She hadn't meant to insult the man's—even now she couldn't bring herself to call it a profession—his work, then, Hester decided. She certainly hadn't meant to make any personal observations. The problem had been that she hadn't been as much on her guard as usual. The man had thrown her off by inviting himself in and joining them for dinner and charming Radley, all in a matter of minutes. She wasn't used to people popping into her life. And she didn't like it.

Radley loved it. Hester picked up a sharpened pencil with

the bank's logo on the side. He'd practically glowed with excitement and hadn't been able to speak of anything else even after Mitch Dempsey had left.

She could be grateful for one thing. The visit had taken Radley's mind off the new school. Radley had always made friends easily, and if this Mitch was willing to give her son some pleasure, she shouldn't criticize. In any case, the man seemed harmless enough. Hester refused to admit to the uncomfortable thrill she'd experienced when his hand had closed over hers. What possible trouble could come from a man who wrote comic books for a living? She caught herself chewing at her lipstick at the question.

The knock on the door was brief and cheerful. Before she could call out, it was pushed open.

"Good morning, Mrs. Wallace. I'm Kay Lorimar, your assistant. Remember, we met for a few minutes a couple of weeks ago."

"Yes, good morning, Kay." Her assistant was everything Hester had always wanted to be herself: petite, well-rounded, blond, with small delicate features. She folded her hands on the fresh blotter and tried to look authoritative.

"Sorry I'm late." Kay smiled and didn't look the least bit sorry. "Everything takes longer than you think it does on Monday. Even if I pretend it's Tuesday, it doesn't seem to help. I don't know why. Would you like some coffee?"

"No, thank you, I've an appointment in a few minutes."

"Just ring if you change your mind." Kay paused at the door. "This place could sure use some cheering up, it's dark as a dungeon. Mr. Blowfield, that's who you're replacing, he liked things dull—matched him, you know." Her smile was ingenuous, but Hester hesitated to answer it. It would hardly do for her to get a reputation as a gossip the first day on the job. "Anyway, if you decide to do any redecorating, let me know. My roommate's into interior design. He's a real artist."

"Thank you." How was she supposed to run an office with a pert little cheerleader in tow? Hester wondered. One day at a time. "Just send Mr. and Mrs. Browning in when they arrive, Kay."

"Yes, ma'am." She sure was more pleasant to look at than old Blowfield, Kay thought. But it looked as if she had the same soul. "Loan application forms are in the bottom left drawer of the desk, arranged according to type. Legal pads in the right. Bank stationery, top right. The list of current interest rates are in the middle drawer. The Brownings are looking for a loan to remodel their loft as they're expecting a child. He's in electronics; she works part-time at Blooming-dale's. They've been advised what papers to bring with them. I can make copies while they're here."

Hester lifted her brow. "Thank you, Kay," she said, not certain whether to be amused or impressed.

When the door closed again, Hester sat back and smiled. The office might be dull, but if the morning was any indication, nothing else at National Trust was going to be.

* * *

Mitch liked having a window that faced the front of the building. That way, whenever he took a break, he could watch the comings and goings. After five years, he figured he knew every tenant by sight and half of them by name. When things were slow or, better, when he was ahead of the game, he whiled away time by sketching the more interesting of them. If his time stretched further, he made a story line to go with the faces.

He considered it the best of practice because it amused him. Occasionally there was a face interesting enough to warrant special attention. Sometimes it was a cabdriver or a delivery boy. Mitch had learned to look close and quick, then sketch from lingering impressions. Years before, he had sketched faces for a living, if a pitiful one. Now he sketched them for entertainment and was a great deal more satisfied.

He spotted Hester and her son when they were still half a block away. The red coat she wore stood out like a beacon. It certainly made a statement, Mitch mused as he picked up his pencil. He wondered if the coolly distant Mrs. Wallace realized what signals she was sending out. He doubted it.

He didn't need to see her face to draw it. Already there were a half-a-dozen rough sketches of her tossed on the table in his workroom. Interesting features, he told himself as his pencil began to fly across the pad. Any artist would be compelled to capture them.

The boy was walking along beside her, his face all but obscured by a woolen scarf and hat. Even from this distance, Mitch could see the boy was chattering earnestly. His head was angled up toward his mother. Every now and again she would glance down as if to comment; then the boy would take over again. A few steps away from the building, she stopped. Mitch saw the wind catch at her hair as she tossed her head back and laughed. His fingers went limp on the pencil as he leaned closer to the window. He wanted to be nearer, near enough to hear the laugh, to see if her eyes lit up with it. He imagined they did, but how? Would that subtle, calm gray go silvery or smoky?

She continued to walk, and in seconds was in the building and out of sight.

Mitch stared down at his sketch pad. He had no more than a few lines and contours. He couldn't finish it, he thought as he set the pencil down. He could only see her laughing now, and to capture that on paper he'd need a closer look.

Picking up his keys, he jangled them in his hand. He'd given her the better part of a week. The aloof Mrs. Wallace might consider another neighborly visit out of line, but he didn't. Besides, he liked the kid. Mitch would have gone upstairs to see him before, but he'd been busy fleshing out his story. He owed the kid for that, too, Mitch considered. The little weekend visit had not only crumbled the block, but had given Mitch enough fuel for three issues. Yeah, he owed the kid.

He pushed the keys into his pocket and walked into his workroom. Taz was there, a bone clamped between his paws as he snoozed. "Don't get up," Mitch said mildly. "I'm going out for a while." As he spoke, he ruffled through papers. Taz opened his eyes to half-mast and grumbled. "I don't know how long I'll be." After wracking through his excuse for a filing system, Mitch found the sketch. Commander Zark in full military regalia, sober faced, sad eyed, his gleaming ship at his back. Beneath it was the caption: "THE MISSION: Capture Princess Leilah—or DESTROY her!!"

Mitch wished briefly that he had the time to ink and color it, but figured the kid would like it as is. With a careless stroke he signed it, then rolled it into a tube.

"Don't wait dinner for me," he instructed Taz.

*   *   *

"I'll get it!" Radley danced to the door. It was Friday, and school was light-years away.

"Ask who it is."

Radley put his hand on the knob and shook his head. He'd been going to ask. Probably. "Who is it?"

"It's Mitch."

"It's Mitch!" Radley shouted, delighted. In the bedroom, Hester scowled and pulled the sweatshirt over her head.

"Hi." Breathless with excitement, Radley opened the door to his latest hero.

"Hi, Rad, how's it going?"

"Fine. I don't have any homework all weekend." He reached out a hand to draw Mitch inside. "I wanted to come down and see you, but Mom said no 'cause you'd be working or something."

"Or something," Mitch muttered. "Look, it's okay with me if you come over. Anytime."

"Really?"

"Really." The kid was irresistible, Mitch thought as he ruffled the boy's hair. Too bad his mother wasn't as friendly. "I thought you might like this." Mitch handed him the rolled sketch.

"Oh, wow." Awestruck, reverent, Radley stared at the drawing. "Jeez, Commander Zark and the *Second Millennium*. Can I have it, really? To keep?"

"Yeah."

"I gotta show Mom." Radley turned and dashed toward the bedroom as Hester came out. "Look what Mitch gave me. Isn't it great? He said I could keep it and everything."

"It's terrific." She put a hand on Radley's shoulder as she studied the sketch. The man was certainly talented, Hester decided. Even if he had chosen such an odd way to show it. Her hand remained on Radley's shoulder as she looked over at Mitch. "That was very nice of you."

He liked the way she looked in the pastel sweats, casual, approachable, if not completely relaxed. Her hair was down too, with the ends just sweeping short of her shoulders. Parted softly on the side and unpinned, it gave her a completely different look.

"I wanted to thank Rad." Mitch forced himself to look away from her face, then smiled at the boy. "You helped me through a block last weekend."

"I did?" Radley's eyes widened. "Honest?"

"Honest. I was stuck, spinning wheels. After I talked to

you that night, I went down and everything fell into place. I appreciate it."

"Wow, you're welcome. You could stay for dinner again. We're just having Chinese chicken, and maybe I could help you some more. It's okay, isn't it, Mom? Isn't it?"

Trapped again. And again she caught the gleam of amusement in Mitch's eyes. "Of course."

"Great. I want to go hang this up right away. Can I call Josh, too, and tell him about it? He won't believe it."

"Sure." She barely had time to run a hand over his hair before he was off and running.

"Thanks, Mitch." Radley paused at the turn of the hallway. "Thanks a lot."

Hester found the deep side pockets in her sweats and slipped her hands inside. There was absolutely no reason for the man to make her nervous. So why did he? "That was really very kind of you."

"Maybe, but I haven't done anything that's made me feel that good in a long time." He wasn't completely at ease himself, Mitch discovered, and he tucked his thumbs into the back pockets of his jeans. "You work fast," he commented as he glanced around the living room.

The boxes were gone. Bright, vivid prints hung on the walls and a vase of flowers, fresh as morning, sat near the window, where sheer curtains filtered the light. Pillows were plumped, furniture gleamed. The only signs of confusion were a miniature car wreck and a few plastic men scattered on the carpet. He was glad to see them. It meant she wasn't the type who expected the boy to play only in his room.

"Dali?" He walked over to a lithograph hung over the sofa.

She caught her bottom lip between her teeth as Mitch studied one of her rare extravagances. "I bought that in a little shop on Fifth that's always going out of business."

"Yeah, I know the one. It didn't take you long to put things together here."

"I wanted everything back to normal as soon as possible. The move wasn't easy for Radley."

"And you?" He turned then, catching her off guard with the sudden sharp look.

"Me? I—ah . . ."

"You know," he began as he crossed over to her, attracted by her simple bafflement. "You're a lot more articulate when you talk about Rad than you are when you talk about Hester."

She stepped back quickly, aware that he would have touched her and totally unsure what her reaction might have been. "I should start dinner."

"Want some help?"

"With what?"

This time she didn't move quickly enough. He cupped her chin in his hand and smiled. "With dinner."

It had been a long time since a man had touched her that way. He had a strong hand with gentle fingers. That had to be the reason her heart leaped up to her throat and pounded there. "Can you cook?"

What incredible eyes she had. So clear, so pale a gray they were almost translucent. For the first time in years he felt the urge to paint, just to see if he could bring those eyes to life on canvas. "I make a hell of a peanut butter sandwich."

She lifted a hand to his wrist, to move his away, she thought. But her fingers lay there lightly a moment, experimenting. "How are you at chopping vegetables?"

"I think I can handle it."

"All right, then." She backed up, amazed that she had allowed the contact to go for so long. "I still don't have any beer, but I do have some wine this time."

"Fine." What the hell were they talking about? Why were they talking at all, when she had a mouth that was made to fit on a man's? A little baffled by his own train of thought, he followed her into the kitchen.

"It's really a simple meal," she began. "But when it's all mixed up, Radley hardly notices he's eating something nutritious. A Twinkie's the true way to his heart."

"My kind of kid."

She smiled a little, more relaxed now that she had her hands full. She set celery and mushrooms on the chopping block. "The trick's in moderation." Hester took the chicken out, then remembered the wine. "I'm willing to concede to Rad's sweet tooth in small doses. He's willing to accept broccoli on the same terms."

"Sounds like a wise arrangement." She opened the wine. Inexpensive, he thought with a glance at the label, but palatable. She filled two glasses, then handed him one. It was silly, but her hands were damp again. It had been some time since she'd shared a bottle of wine or fixed a simple dinner with a man. "To neighbors," he said, and thought she relaxed fractionally as he touched his glass to hers.

"Why don't you sit down while I bone the chicken? Then you can deal with the vegetables."

He didn't sit, but did lean back against the counter. He wasn't willing to give her the distance he was sure she wanted. Not when she smelled so good. She handled the knife like an expert, he noted as he sipped his wine. Impressive. Most of the career women he knew were more experienced in take-outs. "So, how's the new job?"

Hester moved her shoulders. "It's working out well. The manager's a stickler for efficiency, and that trickles down. Rad and I have been having conferences all week so we can compare notes."

Was that what they'd been talking about when they'd walked home today? he wondered. Was that why she'd laughed? "How's Radley taking the new school?"

"Amazingly well." Her lips softened and curved again. He was tempted to touch a fingertip to them to feel the movement. "Whatever happens in Rad's life, he rolls with. He's incredible."

There was a shadow there, a slight one, but he could see it in her eyes. "Divorce is tough," he said, and watched Hester freeze up.

"Yes." She put the boned and cubed chicken in a bowl. "You can chop this while I start the rice."

"Sure." No trespassing, he thought, and let it drop. For now. He'd gone with the law of averages when he'd mentioned divorce, and realized he'd been on the mark. But the mark was still raw. Unless he missed his guess, the divorce had been a lot tougher on her than on Radley. He was also sure that if he wanted to draw her out, it would have to be through the boy. "Rad mentioned that he wanted to come down and visit, but you'd put him off."

Hester handed Mitch an onion before she put a pan on the stove. "I didn't want him disturbing your work."

"We both know what you think of my work."

"I had no intention of offending you the other night," she said stiffly. "It was only that—"

"You can't conceive of a grown man making a living writing comic books."

Hester remained silent as she measured out water. "It's none of my business how you make your living."

"That's right." Mitch took a long sip of wine before he attacked the celery. "In any case, I want you to know that Rad can come see me whenever he likes."

"That's very nice of you, but—"

"No buts, Hester. I like him. And since I'm in the position

of calling my own hours, he won't bother me. What do I do with the mushrooms?"

"Slice." She put the lid on the rice before crossing over to show him. "Not too thin. Just make sure . . ." Her words trailed off when he closed his hand over hers on the knife.

"Like this?" The move was easy. He didn't even have to think about it, but simply shifted until she was trapped between his arms, her back pressed against him. Giving in to the urge, he bent down so that his mouth was close to her ear.

"Yes, that's fine." She stared down at their joined hands and tried to keep her voice even. "It really doesn't matter."

"We aim to please."

"I have to put on the chicken." She turned and found herself in deeper water. It was a mistake to look up at him, to see that slight smile on his lips and that calm, confident look in his eyes. Instinctively she lifted a hand to his chest. Even that was a mistake. She could feel the slow, steady beat of his heart. She couldn't back up, because there was no place to go, and stepping forward was tempting, dangerously so. "Mitch, you're in my way."

He'd seen it. Though it had been free briefly and suppressed quickly, he'd seen the passion come into her eyes. So she could feel and want and wonder. Maybe it was best if they both wondered a little while longer. "I think you're going to find that happening a lot." But he shifted aside and let her pass. "You smell good, Hester, damn good."

That quiet statement did nothing to ease her pulse rate. Humoring Radley or not, she vowed this would be the last time she entertained Mitch Dempsey. Hester turned on the gas under the wok and added peanut oil. "I take it you do your work at home, then. No office?"

He'd let her have it her way for the time being. The minute she'd turned in his arms and looked up at him, he'd known he'd have it his way—have her his way—before too long. "I only have to go a couple of times a week. Some of the writers or artists prefer working in the office. I do better work at home. After I have the story and the sketches, I take them in for editing and inking."

"I see. So you don't do the inking yourself?" she asked, though she'd have been hard-pressed to define what inking was. She'd have to ask Radley.

"Not anymore. We have some real experts in that, and it gives me more time to work on the story. Believe it or not, we shoot for quality, the kind of vocabulary that challenges a kid and a story that entertains."

After adding chicken to the hot oil, Hester took a deep breath. "I really do apologize for anything I said that offended you. I'm sure your work's very important to you, and I know Radley certainly appreciates it."

"Well said, Mrs. Wallace." He slid the vegetable-laden chopping block toward her.

"Josh doesn't believe it." Radley bounced into the room, delighted with himself. "He wants to come over tomorrow and see. Can he? His mom says okay if it's okay with you. Okay, Mom?"

Hester turned from the chicken long enough to give Radley a hug. "Okay, Rad, but it has to be after noon. We have some shopping to do in the morning."

"Thanks. Just wait till he sees. He's gonna go crazy. I'll tell him."

"Dinner's nearly ready. Hurry up and wash your hands."

Radley rolled his eyes at Mitch as he raced from the room again.

"You're a big hit," Hester commented.

"He's nuts about you."

"The feeling's mutual."

"So I noticed." Mitch topped off his wine. "You know, I

was curious. I always thought bankers kept bankers' hours. You and Rad don't get home until five or so." When she turned her head to look at him, he merely smiled. "Some of my windows face the front. I like to watch people going in and out."

It gave her an odd and not entirely comfortable feeling to know he'd watched her walk home. Hester dumped the vegetables in and stirred. "I get off at four, but then I have to pick Rad up from the sitter." She glanced over her shoulder again. "He hates it when I call her a sitter. Anyway, she's over by our old place, so it takes awhile. I have to start looking for someone closer."

"A lot of kids his age and younger come home on their own."

Her eyes did go smoky, he noted. All she needed was a touch of anger. Or passion. "Radley isn't going to be a latchkey child. He isn't coming home to an empty house because I have to work."

Mitch set her glass by her elbow. "Coming home to empty can be depressing," he murmured, remembering his own experiences. "He's lucky to have you."

"I'm luckier to have him." Her tone softened. "If you'd get out the plates, I'll dish this up."

Mitch remembered where she kept her plates, white ones with little violet sprigs along the edges. It was odd to realize they pleased him when he'd become so accustomed to disposable plastic. He took them out, then set them beside her. Most things were best done on impulse, he'd always thought. He went with the feeling now.

"I guess it would be a lot easier on Rad if he could come back here after school."

"Oh, yes. I hate having to drag him across town, though he's awfully good about it. It's just so hard to find someone you can trust and who Radley really likes."

"How about me?"

Hester reached to turn off the gas but stopped to stare at him. Vegetables and chicken popped in hot oil. "I'm sorry?"

"Rad could stay with me in the afternoons." Again Mitch put a hand over hers, this time to turn off the heat. "He'd only be a couple floors away from his own place."

"With you? No, I couldn't."

"Why not?" The more he thought of it, the more Mitch liked the idea. He and Taz could use the company in the afternoons, and as a bonus, he'd be seeing a lot more of the very interesting Mrs. Wallace. "You want references? No criminal record, Hester. Well, there was the case of my motorcycle and the prize roses, but I was only eighteen."

"I didn't mean that—exactly." When he grinned, she began to fuss with the rice. "I mean I couldn't impose that way. I'm sure you're busy."

"Come on, you don't think I do anything all day but doodle. Let's be honest."

"We've already agreed it isn't any of my business," she began.

"Exactly. The point is I'm home in the afternoons, I'm available, and I'm willing. Besides, I may even be able to use Rad as a consultant. He's good, you know." Mitch indicated the drawing on the refrigerator. "The kid could use some art lessons."

"I know. I was hoping I'd be able to swing it this summer, but I don't—"

"Want to look a gift horse in the mouth," Mitch finished. "Look, the kid likes me; I like him. And I'll swear to no more than one Twinkie an afternoon."

She laughed then, as he'd seen her laugh a few hours before from his window. It wasn't easy to hold himself back, but something told him if he made a move now, the door would slam in his face and the bolt would slide shut. "I don't know,

Mitch. I do appreciate the offer, God knows it would make things easier, but I'm not sure you understand what you're asking for."

"I hasten to point out that I was once a small boy." He wanted to do it, he discovered. It was more than a gesture or impulse; he really wanted to have the kid around. "Look, why don't we put this to a vote and ask Rad?"

"Ask me what?" Radley had run some water over his hands after he'd finished talking to Josh, and figured his mother was too busy to give them a close look.

Mitch picked up his wine, then lifted a brow. My ball, Hester thought. She could have put the child off, but she'd always prided herself on being honest with him. "Mitch was just suggesting that you might like to stay with him after school in the afternoons instead of going over to Mrs. Cohen's."

"Really?" Astonishment and excitement warred until he was bouncing with both. "Really, can I?"

"Well, I wanted to think about it and talk to you before—"

"I'll behave." Radley rushed over to wrap his arms around his mother's waist. "I promise. Mitch is much better than Mrs. Cohen. Lots better. She smells like mothballs and pats me on the head."

"I rest my case," Mitch murmured.

Hester sent Mitch a smoldering look. She wasn't accustomed to being outnumbered or to making a decision without careful thought and consideration. "Now, Radley, you know Mrs. Cohen's very nice. You've been staying with her for over two years."

Radley squeezed harder and played his ace. "If I stayed with Mitch, I could come right home. And I'd do my homework first." It was a rash promise, but it was a desperate situation. "You'd get home sooner, too, and everything. Please, Mom, say yes."

She hated to deny him anything, because there were too

many things she'd already had to. He was looking up at her now with his cheeks rosy with pleasure. Bending, she kissed him. "All right, Rad, we'll try it and see how it works out."

"It's going to be great." He locked his arms around her neck before he turned to Mitch. "It's going to be just great."

CHAPTER 3

Mitch liked to sleep late on weekends—whenever he thought of them as weekends. Because he worked in his own home, at his own pace, he often forgot that to the vast majority there was a big difference between Monday mornings and Saturday mornings. This particular Saturday, however, he was spending in bed, largely dead to the world.

He'd been restless the evening before after he'd left Hester's apartment. Too restless to go back to his own alone. On the spur of the moment he'd gone out to the little lounge where the staff of Universal Comics often got together. He'd run into his inker, another artist and one of the staff writers for *The Great Beyond*, Universal's bid for the supernatural market. The music had been loud and none too good, which had been exactly what his mood had called for.

From there he'd been persuaded to attend an all-night horror film festival in Times Square. It had been past six when he'd come home, a little drunk and with only enough energy left to strip and tumble into bed—where he'd promised himself he'd stay for the next twenty-four hours. When the phone rang eight hours later, he answered it mostly because it annoyed him.

"Yeah?"

"Mitch?" Hester hesitated. It sounded as though he'd been asleep. Since it was after two in the afternoon, she dismissed the thought. "It's Hester Wallace. I'm sorry to bother you."

"What? No, it's all right." He rubbed a hand over his face, then pushed at the dog, who had shifted to the middle of the bed. "Damn it, Taz, shove over. You're breathing all over me."

Taz? Hester thought as both brows lifted. She hadn't thought that Mitch would have a roommate. She caught her bottom lip between her teeth. That was something she should have checked out. For Radley's sake.

"I really am sorry," she continued in a voice that had cooled dramatically. "Apparently I've caught you at a bad time."

"No." Give the stupid mutt an inch and he took a mile, Mitch thought as he hefted the phone and climbed to the other side of the bed. "What's up?"

"Are you?"

It was the mild disdain in her voice that had him bristling. That and the fact that it felt as though he'd eaten a sandbox. "Yeah, I'm up. I'm talking to you, aren't I?"

"I only called to give you all the numbers and information you need if you watch Radley next week."

"Oh." He pushed the hair out of his eyes and glanced around, hoping he'd left a glass of watered-down soda or something close at hand. No luck. "Okay. You want to wait until I get a pencil?"

"Well, I . . . ." He heard her put her hand over the receiver and speak to someone—Radley, he imagined from the quick intensity of the voice. "Actually, if it wouldn't put you out, Radley was hoping we could come by for a minute. He wants to introduce you to his friend. If you're busy, I can just drop the information by later."

Mitch started to tell her to do just that. Not only could he go back to sleep, but he might just be able to wrangle five minutes alone with her. Then he thought of Radley standing beside his mother, looking up at her with those big dark eyes. "Give me ten minutes," he muttered, and hung up before Hester could say a word.

Mitch pulled on jeans, then went into the bath to fill the sink with cold water. He took a deep breath and stuck his face in it. He came up swearing but awake. Five minutes later he was pulling on a sweatshirt and wondering if he'd remembered to wash any socks. All the clothes that had come back from the laundry neatly folded had been dumped on the chair in the corner of the bedroom. He briefly considered pushing his way through them, then let it go when he heard the knock. Taz's tail thumped on the mattress.

"Why don't you pick up this place?" Mitch asked him. "It's a pigsty."

Taz grinned, showing a set of big white teeth, then made a series of growls and groans.

"Excuses. Always excuses. And get out of bed. Don't you know it's after two?" Mitch rubbed a hand over his unshaven chin, then went to open the door.

She looked great, just plain great, with a hand on a shoulder of each boy and a half smile on her face. Shy? he thought, a little surprised as he realized it. He had thought her cool and aloof, but now he believed she used that to hide an innate shyness, which he found amazingly sweet.

"Hiya, Rad."

"Hi, Mitch," Radley returned, almost bursting with importance. "This is my friend Josh Miller. He doesn't believe you're Commander Zark."

"Is that so?" Mitch looked down at the doubting Thomas, a skinny towhead about two inches taller than Rad. "Come on in."

"It's nice of you to put up with this," Hester began. "We weren't going to have any peace until Rad and Josh had it settled." The living room looked as though it had exploded. That was Hester's first thought as Mitch closed the door behind them. Papers and clothes and wrappers were everywhere. She imagined there was furniture, too, but she couldn't have described it.

"Tell Josh you're Commander Zark," Radley insisted.

"I guess you could say that." The notion pleased him. "I created him, anyway." He looked down again at Josh, whose pout had gone beyond doubt to true suspicion. "You two go to school together?"

"Used to." Josh stood close to Hester as he studied Mitch. "You don't look like Commander Zark."

Mitch rubbed a hand over his chin again. "Rough night."

"He is too Zark. Hey, look, Mom. Mitch has a VCR." Radley easily overlooked the clutter and homed in on the entertainment center. "I'm saving up my allowance to buy one. I've got seventeen dollars."

"It adds up," Mitch murmured, and flicked a finger down Radley's nose. "Why don't we go into the office? I'll show you what's cooking in the spring issue."

"Wow."

Taking this as an assent, Mitch led the way.

The office, Hester noted, was big and bright and every bit as chaotic as the living room. She was a creature of order, and it was beyond her how anyone could produce under these conditions. Yet there was a drawing board set up, and tacked to it were sketches and captions.

"You can see Zark's going to have his hands full when Leilah teams up with the Black Moth."

"The Black Moth. Holy cow." Faced with the facts, Josh was duly impressed. Then he remembered his comic book history, and suspicion reared again. "I thought he destroyed the Moth five issues ago."

"The Moth only went into hibernation after Zark bombarded the Zenith with experimental ZT-5. Leilah used her scientific genius to bring him out again."

"Wow." This came from Josh as he stared at the oversized words and drawings. "How come you make this so big? It can't fit in a comic book."

"It has to be reduced."

"I read all about that stuff." Radley gave Josh a superior glance. "I got this book out of the library that gave the history of comic books, all the way back to the 1930s."

"The Stone Age." Mitch smiled as the boys continued to admire his work. Hester was doing some admiring of her own. Beneath the clutter, she was certain there was a genuine French rococo cupboard. And books. Hundreds of them. Mitch watched her wander the room. And would have gone on watching if Josh hadn't tugged on his arm.

"Please, can I have your autograph?"

Mitch felt foolishly delighted as he stared down at the earnest face. "Sure." Shuffling through papers, he found a blank one and signed it. Then, with a flourish, he added a quick sketch of Zark.

"Neat." Josh folded the paper reverently and slipped it in his back pocket. "My brother's always bragging because he's got an autographed baseball, but this is better."

"Told ya." With a grin, Radley moved closer to Mitch. "And I'm going to be staying with Mitch after school until Mom gets home from work."

"No kidding?"

"All right, guys, we've taken up enough of Mr. Dempsey's time." Hester started to shoo the boys along when Taz strolled into the room.

"Gee whiz, he's really big." Radley started forward, hand out, when Hester caught him.

"Radley, you know better than to go up to a strange dog."

"Your mom's right," Mitch put in. "But in this case it's okay. Taz is harmless."

And enormous, Hester thought, keeping a firm grip on both boys.

Taz, who had a healthy respect for little people, sat in the doorway and eyed them both. Small boys had a tendency to want to play rough and pull ears, which Taz suffered heroically but could do without. Waiting to see which way the wind blew, he sat and thumped his tail.

"He's anything but an aggressive dog," Mitch reassured Hester. He stepped around her and put a hand on Taz's head. Without, Hester noted, having to bend over.

"Does he do tricks?" Radley wanted to know. It was one of his most secret wishes to own a dog. A big one. But he never asked, because he knew they couldn't keep one shut in an apartment all day alone.

"No, all Taz does is talk."

"Talk?" Josh went into a fit of laughter. "Dogs can't talk."

"He means bark," Hester said, relaxing a little.

"No, I mean talk." Mitch gave Taz a couple of friendly pats. "How's it going, Taz?"

In answer, the dog pushed his head hard against Mitch's leg and began to groan and grumble. Eyes wide and sincere, he looked up at his master and howled and hooted until both boys were nearly rolling with laughter.

"He *does* talk." Radley stepped forward, palm up. "He really does." Taz decided Radley didn't look like an ear puller and nuzzled his long snout in the boy's hand. "He likes me. Look, Mom." It was love at first sight as Radley threw his arms around the dog's neck. Automatically Hester started forward.

"He's as gentle as they come, I promise you." Mitch put a hand on Hester's arm. Even though the dog was already grumbling out his woes in Radley's ear and allowing Josh to pet him, Hester wasn't convinced.

"I don't imagine he's used to children."

"He fools around with kids in the park all the time." As if to prove it, Taz rolled over to expose his belly for stroking. "Added to that is the fact that he's bone lazy. He wouldn't work up the energy to bite anything that hadn't been put in a bowl for him. You aren't afraid of dogs, are you?"

"No, of course not." Not really, she added to herself. Because she hated to show a weakness, Hester crouched down to pet the huge head. Unknowingly she hit the perfect spot, and Taz recognized a patsy when he saw one. He shifted to lay a paw on her thigh and, with his dark, sad eyes on hers, began to moan. Laughing, Hester rubbed behind his ears. "You're just a big baby, aren't you?"

"An operator's more like it," Mitch murmured, wondering what sort of trick he'd have to do to get Hester to touch him with such feeling.

"I can play with him every day, can't I, Mitch?"

"Sure." Mitch smiled down at Radley. "Taz loves attention. You guys want to take him for a walk?"

The response was immediate and affirmative. Hester straightened up, looking doubtfully at Taz. "I don't know, Rad."

"Please, Mom, we'll be careful. You already said me and Josh could play in the park for a little while."

"Yes, I know, but Taz is awfully big. I wouldn't want him to get away from you."

"Taz is a firm believer in conserving energy. Why run if strolling gets you to the same place?" Mitch went back into his office, rooted around and came up with Taz's leash. "He doesn't chase cars, other dogs or park police. He will, however, stop at every tree."

With a giggle, Radley took the leash. "Okay, Mom?"

She hesitated, knowing there was a part of her that wanted to keep Radley with her, within arm's reach. And, for his sake, it was something she had to fight. "A half hour." The words were barely out when he and Josh let out a whoop. "You have to get your coats—and gloves."

"We will. Come on, Taz."

The dog gave a huge sigh before gathering himself up. Grumbling only a little, he stationed himself between the two boys as they headed out.

"Why is it every time I see that kid I feel good?"

"You're very kind to him. Well, I should go upstairs and make sure they bundle up."

"I think they can handle it. Why don't you sit down?" He took advantage of her brief hesitation by taking her arm. "Come over by the window. You can watch them go out."

She gave in because she knew how Radley hated to be hovered over. "Oh, I have my office number for you, and the name and number of his doctor and the school." Mitch took the paper and stuck it in his pocket. "If there's any trouble at all, call me. I can be home in ten minutes."

"Relax, Hester. We'll get along fine."

"I want to thank you again. It's the first time since he started school that Rad's looked forward to a Monday."

"I'm looking forward to it myself."

She looked down, waiting to see the familiar blue cap and coat. "We haven't discussed terms."

"What terms?"

"How much you want for watching him. Mrs. Cohen—"

"Good God, Hester, I don't want you to pay me."

"Don't be ridiculous. Of course I'll pay you."

He put a hand on her shoulder until she'd turned to face him. "I don't need the money; I don't want the money. I made the offer because Rad's a nice kid and I enjoy his company."

"That's very kind of you, but—"

His exasperated sigh cut her off. "Here come the buts again."

"I couldn't possibly let you do it for nothing."

Mitch studied her face. He'd thought her tough at their first meeting, and tough she was —at least on the outside. "Can't you accept a neighborly gesture?"

Her lips curved a bit, but her eyes remained solemn. "I guess not."

"Five bucks a day."

This time the smile reached her eyes. "Thank you."

He caught the ends of her hair between his thumb and forefinger. "You drive a hard bargain, lady."

"So I've been told." Cautiously she took a step away. "Here they come." Radley hadn't forgotten his gloves, she noted as she leaned closer to the window. Nor had he forgotten that he'd been taught to walk to the corner and cross at the light. "He's in heaven, you know. Rad's always wanted a dog." She touched a hand to the window and continued to watch. "He doesn't mention it because he knows we can't keep one in the apartment when no one's home all day. So he's settled for the promise of a kitten."

Mitch put a hand on her shoulder again, but gently this time. "He doesn't strike me as a deprived child, Hester. There's nothing for you to feel guilty about."

She looked at him then, her eyes wide and just a little sad. Mitch discovered he was just as drawn to that as he had been to her laughter. Without planning to, without knowing he'd needed to, he lifted a hand to her cheek. The pale gray of her irises deepened. Her skin warmed. Hester backed away quickly.

"I'd better go. I'm sure they'll want hot chocolate when they get back in."

"They have to bring Taz back here first," Mitch reminded her. "Take a break, Hester. Want some coffee?"

"Well, I—"

"Good. Sit down and I'll get it."

Hester stood in the center of the room a moment, a bit amazed at how smoothly he ran things—his way. She was much too used to setting her own rules to accept anyone else's. Still, she told herself it would be rude to leave, that her son would be back soon and that the least she could do after Mitch had been so good to the boy was bear his company for a little while.

She would have been lying if she'd denied that he interested her. In a casual way, of course. There was something about the way he looked at her, so deep and penetrating, while at the same time he appeared to take most of life as a joke. Yet there was nothing funny about the way he touched her.

Hester lifted fingertips to her cheek, where his had been. She would have to take care to avoid too much of that sort of contact. Perhaps, with effort, she could think of Mitch as a friend, as Radley did already. It might not sit well with her to be obliged to him, but she could swallow that. She'd swallowed worse.

He was kind. She let out a little breath as she tried to relax. Experience had given her a very sensitive antenna. She could recognize the kind of man who tried to ingratiate himself with the child to get to the mother. If she was sure of anything, it was that Mitch genuinely liked Radley. That, if nothing else, was a point in his favor.

But she wished he hadn't touched her that way, looked at her that way, made her feel that way.

"It's hot. Probably lousy, but hot." Mitch walked in with two mugs. "Don't you want to sit down?"

Hester smiled at him. "Where?"

Mitch set the mugs down on a stack of papers, then pushed magazines from the sofa. "Here."

"You know . . ." She stepped over a stack of old newspapers. "Radley's very good at tidying. He'd be glad to help you."

"I function best in controlled confusion."

Hester joined him on the sofa. "I can see the confusion but not the controlled."

"It's here, believe me. I didn't ask if you wanted anything in the coffee, so I brought it black."

"Black's fine. This table—it's Queen Anne, isn't it?"

"Yeah." Mitch set his bare feet on it, then crossed them at the ankles. "You've got a good eye."

"One would have to under the circumstances." Because he laughed, she smiled as she took her first sip. "I've always loved antiques. I suppose it's the endurance. Not many things last."

"Sure they do. I once had a cold that lasted six weeks." He settled back as she laughed. "When you do that, you get a dimple at the corner of your mouth. Cute."

Hester was immediately self-conscious again. "You have a very natural way with children. Did you come from a large family?"

"No. Only child." He continued to study her, curious about her reaction to the most casual of compliments.

"Really? I wouldn't have guessed it."

"Don't tell me you're of the school who believes only a woman can relate to children?"

"No, not really," she hedged, because that had been her experience thus far. "It's just that you're particularly good with them. No children of your own?" The question came out quickly, amazing and embarrassing her.

"No. I guess I've been too busy being a kid myself to think about raising any."

"That hardly makes you unusual," she said coolly.

He tilted his head as he studied her. "Tossing me in with Rad's father, Hester?"

Something flashed in her eyes. Mitch shook his head as he sipped again. "Damn, Hester, what did the bastard do to you?" She froze instantly. Mitch was quicker. Even as she started to rise, he put a restraining hand on her arm. "Okay, hands off that one until you're ready. I apologize if I hit a sore spot, but I'm curious. I've spent a couple of evenings with Rad now, and he's never mentioned his father."

"I'd appreciate it if you wouldn't ask him any questions."

"Fine." Mitch was capable of being just as snotty. "I didn't intend to grill the kid."

Hester was tempted to get up and excuse herself. That would be the easiest way. But the fact was that she was trusting her son to this man every afternoon. She supposed it would be best if he had some background.

"Rad hasn't seen his father in almost seven years."

"At all?" He couldn't help his surprise. His own family had been undemonstrative and distant, but he never went more than a year without seeing his parents. "Must be rough on the kid."

"They were never close. I think Radley's adjusted very well."

"Hold on. I wasn't criticizing you." He'd placed his hand over hers again, too firmly to be shaken off. "I know a happy, well-loved boy when I see one. You'd walk through fire for him. Maybe you don't think it shows, but it does."

"There's nothing that's more important to me than Radley." She wanted to relax again, but he was sitting too close, and his hand was still on hers. "I only told you this so that you wouldn't ask him questions that might upset him."

"Does that sort of thing happen often?"

"Sometimes." His fingers were linked with hers now. She

couldn't quite figure out how he'd managed it. "A new friend, a new teacher. I really should go."

"How about you?" He touched her cheek gently and turned her face toward him. "How have you adjusted?"

"Just fine. I have Rad and my work."

"And no relationships?"

She wasn't sure if it was embarrassment or anger, but the sensation was very strong. "That's none of your business."

"If people only talked about what was their business, they wouldn't get very far. You don't strike me as a man-hater, Hester."

She lifted a brow. When pushed, she could play the game by someone else's rules. And she could play it well. "I went through a period of time when I despised men on principle. Actually, it was a very rewarding time of my life. Then, gradually, I came to the opinion that some members of your species weren't lower forms of life."

"Sounds promising."

She smiled again, because he made it easy. "The point is, I don't blame all men for the faults of one."

"You're just cautious."

"If you like."

"The one thing I'm sure I like is your eyes. No, don't look away." Patiently, he turned her face back to his. "They're fabulous—take it from an artist's standpoint."

She had to stop being so jumpy, Hester ordered herself. With an effort, she remained still. "Does that mean they're going to appear in an upcoming issue?"

"They just might." He smiled, appreciating the thought and the fact that though tense, she was able to hold her own. "Poor old Zark deserves to meet someone who understands him. These eyes would."

"I'll take that as a compliment." And run. "The boys will be back in a minute."

"We've got some time yet. Hester, do you ever have fun?"

"What a stupid question. Of course I do."

"Not as Rad's mother, but as Hester." He ran a hand through her hair, captivated.

"I *am* Rad's mother." Though she managed to rise, he stood with her.

"You're also a woman. A gorgeous one." He saw the look in her eyes and ran his thumb along her jawline. "Take my word for it. I'm an honest man. You're one gorgeous bundle of nerves."

"That's silly. I don't have anything to be nervous about." Other than the fact that he was touching her, and his voice was quiet, and the apartment was empty.

"I'll take the shaft out of my heart later," he murmured. He bent to kiss her, then had to catch her when she nearly stumbled over the newspapers. "Take it easy. I'm not going to bite you. This time."

"I have to go." She was as close to panic as she ever allowed herself to come. "I have a dozen things to do."

"In a minute." He framed her face. She was trembling, he realized. It didn't surprise him. What did was that he wasn't steady himself. "What we have here, Mrs. Wallace, is called attraction, chemistry, lust. It doesn't really matter what label you put on it."

"Maybe not to you."

"Then we'll let you pick the label later." He stroked his thumbs over her cheekbones, gently, soothingly. "I already told you I'm not a maniac. I'll have to remember to get those references."

"Mitch, I told you I appreciate what you're doing for Rad, but I wish you'd—"

"Here and now doesn't concern Rad. This is you and me, Hester. When was the last time you let yourself be alone with a man who wanted you?" He casually brushed his thumb over her lips. Her eyes went to smoke. "When was the last time you let anyone do this?"

His mouth covered hers quickly, with a force that came as a shock. She hadn't been prepared for violence. His hands had been so gentle, his voice so soothing. She hadn't expected this edgy passion. But God, how she'd wanted it. With the same reckless need, she threw her arms around his neck and answered demand for demand.

"Too long," Mitch managed breathlessly when he tore his mouth from hers. "Thank God." Before she could utter more than a moan, he took her mouth again.

He hadn't been sure what he'd find in her—ice, anger, fear. The unrestrained heat came as much of a shock to his system as to hers. Her wide, generous mouth was warm and willing, with all traces of shyness swallowed by passion. She gave more than he would have asked for, more than he'd been prepared to take.

His head spun, a fascinating and novel sensation he couldn't fully appreciate as he struggled to touch and taste. He dragged his hands through her hair, scattering the two thin silver pins she'd used to pull it back from her face. He wanted it free and wild in his hands, just as he wanted her free and wild in his bed. His plans to go slowly, to test the waters, evaporated in an overwhelming desire to dive in head-first. Thinking only of this, he slipped his hands under her sweater. The skin there was tender and warm. The silky little concoction she wore was cool and soft. He slid his hands around her waist and up to cup her breasts.

She stiffened, then shuddered. She hadn't known how much she'd wanted to be touched like this. Needed like this. His taste was so dark, so tempting. She'd forgotten what it was like to hunger for such things. It was madness, the sweet release of madness. She heard him murmur her name as he moved his mouth down her throat and back again.

Madness. She understood it. She'd been there before, or thought she had. Though it seemed sweeter now, richer now, she knew she could never go there again.

"Mitch, please." It wasn't easy to resist what he was offering. It surprised Hester how difficult it was to draw away, to put the boundaries back. "We can't do this."

"We are," he pointed out, and drew the flavor from her lips again. "And very well."

"*I* can't." With the small sliver of willpower she had left, she struggled away. "I'm sorry. I should never have let this happen." Her cheeks were hot. Hester put her hands to them, then dragged them up through her hair.

His knees were weak. That was something to think about. But for the moment he concentrated on her. "You're taking a lot on yourself, Hester. It seems to be a habit of yours. I kissed you, and you just happened to kiss me back. Since we both enjoyed it, I don't see where apologies are necessary on either side."

"I should have made myself clear." She stepped back, hit the newspapers again, then skirted around them. "I do appreciate what you're doing for Rad—"

"Leave him out of this, for God's sake."

"I can't." Her voice rose, surprising her again. She knew better than to lose control. "I don't expect you to understand, but I can't leave him out of it." She took a deep breath, amazed that it did nothing to calm her pulse rate. "I'm not interested in casual sex. I have Rad to think about, and myself."

"Fair enough." He wanted to sit down until he'd recovered, but figured the situation called for an eye-to-eye discussion. "I wasn't feeling too casual about it myself."

That was what worried her. "Let's just drop it."

Anger was an amazing stimulant. Mitch stepped forward and caught her chin in his hand. "Fat chance."

"I don't want to argue with you. I just think that—" The knock came as a blessed reprieve. "That's the boys."

"I know." But he didn't release her. "Whatever you're interested in, have time for, room for, might just have to be adjusted." He was angry, really angry, Mitch realized. It wasn't like him to lose his temper so quickly. "Life's full of adjustments, Hester." Letting her go, he opened the door.

"It was great." Rosy-cheeked and bright-eyed, Radley tumbled in ahead of Josh and the dog. "We even got Taz to run once, for a minute."

"Amazing." Mitch bent to unclip the leash. Grumbling with exhaustion, Taz walked to a spot by the window, then collapsed.

"You guys must be freezing." Hester kissed Radley's forehead. "It must be time for hot chocolate."

"Yeah!" Radley turned his beaming face to Mitch. "Want some? Mom makes real good hot chocolate."

It was tempting to put her on the spot. Perhaps it was a good thing for both of them that his temper was already fading. "Maybe next time." He pulled Radley's cap over his eyes. "I've got some things to do."

"Thanks a lot for letting us take Taz out. It was really neat, wasn't it, Josh?"

"Yeah. Thanks, Mr. Dempsey."

"Anytime. See you Monday, Rad."

"Okay." The boys fled, laughing and shoving. Mitch looked, but Hester was already gone.

CHAPTER 4

Mitchell Dempsey II had been born rich, privileged and, according to his parents, with an incorrigible imagination. Maybe that was why he'd taken to Radley so quickly. The boy was far from rich, not even privileged enough to have a set of parents, but his imagination was first-class.

Mitch had always liked crowds as much as one-on-one social situations. He was certainly no stranger to parties, given his mother's affection for entertaining and his own gregarious nature, and no one who knew him would ever have classed him as a loner. In his work, however, he had always preferred the solitary. He worked at home not because he didn't like distractions—he was really fond of them—but because he didn't care to have anyone looking over his shoulder or timing his progress. He'd never considered working any way other than alone. Until Radley.

They made a pact the first day. If Radley finished his homework, with or without Mitch's dubious help, he could then choose to either play with Taz or give his input into Mitch's latest story line. If Mitch had decided to call it quits for the day, they could entertain themselves with his extensive collection of videotapes or with Radley's growing army of plastic figures.

To Mitch, it was natural—to Radley, fantastic. For the first time in his young life he had a man who was part of his daily routine, one who talked to him and listened to him. He had someone who was not only as willing to spend time to set up a battle or wage a war as his mother was, but someone who understood his military strategy.

By the end of their first week, Mitch was not only a hero, creator of Zark and owner of Taz, but the most solid and dependable person in his life other than his mother. Radley loved, without guards or restrictions.

Mitch saw it, wondered at it and found himself just as captivated. He had told Hester no less than the truth when he'd said that he'd never thought about having children. He'd run his life on his own clock for so long that he'd never considered doing things differently. If he'd known what it was to love a small boy, to find pieces of himself in one, he might have done things differently.

Perhaps it was because of his discoveries that he thought of Radley's father. What kind of man could create something that special and then walk away from it? His own father had been stern and anything but understanding, but he'd been there. Mitch had never questioned the love.

A man didn't get to be thirty-five without knowing several contemporaries who'd been through divorces—many of them bitter. But he also was acquainted with several who'd managed to call a moratorium with their ex-wives in order to remain fathers. It was difficult enough to understand how Radley's father not only could have walked out, but could have walked away. After a week in Radley's company, it was all but impossible.

And what of Hester? What kind of man left a woman to struggle alone to raise a child they had brought into the world together? How much had she loved him? That was a thought that dug into his brain too often for comfort. The results of the experience were obvious. She was tense and overly cautious around men. Around him, certainly, Mitch thought with a grimace as he watched Radley sketch. So cautious that she'd stayed out of his path throughout the week.

Every day between 4:15 and 4:25, he received a polite call. Hester would ask him if everything had gone well, thank him for watching Radley, then ask him to send her son upstairs. That afternoon. Radley had handed him a neatly written check for twenty-five dollars drawn on the account of Hester Gentry Wallace. It was still crumpled in Mitch's pocket.

Did she really think he was going to quietly step aside after she'd knocked the wind out of him? He hadn't forgotten what she'd felt like pressed against him, inhibitions and caution stripped away for one brief, stunning moment. He intended to live that moment again as well as the others his incorrigible imagination had conjured up.

If she did think he'd bow out gracefully, Mrs. Hester Wallace was in for a big surprise.

"I can't get the retro rockets right," Radley complained. "They never look right."

Mitch set aside his own work, which had stopped humming along the moment he'd started to think of Hester. "Let's have a look." He took the spare sketch pad he'd lent to Radley. "Hey, not bad." He grinned, foolishly pleased with Radley's attempt at the *Defiance*. It seemed the few pointers he'd given the kid had taken root. "You're a real natural, Rad."

The boy blushed with pleasure, then frowned again. "But see, the boosters and retros are all wrong. They look stupid."

"Only because you're trying to detail too soon. Look, light strokes, impressions first." He put a hand over the boy's to guide it. "Don't be afraid to make mistakes. That's why they make those big gum erasers."

"You don't make mistakes." Radley caught his tongue

between his teeth as he struggled to make his hand move as expertly as Mitch's.

"Sure I do. This is my fifteenth eraser this year."

"You're the best artist in the whole world," Radley said, looking up, his heart in his eyes.

Moved and strangely humbled, Mitch ruffled the boy's hair. "Maybe one of the top twenty, but thanks." When the phone rang, Mitch felt a strange stab of disappointment. The weekend meant something different now—no Radley. For a man who had lived his entire adult life without responsibilities, it was a sobering thought to realize he would miss one. "That should be your mother."

"She said we could go out to the movies tonight 'cause it's Friday and all. You could come with us."

Giving a noncommittal grunt, Mitch answered the phone. "Hi, Hester."

"Mitch, I—everything okay?"

Something in her tone had his brows drawing together. "Just dandy."

"Did Radley give you the check?"

"Yeah. Sorry, I haven't had a chance to cash it yet."

If there was one thing she wasn't in the mood for at the moment, it was sarcasm. "Well, thanks. If you'd send Radley upstairs, I'd appreciate it."

"No problem." He hesitated. "Rough day, Hester?"

She pressed a hand to her throbbing temple. "A bit. Thank you, Mitch."

"Sure." He hung up, still frowning. Turning to Radley, he made the effort to smile. "Time to transfer your equipment, Corporal."

"Sir, yes, sir!" Radley gave a smart salute. The intergalactic army he'd left at Mitch's through the week was tossed into his backpack. After a brief search, both of his gloves were located and pushed in on top of the plastic figures.

Radley stuffed his coat and hat in before kneeling down to hug Taz. "Bye, Taz. See ya." The dog rumbled a goodbye as he rubbed his snout into Radley's shoulder. "Bye, Mitch." He went to the door, then hesitated. "I guess I'll see you Monday."

"Sure. Hey, maybe I'll just walk up with you. Give your mom a full report."

"Okay!" Radley brightened instantly. "You left your keys in the kitchen. I'll get them." Mitch watched the tornado pass, then swirl back. "I got an A in spelling. When I tell Mom, she'll be in a real good mood. We'll probably get sodas."

"Sounds like a good deal to me," Mitch said, and let himself be dragged along.

* * *

Hester heard Radley's key in the lock and set down the ice pack. Leaning closer, she checked her face in the bathroom mirror, saw a bruise was already forming, and swore. She'd hoped to be able to tell Radley about the mishap, gloss over it and make it a joke before any battle scars showed. Hester downed two aspirin and prayed the headache would pass.

"Mom! Hey, Mom!"

"Right here, Radley." She winced at her own raised voice, then put on a smile as she walked out to greet him. The smile faded when she saw her son had brought company.

"Mitch came up to report," Radley began as he shrugged out of his backpack.

"What the hell happened to you?" Mitch crossed over to her in two strides. He had her face in his hands and fury in his eyes. "Are you all right?"

"Of course I am." She shot him a quick warning look, then turned to Radley. "I'm fine."

Radley stared up at her, his eyes widening, then his bottom lip trembling as he saw the black-and-blue mark under her eye. "Did you fall down?"

She wanted to lie and say yes, but she'd never lied to him. "Not exactly." She forced a smile, annoyed to have a witness to her explanation. "It seems that there was a man at the subway station who wanted my purse. I wanted it, too."

"You were mugged?" Mitch wasn't sure whether to swear at her or gather her close and check for injuries. Hester's long, withering look didn't give him the chance to do either.

"Sort of." She moved her shoulders to show Radley it was of little consequence. "It wasn't all that exciting, I'm afraid. The subway was crowded. Someone saw what was going on and called security, so the man changed his mind about my purse and ran away."

Radley looked closer. He'd seen a black eye before. Joey Phelps had had a really neat one once. But he'd never seen one on his mother. "Did he hit you?"

"Not really. That part was sort of an accident." An accident that hurt like the devil. "We were having this tug-of-war over my purse, and his elbow shot up. I didn't duck quick enough, that's all."

"Stupid," Mitch muttered loud enough to be heard.

"Did you hit him?"

"Of course not," Hester answered, and thought longingly of her ice pack. "Go put your things away now, Radley."

"But I want to know about—"

"Now," his mother interrupted in a tone she used rarely but to great effect.

"Yes, ma'am," Radley mumbled, and lugged the backpack off the couch.

Hester waited until he'd turned the corner into his room. "I want you to know I don't appreciate your interference."

"You haven't begun to see interference. What the hell's

wrong with you? You know better than to fight with a mugger over a purse. What if he'd had a knife?" Even the thought of it had his reliable imagination working overtime.

"He didn't have a knife." Hester felt her knees begin to tremble. The damnedest thing was that the reaction had chosen the most inopportune moment to set in. "And he doesn't have my purse, either."

"Or a black eye. For God's sake, Hester, you could have been seriously hurt, and I doubt there's anything in your purse that would warrant it. Credit cards can be canceled, a compact or a lipstick replaced."

"I suppose if someone had tried to lift your wallet you'd have given him your blessing."

"That's different."

"The hell it is."

He stopped pacing long enough to give her a long study. Her chin was thrust out, in the same way he'd seen Radley's go a few times. He'd expected the stubbornness, but he had to admit he hadn't expected the ready temper, or his admiration for it. But that was beside the point, he reminded himself as his gaze swept over her bruised cheekbone again.

"Let's just back up a minute. In the first place, you've got no business taking the subway alone."

She let out what might have been a laugh. "You've got to be kidding."

The funny thing was, he couldn't remember ever having said anything quite that stupid. It brought his own temper bubbling over. "Take a cab, damn it."

"I have no intention of taking a cab."

"Why?"

"In the first place it would be stupid, and in the second I can't afford it."

Mitch dragged the check out of his pocket and pushed it

into her hand. "Now you can afford it, along with a reason-able tip."

"I have no intention of taking this." She shoved the crum-pled check back at him. "Or of taking a taxi when the sub-way is both inexpensive and convenient. And I have less intention of allowing you to take a small incident and blow it into a major calamity. I don't want Radley upset."

"Fine, then take a cab. For the kid's sake, if not your own. Think how it would have been for him if you'd really been hurt."

The bruise stood out darkly as her cheeks paled. "I don't need you or anyone to lecture me on the welfare of my son."

"No, you do just fine by him. It's when it comes to Hester that you've got a few loose screws." He jammed his hands into his pockets. "Okay, you won't take a cab. At least promise you won't play Sally Courageous the next time some lowlife decides he likes the color of your purse."

Hester brushed at the sleeve of her jacket. "Is that the name of one of your characters?"

"It might be." He told himself to calm down. He didn't have much of a temper as a rule, but when it started to perk, it could come to a boil in seconds. "Look, Hester, did you have your life savings in your bag?"

"Of course not."

"Family heirlooms?"

"No."

"Any microchips vital to national security?"

She let out an exasperated sigh and dropped onto the arm of a chair. "I left them at the office." She pouted as she looked up at him. "Don't give me that disgusting smile now."

"Sorry." He changed it to a grin.

"I just had such a rotten day." Without realizing it, she slipped off her shoe and began to massage her instep. "The first thing this morning Mr. Rosen went on an efficiency campaign. Then there was the staff meeting, then the idiot settlement clerk who made a pass at me."

"What idiot settlement clerk?"

"Never mind." Tired, she rubbed her temple. "Just take it that things went from bad to worse until I was ready to bite someone's head off. Then that jerk grabbed my purse, and I just exploded. At least I have the satisfaction of knowing he'll be walking with a limp for a few days."

"Got in a few licks, did you?"

Hester continued to pout as she gingerly touched her eye with her fingertips. "Yeah."

Mitch walked over, then bent down to her level. With a look more of curiosity than sympathy, he examined the damage. "You're going to have a hell of a shiner."

"Really?" Hester touched the bruise again. "I was hoping this was as bad as it would get."

"Not a chance. It's going to be a beaut."

She thought of the stares and the explanations that would be necessary the following week. "Terrific."

"Hurt?"

"Yes."

Mitch touched his lips to the bruise before she could evade him. "Try some ice."

"I've already thought of that."

"I put my things away." Radley stood in the hallway looking down at his shoes. "I had homework, but I already did it."

"That's good. Come here." Radley continued to look at his shoes as he walked to her. Hester put her arms around his neck and squeezed. "Sorry."

"'S okay. I didn't mean to make you mad."

"You didn't make me mad. Mr. Rosen made me mad. That man who wanted my purse made me mad, but not you, baby."

"I could get you a wet cloth the way you do when my head hurts."

"Thanks, but I think I need a hot bath and an ice pack." She gave him another squeeze, then remembered. "Oh, we had a date didn't we? Cheeseburgers and a movie."

"We can watch TV instead."

"Well, why don't we see how I feel in a little while?"

"I got an A on my spelling test."

"My hero," Hester said, laughing.

"You know, that hot bath's a good idea. Ice, too." Mitch was already making plans. "Why don't you get started on that while I borrow Rad for a little while."

"But he just got home."

"It'll only take a little while." Mitch took her arm and started to lead her toward the hall. "Put some bubbles in the tub. They're great for the morale. We'll be back in half an hour."

"But where are you going?"

"Just an errand I need to run. Rad can keep me company, can't you, Rad?"

"Sure."

The idea of a thirty-minute soak was too tempting. "No candy, it's too close to dinner."

"Okay, I won't eat any," Mitch promised, and scooted her into the bath. Putting a hand on Radley's shoulder, he marched back into the living room. "Ready to go out on a mission, Corporal?"

Radley's eyes twinkled as he saluted. "Ready and willing, sir."

* * *

The combination of ice pack, hot bath and aspirin proved successful. By the time the water had cooled in the tub, Hester's headache was down to dull and manageable. She supposed she owed Mitch for giving her a few minutes to herself, Hester admitted as she pulled on jeans. Along with most of the pain, the shakiness had drained away in the hot water. In fact, when she took the time to examine her bruised eye, she felt downright proud of herself. Mitch had been right; bubbles had been good for the morale.

She pulled a brush through her hair and wondered how disappointed Radley would be if they postponed their trip to the movies. Hot bath or no, the last thing she felt like doing at the moment was braving the cold to sit in a crowded theater. She thought a matinee the next day might satisfy him. It would mean adjusting her schedule a bit, but the idea of a quiet evening at home after the week she'd put in made doing the laundry after dinner a lot more acceptable.

And what a week, Hester thought as she pulled on slippers. Rosen was a tyrant, and the settlement clerk was a pest. She'd spent almost as much time during the last five days placating one and discouraging the other as she had processing loans. She wasn't afraid of work, but she did resent having to account for every minute of her time. It was nothing personal; Hester had discovered that within the first eight-hour stretch. Rosen was equally overbearing and fussy with everyone on his staff.

And that fool Cummings. Hester pushed the thought of the overamorous clerk out of her mind and sat on the edge of the bed. She'd gotten through the first two weeks, hadn't she? She touched her cheekbone gingerly. With the scars to prove it. It would be easier now. She wouldn't have the strain of meeting all those new people. The biggest relief of all was that she didn't have to worry about Radley.

She'd never admit it to anyone, but she'd waited for Mitch to call every day that week to tell her Radley was too much trouble, he'd changed his mind, he was tired of spending his afternoons with a nine-year-old. But the fact was that every afternoon when Radley had come upstairs, the boy had been full of stories about Mitch and Taz and what they'd done.

Mitch had showed him a series of sketches for the big anniversary issue. They'd taken Taz to the park. They'd watched the original, uncut, absolutely classic *King Kong* on the VCR. Mitch had showed him his comic book collection, which included the first issues of *Superman* and *Tales From the Crypt*, which everyone knew, she'd been informed, were practically priceless. And did she know that Mitch had an original, honest-to-God *Captain Midnight* decoder ring? Wow.

Hester rolled her eyes, then winced when the movement reminded her of the bruise. The man might be odd, she decided, but he was certainly making Radley happy. Things would be fine as long as she continued to think of him as Radley's friend, and forgot about that unexpected and unexplainable connection they'd made last weekend.

Hester preferred to think about it as a connection rather than any of the terms Mitch had used. Attraction, chemistry, lust. No, she didn't care for any of those words, or for her immediate and unrestrained reaction to him. She knew what she'd felt. Hester was too honest to deny that for one crazed moment she'd welcomed the sensation of being held and kissed and desired. It wasn't something to be ashamed of. A woman who'd been alone as long as she had was bound to feel certain stirrings around an attractive man.

Then why didn't she feel any of those stirrings around Cummings?

Don't answer that, she warned herself. Sometimes it was best not to dig too deeply when you really didn't want to know.

Think about dinner, she decided. Poor Radley was going to have to make do with soup and a sandwich instead of his beloved cheeseburger tonight. With a sigh, she rose as she heard the front door open.

"Mom! Mom, come see the surprise."

Hester made sure she was smiling, though she wasn't sure she could take any more surprises that day. "Rad, did you thank Mitch for . . . oh." He was back, Hester saw, automatically adjusting her sweater. The two of them stood just inside the doorway with identical grins on their faces. Radley carried two paper bags, and Mitch hefted what looked suspiciously like a tape machine with cables dangling.

"What's all this?"

"Dinner and a double feature," Mitch informed her. "Rad said you like chocolate shakes."

"Yes, I do." The aroma finally carried to her. Sniffing, she eyed Radley's bags. "Cheeseburgers?"

"Yeah, and fries. Mitch said we could have double orders. We took Taz for a walk. He's eating his downstairs."

"He's got lousy table manners." Mitch carried the unit over to Hester's television.

"And I helped Mitch unhook the VCR. We got *Raiders of the Lost Ark*. Mitch has millions of movies."

"Rad said you like musical junk."

"Well, yes, I—"

"We got one of them, too." Rad set the bags down to go over and sit with Mitch on the floor. "Mitch said it's pretty funny, so I guess it'll be okay." He put a hand on Mitch's leg and leaned closer to watch the hookup.

"*Singin' in the Rain*." Handing Radley a cable, Mitch sat back to let him connect it.

"Really?"

He had to smile. There were times she sounded just like the kid. "Yeah. How's the eye?"

"Oh, it's better." Unable to resist, Hester walked over

to watch. How odd it seemed to see her son's small hands working with those of a man.

"It's a tight squeeze, but the VCR just about fits under your television stand." Mitch gave Radley's shoulder a quick squeeze before he rose. "Colorful." With a finger under her chin, he turned Hester's face to the side to examine her eye. "Rad and I thought you looked a little beat, so we figured we'd bring the movie to you."

"I was." She touched her hand to his wrist a moment. "Thanks."

"Anytime." He wondered what her reaction, and Radley's, would be if he kissed her right now. Hester must have seen the question in his eyes, because she backed up quickly.

"Well, I guess I'd better get some plates so the food doesn't get cold."

"We've got plenty of napkins." He gestured toward the couch. "Sit down while my assistant and I finish up."

"I did it." Flushed with success, Radley scrambled back on all fours. "It's all hooked up."

Mitch bent to check the connections. "You're a regular mechanic, Corporal."

"We get to watch *Raiders* first, right?"

"That was the deal." Mitch handed him the tape. "You're in charge."

"It looks like I have to thank you again," Hester said when Mitch joined her on the couch.

"What for? I figured to wangle myself in on your date with Rad tonight." He pulled a burger out of the bag. "This is cheaper."

"Most men wouldn't choose to spend a Friday night with a small boy."

"Why not?" He took a healthy bite, and after swallowing continued, "I figure he won't eat half his fries, and I'll get the rest."

Radley took a running leap and plopped onto the couch between them. He gave a contented and very adult sigh as he snuggled down. "This is better than going out. Lots better."

He was right, Hester thought as she relaxed and let herself become caught up in Indiana Jones's adventures. There had been a time when she'd believed life could be that thrilling, romantic, heart-stopping. Circumstances had forced her to set those things aside, but she'd never lost her love of the fantasy of films. For a couple of hours it was possible to close off reality and the pressures that went with it and be innocent again.

Radley was bright-eyed and full of energy as he switched tapes. Hester had no doubt his dreams that night would revolve around lost treasures and heroic deeds. Snuggling against her, he giggled at Donald O'Connor's mugging and pratfalls, but began to nod off soon after Gene Kelly's marvelous dance through the rain.

"Fabulous, isn't it?" Mitch murmured. Radley had shifted so that his head rested against Mitch's chest.

"Absolutely. I never get tired of this movie. When I was a little girl, we'd watch it whenever it came on TV. My father's a big movie buff. You can name almost any film, and he'll tell you who was in it. But his first love was always the musical."

Mitch fell silent again. It took very little to learn how one person felt about another—a mere inflection in their voice, a softening of their expression. Hester's family had been close, as he'd always regretted his hadn't been. His father had never shared Mitch's love of fantasy or film, as he had never shared his father's devotion to business. Though he would never have considered himself a lonely child—his imagination had been company enough—he'd always missed the warmth and affection he'd heard so clearly in Hester's voice when she'd spoken of her father.

When the credits rolled, he turned to her again. "Your parents live in the city?"

"Here? Oh, no." She had to laugh as she tried to picture either of her parents coping with life in New York. "No, I grew up in Rochester, but my parents moved to the Sunbelt almost ten years ago—Fort Worth. Dad's still in banking, and my mother has a part-time job in a bookstore. We were all amazed when she went to work. I guess all of us thought she didn't know how to do anything but bake cookies and fold sheets."

"How many's we?"

Hester sighed a little as the screen went blank. She couldn't honestly remember when she'd enjoyed an evening more. "I have a brother and a sister. I'm the oldest. Luke's settled in Rochester with a wife and a new baby on the way, and Julia's in Atlanta. She's a disc jockey."

"No kidding?"

"Wake up, Atlanta, it's 6:00 a.m., time for three hits in a row." She laughed a little as she thought of her sister. "I'd give anything to take Rad down for a visit."

"Miss them?"

"It's just hard thinking how spread out we all are. I know how nice it would be for Rad to have more family close by."

"What about Hester?"

She looked over at him, a bit surprised to see how natural Radley looked dozing in the crook of his arm. "I have Rad."

"And that's enough?"

"More than." She smiled; then, uncurling her legs, she rose. "And speaking of Rad, I'd better take him in to bed."

Mitch picked the boy up and settled him over his shoulder. "I'll carry him."

"Oh, that's all right. I do it all the time."

"I've got him." Radley turned his face into Mitch's neck.

What an amazing feeling, he thought, a little shaken by it. "Just show me where."

Telling herself it was silly to feel odd, Hester led him into Radley's bedroom. The bed had been made à la Rad, which meant the *Star Wars* spread was pulled up over rumpled sheets. Mitch narrowly missed stepping on a pint-size robot and a worn rag dog. There was a night-light burning by the dresser, because for all Radley's bravado he was still a bit leery about what might or might not be in the closet.

Mitch laid him down on the bed, then began to help Hester take off the boy's sneakers. "You don't have to bother." Hester untangled a knot in the laces with the ease of experience.

"It's not a bother. Does he use pajamas?" Mitch was already tugging off Radley's jeans. In silence, Hester moved over to Radley's dresser and took out his favorites. Mitch studied the bold imprint of Commander Zark. "Good taste. It always ticked me off they didn't come in my size."

The laugh relaxed her again. Hester bundled the top over Radley's head while Mitch pulled the bottoms over his legs.

"Kid sleeps like a rock."

"I know. He always has. He rarely woke up during the night even as a baby." As a matter of habit, she picked up the rag dog and tucked it in beside him before kissing his cheek. "Don't mention Fido," she murmured. "Radley's a bit sensitive about still sleeping with him."

"I never saw a thing." Then, giving in to the need, he brushed a hand over Radley's hair. "Pretty special, isn't he?"

"Yes, he is."

"So are you." Mitch turned and touched her hair in turn. "Don't close up on me, Hester," he said as she shifted her gaze away from his. "The best way to accept a compliment is to say thank you. Give it a shot."

Embarrassed more by her reaction to him than by his words, she made herself look at him. "Thank you."

"That's a good start. Now let's try it again." He slipped his arms around her. "I've been thinking about kissing you again for almost a week."

"Mitch, I—"

"Did you forget your line?" She'd lifted her hands to his shoulders to hold him off. But her eyes . . . He much preferred the message he read in them. "That was another compliment. I don't make a habit of thinking about a woman who goes out of her way to avoid me."

"I haven't been. Exactly."

"That's okay, because I figured it was because you couldn't trust yourself around me."

That had her eyes locking on his again, strong and steady. "You have an amazing ego."

"Thanks. Let's try another angle, then." As he spoke, he moved his hand up and down her spine, lighting little fingers of heat. "Kiss me again, and if the bombs don't go off this time, I'll figure I was wrong."

"No." But despite herself she couldn't dredge up the will to push him away. "Radley's—"

"Sleeping like a rock, remember?" He touched his lips, very gently, to the swelling under her eye. "And even if he woke up, I don't think the sight of me kissing his mother would give him nightmares."

She started to speak again, but the words were only a sigh as his mouth met hers. He was patient this time, even . . . tender. Yet the bombs went off. She would have sworn they shook the floor beneath her as she dug her fingers hard into his shoulders.

It was incredible. Impossible. But the need was there, instant, incendiary. It had never been so strong before, not for anyone. Once, when she'd been very young, she'd had a hint of what true, ripe passion could be. And then it had been over. She had come to believe that, like so many other things, such passions were only temporary. But this—this felt like forever.

He'd thought he knew all there was to know about women. Hester was proving him wrong. Even as he felt himself sliding down that warm, soft tunnel of desire, he warned himself not to move too quickly or take too much. There was a hurricane in her, one he had already realized had been channeled and repressed for a long, long time. The first time he'd held her he'd known he had to be the one to free it. But slowly. Carefully. Whether she knew it or not, she was as vulnerable as the child sleeping beside them.

Then her hands were in his hair, pulling him closer. For one mad moment, he dragged her hard against him and let them both taste of what might be.

"Bombs, Hester." She shuddered as he traced his tongue over her ear. "The city's in shambles."

She believed him. With his mouth hot on hers, she believed him. "I have to think."

"Yeah, maybe you do." But he kissed her again. "Maybe we both do." He ran his hands down her body in one long, possessive stroke. "But I have a feeling we're going to come up with the same answer."

Shaken, she backed away. And stumbled over the robot. The crash didn't penetrate Radley's dreams.

"You know, you run into things every time I kiss you." He was going to have to go now or not at all. "I'll pick up the VCR later."

There was a little breath of relief as she nodded. She'd been afraid he'd ask her to sleep with him, and she wasn't at all sure what her answer would have been. "Thank you for everything."

"Good, you're learning." He stroked a finger down her cheek. "Take care of the eye."

Cowardly or not, Hester stayed by Radley's bed until she heard the front door shut. Then, easing down, she put a hand on her sleeping son's shoulder. "Oh, Rad, what have I gotten into?"

CHAPTER 5

When the phone rang at 7:25, Mitch had his head buried under a pillow. He would have ignored it, but Taz rolled over, stuck his snout against Mitch's cheek and began to grumble in his ear. Mitch swore and shoved at the dog, then snatched up the receiver and dragged it under the pillow.

"What?"

On the other end of the line, Hester bit her lip. "Mitch, it's Hester."

"So?"

"I guess I woke you up."

"Right."

It was painfully obvious that Mitch Dempsey wasn't a morning person. "I'm sorry. I know it's early."

"Is that what you called to tell me?"

"No . . . I guess you haven't looked out the window yet."

"Honey, I haven't even looked past my eyelids yet."

"It's snowing. We've got about eight inches, and it's not expected to let up until around midday. They're calling for twelve to fifteen inches."

"Who are they?"

Hester switched the phone to her other hand. Her hair was

still wet from the shower, and she'd only had a chance to gulp down one cup of coffee. "The National Weather Service."

"Well, thanks for the bulletin."

"Mitch! Don't hang up."

He let out a long sigh, then shifted away from Taz's wet nose. "Is there more news?"

"The schools are closed."

"Whoopee."

She was tempted, very tempted to hang up the phone in his ear. The trouble was, she needed him. "I hate to ask, but I'm not sure I can get Radley all the way over to Mrs. Cohen's. I'd take the day off, but I have back-to-back appointments most of the day. I'm going to try to shift things around and get off early, but—"

"Send him down."

There was the briefest of hesitations. "Are you sure?"

"Did you want me to say no?"

"I don't want to interfere with any plans you had."

"Got any hot coffee?"

"Well, yes, I—"

"Send that, too."

Hester stared at the phone after it clicked in her ear, and tried to remind herself to be grateful.

Radley couldn't have been more pleased. He took Taz for his morning walk, threw snowballs—which the dog, on principle, refused to chase—and rolled in the thick blanket of snow until he was satisfactorily covered.

Since Mitch's supplies didn't run to hot chocolate, Radley raided his mother's supply, then spent the rest of the morning happily involved with Mitch's comic books and his own sketches.

As for Mitch, he found the company appealing rather than distracting. The boy lay sprawled on the floor of his office and, between his reading or sketching, rambled on about whatever struck his fancy. Because he spoke to either Mitch or Taz, and seemed to be content to be answered or not, it suited everyone nicely.

By noon the snow had thinned to occasional flurries, dashing Radley's fantasy about another holiday. In tacit agreement, Mitch pushed away from his drawing board.

"You like tacos?"

"Yeah." Radley turned away from the window. "You know how to make them?"

"Nope. But I know how to buy them. Get your coat, Corporal, we've got places to go."

Radley was struggling into his boots when Mitch walked out with a trio of cardboard tubes. "I've got to stop by the office and drop these off."

Radley's mouth dropped down to his toes. "You mean the place where they make the comics?"

"Yeah." Mitch shrugged into his coat. "I guess I could do it tomorrow if you don't want to bother."

"No, I want to." The boy was up and dragging Mitch's sleeve. "Can we go today? I won't touch anything, I promise. I'll be real quiet, too."

"How can you ask questions if you're quiet?" He pulled the boy's collar up. "Get Taz, will you?"

It was always a bit of a trick, and usually an expensive one, to find a cabdriver who didn't object to a hundred-and-fifty pound dog as a passenger. Once inside, however, Taz sat by the window and morosely watched New York pass by.

"It's a mess out here, isn't it?" The cabbie shot a grin in the rearview mirror, pleased with the tip Mitch had given him in advance. "Don't like the snow myself, but my kids do." He gave a tuneless whistle to accompany the big-band music on his radio. "I guess your boy there wasn't doing any complaining about not going to school. No, sir," the driver continued, without any need for an answer. "Nothing a kid likes better than a day off from school, is there? Even going to the office with your dad's better than school, isn't it, kid?" The cabbie let out a chuckle as he pulled to the curb. The snow there had already turned gray. "Here you go. That's a right nice dog you got there, boy." He gave Mitch his change and continued to whistle as they got out. He had another fare when he pulled away.

"He thought you were my dad," Radley murmured as they walked down the sidewalk.

"Yeah." He started to put a hand on Radley's shoulder, then waited. "Does that bother you?"

The boy looked up, wide-eyed and, for the first time, shy. "No. Does it bother you?"

Mitch bent down so they were at eye level. "Well, maybe it wouldn't if you weren't so ugly."

Radley grinned. As they continued to walk, he slipped his hand into Mitch's. He'd already begun to fantasize about Mitch as his father. He'd done it once before with his second grade teacher, but Mr. Stratham hadn't been nearly as neat as Mitch.

"Is this it?" He stopped as Mitch walked toward a tall, scarred brownstone.

"This is it."

Radley struggled with disappointment. It looked so— ordinary. He'd thought they would at least have the flag of Perth or Ragamond flying. Understanding perfectly, Mitch led him inside.

There was a guard in the lobby who lifted a hand to Mitch and continued to eat his pastrami sandwich. Acknowledging the greeting, Mitch took Radley to an elevator and drew open the iron gate.

"This is pretty neat," Radley decided.

"It's neater when it works." Mitch pushed the button for the fifth floor, which housed the editorial department. "Let's hope for the best."

"Has it ever crashed?" The question was half wary, half hopeful.

"No, but it has been known to go on strike." The car shuddered to a stop on five. Mitch swung the gate open again. He put a hand on Radley's head. "Welcome to bedlam."

It was precisely that. Radley forgot his disappointment with the exterior in his awe at the fifth floor. There was a reception area of sorts. In any case, there was a desk and a bank of phones manned by a harassed-looking black woman in a Princess Leilah sweatshirt. The walls around her were crammed with posters depicting Universal's most enduring characters: the Human Scorpion, the Velvet Saber, the deadly Black Moth and, of course, Commander Zark.

"How's it going, Lou?"

"Don't ask." She pushed a button on a phone. "I ask you, is it my fault the deli won't deliver his corned beef?"

"If I put him in a good mood, will you dig up some samples for me?"

"Universal Comics, please hold." The receptionist pushed another button. "You put him in a good mood, you've got my firstborn."

"Just the samples, Lou. Put on your helmet, Corporal. This could be messy." He led Radley down a short hall into the big, brightly lit hub of activity. It was a series of cubicles with a high noise level and a look of chaos. Pinned to the corkboard walls were sketches, rude messages and an occasional photograph. In a corner was a pyramid made of empty soda cans. Someone was tossing wadded-up balls of paper at it.

"Scorpion's never been a joiner. What's his motivation for hooking up with Worldwide Law and Justice?"

A woman with pencils poking out of her wild red hair at

dangerous angles shifted in her swivel chair. Her eyes, already huge, were accented by layers of liner and mascara. "Look, let's be real. He can't save the world's water supply on his own. He needs someone like Atlantis."

A man sat across from her, eating an enormous pickle. "They hate each other. Ever since they bumped heads over the Triangular Affair."

"That's the point, dummy. They'll have to put personal feelings aside for the sake of mankind. It's a moral." Glancing over, she caught sight of Mitch. "Hey, Dr. Deadly's poisoned the world's water supply. Scorpion's found an antidote. How's he going to distribute it?"

"Sounds like he'd better mend fences with Atlantis," Mitch replied. "What do you think, Radley?"

For a moment, Rad was so tongue-tied he could only stare. Then, taking a deep breath, he let the words blurt out. "I think they'd make a neat team, 'cause they'd always be fighting and trying to show each other up."

"I'm with you, kid." The redhead held out her hand. "I'm M. J. Jones."

"Wow, really?" He wasn't sure whether he was more impressed with meeting M. J. Jones or with discovering she was a woman. Mitch didn't see the point in mentioning that she was one of the few in the business.

"And this grouch over here is Rob Myers. You bring him as a shield, Mitch?" she asked without giving Rob time to swallow his pickle. They'd been married for six years, and she obviously enjoyed frustrating him.

"Do I need one?"

"If you don't have something terrific in those tubes, I'd advise you to slip back out again." She shoved aside a stack of preliminary sketches. "Maloney just quit, defected to Five Star."

"No kidding?"

"Skinner's been muttering about traitors all morning. And the snow didn't help his mood. So if I were you . . . Oops, too late." Respecting rats who deserted tyrannically captained ships, M.J. turned away and fell into deep discussion with her husband.

"Dempsey, you were supposed to be in two hours ago."

Mitch gave his editor an ingratiating smile. "My alarm didn't go off. This is Radley Wallace, a friend of mine. Rad, this is Rich Skinner."

Radley stared. Skinner looked exactly like Hank Wheeler, the tanklike and overbearing boss of Joe David, alias the Fly. Later, Mitch would tell him that the resemblance was no accident. Radley switched Taz's leash to his other hand.

"Hello, Mr. Skinner. I really like your comics. They're lots better than Five Star. I hardly ever buy Five Star, because the stories aren't as good."

"Right." Skinner dragged a hand through his thinning hair. "Right," he repeated with more conviction. "Don't waste your allowance on Five Star, kid."

"No, sir."

"Mitch, you know you're not supposed to bring that mutt in here."

"You know how Taz loves you." On cue, Taz lifted his head and howled.

Skinner started to swear, then remembered the boy. "You got something in those tubes, or did you just come by to brighten up my dull day?"

"Why don't you take a look for yourself?"

Grumbling, Skinner took the tubes and marched off. As Mitch started to follow, Radley grabbed at his hand. "Is he really mad?"

"Sure. He likes being mad best."

"Is he going to yell at you like Hank Wheeler yells at the Fly?"

"Maybe."

Radley swallowed and buried his hand in Mitch's. "Okay."

Amused, Mitch led Radley into Skinner's office, where the venetian blinds had been drawn to shut off any view of the snow. Skinner unrolled the contents of the first tube and spread them over his already cluttered desk. He didn't sit, but loomed over them while Taz plopped down on the linoleum and went to sleep.

"Not bad," Skinner announced after he had studied the series of sketches and captions. "Not too bad. This new character, Mirium, you have plans to expand her?"

"I'd like to. I think Zark's ready to have his heart tugged from a different direction. Adds more emotional conflict. He loves his wife, but she's his biggest enemy. Now he runs into this empath and finds himself torn up all over again because he has feelings for her as well."

"Zark never gets much of a break."

"I think he's the best," Radley piped in, forgetting himself.

Skinner lifted his bushy brows and studied Radley carefully. "You don't think he gets carried away with this honor and duty stuff?"

"Uh-uh." He wasn't sure if he was relieved or disappointed that Skinner wasn't going to yell. "You always know Zark's going to do the right thing. He doesn't have any super powers and stuff, but he's real smart."

Skinner nodded, accepting the opinion. "We'll give your Mirium a shot, Mitch, and see what the reader response is like." He let the papers roll into themselves again. "This is the first time I can remember you being this far ahead of deadline."

"That's because I have an assistant now." Mitch laid a hand on Radley's shoulder.

"Good work, kid. Why don't you take your assistant on a tour?"

It would take Radley weeks to stop talking about his hour at Universal Comics. When they left, he carried a shopping bag full of pencils with Universal's logo, a Mad Matilda mug that had been unearthed from someone's storage locker, a half-dozen rejected sketches and a batch of comics fresh off the presses.

"This was the best day in my whole life," Radley said, dancing down the snow-choked sidewalk. "Wait until I show Mom. She won't believe it."

Oddly enough, Mitch had been thinking of Hester himself. He lengthened his stride to keep up with Radley's skipping pace. "Why don't we go by and pay her a visit?"

"Okay." He slipped his hand into Mitch's again. "The bank's not nearly as neat as where you work, though. They don't let anyone play radios or yell at each other, but they have a vault where they keep lots of money—millions of dollars—and they have cameras everywhere so they can see anybody who tries to rob them. Mom's never been in a bank that's been robbed."

Since the statement came out as an apology, Mitch laughed. "We can't all be blessed." He ran a hand over his stomach. He hadn't put anything into it in at least two hours. "Let's grab that taco first."

*   *   *

Inside the staid and unthreatened walls of National Trust, Hester dealt with a stack of paperwork. She enjoyed this part of her job, the organized monotony of it. There was also the challenge of sorting through the facts and figures and translating them into real estate, automobiles, business equipment, stage sets or college funds. Nothing gave her greater pleasure than to be able to stamp a loan with her approval.

She'd had to teach herself not to be softhearted. There were times the facts and figures told you to say no, no matter how earnest the applicant might be. Part of her job was to dictate polite and impersonal letters of refusal. Hester might not have cared for it, but she accepted that responsibility, just as she accepted the occasional irate phone call from the recipient of a loan refusal.

At the moment she was stealing half an hour, with the muffin and coffee that would be her lunch, to put together three loan packages she wanted approved by the board when they met the following day. She had another appointment in fifteen minutes. And, with that and a lack of interruptions, she could just finish. She wasn't particularly pleased when her assistant buzzed through.

"Yes, Kay."

"There's a young man out here to see you, Mrs. Wallace."

"His appointment isn't for fifteen minutes. He'll have to wait."

"No, it isn't Mr. Greenburg. And I don't think he's here for a loan. Are you here for a loan, honey?"

Hester heard the familiar giggle and hurried to the door. "Rad? Is everything all right—oh."

He wasn't alone. Hester realized she'd been foolish to think Radley would have made the trip by himself. Mitch was with him, along with the huge, mild-eyed dog.

"We just ate tacos."

Hester eyed the faint smudge of salsa on Radley's chin. "So I see." She bent to hug him, then glanced up at Mitch. "Is everything okay?"

"Sure. We were just out taking care of a little business and decided to drop by." He took a good long look. She'd covered most of the colorful bruise with makeup. Only a hint of yellow and mauve showed through. "The eye looks better."

"I seem to have passed the crisis."

"That your office?" Without invitation, he strolled over to stick his head inside. "God, how depressing. Maybe you can talk Radley into giving you one of his posters."

"You can have one," Radley agreed immediately. "I got a bunch of them when Mitch took me to Universal. Wow, Mom you should see it. I met M. J. Jones and Rich Skinner, and I saw this room where they keep zillions of comics. See what I got." He held up his shopping bag. "For free. They said I could."

Her first feeling was one of discomfort. It seemed her obligation to Mitch grew with each day. Then she looked down at Radley's eager, glowing face. "Sounds like a pretty great morning."

"It was the best ever."

"Yellow alert," Kay murmured. "Rosen at three o'clock."

It didn't take words to show Mitch that Rosen was a force to be reckoned with. He saw Hester's face poker up instantly as she smoothed a hand over her hair to be sure it was in place.

"Good afternoon, Mrs. Wallace." He glanced meaningfully at the dog, who sniffed the toe of his shoe. "Perhaps you've forgotten that pets are not permitted inside the bank."

"No, sir. My son was just—"

"Your son?" Rosen gave Radley a brief nod. "How do you do, young man. Mrs. Wallace, I'm sure you remember that bank policy frowns on personal visits during working hours."

"Mrs. Wallace, I'll just put these papers on your desk for your signature—when your lunch break is over." Kay shuffled some forms importantly, then winked at Radley.

"Thank you, Kay."

Rosen harrumphed. He couldn't argue with a lunch break, but it was his duty to deal with other infractions of policy. "About this animal—"

Finding Rosen's tone upsetting, Taz pushed his nose

against Radley's knee and moaned. "He's mine." Mitch stepped forward, his smile charming, his hand outstretched. Hester had time to think that with that look he could sell Florida swampland. "Mitchell Dempsey II. Hester and I are good friends, very good friends. She's told me so much about you and your bank." He gave Rosen's hand a hearty political shake. "My family has several holdings in New York. Hester's convinced me I should use my influence to have them transfer to National Trust. You might be familiar with some of the family companies. Trioptic, D and H Chemicals, Dempsey Paperworks?"

"Well, of course, of course." Rosen's limp grip on Mitch's hand tightened. "It's a pleasure to meet you, a real pleasure."

"Hester persuaded me to come by and see for myself how efficiently National Trust ticked." He definitely had the man's number, Mitch thought. Dollar signs were already flitting through the pudgy little brain. "I am impressed. Of course, I could have taken Hester's word for it." He gave her stiff shoulder an intimate little squeeze. "She's just a whiz at financial matters. I can tell you, my father would snatch her up as a corporate adviser in a minute. You're lucky to have her."

"Mrs. Wallace is one of our most valued employees."

"I'm glad to hear it. I'll have to bring up National Trust's advantages when I speak with my father."

"I'll be happy to take you on a tour personally. I'm sure you'd like to see the executive offices."

"Nothing I'd like better, but I am a bit pressed for time." If he'd had days stretching out before him, he wouldn't have spent a minute of them touring the stuffy corners of a bank. "Why don't you work up a package I can present at the next board meeting?"

"Delighted." Rosen's face beamed with pleasure. Bringing an account as large and diversified as Dempsey's to National Trust would be quite a coup for the stuffy bank manager.

"Just send it through Hester. You don't mind playing messenger, do you, darling?" Mitch said cheerfully.

"No," she managed.

"Excellent," Rosen said, the excitement evident in his voice. "I'm sure you'll find we can serve all your family's needs. We are the bank to grow with, after all." He patted Taz's head. "Lovely dog," he said and strode off with a new briskness in his step.

"What a fusty old snob," Mitch decided. "How do you stand it?"

"Would you come into my office a moment?" Hester's voice was as stiff as her shoulders. Recognizing the tone, Radley rolled his eyes at Mitch. "Kay, if Mr. Greenburg comes in, please have him wait."

"Yes, ma'am."

Hester led the way into her office, then closed the door and leaned against it. There was a part of her that wanted to laugh, to throw her arms around Mitch and howl with delight over the way he'd handled Rosen. There was another part— the part that needed a job, a regular salary and employee benefits—that cringed.

"How could you do that?"

"Do what?" Mitch took a look around the office. "The brown carpet has to go. And this paint. What do you call this?"

"Yuck," Radley ventured as he settled in a chair with Taz's head in his lap.

"Yeah, that's it. You know, your work area has a lot to do with your work production. Try that on Rosen."

"I won't be trying anything with Rosen once he finds out what you did. I'll be fired."

"Don't be silly. I never promised my family would move their interests to National Trust. Besides, if he puts together an intriguing enough package, they just might." He shrugged, indicating it made little difference to him. "If it'll make you happier, I can move my personal accounts here. A bank's a bank as far as I'm concerned."

"Damn it." It was very rare for her to swear out loud and with heat. Radley found the fur on Taz's neck of primary interest. "Rosen's got corporate dynasty on his mind, thanks to you. He's going to be furious with me when he finds out you made all that up."

Mitch tapped a hand on a tidy stack of papers. "You're obsessively neat, did you know that? And I didn't make anything up. I could have," he said thoughtfully. "I'm good at it, but there didn't seem to be any reason to."

"Would you stop?" Frustrated, she moved to him to slap his hands away from her work. "All that business about Trioptic, and D and H Chemicals." Letting out a long sigh, she dropped down on the edge of the desk. "I know you did it to try to help me, and I appreciate the thought, but—"

"You do?" With a smile, he fingered the lapel of her suit jacket.

"You mean well, I suppose," Hester murmured.

"Sometimes." He leaned a little closer. "You smell much too good for this office."

"Mitch." She put a hand on his chest and glanced nervously at Radley. The boy had an arm hooked around Taz and was already deeply involved in one of his new comic books.

"Do you really think it would be a traumatic experience if the kid saw me kiss you?"

"No." At his slight movement, she pressed harder. "But that's beside the point."

"What *is* the point?" He took his hand from her jacket to fiddle with the gold triangle at her ear.

"The point is I'm going to have to see Rosen and explain to him that you were just . . ." What was the word she wanted? "Fantasizing."

"I've done a lot of that," he admitted as he moved his thumb down her jawline. "But I'm damned if I think it's any of his business. Want me to tell you the one about you and me in the life raft on the Indian Ocean?"

"No." This time she had to laugh, though the reaction in her stomach had more to do with heat than humor. Curiosity pricked at her so that she met his eyes, then looked quickly away again. "Why don't you and Rad go home? I have another appointment, then I'll go and explain things to Mr. Rosen."

"You're not mad anymore?"

She shook her head and gave in to the urge to touch his face. "You were just trying to help. It was sweet of you."

He imagined she'd have taken the same attitude with Radley if he'd tried to wash the dishes and had smashed her violet-edged china on the floor. Telling himself it was a kind of test, he pressed his lips firmly to hers. He felt each layer of reaction—the shock, the tension, the need. When he drew back, he saw more than indulgence in her eyes. The fire flickered briefly, but with intensity.

"Come on, Rad, your mom has to get back to work. If we're not in the apartment when you get home, we're in the park."

"Fine." Unconsciously she pressed her lips together to seal in the warmth. "Thanks."

"Anytime."

"Bye, Rad, I'll be home soon."

"Okay." He lifted his arms to squeeze her neck. "You're not mad at Mitch anymore?"

"No," she answered in the same carrying whisper. "I'm not mad at anyone."

She was smiling when she straightened, but Mitch saw the worried look in her eye. He paused with his hand on the knob. "You're really going to go up to Rosen and tell him I made that business up?"

"I have to." Then, because she felt guilty about launching her earlier attack, she smiled. "Don't worry. I'm sure I can handle him."

"What if I told you I didn't make it up, that my family founded Trioptic forty-seven years ago?"

Hester lifted a brow. "I'd say don't forget your gloves. It's cold out there."

"Okay, but do yourself a favor before you bare your soul to Rosen. Look it up in *Who's Who*."

With her hands in her pockets, Hester walked to her office door. From there she saw Radley reach up to put a gloved hand into Mitch's bare one.

"Your son's adorable," Kay said, offering Hester a file. The little skirmish with Rosen had completely changed her opinion of the reserved Mrs. Wallace.

"Thanks." When Hester smiled, Kay's new opinion was cemented. "And I do appreciate you covering for me that way."

"That's no big deal. I don't see what's wrong with your son dropping by for a minute."

"Bank policy," Hester murmured under her breath, and Kay let out a snort.

"Rosen policy, you mean. Beneath that gruff exterior is a gruff interior. But don't worry about him. I happen to know he considers your work production far superior to your predecessor's. As far as he's concerned, that's the bottom line."

Kay hesitated a moment as Hester nodded and flipped through the file. "It's tough raising a kid on your own. My sister has a little girl, she's just five. I know some nights Annie's just knocked out from wearing all the badges, you know."

"Yes, I do."

"My parents want her to move back home so Mom can watch Sarah while Annie works, but Annie's not sure it's the best thing."

"Sometimes it's hard to know if accepting help's right," Hester murmured, thinking of Mitch. "And sometimes we forget to be grateful that someone's there to offer it." She shook herself and tucked the file under her arm. "Is Mr. Greenburg here?"

"Just came in."

"Fine, send him in, Kay." She started for her office, then stopped. "Oh, and Kay, dig me up a copy of *Who's Who*."

CHAPTER 6

He was loaded.
Hester was still dazed when she let herself into her apartment. Her downstairs neighbor with the bare feet and the holes in his jeans was an heir to one of the biggest fortunes in the country.

Hester took off her coat and, out of habit, went to the closet to hang it up. The man who spent his days writing the further adventures of Commander Zark came from a family who owned polo ponies and summer houses. Yet he lived on the fourth floor of a very ordinary apartment building in Manhattan.

He was attracted to her. She'd have had to be blind and deaf not to be certain of that, and yet she'd known him for weeks and he hadn't once mentioned his family or his position in an effort to impress her.

Who was he? she wondered. She'd begun to think she had a handle on him, but now he was a stranger all over again.

She had to call him, tell him she was home and to send Radley up. Hester looked at the phone with a feeling of acute embarrassment. She'd lectured him about spinning a tale to Mr. Rosen; then, in her softhearted and probably condescending way, she'd forgiven him. It all added up to her doing what she hated most. Making a fool of herself.

Swearing, Hester snatched up the phone. She would have felt much better if she could have rapped Mitchell Dempsey II over the head with it.

She'd dialed half the numbers when she heard Radley's howl of laughter and the sound of stomping feet in the hall outside. She opened the door just as Radley was digging his key out of his pocket.

Both of them were covered with snow. Some that was beginning to melt dripped from Radley's ski cap and boot tops. They looked unmistakably as if they'd been rolling in it.

"Hi, Mom. We've been in the park. We stopped by Mitch's to get my bag, then came on up because we thought you'd be home. Come on out with us."

"I don't think I'm dressed for snow wars."

She smiled and peeled off her son's snow-crusted cap, but Mitch noted, she didn't look up. "So change." He leaned against the doorjamb, ignoring the snow that fell at his feet.

"I built a fort. Please come out and see. I already started a snow warrior, but Mitch said we should check in so you wouldn't worry."

His consideration forced her to look up. "I appreciate that."

He was watching her thoughtfully—too thoughtfully, Hester decided. "Rad says you build a pretty good snow warrior yourself."

"Please, Mom. What if we got a freak heat wave and the snow was all gone tomorrow? It's like the greenhouse effect, you know. I read all about it."

She was trapped and knew it. "All right, I'll change. Why don't you fix Mitch some hot chocolate and warm up?"

"All right!" Radley dropped down on the floor just inside the door. "You have to take off your boots," he told Mitch. "She gets mad if you track up the carpet."

Mitch unbuttoned his coat as Hester walked away. "We wouldn't want to make her mad."

Within fifteen minutes, Hester had changed into corduroys, a bulky sweater and old boots. In place of her red coat was a blue parka that showed some wear. Mitch kept one hand on Taz's leash and the other in his pocket as they walked across to the park. He couldn't say why he enjoyed seeing her dressed casually with Radley's hand joined tight with hers. He couldn't say for certain why he'd wanted to spend this time with her, but it had been he who'd planted the idea of another outing in Radley's head, and he who'd suggested that they go up together to persuade her to come outside.

He liked the winter. Mitch took a deep gulp of cold air as they walked through the soft, deep snow of Central Park. Snow and stinging air had always appealed to him, particularly when the trees were draped in white and there were snow castles to be built.

When he'd been a boy, his family had often wintered in the Caribbean, away from what his mother had termed the "mess and inconvenience." He'd picked up an affection for scuba and white sand, but had never felt that a palm tree replaced a pine at Christmas.

The winters he'd liked best had been spent in his uncle's country home in New Hampshire, where there'd been woods to walk in and hills to sled. Oddly enough, he'd been thinking of going back there for a few weeks—until the Wallaces popped up two floors above, that is. He hadn't realized until today that he'd shuffled those plans to the back of his mind as soon as he'd seen Hester and her son.

Now she was embarrassed, annoyed and uncomfortable. Mitch turned to study her profile. Her cheeks were already rosy with cold, and she'd made certain that Radley walked between them. He wondered if she realized how obvious her strategies were. She didn't use the boy, not in the way some parents used their offspring for their own ambitions or purposes. He respected her for that more than he could have explained. But she had, by putting Radley in the center, relegated Mitch to the level of her son's friend.

And so he was, Mitch thought with a smile. But he'd be damned if he was going to let it stop there.

"There's the fort. See?" Radley tugged on Hester's hand, then let it go to run, too impatient to wait any longer.

"Pretty impressive, huh?" Before she could avoid it, Mitch draped a casual arm over her shoulder. "He's really got a knack."

Hester tried to ignore the warmth and pressure of his arm as she looked at her son's handiwork. The walls of the fort were about two feet high, smooth as stone, with one end sloping nearly a foot higher in the shape of a round tower. They'd made an arched doorway high enough for Radley to crawl through. When Hester reached the fort, she saw him pass through on his hands and knees and pop up inside, his arms held high.

"It's terrific, Rad. I imagine you had a great deal to do with it," she said quietly to Mitch.

"Here and there." Then he smiled, as though he was laughing at himself. "Rad's a better architect than I'll ever be."

"I'm going to finish my snow warrior." Belly down, Rad crawled through the opening again. "Build one, Mom, on the other side of the fort. They'll be the sentries." Rad began to pack and smooth snow on his already half-formed figure. "You help her, Mitch, 'cause I've got a head start."

"Fair's fair." Mitch scooped up a handful of snow. "Any objections to teamwork?"

"No, of course not." Still avoiding giving him a straight look, Hester knelt in the snow. Mitch dropped the handful of snow on her head.

"I figured that was the quickest way to get you to look at me." She glared, then began to push the snow into a mound. "Problem, Mrs. Wallace?"

Seconds ticked by as she pushed at the snow. "I got a copy of *Who's Who*."

"Oh?" Mitch knelt down beside her.

"You were telling the truth."

"I've been known to from time to time." He shoved some more snow on the mound she was forming. "So?"

Hester frowned and punched the snow into shape. "I feel like an idiot."

"I told the truth, and you feel like an idiot." Patiently Mitch smoothed over the base she was making. "Want to explain the correlation?"

"You let me lecture you."

"It's kinda hard to stop you when you get rolling."

Hester began to dig out snow with both hands to form the legs. "You let me think you were some poor, eccentric Good Samaritan. I was even going to offer to put patches on your jeans."

"No kidding." Incredibly touched, Mitch caught her chin in his snow-covered glove. "That's sweet."

There was no way she was going to let his charm brush away the discomfort of her embarrassment. "The fact is, you're a rich, eccentric Good Samaritan." She shoved his hand away and began to gather snow for the torso.

"Does this mean you won't patch my jeans?"

Hester's long-suffering breath came out in a white plume. "I don't want to talk about it."

"Yes, you do." Always helpful, Mitch packed on more snow and succeeded in burying her up to the elbows. "Money shouldn't bother you, Hester. You're a banker."

"Money doesn't bother me." She yanked her arms free and

tossed two good-sized hunks of snow into his face. Because she had to fight back a giggle, she turned her back. "I just wish the situation had been made clear earlier, that's all."

Mitch wiped the snow from his face, then scooped up more, running his tongue along the inside of his lip. He'd had a lot of experience in forming what he considered the ultimate snowball. "What's the situation, Mrs. Wallace?"

"I wish you'd stop calling me that in that tone of voice." She turned, just in time to get the snowball right between the eyes.

"Sorry." Mitch smiled, then began to brush off her coat. "Must've slipped. About this situation . . ."

"There is no situation between us." Before she realized it, she'd shoved him hard enough to send him sprawling in the snow. "Excuse me." Her laughter came out in hitches that were difficult to swallow. "I didn't mean to do that. I don't know what it is about you that makes me do things like that." He sat up and continued to stare at her. "I *am* sorry," she repeated. "I think it's best if we just let this other business drop. Now, if I help you up, will you promise not to retaliate?"

"Sure." Mitch held out a gloved hand. The moment he closed it over hers, he yanked her forward. Hester went down, face first. "I don't *always* tell the truth, by the way." Before she could respond, he wrapped his arms around her and began to roll.

"Hey, you're supposed to be building another sentry."

"In a minute," Mitch called to Rad, while Hester tried to catch her breath. "I'm teaching your mom a new game. Like it?" he asked her as he rolled her underneath him again.

"Get off me. I've got snow down my sweater, down my jeans—"

"No use trying to seduce me here. I'm stronger than that."

"You're crazy." She tried to sit up, but he pinned her beneath him.

"Maybe." He licked a trace of snow from her cheek and

felt her go utterly still. "But I'm not stupid." His voice had changed. It wasn't the easy, carefree voice of her neighbor now, but the slow, soft tones of a lover. "You feel something for me. You may not like it, but you feel it."

It wasn't the unexpected exercise that had stolen her breath, and she knew it. His eyes were so blue in the lowering sunlight, and his hair glistened with a dusting of snow. And his face was close, temptingly close. Yes, she felt something, she felt something almost from the first minute she saw him, but she wasn't stupid, either.

"If you let go of my arms, I'll show you just how I feel."

"Why do I think I wouldn't like it? Never mind." He brushed his lips over hers before she could answer. "Hester, the situation is this. You have feelings for me that have nothing to do with my money, because you didn't know until a few hours ago that I had any to speak of. Some of those feelings don't have anything to do with the fact that I'm fond of your son. They're very personal, as in you and me."

He was right, absolutely and completely right. She could have murdered him for it. "Don't tell me how I feel."

"All right." After he spoke, he surprised her by rising and helping her to her feet. Then he took her in his arms again. "I'll tell you how *I* feel then. I care for you—more than I'd counted on."

She paled beneath her cold-tinted cheeks. There was more than a hint of desperation in her eyes as she shook her head and tried to back away. "Don't say that to me."

"Why not?" He struggled against impatience as he lowered his brow to hers. "You'll have to get used to it. I did."

"I don't want this. I don't want to feel this way."

He tipped her head back, and his eyes were very serious. "We'll have to talk about that."

"No. There's nothing to talk about. This is just getting out of hand."

"It's not out of hand yet." He tangled his fingers in the tips of her hair, but his eyes never left hers. "I'm almost certain it will be before long, but it isn't yet. You're too smart and too strong for that."

She'd be able to breathe easier in a moment. She was sure of it. She'd be able to breathe easier as soon as she was away from him. "No, I'm not afraid of you." Oddly, she discovered that much was true.

"Then kiss me." His voice was coaxing now, gentle. "It's nearly twilight. Kiss me, once, before the sun goes down."

She found herself leaning into him, lifting her lips up and letting her lashes fall without questioning why it should seem so right, so natural to do as he asked. There would be questions later, though she was certain the answers wouldn't come as easily. For now, she touched her lips to his and found them cool, cool and patient.

The world was all ice and snow, forts and fairylands, but his lips were real. They fit on hers firmly, warming her soft, sensitive skin while the racing of her heart heated her body. There was the rushing whoosh of traffic in the distance, but closer, more intimate, was the whisper of her coat sliding against his as they pressed tighter together.

He wanted to coax, to persuade, and just once to see her lips curve into a smile as he left them. He knew there were times when a man who preferred action and impulse had to go step by step. Especially when the prize at the top was precious.

He hadn't been prepared for her, but he knew he could accept what was happening between them with more ease than she. There were still secrets tucked inside her, hurts that had only partially healed. He knew better than to wish for the power to wipe all that aside. How she'd lived and what had happened to her were all part of the woman she was. The woman he was very, very close to falling in love with.

So he would take it step by step, Mitch told himself as he placed her away from him. And he would wait.

"That might have cleared up a few points, but I think we still have to talk." He took her hand to keep her close another moment. "Soon."

"I don't know." Had she ever been this confused before? She'd thought she'd left these feelings, these doubts behind her long ago.

"I'll come up or you can come down, but we'll talk."

He was jockeying her into a corner, one she knew she'd be backed into sooner or later. "Not tonight," she said, despising herself for being a coward. "Rad and I have a lot to do."

"Procrastination's not your style."

"It is this time," she murmured, and turned away quickly. "Radley, we have to go in."

"Look, Mom, I just finished, isn't it great?" He stood back to show off his warrior. "You hardly started yours."

"Maybe we'll finish it tomorrow." She walked to him quickly and took him by the hand. "We have to go in and fix dinner now."

"But can't we just—"

"No, it's nearly dark."

"Can Mitch come?"

"No, he can't." She shot a glance over her shoulder as they walked. He was hardly more than a shadow now, standing beside her son's fort. "Not tonight."

Mitch put a hand on his dog's head as Taz whined and started forward. "Nope. Not this time."

* * *

There didn't seem any way of avoiding him, Hester thought as she started down to Mitch's apartment at her son's request. She had to admit it had been foolish of her to try. On

the surface, anyone would think that Mitch Dempsey was the
solution to many of her problems. He was genuinely fond of
Radley, and gave her son both a companion and a safe and
convenient place to stay while she worked. His time was flex-
ible, and he was very generous with it.

The truth was, he'd complicated her life. No matter how
much she tried to look at him as Radley's friend or her
slightly odd neighbor, he brought back feelings she hadn't
experienced in almost ten years. Fluttery pulses and warm
surges were things Hester had attributed to the very young
or the very optimistic. She'd stopped being either when Radley's father had left them.

In all the years that had followed that moment, she'd devoted herself to her son—to making the best possible home
for him, to make his life as normal and well-balanced as possible. If Hester the woman had gotten lost somewhere in the
shuffle, Radley's mother figured it was a fair exchange. Now
Mitch Dempsey had come along and made her feel and,
worse, had made her wish.

Taking a deep breath, Hester knocked on Mitch's door.
Radley's friend's door, she told herself firmly. The only reason she was here was because Radley had been so excited
about showing her something. She wasn't here to see Mitch;
she wasn't hoping he would reach out and run his fingertips
along her cheek as he sometimes did. Hester's skin warmed
at the thought of it.

Hester linked her hands together and concentrated on Radley. She would see whatever it was he was so anxious for her
to see, and then she would get them both back upstairs to
their own apartment—and safety.

Mitch answered the door. He wore a sweatshirt sporting a
decal of a rival super hero across the chest, and sweatpants
with a gaping hole in one knee. There was a towel slung over

his shoulders. He used one end of it to dry the sweat off his face.

"You haven't been out running in this weather?" she asked before she'd allowed herself to think, immediately regretting the question and the obvious concern in her voice.

"No." He took her hand to draw her inside. She smelled like the springtime that was still weeks and weeks away. Her dark blue suit gave her a look of uncreased professionalism he found ridiculously sexy. "Weights," he told her. The fact was, he'd been lifting weights a great deal since he'd met Hester Wallace. Mitch considered it the second best way to decrease tension and rid the body of excess energy.

"Oh." So that explained the strength she'd felt in his arms. "I didn't realize you went in for that sort of thing."

"The Mr. Macho routine?" he said, laughing. "No, I don't, actually. The thing is, if I don't work out regularly, my body turns into a toothpick. It's not a pretty sight." Because she looked nervous enough to jump out of her skin, Mitch couldn't resist. He leered and flexed his arm. "Want to feel my pecs?"

"I'll pass, thanks." Hester kept her hands by her sides. "Mr. Rosen sent this package." She slipped the fat bank portfolio out from where she'd held it at her side. "Just remember, you asked for it."

"So I did." Mitch accepted it, then tossed it on a pile of magazines on the coffee table. "Tell him I'll pass it along."

"And will you?"

He lifted a brow. "I usually keep my word."

She was certain of that. It reminded her that he'd said they would talk, and soon. "Radley called and said there was something he had to show me."

"He's in the office. Want some coffee?"

It was such a casual offer, so easy and friendly, that she

nearly agreed. "Thanks, but we really can't stay. I had to bring some paperwork home with me."

"Fine. Just go on in. I need a drink."

"Mom!" The minute she stepped into the office, Radley jumped up and grabbed her hands. "Isn't it great? It's the neatest present I ever got in my life." With his hands still locked on hers, Radley dragged her over to a scaled-down drawing board.

It wasn't a toy. Hester could see immediately that it was top-of-the-line equipment, if child size. The small swivel stool was worn, but the seat was leather. Radley already had graph paper tacked to the board, and with compass and ruler had begun what appeared to be a set of blueprints.

"Is this Mitch's?"

"It was, but he said I could use it now, for as long as I wanted. See, I'm making the plans for a space station. This is the engine room. And over here and here are the living quarters. It's going to have a greenhouse, sort of like the one they had in this movie Mitch let me watch. Mitch showed me how to draw things to scale with these squares."

"I see." Pride in her son overshadowed any tension as she crouched down for a better look. "You catch on fast, Rad. This is wonderful. I wonder if NASA has an opening."

He chuckled, facedown, as he did when he was both pleased and embarrassed. "Maybe I could be an engineer."

"You can be anything you want." She pressed a kiss to his temple. "If you keep drawing like this, I'm going to need an interpreter to know what you're doing. All these tools." She picked up a square. "I guess you know what they're for."

"Mitch told me. He uses them sometimes when he draws."

"Oh?" She turned the square over in her hand. It looked so—professional.

"Even comic art needs a certain discipline," Mitch said from the doorway. He held a large glass of orange juice, which was already half gone. Hester rose. He looked—virile, she realized.

There was a faint vee of dampness down the center of his shirt. His hair had been combed through with no more than his fingers, and not for the first time, he hadn't bothered to shave off the night's growth of beard. Beside her, her son was happily remodeling his blueprint.

Virile, dangerous, nerve-wracking he might be, but a kinder man she'd never met. Concentrating on that, Hester stepped forward. "I don't know how to thank you."

"Rad already has."

She nodded, then laid a hand on Radley's shoulder.

"You finish that up, Rad. I'll be in the other room with Mitch."

Hester walked into the living room. It was, as she'd come to expect, cluttered and chaotic. Taz nosed around the carpet looking for cookie crumbs. "I thought I knew Rad inside and out," Hester began. "But I didn't know a drawing board would mean so much to him. I guess I would have thought him too young to appreciate it."

"I told you once he had a natural talent."

"I know." She gnawed on her lip. She wished she had accepted the offer of coffee so that she'd have something to do with her hands. "Rad told me that you were giving him some art lessons. You've done more for him than I ever could have expected. Certainly much more than you're obligated to."

He gave her a long, searching look. "It hasn't got anything to do with obligation. Why don't you sit down?"

"No." She linked her hands together, then pulled them apart again. "No, that's all right."

"Would you rather pace?"

It was the ease of his smile that had her unbending another notch. "Maybe later. I just wanted to tell you how grateful I am. Rad's never had . . ." A father. The words had nearly

come out before Hester had swallowed them in a kind of horror. She hadn't meant that, she assured herself. "He's never
had anyone to give him so much attention—besides me." She
let out a little breath. That was what she'd meant to say. Of
course it was. "The drawing board was very generous. Rad
said it was yours."

"My father had it made for me when I was about Rad's
age. He'd hoped I'd stop sketching monsters and start doing
something productive." He said it without bitterness, but with
a trace of amusement. Mitch had long since stopped resent-
ing his parents' lack of understanding.

"It must mean a great deal to you for you to have kept it
all this time. I know Rad loves it, but shouldn't you keep it
for your own children?"

Mitch took a sip of juice and glanced around the apartment. "I don't seem to have any around at the moment."

"But still—"

"Hester, I wouldn't have given it to him if I hadn't wanted
him to have it. It's been in storage for years, gathering dust.
It gives me a kick to see Rad putting it to use." He finished
off the juice, then set the glass down before he crossed to
her. "The present's for Rad, with no strings attached to his
mother."

"I know that. I didn't mean—"

"No, I don't think you did, exactly." He was watching her
now, unsmiling, with that quiet intensity he drew out at unexpected moments. "I doubt if it was even in the front of your
mind, but it was milling around in there somewhere."

"I don't think you're using Radley to get to me, if that's
what you mean."

"Good." He did as she'd imagined he might, and ran a finger along her jawline. "Because the fact is, Mrs. Wallace,
I'd like the kid without you, or you without the kid. It just so
happens that in this case, you came as a set."

"That's just it. Radley and I are a unit. What affects him affects me."

Mitch tilted his head as a new thought began to dawn. "I think I'm getting a signal here. You don't think I'm playing pals and buddies with Rad to get Rad's mother between the sheets?"

"Of course not." She drew back sharply, looking toward the office. "If I had thought that, Radley wouldn't be within ten feet of you."

"But . . ." He laid his arms on her shoulders, linking his hands loosely behind her neck. "You're wondering if your feelings for me might be residual of Radley's feelings."

"I never said I had feelings for you."

"Yes, you did. And you say it again every time I manage to get this close. No, don't pull away, Hester." He tightened his hands. "Let's be upfront. I want to sleep with you. It has nothing to do with Rad, and less than I figured to do with the primal urge I felt the first time I saw your legs." Her eyes lifted warily to his, but held. "It has to do with the fact that I find you attractive in a lot of ways. You're smart, you're strong, and you're stable. It might not sound very romantic, but the fact is, your stability is very alluring. I've never had a lot of it myself."

He brushed his linked hands up the back of her neck. "Now, maybe you're not ready to take a step like this at the moment. But I'd appreciate it if you'd take a straight look at what you want, at what you feel."

"I'm not sure I can. You only have yourself. I have Rad. Whatever I do, whatever decisions I make, ripple down to affect him. I promised myself years ago that he would never be hurt by another one of his parents. I'm going to keep that promise."

He wanted to demand that she tell him about Radley's father then and there, but the boy was just in the next room.

"Let me tell you what I believe. You could never make a decision that could hurt Rad. But I do think you could make one that could hurt yourself. I want to be with you, Hester, and I don't think our being together is going to hurt Radley."

"It's all done." Radley streamed out of the office, the graph paper in both hands. Hester immediately started to move away. To prove a point to both of them, Mitch held her where she was. "I want to take it and show Josh tomorrow. Okay?"

Knowing a struggle would be worse than submission, Hester stayed still with Mitch's arms on her shoulders. "Sure you can."

Radley studied them a moment. He'd never seen a man with his arms around his mother, except his grandpa or his uncle. He wondered if this made Mitch like family. "I'm going over to Josh's tomorrow afternoon, and I'm staying for a sleepover. We're going to stay up all night."

"Then I'll just have to look after your mom, won't I?"

"I guess." Radley began to roll the graph paper into a tube as Mitch had shown him.

"Radley knows I don't have to be looked after."

Ignoring her, Mitch continued to speak to Radley. "How about if I took your mom on a date?"

"You mean get dressed up and go to a restaurant and stuff?"

"Something like that."

"That'd be okay."

"Good. I'll pick her up at seven."

"I really don't think—"

"Seven's not good?" Mitch interrupted Hester. "All right, seven thirty, but that's as late as it gets. If I don't eat by eight, I get nasty." He gave Hester a quick kiss on the temple before releasing her. "Have a good time at Josh's."

"I will." Radley gathered up his coat and backpack. Then he walked to Mitch and hugged him. The words that had been on the tip of Hester's tongue dried up. "Thanks for the drawing board and everything. It's really neat."

"You're welcome. See you Monday." He waited until Hester was at the door. "Seven thirty."

She nodded and closed the door quietly behind her.

CHAPTER 7

She could have made excuses, but the fact was, Hester didn't want to. She knew Mitch had hustled her into this dinner date, but as she crossed the wide leather belt at her waist and secured it, she discovered she didn't mind. In fact, she was relieved that he'd made the decision for her—almost.

The nerves were there. She stood in front of the bureau mirror and took a few long, deep breaths. Yes, there were nerves, but they weren't the stomach-roiling sort she experienced when she went on job interviews. Though she wasn't quite sure where her feelings lay when it came to Mitch Dempsey, she was glad to be certain she wasn't afraid.

Picking up her brush, she studied her reflection as she smoothed her hair. She didn't look nervous, Hester decided. That was another point in her favor. The black wool dress was flattering with its deep cowl neck and nipped-in waist. The red slash of belt accented the line before the skirt flared out. For some reason, red gave her confidence. She considered the bold color another kind of defense for a far-from-bold person.

She fixed oversized scarlet swirls at her ears. Like most of her wardrobe, the dress was practical. It could go to the office, to a PTA meeting or a business lunch. Tonight, she thought with a half smile, it was going on a date.

Hester tried not to dwell on how long it had been since she'd been on a date, but comforted herself with the fact that she knew Mitch well enough to keep up an easy conversation through an evening. An adult evening. As much as she adored Radley, she couldn't help but look forward to it.

When she heard the knock, she gave herself a last quick check, then went to answer. The moment she opened the door, her confidence vanished.

He didn't look like Mitch. Gone were the scruffy jeans and baggy sweatshirts. This man wore a dark suit with a pale blue shirt. And a tie. The top button of the shirt was open, and the tie of dark blue silk was knotted loose and low, but it was still a tie. He was clean-shaven, and though some might have thought he still needed a trim, his hair waved dark and glossy over his ears and the collar of his shirt.

Hester was suddenly and painfully shy.

She looked terrific. Mitch felt a moment's awkwardness himself as he looked at her. Her evening shoes put her to within an inch of his height so that they were eye to eye. It was the wariness in hers that had him relaxing with a smile.

"Looks like I picked the right color." He offered her an armful of red roses.

She knew it was foolish for a woman of her age to be flustered by something as simple as flowers. But her heart rushed up to her throat as she gathered them to her.

"Did you forget your line again?" he murmured.

"My line?"

"Thank you."

The scent of the roses flowed around her, soft and sweet. "Thank you."

He touched one of the petals. He already knew her skin

felt much the same. "Now you're supposed to put them in water."

Feeling a great deal more than foolish, Hester stepped back. "Of course. Come in."

"The apartment feels different without Rad," he commented when Hester went to get a vase.

"I know. Whenever he goes to a sleepover, it takes me hours to get used to the quiet." He'd followed her into the kitchen. Hester busied herself with arranging the roses. I am a grown woman, she reminded herself, and just because I haven't been on a date since high school doesn't mean I don't remember how.

"What do you usually do when you have a free evening?"

"Oh, I read, watch a late movie." She turned with the vase and nearly collided with him. Water sloshed dangerously close to the top of the vase.

"The eye's barely noticeable now." He lifted a fingertip to where the bruise had faded to a shadow.

"It wasn't such a calamity." Her throat had tightened. Grown woman or not, she found herself enormously glad that the vase of roses was between them. "I'll get my coat."

After carrying the roses to the table beside the sofa, Hester went to the closet. She slipped one arm into the sleeve before Mitch came up behind her to help her finish. He made such an ordinary task sensual, she thought as she stared straight ahead. He brushed his hands over her shoulders, lingered, then trailed them down her arms before bringing them up again to gently release her hair from the coat collar.

Hester's hands were balled into fists as she turned her head. "Thank you."

"You're welcome." With his hands on her shoulders, Mitch turned her to face him. "Maybe you'll feel better if we get this out of the way now." He kept his hands where they were and touched his lips, firm and warm, to hers. Hester's rigid hands went lax. There was nothing demanding or passionate in the kiss. It moved her unbearably with its understanding.

"Feel better?" Mitch murmured.

"I'm not sure."

With a laugh, he touched his lips to hers again. "Well, I do." Linking his hand with hers, he walked to the door.

* * *

The restaurant was French, subdued and very exclusive. The pale flowered walls glowed in the quiet light and the flicker of candles. Diners murmured their private conversations over linen cloths and crystal stemware. The hustle and bustle of the streets were shut out by beveled glass doors.

"Ah, Monsieur Dempsey, we haven't seen you in some time." The maître d' stepped forward to greet him.

"You know I always come back for your snails."

With a laugh, the maître d' waved a waiter aside.

"Good evening, *mademoiselle*. I'll take you to your table."

The little booth was candlelit and secluded, a place for hand-holding and intimate secrets. Hester's leg brushed Mitch's as they settled.

"The sommelier will be right with you. Enjoy your evening."

"No need to ask if you've been here before."

"From time to time I get tired of frozen pizza. Would you like champagne?"

"I'd love it."

He ordered a bottle, pleasing the wine steward with the vintage. Hester opened her menu and sighed over the elegant foods. "I'm going to remember this the next time I'm biting into half a tuna sandwich between appointments."

"You like your job?"

"Very much." She wondered if *soufflé de crabe* was what

it sounded like. "Rosen can be a pain, but he does push you to be efficient."

"And you like being efficient."

"It's important to me."

"What else is, other than Rad?"

"Security." She looked over at him with a half smile. "I suppose that has to do with Rad. The truth is, anything that's been important to me over the last few years has to do with Rad."

She glanced up as the steward brought the wine and began his routine for Mitch's approval. Hester watched the wine rise in her fluted glass, pale gold and frothy. "To Rad, then," Mitch said as he lifted his glass to touch hers. "And his fascinating mother."

Hester sipped, a bit stunned that anything could taste so good. She'd had champagne before, but like everything that had to do with Mitch, it hadn't been quite like this. "I've never considered myself fascinating."

"A beautiful woman raising a boy on her own in one of the toughest cities in the world fascinates me." He sipped and grinned. "Added to that, you do have terrific legs, Hester."

She laughed, and even when he slipped his hand over hers, felt no embarrassment. "So you said before. They're long, anyway. I was taller than my brother until he was out of high school. It infuriated him, and I had to live down the name Stretch."

"Mine was String."

"String?"

"You know those pictures of the eighty-pound weakling? That was me."

Over the rim of her glass, Hester studied the way he filled out the suit jacket. "I don't believe it."

"One day, if I'm drunk enough, I'll show you pictures."

Mitch ordered in flawless French that had Hester staring.

This was the comic book writer, she thought, who built snow forts and talked to his dog. Catching the look, Mitch lifted a brow. "I spent a couple of summers in Paris during high school."

"Oh." It reminded her forcefully where he'd come from. "You said you didn't have any brothers or sisters. Do your parents live in New York?"

"No." He broke off a hunk of crusty French bread. "My mother zips in from time to time to shop or go to the theater, and my father might come in occasionally on business, but New York isn't their style. They still live most of the year in Newport, where I grew up."

"Oh, Newport. We drove through once when I was a kid. We'd always take these rambling car vacations in the summer." She tucked her hair behind her ear in an unconscious gesture that gave him a tantalizing view of her throat. "I remember the houses, the enormous mansions with the pillars and flowers and ornamental trees. We even took pictures. It was hard to believe anyone really lived there." Then she caught herself up abruptly and glanced over at Mitch's amused face. "You did."

"It's funny. I spent some time with binoculars watching the tourists in the summer. I might have homed in on your family."

"We were the ones in the station wagon with the suitcases strapped to the roof."

"Sure, I remember you." He offered her a piece of bread. "I envied you a great deal."

"Really?" She paused with her butter knife in midair. "Why?"

"Because you were going on vacation and eating hot dogs. You were staying in motels with soda machines outside the door and playing car bingo between cities."

"Yes," she murmured. "I suppose that sums it up."

"I'm not pulling poor-little-rich boy," he added when he saw the change in her eyes. "I'm just saying that having a big house isn't necessarily better than having a station wagon." He added more wine to her glass. "In any case, I finished my rebellious money-is-beneath-me stage a long time ago."

"I don't know if I can believe that from someone who lets dust collect on his Louis Quinze."

"That's not rebellion, that's laziness."

"Not to mention sinful," she put in. "It makes me itch for a polishing cloth and lemon oil."

"Any time you want to rub my mahogany, feel free."

She lifted a brow when he smiled at her. "So what did you do during your rebellious stage?"

Her fingertips grazed his. It was one of the few times she'd touched him without coaxing. Mitch lifted his gaze from their hands to her face. "You really want to know?"

"Yes."

"Then we'll make a deal. One slightly abridged life story for another."

It wasn't the wine that was making her reckless, Hester knew, but him. "All right. Yours first."

"We'll start off by saying my parents wanted me to be an architect. It was the only practical and acceptable profession they could see me using my drawing abilities for. The stories I made up didn't really appall them; they merely baffled them—so they were easily ignored. Straight out of high school, I decided to sacrifice my life to art."

Their appetizers were served. Mitch sighed approvingly over his escargots.

"So you came to New York?"

"No, New Orleans. At that time my money was still in trusts, though I doubt I would have used it, in any case. Since I refused to use my parents' financial backing, New Orleans was as close to Paris as I could afford to get. God, I loved it.

I starved, but I loved the city. Those dripping, steamy after-noons, the smell of the river. It was my first great adventure. Want one of these? They're incredible."

"No, I—"

"Come on, you'll thank me." He lifted his fork to her lips. Reluctantly, Hester parted them and accepted.

"Oh." The flavor streamed, warm and exotic, over her tongue. "It's not what I expected."

"The best things usually aren't."

She lifted her glass and wondered what Radley's reaction would be when she told him she'd eaten a snail. "So what did you do in New Orleans?"

"I set up an easel in Jackson Square and made my living sketching tourists and selling watercolors. For three years I lived in one room where I baked in the summer and froze in the winter and considered myself one lucky guy."

"What happened?"

"There was a woman. I thought I was crazy about her and vice versa. She modeled for me when I was going through my Matisse period. You should have seen me then. My hair was about your length, and I wore it pulled back and fastened with a leather thong. I even had a gold earring in my left ear."

"You wore an earring?"

"Don't smirk, they're very fashionable now. I was ahead of my time." Appetizers were cleared away to make room for green salads. "Anyway, we were going to play house in my miserable little room. One night, when I'd had a little too much wine, I told her about my parents and how they'd never understood my artistic drive. She got absolutely furious."

"She was angry with your parents?"

"You are sweet," he said unexpectedly, and kissed her hand. "No, she was angry with me. I was rich and hadn't told her. I had piles of money and expected her to be satisfied with one filthy little room in the Quarter where she had to cook red beans and rice on a hot plate. The funny thing was she really cared for me when she'd thought I was poor, but when she found out I wasn't and that I didn't intend to use what was available to me—and, by association, to her—she was infuriated. We had one hell of a fight, where she let me know what she really thought of me and my work."

Hester could picture him, young, idealistic and struggling. "People say things they don't mean when they're angry."

He lifted her hand and kissed her fingers. "Yes, very sweet." His hand remained on hers as he continued. "Anyway, she left and gave me the opportunity to take stock of myself. For three years I'd been living day to day, telling myself I was a great artist whose time was coming. The truth was I wasn't a great artist. I was a clever one, but I'd never be a great one. So I left New Orleans for New York and commercial art. I was good. I worked fast tucked in my little cubicle and generally made the client happy—and I was miserable. But my credentials there got me a spot at Universal, originally as an inker, then as an artist. And then"—he lifted his glass in salute—"there was Zark. The rest is history."

"You're happy." She turned her hand under his so their palms met. "It shows. Not everyone is as content with themselves as you are, as at ease with himself and what he does."

"It took me awhile."

"And your parents? Have you reconciled with them?"

"We came to the mutual understanding that we'd never understand each other. But we're family. I have my stock portfolio, so they can tell their friends the comic book business is something that amuses me. Which is true enough."

Mitch ordered another bottle of champagne with the main course. "Now it's your turn."

She smiled and let the delicate soufflé melt on her tongue. "Oh, I don't have anything so exotic as an artist's garret in New Orleans. I had a very average childhood with a very average family. Board games on Saturday nights, pot roast on Sundays. Dad had a good job, Mom stayed home and kept the house. We loved each other very much but didn't always get along. My sister was very outgoing, head cheerleader, that sort of thing. I was miserably shy."

"You're still shy," Mitch murmured as he wound his fingers around hers.

"I didn't think it showed."

"In a very appealing way. What about Rad's father?" He felt her hand stiffen in his. "I've wanted to ask, Hester, but we don't have to talk about it now if it upsets you."

She drew her hand from his to reach for her glass. The champagne was cold and crisp. "It was a long time ago. We met in high school. Radley looks a great deal like his father, so you can understand that he was very attractive. He was also just a little wild, and I found that magnetic."

She moved her shoulders a little, restlessly, but was determined to finish what she'd started. "I really was painfully shy and a bit withdrawn, so he seemed like something exciting to me, even a little larger than life. I fell desperately in love with him the first time he noticed me. It was as simple as that. In any case, we went together for two years and were married a few weeks after graduation. I wasn't quite eighteen and was absolutely sure that marriage was going to be one adventure after another."

"And it wasn't?" he asked when she paused.

"For a while it was. We were young, so it never seemed terribly important that Allan moved from one job to another or quit altogether for weeks at a time. Once he sold the living room set that my parents had given us as a wedding present so that we could take a trip to Jamaica. It seemed impetuous and romantic, and at that time we didn't have any responsibilities except to ourselves. Then I got pregnant."

She paused again and, looking back, remembered her

own excitement and wonder and fear at the idea of carrying a child. "I was thrilled. Allan got a tremendous kick out of it and started buying strollers and high chairs on credit. Money was tight, but we were optimistic, even when I had to cut down to part-time work toward the end of my pregnancy and then take maternity leave after Radley was born. He was beautiful." She laughed a little. "I know all mothers say that about their babies, but he was honestly the most beautiful, the most precious thing I'd ever seen. He changed my life. He didn't change Allan's."

She toyed with the stem of her glass and tried to work out in her mind what she hadn't allowed herself to think about for a very long time. "I couldn't understand it at the time, but Allan resented having the burden of responsibility. He hated it that we couldn't just stroll out of the apartment and go to the movies or go dancing whenever we chose. He was still unbelievably reckless with money, and because of Rad I had to compensate."

"In other words," Mitch said quietly, "you grew up."

"Yes." It surprised her that he saw that so quickly, and it relieved her that he seemed to understand. "Allan wanted to go back to the way things were, but we weren't children anymore. As I look back, I can see that he was jealous of Radley, but at the time I just wanted him to grow up, to be a father, to take charge. At twenty he was still the sixteen-year-old boy I'd known in high school, but I wasn't the same girl. I was a mother. I'd gone back to work because I'd thought the extra income would ease some of the strain. One day I came home after picking Radley up at the sitter's, and Allan was gone. He'd left a note saying he just couldn't handle being tied down any longer."

"Did you know he was leaving?"

"No, I honestly didn't. In all probability it was done on impulse, the way Allan did most things. It would never have occurred to him that it was desertion, to him it would've meant moving on. He thought he was being fair by taking only half the money, but he left all the bills. I had to get another part-time job in the evenings. I hated that; leaving Rad with a sitter and not seeing him. That six months was the worst time of my life."

Her eyes darkened a moment; then she shook her head and pushed it all back into the past. "After a while I'd straightened things out enough to quit the second job. About that time, Allan called. It was the first I'd heard from him since he'd left. He was very amiable, as if we'd been nothing more than passing acquaintances. He told me he was heading up to Alaska to work. After he hung up, I called a lawyer and got a very simple divorce."

"It must have been difficult for you." Difficult? he thought—he couldn't even imagine what kind of hell it had been. "You could have gone home to your parents."

"No. I was angry for a long, long time. The anger made me determined to stay right here in New York and make it work for me and Radley. By the time the anger had died down, I was making it work."

"He's never come back to see Rad?"

"No, never."

"His loss." He cupped her chin, then leaned over to kiss her lightly. "His very great loss."

She found it easy to lift a hand to his cheek. "The same can be said about that woman in New Orleans."

"Thanks." He nibbled her lips again, enjoying the faint hint of champagne. "Dessert?"

"Hmmm?"

He felt a wild thrill of triumph at her soft, distracted sigh. "Let's skip it." Moving back only slightly, he signaled the waiter for the check, then handed Hester the last of the champagne. "I think we should walk awhile."

The air was biting, almost as exhilarating as the wine. Yet the wine warmed her, making her feel as though she could walk for miles without feeling the wind. She didn't object to Mitch's arm around her shoulders or to the fact that he set the direction. She didn't care where they walked as long as the feelings that stirred inside her didn't fade.

She knew what it was like to fall in love—to be in love. Time slowed down. Everything around you went quickly, but not in a blur. Colors were brighter, sounds sharper, and even in midwinter you could smell flowers. She had been there once before, had felt this intensely once before, but had thought she would never find that place again. Even as a part of her mind struggled to remind her that this couldn't be love—or certainly shouldn't be—she simply ignored it. Tonight she was just a woman.

There were skaters at Rockefeller Center, swirling around and around the ice as the music flowed. Hester watched them, tucked in the warmth of Mitch's arms. His cheek rested on her hair, and she could feel the strong, steady rhythm of his heart.

"Sometimes I bring Rad here on Sundays to skate or just to watch like this. It seems different tonight." She turned her head, and her lips were barely a whisper from his. "Everything seems different tonight."

If she looked at him like that again, Mitch knew he'd break his vow to give her enough time to clear her head and would bundle her into the nearest cab so that he could have her home and in bed before the look broke. Calling on willpower, he shifted her so he could brush his lips over her temple. "Things look different at night, especially after champagne." He relaxed again, her head against his shoulder. "It's a nice difference. Not necessarily steeped in reality, but nice. You can get enough reality from nine to five."

"Not you." Unaware of the tug-of-war she was causing inside him, she turned in his arms. "You make fantasies from nine to five, or whatever hours you choose."

"You should hear the one I'm making up now." He drew another deep breath. "Let's walk some more, and you can tell me about one of yours."

"A fantasy?" Her stride matched his easily. "Mine isn't nearly as earthshaking as yours, I imagine. It's just a house."

"A house." He walked toward the park, hoping they'd both be a little steadier on their feet by the time they reached home. "What kind of house?"

"A country house, one of those big old farmhouses with shutters at the windows and porches all around. Lots of windows so you could look at the woods—there would have to be woods. Inside there would be high ceilings and big fireplaces. Outside would be a garden with wisteria climbing on a trellis." She felt the sting of winter on her cheeks, but could almost smell the summer.

"You'd be able to hear the bees hum in it all summer long. There'd be a big yard for Radley, and he could have a dog. I'd have a swing on the porch so I could sit outside in the evening and watch him catch lightning bugs in a jar." She laughed and let her head rest on his shoulder. "I told you it wasn't earthshaking."

"I like it." He liked it so well he could picture it, white shuttered and hip roofed, with a barn off in the distance. "But you need a stream so Rad could fish."

She closed her eyes a moment, then shook her head. "As much as I love him, I don't think I could bait a hook. Build a tree house maybe, or throw a curveball, but no worms."

"You throw a curveball?"

She tilted her head and smiled. "Right in the strike zone. I helped coach Little League last year."

"The woman's full of surprises. You wear shorts in the dugout?"

"You're obsessed with my legs."

"For a start."

He steered her into their building and toward the elevators. "I haven't had an evening like this in a very long time."

"Neither have I."

She drew back far enough to study him as they began the ride to her floor. "I've wondered about that, about the fact that you don't seem to be involved with anyone."

He touched her chin with his fingertip. "Aren't I?"

She heard the warning signal but wasn't quite sure what to do about it. "I mean, I haven't noticed you dating or spending any time with women."

Amused, he flicked the finger down her throat. "Do I look like a monk?"

"No." Embarrassed and more than a little unsettled, she looked away. "No, of course not."

"The fact is, Hester, after you've had your share of wild oats, you lose your taste for them. Spending time with a woman just because you don't want to be alone isn't very satisfying."

"From the stories I hear around the office from the single women, there are plenty of men who disagree with you."

He shrugged as they stepped off the elevator. "It's obvious you haven't played the singles scene." Her brows drew together as she dug for her key. "That was a compliment, but my point is it gets to be a strain or a bore—"

"And this is the age of the meaningful relationship."

"You say that like a cynic. Terribly uncharacteristic, Hester." He leaned against the jamb as she opened the door. "In any case, I'm not big on catchphrases. Are you going to ask me in?"

She hesitated. The walk had cleared her head enough for

the doubts to seep through. But along with the doubts was the echo of the way she'd felt when they'd stood together in the cold. The echo was stronger. "All right. Would you like some coffee?"

"No." He shrugged out of his coat as he watched her.

"It's no trouble. It'll only take a minute."

He caught her hands. "I don't want coffee, Hester. I want you." He slipped her coat from her shoulders. "And I want you so bad it makes me jumpy."

She didn't back away, but stood, waiting. "I don't know what to say. I'm out of practice."

"I know." For the first time his own nerves were evident as he dragged a hand through his hair. "That's given me some bad moments. I don't want to seduce you." Then he laughed and walked a few paces away. "The hell I don't."

"I knew— I tried to tell myself I didn't, but I knew when I went out with you tonight that we'd come back here like this." She pressed a hand to her stomach, surprised that it was tied in knots. "I think I was hoping you'd just sort of sweep me away so I wouldn't have to make a decision."

He turned to her. "That's a cop-out, Hester."

"I know." She couldn't look at him then, wasn't certain she dared. "I've never been with anyone but Rad's father. The truth is, I've never wanted to be."

"And now?" He only wanted a word, one word.

She pressed her lips together. "It's been so long, Mitch. I'm frightened."

"Would it help if I told you I am too?"

"I don't know."

"Hester." He crossed to her to lay his hands on her shoulders. "Look at me." When she did, her eyes were wide and achingly clear. "I want you to be sure, because I don't want regrets in the morning. Tell me what you want."

It seemed her life was a series of decisions. There was no

one to tell her which was right or which was wrong. As always, she reminded herself that once the decision was made, she alone would deal with the consequences and accept the responsibility.

"Stay with me tonight," she whispered. "I want you."

CHAPTER 8

He cupped her face in his hands and felt her tremble. He touched his lips to hers and heard her sigh. It was a moment he knew he would always remember. Her acceptance, her desire, her vulnerability.

The apartment was silent. He would have given her music. The scent of the roses she'd put in a vase was pale next to the fragrance of the garden he imagined for her. The lamp burned brightly. He wouldn't have chosen the secrets of the dark, but rather the mystery of candlelight.

How could he explain to her that there was nothing ordinary, nothing casual in what they were about to give each other? How could he make her understand that he had been waiting all his life for a moment like this? He wasn't certain he could choose the right words or that the words he did choose would reach her.

So he would show her.

With his lips still lingering on hers, he swept her up into his arms. Though he heard her quick intake of breath, she wrapped her arms around him.

"Mitch—"

"I'm not much of a white knight." He looked at her, half smiling, half questioning. "But for tonight we can pretend."

He looked heroic and strong and incredibly, impossibly sweet. Whatever doubts had remained slipped quietly away. "I don't need a white knight."

"Tonight I need to give you one." He kissed her once more before he carried her into the bedroom.

There was a part of him that needed, ached with that need, so much so that he wanted to lay her down on the bed and cover her with his body. There were times that love ran swiftly, even violently. He understood that and knew that she would too. But he set her down on the floor beside the bed and touched only her hand.

He drew away just a little. "The light."

"But—"

"I want to see you, Hester."

It was foolish to be shy. It was wrong, she knew, to want to have this moment pass in the dark, anonymously. She reached for the bedside lamp and turned the switch.

The light bathed them, capturing them both standing hand in hand and eye to eye. The quick panic returned, pounding in her head and her heart. Then he touched her and quieted it. He drew off her earrings and set them on the bedside table so that the metal clicked quietly against the wood. She felt a rush of heat, as though with that one simple, intimate move he had already undressed her.

He reached for her belt, then paused when her hands fluttered nervously to his. "I won't hurt you."

"No." She believed him and let her hands drop away. He unhooked her belt to let it slide to the floor. When he lowered his lips to hers again, she slipped her arms around his waist and let the power guide her.

This was what she wanted. She couldn't lie to herself or make excuses. For tonight, she wanted to think only as a woman, to be thought of only as a woman. To be desired, enjoyed, wondered over. When their lips parted, their eyes met. And she smiled.

"I've been waiting for that." He touched a finger to her lips, overcome with a pleasure that was so purely emotional even he couldn't describe it.

"For what?"

"For you to smile at me when I kiss you." He brought his hand to her face. "Let's try it again."

This time the kiss went deeper, edging closer to those uncharted territories. She lifted her hands to his shoulders, then slid them around to encircle his neck. He felt her fingers touch the skin there, shyly at first, then with more confidence.

"Still afraid?"

"No." Then she smiled again. "Yes, a little. I'm not—" she looked away, and he once more brought her face back to his.

"What?"

"I'm not sure what to do. What you like."

He wasn't stunned by her words so much as humbled. He'd said he'd cared for her, and that was true. But now his heart, which had been teetering on the edge, fell over into love.

"Hester, you leave me speechless." He drew her against him, hard, and just held her there. "Tonight, just do what seems right. I think we'll be fine."

He began by kissing her hair, drawing in the scent that had so appealed to him. The mood was already set, seduction on either side unnecessary. He felt her heart begin to race against his; then she turned her head and found his lips with her own.

His hands weren't steady as he drew down the long zipper at her back. He knew it was an imperfect world but needed badly to give her one perfect night. No one would ever have called him a selfish man, but it was a fact that he'd never before put someone else's needs so entirely before his own.

He drew the wool from her shoulders, down her arms. She wore a simple chemise beneath it, plain white without frills or lace. No fantasy of silk or satin could have excited him more.

"You're lovely." He pressed a kiss to one shoulder, then the other. "Absolutely lovely."

She wanted to be. It had been so long since she'd felt the need to be any more than presentable. When she saw his eyes, she felt lovely. Gathering her courage together, she began to undress him in turn.

He knew it wasn't easy for her. She drew his jacket off, then began to unknot his tie before she was able to lift her gaze to his again. He could feel her fingers tremble lightly against him as she unbuttoned his shirt.

"You're lovely, too," she murmured. The last, the only man she had ever touched this way had been little more than a boy. Mitch's muscles were subtle but hard, and though his chest was smooth, it was that of a man. Her movements were slow, from shyness rather than a knowledge of arousal. His stomach muscles quivered as she reached for the hook of his slacks.

"You're driving me crazy."

She drew her hands back automatically. "I'm sorry."

"No." He tried to laugh, but it sounded like a groan. "I like it."

Her fingers trembled all the more as she slid his slacks over his hips. Lean hips, with the muscles long and hard. She felt a surge that was both fascination and delight as she brought her hands to them. Then she was against him, and the shock of flesh against flesh vibrated through her.

He was fighting every instinct that pushed him to move quickly, to take quickly. Her shy hands and wondering eyes had taken him to the brink, and he had to claw his way back.

She sensed a war going on inside him, felt the rigidity of his muscles and heard the raggedness of his breathing.

"Mitch?"

"Just a minute." He buried his face in her hair. The battle for control was hard won. He felt weakened by it, weakened and stunned. When he found the soft, sensitive skin of her neck, he concentrated on that alone.

She strained against him, turning her head instinctively to give him freer access. It seemed as though a veil had floated down over her eyes so that the room, which had become so familiar to her, was hazy. She could feel her blood begin to pound where his lips rubbed and nibbled; then it was throbbing hot, close to the skin, softening it, sensitizing it. Her moan sounded primitive in her own ears. Then it was she who was drawing him down to the bed.

He'd wanted another minute before he let his body spread over hers. There were explosions bombarding his system, from head to heart to loins. He knew he had to calm them before they shattered his senses. But her hands were moving over him, her hips straining upward. With an effort, Mitch rolled so that they were side by side.

He brought his lips down on her, and for a moment all the needs, the fantasies, the darker desires centered there. Her mouth was moist and hot, pounding into his brain how she would be when he filled her. He was already dragging the thin barrier of her chemise aside so that she gasped when her breasts met him unencumbered. As his lips closed over the first firm point, he heard her cry out his name.

This was abandonment. She'd been sure she'd never wanted it, but now, as her body went fluid in her movements against his, she thought she might never want anything else. The feelings of flesh against flesh, growing hot and damp, were new and exhilarating. As were the avid seeking of mouths and the tastes they found and drew in. His murmurs to her were hot and incoherent, but she responded. The light played over his hands as he showed her how a touch could make the soul soar.

She was naked, but the shyness was gone. She wanted him to touch and taste and look his fill, just as she was driven to. His body was a fascination of muscle and taut skin. She hadn't known until now that to touch another, to please another, could bring on such wild waves of passion. He cupped a hand over her, and the passion contracted into a ball of flame in her center that abruptly, almost violently, burst. Gasping for breath, she reached for him.

He'd never had a woman respond so utterly. Watching her rise and peak had given him a delirious thrust of pleasure. He wanted badly to take her up and over again and again, until she was limp and mindless. But his control was slipping, and she was calling for him.

His body covered hers, and he filled her.

He couldn't have said how long they moved together— minutes, hours. But he would never forget how her eyes had opened and stared into his.

* * *

He was a little shaken as he lay with her on top of the crumpled spread with drops of freezing rain striking the windows. He turned his head toward the hiss and wondered idly how long it had been going on. As far as he could remember, he'd never been so involved with a woman that the outside world, and all its sights and sounds, had simply ceased to exist.

He turned away again and drew Hester against him. His body was cooling rapidly, but he had no desire to move. "You're quiet," he murmured.

Her eyes were closed. She wasn't ready to open them again. "I don't know what to say."

"How about 'Wow'?"

She was surprised she could laugh after such intensity. "Okay. Wow."

"Try for more enthusiasm. How about 'Fantastic, incredible, earth-shattering?' "

She opened her eyes now and looked into his. "How about beautiful?"

He caught her hand in his and kissed it. "Yeah, that'll do." When he propped himself up on his elbow to look down at her, she shifted. "Too late to be shy now," he told her. Then he ran a hand, light and possessively, down her body. "You know, I was right about your legs. I don't suppose I could talk you into putting on a pair of shorts and those little socks that stop at the ankles."

"I beg your pardon?"

Her tone had him gathering her to him and covering her face with kisses. "I have a thing about long legs in shorts and socks. I drive myself crazy watching women jog in the park in the summer. When they color-coordinate them, I'm finished."

"You're crazy."

"Come on, Hester, don't you have some secret turn-on? Men in muscle shirts, in tuxedos with black tie and studs undone?"

"Don't be silly."

"Why not?"

Why not, indeed, she thought, catching her bottom lip between her teeth. "Well, there is something about jeans riding low on the hips with the snap undone."

"I'll never snap my jeans again as long as I live."

She laughed again. "That doesn't mean I'm going to start wearing shorts and socks."

"That's okay. I get excited when I see you in a business suit."

"You do not."

"Oh, yes, I do." He rolled her on top of him and began to play with her hair. "Those slim lapels and high-collar blouses. And you always wear your hair up." With it caught in his hands, he lifted it on top of her head. It wasn't the same look at all, but one that still succeeded in making his mouth dry. "The efficient and dependable Mrs. Wallace. Every time I see you dressed that way I imagine how fascinating it would be to peel off those professional clothes and take out those tidy little pins." He let her hair slide down through his fingers.

Thoughtful, Hester rested her cheek against his cheek. "You're a strange man, Mitch."

"More than likely."

"You depend so much on your imagination, on what it might be, on fantasies and make-believe. With me it's facts and figures, profit and loss, what is or what isn't."

"Are you talking about our jobs or our personalities?"

"Isn't one really the same as the other?"

"No. I'm not Commander Zark, Hester."

She shifted, lulled by the rhythm of his heart. "I suppose what I mean is that the artist in you, the writer in you, thrives on imagination or possibilities. I guess the banker in me looks for checks and balances."

He was silent for a moment, stroking her hair. Didn't she realize how much more there was to her? This was the woman who fantasized about a home in the country, the one who threw a curveball, the one who had just taken a man of flesh and blood, and turned him into a puddle of need.

"I don't want to get overly philosophical, but why do you think you chose to deal with loans? Do you get the same feeling when you turn down an application as you do when you approve one?"

"No, of course not."

"Of course not," he repeated. "Because when you approve one, you've had a hand in the possibilities. I have no doubt that you play by the book, that's part of your charm, but I'd wager you get a great deal of personal satisfaction by being able to say, 'Okay, buy your home, start your business, expand.'"

She lifted her head. "You seem to understand me very well." No one else had, she realized with a jolt. Ever.

"I've been giving you a great deal of thought." He drew her to him, wondering if she could feel how well their bodies fit. "A very great deal. In fact, I haven't thought about another woman since I delivered your pizza."

She smiled at that and would have settled against him again, but he held her back. "Hester . . ." It was one of the few times in his life he'd ever felt self-conscious. She was looking at him expectantly, even patiently, while he struggled for the right words. "The thing is, I don't want to think about another woman or be with another woman—this way." He struggled again, then swore. "Damn, I feel like I'm back in high school."

Her smile was cautious. "Are you going to ask me to go steady?"

It wasn't exactly what he'd had in mind, but he could see by the look in her eyes that he'd better go slowly. "I could probably find my class ring if you want."

She looked down at her hand, which was resting so naturally on his heart. Was it foolish to be so moved? If not, it was certainly dangerous. "Maybe we can just leave it that there's no one else I want to be with this way, either."

He started to speak, then stopped himself. She needed time to be sure that was true, didn't she? There had only been one other man in her life, and she'd been no more than a girl then. To be fair, he had to give her room to be certain. But he didn't want to be fair. No, Mitch Dempsey was no self-sacrificing Commander Zark.

"All right." He'd devised and won enough wars to know how to plan strategy. He'd win Hester before she realized there'd been a battle.

Drawing her down to him, he closed his mouth over hers and began the first siege.

* * *

It was an odd and rather wonderful feeling to wake up in the morning beside a lover—even one who nudged you over to the edge of the mattress. Hester opened her eyes and, lying very still, savored it.

His face was buried against the back of her neck, and his arm was wrapped tightly around her waist—which was fortunate, as without it she would have rolled onto the floor. Hester shifted slightly and experienced the arousing sensation of having her sleep-warmed skin rub cozily against his.

She'd never had a lover. A husband, yes, but her wedding night, her first initiation into womanhood, had been nothing like the night she'd just shared with Mitch. Was it fair to compare them? she wondered. Would she be human if she didn't?

That first night so long ago had been frenzied, complicated by her nerves and her husband's hurry. Last night the passion had built layer by layer, as though there'd been all the time in the world to enjoy it. She'd never known that making love could be so liberating. In truth, she hadn't known a man could sincerely want to give pleasure as much as he desired to take it.

She snuggled into the pillow and watched the thin winter light come through the windows. Would things be different this morning? Would there be an awkwardness between them or, worse, a casualness that would diminish the depth of what they'd shared? The simple fact was she didn't know what it was like to have a lover—or to be one.

She was putting too much emphasis on one evening, she told herself, sighing. How could she not, when the evening had been so special?

Hester touched a hand to his, let it linger a moment, then shifted to rise. Mitch's arm clamped down.

"Going somewhere?"

She tried to turn over, but discovered his legs had pinned her. "It's almost nine."

"So?" His fingers spread out lazily to stroke.

"I have to get up. I need to pick Rad up in a couple of hours."

"Hmmm." He watched his little dream bubble of a morning in bed with her deflate, then reconstructed it to fit two hours. "You feel so good." He released his hold, but only so he could turn her around so they were face-to-face. "Look good, too," he decided as he studied her face through half-closed eyes. "And taste"—he touched his lips to hers, and there was nothing awkward, nothing casual—"wonderful. Imagine this." He ran a hand down her flank. "We're on an island—the South Seas, let's say. The ship was wrecked a week ago, and we're the only survivors." His eyes closed as he pressed a kiss to her forehead. "We've been living on fruit and the fish I cleverly catch with my pointed stick."

"Who cleans them?"

"This is a fantasy; you don't worry about details like that. Last night there was a storm—a big, busting tropical storm—and we had to huddle together for warmth and safety under the lean-to I built."

"You built?" Her lips curved against his. "Do I do anything useful?"

"You can do all you want in your own fantasy. Now shut up." He snuggled closer and could almost smell the salt air. "It's morning, and the storm washed everything clean. There are gulls swooping down near the surf. We're lying together on an old blanket."

"Which you heroically salvaged from the wreck."

"Now you're catching on. When we wake up, we discover we'd tangled together during the night, drawn together despite ourselves. The sun's hot—it's already warmed our half-naked bodies. Still dazed with sleep, already aroused, we come together. And then . . ." His lips hovered a breath away from hers. Hester let her eyes close as she found herself caught up in the picture he painted. "And then a wild boar attacks, and I have to wrestle him."

"Half naked and unarmed?"

"That's right. I'm badly bitten, but I kill him with my bare hands."

Hester opened her eyes again to narrow slits. "And while you're doing that, I put the blanket over my head and whimper."

"Okay." Mitch kissed the tip of her nose. "But afterward you're very, very grateful that I saved your life."

"Poor, defenseless female that I am."

"That's the ticket. You're so grateful you tear the rags of your skirt to make bandages for my wounds, and then . . ." He paused for impact. "You make me coffee."

Hester drew back, not certain whether to be amazed or amused. "You went through that whole scenario so I'd offer to make you coffee?"

"Not just coffee, morning coffee, the first cup of coffee. Life's blood."

"I'd have made it even without the story."

"Yeah, but did you like the story?"

She combed the hair away from her face as she considered. "Next time I get to catch the fish."

"Deal."

She rose and, though she knew it was foolish, wished that she'd had her robe within arm's reach. Going to the closet, she slipped it on with her back still to him. "Do you want some breakfast?"

He was sitting up, rubbing his hands over his face when she turned. "Breakfast? You mean likes eggs or something? Hot food?" The only time he managed a hot breakfast was when he had the energy to drag himself to the corner diner. "Mrs. Wallace, for a hot breakfast you can have the crown jewels of Perth."

"All that for bacon and eggs?"

"Bacon, too? God, what a woman."

She laughed, sure he was joking. "Go ahead and get a shower if you want. It won't take long."

He hadn't been joking. Mitch watched her walk from the room and shook his head. He didn't expect a woman to offer to cook for him, or for one to offer as though he had a right to expect it. But this, he remembered, was the woman who would have sewed patches on his jeans because she'd thought he couldn't afford new ones.

Mitch climbed out of bed, then slowly, thoughtfully ran a hand through his hair. The aloof and professional Hester Wallace was a very warm and special woman, and he had no intention of letting her get away.

* * *

She was stirring eggs in a skillet when he came into the kitchen. Bacon was draining on a rack, and coffee was already hot. He stood in the doorway a moment, more than a little surprised that such a simple domestic scene would affect him so strongly. Her robe was flannel and covered her from neck to ankle, but to him Hester had never looked more alluring. He hadn't realized he'd been looking for this—the morning smells, the morning sounds of the Sunday news on the radio on the counter, the morning sights of the woman who'd shared his night moving competently in the kitchen.

As a child, Sunday mornings had been almost formal affairs—brunch at eleven, served by a uniformed member of the staff. Orange juice in Waterford, shirred eggs on Wedgwood. He'd been taught to spread the Irish linen on his lap and make polite conversation. In later years, Sunday mornings had meant a bleary-eyed search through the cupboards or a dash down to the nearest diner.

He felt foolish, but he wanted to tell Hester that the simple meal at her kitchen counter meant as much to him as the long night in her bed. Crossing to her, he wrapped his arms around her waist and pressed a kiss to her neck.

Strange how a touch could speed up the heart rate and warm the blood. Absorbing the sensation, she leaned back against him. "It's almost done. You didn't say how you liked your eggs, so you've got them scrambled with a little dill and cheese."

She could have offered him cardboard and told him to eat it with a plastic fork. Mitch turned her to face him and kissed her long and hard. "Thanks."

He'd flustered her again. Hester turned to the eggs in time to prevent them from burning. "Why don't you sit down?" She poured coffee into a mug and handed it to him. "With your life's blood."

He finished half the mug before he sat. "Hester, you know what I said about your legs?"

She glanced over as she heaped eggs on a plate. "Yes?"

"Your coffee's almost as good as they are. Tremendous qualities in a woman."

"Thanks." She set the plate in front of him before moving to the toaster.

"Aren't you eating any of this?"

"No, just toast."

Mitch looked down at the pile of golden eggs and crisp bacon. "Hester, I didn't expect you to fix me all this when you aren't eating."

"It's all right." She arranged a stack of toast on a plate. "I do it for Rad all the time."

He covered her hand with his as she sat beside him. "I appreciate it."

"It's only a couple of eggs," she said, embarrassed. "You should eat them before they get cold."

"The woman's a marvel," Mitch commented as he obliged her. "She raises an interesting and well-balanced son, holds down a demanding job, and cooks." Mitch bit into a piece of bacon. "Want to get married?"

She laughed and added more coffee to both mugs. "If it only takes scrambled eggs to get you to propose, I'm surprised you don't have three or four wives hidden in the closet."

He hadn't been joking. She would have seen it in his eyes if she'd looked at him, but she was busy spreading butter on toast. Mitch watched her competent, ringless hands a moment. It had been a stupid way to propose and a useless way to make her see he was serious. It was also too soon, he admitted as he scooped up another forkful of eggs.

The trick would be first to get her used to having him around, then to have her trust him enough to believe he would stay around. Then there was the big one, he mused as he lifted his cup. She had to need him. She wouldn't ever need him for the roof over her head or the food in her cupboards. She was much too self-sufficient for that, and he admired it. In time, she might come to need him for emotional support and companionship. It would be a start.

The courting of Hester would have to be both complex and subtle. He wasn't certain he knew exactly how to go about it, but he was more than ready to start. Today was as good a time as any.

"Got any plans for later?"

"I've got to pick up Rad around noon." She lingered over her toast, realizing it had been years since she had shared adult company over breakfast and that it had an appeal all its own. "Then I promised that I'd take him and Josh to a matinee. *The Moon of Andromeda*."

"Yeah? Terrific movie. The special effects are tremendous."

"You've seen it?" She felt a twinge of disappointment. She'd been wondering if he might be willing to come along.

"Twice. There's a scene between the mad scientist and the sane scientist that'll knock you out. And there's this mutant that looks like a carp. Fantastic."

"A carp." Hester sipped her coffee. "Sounds wonderful."

"A cinematic treat for the eyes. Can I tag along?"

"You just said you've seen it twice already."

"So? The only movies I see once are dogs. Besides, I'd like to see Rad's reaction to the laser battle in deep space."

"Is it gory?"

"Nothing Rad can't handle."

"I wasn't asking for him."

With a laugh, Mitch took her hand. "I'll be there to protect you. How about it? I'll spring for the popcorn." He brought her hand up to his lips. "Buttered."

"How could I pass up a deal like that?"

"Good. Look, I'll give you a hand with the dishes, then I've got to go down and take Taz out before his bladder causes us both embarrassment."

"Go on ahead. There isn't that much, and Taz is probably moaning at the door by this time."

"Okay." He stood with her. "But next time I cook."

Hester gathered up the plates. "Peanut butter and jelly?"

"I can do better than that if it impresses you."

She smiled and reached for his empty mug. "You don't have to impress me."

He caught her face in his hands while she stood with her hands full of dishes. "Yes, I do." He nibbled at her lips, then abruptly deepened the kiss until they were both breathless. She was forced to swallow when he released her.

"That's a good start."

He was smiling as he brushed his lips over her forehead. "I'll be up in an hour."

Hester stood where she was until she heard the door close, then quietly set the dishes down again. How in the world had it happened? she wondered. She'd fallen in love with the man. He'd be gone only an hour, yet she wanted him back already.

Taking a deep breath, she sat down again. She had to keep herself from overreacting, from taking this, as she took too many other things, too seriously. He was fun, he was kind, but he wasn't permanent. There was nothing permanent but her and Radley. She'd promised herself years ago that she would never forget that again. Now, more than ever, she had to remember it.

CHAPTER 9

"Rich, you know I hate business discussions before noon."
Mitch sat in Skinner's office with Taz snoozing at his feet. Though it was after ten and he'd been up working for a couple of hours, he hadn't been ready to venture out and talk shop. He'd had to leave his characters on the drawing board in a hell of a predicament, and Mitch imagined they resented being left dangling as much as he resented leaving them.

"If you're going to give me a raise, that's fine by me, but you could've waited until after lunch."

"You're not getting a raise." Skinner ignored the phone that rang on his desk. "You're already overpaid."

"Well, if I'm fired, you could definitely have waited a couple of hours."

"You're not fired." Skinner drew his brows together until they met above his nose. "But if you keep bringing that hound in here, I could change my mind."

"I made Taz my agent. Anything you say to me you can say in front of him."

Skinner sat back in his chair and folded hands that were swollen at the knuckles from years of nervous cracking. "You know, Dempsey, someone who didn't know you so well would think you were joking. The problem is, I happen to know you're crazy."

"That's why we get along so well, right? Listen, Rich, I've got Mirium trapped in a roomful of wounded rebels from Zirial. Being an empath, she's not feeling too good herself. Why don't we wrap this up so I can get back and take her to the crisis point?"

"Rebels from Zirial," Skinner mused. "You aren't thinking of bringing back Nimrod the Sorceror?"

"It's crossed my mind, and I could get back and figure out what he's got up his invisible sleeve if you'd tell me why you dragged me in here."

"You work here," Skinner pointed out.

"That's no excuse."

Skinner puffed out his cheeks and let the subject drop. "You know Two Moon Pictures has been negotiating with Universal for the rights to produce Zark as a full-length film?"

"Sure. That's been going on a year, a year and a half now." Since the wheeling and dealing didn't interest him, Mitch stretched out a leg and began to massage Taz's flank with his foot. "The last thing you told me was that the alfalfa sprouts from L.A. couldn't get out of their hot tubs long enough to close the deal." Mitch grinned. "You've got a real way with words, Rich."

"The deal closed yesterday," Rich said flatly. "Two Moon wants to go with Zark."

Mitch's grin faded. "You're serious?"

"I'm always serious," Rich said, studying Mitch's reaction. "I thought you'd be a little more enthusiastic. Your baby's going to be a movie star."

"To tell you the truth, I don't know how I feel." Pushing himself out of the chair, Mitch began to pace Rich's cramped office. As he passed the window, he pulled open the blinds to let in slants of hard winter light. "Zark's always been personal. I don't know how I feel about him going Hollywood."

"You got a kick out of when B. C. Toys made the dolls."

"Action figures," Mitch corrected automatically. "I guess that's because they stayed pretty true to the theme." It was silly, he knew. Zark didn't belong to him. He'd created him, true, but Zark belonged to Universal, just like all the other heroes and villains of the staff's fertile imaginations. If, like Maloney, Mitch decided to move on, Zark would stay behind, the responsibility of someone else's imagination. "Did we retain any creative leeway?"

"Afraid they're going to exploit your firstborn?"

"Maybe."

"Listen, Two Moon bought the rights to Zark because he has potential at the box office—the way he is. It wouldn't be smart businesswise to change him. Let's look at the bottom line—comics are big business. A hundred and thirty million a year isn't something to shrug off. The business is thriving now the way it hasn't since the forties, and even though it's bound to level off, it's going to stay hot. Those jokers on the coast might dress funny, but they know a winner when they see one. Still, if you're worried, you could take their offer."

"What offer?"

"They want you to write the screenplay."

Mitch stopped where he was. "Me? I don't write movies."

"You write Zark—apparently that's enough for the producers. Our publishers aren't stupid, either. Stingy," he added with a glance at his worn linoleum, "but not stupid. They wanted the script to come from in-house, and there's a clause in the contract that says we have a shot. Two Moon agreed to accept a treatment from you first. If it doesn't pan out, they still want you on the project as a creative consultant."

"Creative consultant." Mitch rolled the title around on his tongue.

"If I were you, Dempsey, I'd get myself a two-legged agent."

"I just might. Look, I'm going to have to think about it. How long are they giving me?"

"Nobody mentioned a time frame. I don't think the possibility of your saying no occurred to them. But then, they don't know you like I do."

"I need a couple of days. There's someone I have to talk to."

Skinner waited until he'd started out. "Mitch, opportunity doesn't often kick down your door this way."

"Just let me make sure I'm at home first. I'll be in touch."

When it rains it pours, Mitch thought as he and Taz walked. It had started off as a fairly normal, even ordinary new year. He'd planned to dig his heels in a bit and get ahead of schedule so that he could take three or four weeks off to ski, drink brandy and kick up some snow on his uncle's farm. He'd figured on meeting one or two attractive women on the slopes to make the evenings interesting. He'd thought to sketch a little, sleep a lot and cruise the lodges. Very simple.

Then, within weeks, everything had changed. In Hester he'd found everything he'd ever wanted in his personal life, but he'd only begun to convince her that he was everything she'd ever wanted in hers. Now he was being offered one of the biggest opportunities of his professional life, but he couldn't think of one without considering the other.

In truth, he'd never been able to draw a hard line of demarcation between his professional and personal lives. He was the same man whether he was having a couple of drinks with friends or burning the midnight oil with Zark. If he'd changed at all, it had been Hester and Radley who had caused it. Since he'd fallen for them, he wanted the strings he'd always avoided, the responsibilities he'd always blithely shrugged off.

So he went to her first.

Mitch strolled into the bank with his ears tingling from the cold. The long walk had given him time to think through everything Skinner had told him, and to feel the first twinges of excitement. Zark, in Technicolor, in stereophonic sound, in Panavision.

Mitch stopped at Kay's desk. "She had lunch yet?"

Kay rolled back from her terminal. "Nope."

"Anybody with her now?"

"Not a soul."

"Good. When's her next appointment?"

Kay ran her finger down the appointment book. "Two fifteen."

"She'll be back. If Rosen stops by, tell him I took Mrs. Wallace to lunch to discuss some refinancing."

"Yes, sir."

She was working on a long column of figures when Mitch opened the door. She moved her fingers quickly over the adding machine, which clicked as it spewed out a stream of tape. "Kay, I'm going to need Lorimar's construction estimate. And would you mind ordering me a sandwich? Anything as long as it's quick. I'd like to have these figures upstairs by the end of the day. Oh, and I'll need the barter exchange transactions on the Duberry account. Look up the 1099."

Mitch shut the door at his back. "God, all this bank talk excites me."

"Mitch." Hester glanced up with the last of the figures still rolling through her head. "What are you doing here?"

"Breaking you out, and we have to move fast. Taz'll distract the guards." He was already taking her coat from the rack behind the door. "Let's go. Just keep your head down and look natural."

"Mitch, I've got—"

"To eat Chinese takeout and make love with me. In whatever order you like. Here, button up."

"I've only half finished with these figures."

"They won't run away." He buttoned her coat, then closed his hands over her collar. "Hester, do you know how long it's been since we had an hour alone? Four days."

"I know. I'm sorry, things have been busy."

"Busy." He nodded toward her desk. "No one's going to argue with you there, but you've also been holding me off."

"No, I haven't." The truth was she'd been holding herself off, trying to prove to herself that she didn't need him as badly as it seemed. It hadn't been working as well as she'd hoped. There was tangible proof of that now as she stood facing him with her heart beating fast. "Mitch, I explained how I felt about . . . being with you with Radley in the apartment."

"And I'm not arguing that point, either." Though he would have liked to. "But Rad's in school and you have a constitutional right to a lunch hour. Come with me, Hester." He let his brow rest on hers. "I need you."

She couldn't resist or refuse or pretend she didn't want to be with him. Knowing she might regret it later, she turned her back on her work. "I'd settle for a peanut butter and jelly. I'm not very hungry."

"You got it."

Fifteen minutes later, they were walking into Mitch's apartment. As usual, his curtains were open wide so that the sun poured through. It was warm, Hester thought as she slipped out of her coat. She imagined he kept the thermostat up so that he could be comfortable in his bare feet and short-sleeved sweatshirts. Hester stood with her coat in her hands and wondered what to do next.

"Here, let me take that." Mitch tossed her coat carelessly

over a chair. "Nice suit, Mrs. Wallace," he murmured, finger-ing the lapel of the dark blue pinstripe.

She put a hand over his, once again afraid that things were moving too fast. "I feel . . ."

"Decadent?"

Once again, it was the humor in his eyes that relaxed her. "More like I've just climbed out my bedroom window at mid-night."

"Did you ever?"

"No. I thought about it a lot, but I could never figure out what I was supposed to do once I climbed down."

"That's why I'm nuts about you." He kissed her cautious smile and felt her lips soften and give under his. "Climb out the bedroom window to me, Hester. I'll show you what to do." Then his hands were in her hair, and her control scattered as quickly as the pins.

She wanted him. Perhaps it had a great deal to do with madness, but oh, how she wanted him. In the long nights since they'd been together like this, she'd thought of him, of how he touched her, where he touched her, and now his hands were there, just as she remembered. This time she moved faster than he, pulling his sweater up over his head to feast on the warm, taut flesh beneath. Her teeth nipped into his lip, insisting, inciting, until he was dragging the jacket from her and fumbling with the buttons that ranged down the back of her blouse.

His touch wasn't as gentle when he found her, nor was he as patient. But she had long since thrown caution aside. Now, pressed hard against him, she gripped passion with both hands. Whether it was day or night no longer mattered. She was where she wanted to be, where, no matter how she struggled to pretend otherwise, she needed to be.

Madness, yes, it was madness. She wondered how she'd lived so long without it.

He unfastened her skirt so that it flowed over her hips and onto the floor. With a groan of satisfaction he pressed his mouth to her throat. Four days? Had it only been four days? It seemed like years since he had had her close and alone. She was as hot and as desperate against him as he'd dreamed she would be. He could savor the feel of her even as desire clamped inside his gut and swam in his head. He wanted to spend hours touching, being touched, but the intensity of the moment, the lack of time and her urgent murmurs made it impossible.

"The bedroom," she managed as he pulled the thin straps of her lingerie over her shoulders.

"No, here. Right here." He fastened his mouth on hers and pulled her to the floor.

He would have given her more. Even though his own system was straining toward the breaking point, he would have given her more, but she was wrapped around him. Before he could catch his breath, her hands were on his hips, guiding him to her. She dug her fingers into his flesh as she murmured his name, and whole galaxies seemed to explode inside his head.

When she could think again, Hester stared at the dust motes that danced in a beam of sunlight. She was lying on a priceless Aubusson with Mitch's head pillowed between her breasts. It was the middle of the day, she had a pile of paperwork on her desk, and she'd just spent the better part of her lunch making love on the floor. She couldn't remember ever being more content.

She hadn't known life could be like this—an adventure, a carnival. For years she hadn't believed there was room for the madness of love and lovemaking in a world that revolved around responsibilities. Now, just now, she was beginning to realize she could have both. For how long, she couldn't be sure. Perhaps one day would be enough. She combed her fingers through his hair.

"I'm glad you came to take me to lunch."

"If this is any indication, we're going to have to make it a habit. Still want that sandwich?"

"Uh-uh. I don't need anything." But you. Hester sighed, realizing she was going to have to accept that. "I'm going to have to get back."

"You don't have an appointment until after two. I checked. Your barter exchange transactions can wait a few more minutes, can't they?"

"I suppose."

"Come on." He was up and pulling her to her feet.

"Where?"

"We'll have a quick shower, then I need to talk to you."

Hester accepted his offer of a robe and tried not to worry about what he had to say. She understood Mitch well enough to know he was full of surprises. The trouble was, she wasn't certain she was ready for another. Shoulders tense, she sat beside him on the couch and waited.

"You look like you're waiting for the blindfold and your last cigarette."

Hester shook back her hair and tried to smile. "No, it's just that you sounded so serious."

"I've told you before, I have my serious moments." He shoved magazines off the table with his foot. "I had some news today, and I haven't decided how I feel about it. I wanted to see what you thought."

"Your family?" she began, instantly concerned.

"No." He took her hand. "I guess I'm making it sound like bad news, and it's not. At least I don't think it is. A production company in Hollywood just cut a deal with Universal to make a movie out of Zark."

Hester stared at him a moment, then blinked. "A movie. Well, that's wonderful. Isn't it? I mean, I know he's very popular in comics, but a movie would be even bigger. You should be thrilled and very proud that your work can translate that way."

"I just don't know if they can pull it off, if they can bring him to the screen with the right tone, the right emotion. Don't look at me that way."

"Mitch, I know how you feel about Zark. At least I think I do. He's your creation, and he's important to you."

"He's real to me," Mitch corrected. "Up here," he said, tapping his temple. "And, as corny as it might sound, in here." He touched a hand to his heart. "He made a difference in my life, made a difference in how I looked at myself and my work. I don't want to see them screw him up and make him into some cardboard hero or, worse, into something infallible and perfect."

Hester was silent a moment. She began to understand that giving birth to an idea might be as life-altering as giving birth to a child. "Let me ask you something: why did you create him?"

"I wanted to make a hero—a very human one—with flaws and vulnerabilities, and I guess with high standards. Someone kids could relate to because he was just flesh and blood, but powerful enough inside to fight back. Kids don't have a hell of a lot of choices, you know. I remember when I was young I wanted to be able to say, 'No, I don't want to. I don't like that.' When I read, I could see there were possibilities, ways out. That's what I wanted Zark to be."

"Do you think you succeeded?"

"Yeah. On a personal level, I succeeded when I came up with the first issue. Professionally, Zark has pushed Universal to the top. He translates into millions of dollars a year for the business."

"Do you resent that?"

"No, why should I?"

"Then you shouldn't resent seeing him take the next step."

Mitch fell silent, thinking. He might have known Hester would see things more clearly and be able to cut through everything to the most practical level. Wasn't that just one more reason he needed her?

"They offered to let me do the screenplay."

"What?" She was sitting straight up now, eyes wide. "Oh, Mitch, that's wonderful. I'm so proud of you."

He continued to play with her fingers. "I haven't done it yet."

"Don't you think you can?"

"I'm not sure."

She started to speak, then caught herself. After a moment, she spoke carefully. "Strange, if anyone had asked, I would have said you were the most self-confident man I'd ever met. Added to that, I'd have said that you'd be much too selfish with Zark to let anyone else write him."

"There's a difference between writing a story line for a comic series and writing a screenplay for a major motion picture."

"So?"

He had to laugh. "Tossing my own words back at me, aren't you?"

"You can write, I'd be the first to say that you have a very fluid imagination, and you know your character better than anyone else. I don't see the problem."

"Screwing up is the problem. Anyway, if I don't do the script, they want me as creative consultant."

"I can't tell you what to do, Mitch."

"But?"

She leaned forward, putting her hands on his shoulders. "Write the script, Mitch. You'll hate yourself if you don't try. There aren't any guarantees, but if you don't take the risk, there's no reward, either."

He lifted a hand to hers and held it firmly as he watched her. "Do you really feel that way?"

"Yes, I do. I also believe in you." She leaned closer and touched her mouth to his.

"Marry me, Hester."

With her lips still on his, she froze. Slowly, very slowly, she drew away. "What?"

"Marry me." He took her hands in his to hold them still. "I love you."

"Don't. Please don't do this."

"Don't what? Don't love you?" He tightened his grip as she struggled to pull away. "It's a great deal too late for that, and I think you know it. I'm not lying when I tell you that I've never felt about anyone the way I feel about you. I want to spend my life with you."

"I can't." Her voice was breathless. It seemed each word she pushed out seared the back of her throat. "I can't marry you. I don't want to marry anyone. You don't understand what you're asking."

"Just because I haven't been there doesn't mean I don't know." He'd expected surprise, even some resistance. But he could see now he'd totally miscalculated. There was out-and-out fear in her eyes and full panic in her voice. "Hester, I'm not Allan, and we both know you're not the same woman you were when you were married to him."

"It doesn't matter. I'm not going through that again, and I won't put Radley through it." She pulled away and started to dress. "You're not being reasonable."

"*I'm not?*" Struggling for calm, he walked behind her and began to do up her buttons. Her back went rigid. "You're the one who's basing her feelings now on something that happened years ago."

"I don't want to talk about it."

"Maybe not, and maybe now's not the best time, but you're going to have to." Though she resisted, he turned her around. "We're going to have to."

She wanted to get away, far enough that she could bury everything that had been said. But for the moment she had to face it. "Mitch, we've known each other for a matter of weeks, and we've just begun to be able to accept what's happening between us."

"What *is* happening?" he demanded. "Aren't you the one who said at the beginning that you weren't interested in casual sex?"

She paled a bit, then turned away to pick up her suit jacket. "There wasn't anything casual about it."

"No, there wasn't, not for either of us. You understand that?"

"Yes, but—"

"Hester, I said I loved you. Now I want to know how you feel about me."

"I don't know." She let out a gasp when he grabbed her shoulders again. "I tell you I don't know. I think I love you. Today. You're asking me to risk everything I've done, the life I've built for myself and Rad, over an emotion I already know can change overnight."

"Love doesn't change overnight," he corrected. "It can be killed or it can be nurtured. That's up to the people involved. I want a commitment from you, a family, and I want to give those things back to you."

"Mitch, this is all happening too fast, much too fast for both of us."

"Damn it, Hester, I'm thirty-five years old, not some kid with hot pants and no brains. I don't want to marry you so I can have convenient sex and a hot breakfast, but because I know we could have something together, something real, something important."

"You don't know what marriage is like; you're only imagining."

"And you're only remembering a bad one. Hester, look at me. Look at me," he demanded again. "When the hell are you going to stop using Radley's father as a yardstick?"

"He's the only one I've got." She shook him off again and tried to catch her breath. "Mitch, I'm flattered that you want me."

"The hell with that."

"Please." She dragged a hand through her hair. "I do care about you, and the only thing I'm really sure of is that I don't want to lose you."

"Marriage isn't the end of a relationship, Hester."

"I can't think about marriage. I'm sorry." The panic flowed in and out of her voice until she was forced to stop and calm it. "If you don't want to see me anymore, I'll try to understand. But I'd rather . . . I hope we can just let things go on the way they are."

He dug his hands into his pockets. He had a habit of pushing too far too fast and knew it. But he hated to waste the time he could already imagine them having together. "For how long, Hester?"

"For as long as it lasts." She closed her eyes. "That sounds hard. I don't mean it to. You mean a great deal to me, more than I thought anyone ever would again."

Mitch brushed a finger over her cheek and brought it away wet. "A low blow," he murmured, studying the tear.

"I'm sorry. I don't mean to do this. I had no idea that you were thinking along these lines."

"I can see that." He gave a self-deprecating laugh. "In three dimensions."

"I've hurt you. I can't tell you how much I regret that."

"Don't. I asked for it. The truth is, I hadn't planned on asking you to marry me for at least a week."

She started to touch his hand, then stopped. "Mitch, can we just forget all this, go on as we were?"

He reached out and straightened the collar of her jacket. "I'm afraid not. I've made up my mind, Hester. That's something I try to do only once or twice a year. Once I've done it, there's no turning back." His gaze came up to hers with that rush of intensity she felt to the bone. "I'm going to marry you, sooner or later. If it has to be later, that's fine. I'll just give you some time to get used to it."

"Mitch, I won't change my mind. It wouldn't be fair if I let you think I would. It isn't a matter of a whim, but of a promise I made to myself."

"Some promises are best broken."

She shook her head. "I don't know what else to say. I just wish—"

He pressed his finger to her lips. "We'll talk about it later. I'll take you back to work."

"No, don't bother. Really," she said when he started to argue. "I'd like some time to think, anyway. Being with you makes that difficult."

"That's a good start." He took her chin in his hand and studied her face. "You look fine, but next time don't cry when I ask you to marry me. It's hell on the ego." He kissed her before she could speak. "See you later, Mrs. Wallace. Thanks for lunch."

A little dazed, she walked out into the hall. "I'll call you later."

"Do that. I'll be around."

He closed the door, then turned to lean back against it. Hurt? He rubbed a spot just under his heart. Damn right it hurt. If anyone had told him that being in love could cause the heart to twist, he'd have continued to avoid it. He'd had a twinge when his long-ago love in New Orleans had deserted him. It hadn't prepared him for this sledgehammer blow. What could possibly have?

But he wasn't giving up. What he had to do was figure out a plan of attack—subtle, clever and irresistible. Mitch glanced down at Taz consideringly.

"Where do you think Hester would like to go on our honeymoon?"

The dog grumbled, then rolled over on his back.

"No," Mitch decided. "Bermuda's overdone. Never mind, I'll come up with something."

CHAPTER 10

"Radley, you and your friends have to tone down the volume on the war, please." Hester took the measuring tape from around her neck and stretched it out over the wall space. Perfect, she thought with a satisfied nod. Then she took the pencil from behind her ear to mark two Xs where the nails would go.

The little glass shelves she would hang were a present to herself, one that was completely unnecessary and pleased her a great deal. She didn't consider the act of hanging them herself a show of competence or independence, but simply one more of the ordinary chores she'd been doing on her own for years. With a hammer in one hand, she lined up the first nail. She'd given it two good whacks when someone knocked on the door.

"Just a minute." She gave the nail a final smack. From Radley's bedroom came the sounds of antiaircraft and whistling missiles. Hester took the second nail out of her mouth and stuck it in her pocket. "Rad, we're going to be arrested for disturbing the peace." She opened the door to Mitch. "Hi."

The pleasure showed instantly, gratifying him. It had been two days since he'd seen her, since he'd told her he loved her and wanted to marry her. In two days he'd done a lot of hard thinking and could only hope that, despite herself, Hester had done some thinking too.

"Doing some remodeling?" he asked with a nod at the hammer.

"Just hanging a shelf." She wrapped both hands around the handle of the hammer, feeling like a teenager. "Come in."

He glanced toward Radley's room as she shut the door. It sounded as though a major air strike was in progress. "You didn't mention you were opening a playground."

"It's been a lifelong dream of mine. Rad, they've just signed a treaty—hold your fire!" With a cautious smile for Mitch, she waved him toward a chair. "Radley has Josh over today, and Ernie—Ernie lives upstairs and goes to school with Rad."

"Sure, the Bitterman kid. I know him. Nice," he commented as he looked at the shelves.

"They're a present for completing a successful month at National Trust." Hester ran a finger along a beveled edge. She really did want this more than a new outfit.

"You're on the reward program?"

"Self-reward."

"The best kind. Want me to finish that for you?"

"Oh?" She glanced down at the hammer. "Oh, no, thanks. I can do it. Why don't you sit down? I'll get you some coffee."

"You hang the shelf; I'll get the coffee." He kissed the tip of her nose. "And relax, will you?"

"Mitch." He'd taken only two steps away when she reached for his arm. "I'm awfully glad to see you. I was afraid, well, that you were angry."

"Angry?" He gave her a baffled look. "About what?"

"About . . ." She trailed off as he continued to stare at her in a half-interested, half-curious way that made her wonder if she'd imagined everything he'd said. "Nothing." She dug the nail out of her pocket. "Help yourself to the coffee."

"Thanks." He grinned at the back of her head. He'd done exactly what he'd set out to do—confuse her. Now she'd be thinking about him, about what had been said between them. The more she thought about it, the closer she'd be to seeing reason.

Whistling between his teeth, he strolled into the kitchen while Hester banged in the second nail.

He *had* asked her to marry him. She remembered everything he'd said, everything she'd said in return. And she knew that he'd been angry and hurt. Hadn't she spent two days regretting that she'd had to cause that? Now he strolled in as though nothing had happened.

Hester set down the hammer, then lifted the shelves. Maybe he'd cooled off enough to be relieved that she'd said no. That could be it, she decided, wondering why the idea didn't ease her mind as much as it should have.

"You made cookies." Mitch came in carrying two mugs, with a plate of fresh cookies balanced on top of one.

"This morning." She smiled over her shoulder as she adjusted the shelves.

"You want to bring that up a little on the right." He sat on the arm of a chair, then set her mug down so his hands would be free for the chocolate-chip cookies. "Terrific," he decided after the first bite. "And, if I say so myself, I'm an expert."

"I'm glad they pass." With her mind on her shelves, Hester stepped back to admire them.

"It's important. I don't know if I could marry a woman who made lousy cookies." He picked up a second one and examined it. "Yeah, maybe I could," he said as Hester turned slowly to stare at him. "But it would be tough." He devoured the second one and smiled at her. "Luckily, it won't have to be an issue."

"Mitch." Before she could work out what to say, Radley came barreling in, his two friends behind him.

"Mitch!" Delighted with the company, Radley screeched to a halt beside him so that Mitch's arm went naturally around his shoulders. "We just had the neatest battle. We're the only survivors."

"Hungry work. Have a cookie."

Radley took one and shoved it into his mouth. "We've got to go up to Ernie's and get more weapons." He reached for another cookie, then caught his mother's eye. "You didn't bring Taz up."

"He stayed up late watching a movie. He's sleeping in today."

"Okay." Radley accepted this before turning to his mother. "Is it okay if we go up to Ernie's for a while?"

"Sure. Just don't go outside unless you let me know."

"We won't. You guys go ahead. I gotta get something."

He raced back to the bedroom while his friends trooped to the door.

"I'm glad he's making some new friends," Hester commented as she reached for her mug. "He was worried about it."

"Radley's not the kind of kid who has trouble making friends."

"No, he's not."

"He's also fortunate to have a mother who lets them come around and bakes cookies for them." He took another sip of coffee. His mother's cook had baked little cakes. He thought Hester would understand it wasn't quite the same thing. "Of course, once we're married, we'll have to give him some brothers and sisters. What are you going to put on the shelf?"

"Useless things," she murmured, staring at him. "Mitch, I don't want to fight, but I think we should clear this up."

"Clear what up? Oh, I meant to tell you I started on the script. It's going pretty well."

"I'm glad." And confused. "Really, that's wonderful, but I think we should talk about this business first."

"Sure, what business was that?"

She opened her mouth and was once more interrupted by her son. When Radley came in, Hester walked away to put a small china cat on the bottom shelf.

"I made something for you in school." Embarrassed, Radley held his hands behind his back.

"Yeah?" Mitch set his coffee down. "Do I get to see it?"

"It's Valentine's Day, you know." After a moment's hesitation, he handed Mitch a card fashioned out of construction paper and blue ribbon. "I made Mom this heart with lace stuff, but I thought the ribbon was better for guys." Radley shuffled his feet. "It opens."

Not certain he could trust his voice, Mitch opened the card. Radley had used his very best block printing.

"To my best friend, Mitch. I love you, Radley." He had to clear his throat, and hoped he wouldn't make a fool out of himself. "It's great. I, ah, nobody ever made me a card before."

"Really?" Embarrassment faded with surprise. "I make them for Mom all the time. She says she likes them better than the ones you buy."

"I like this one a lot better," Mitch told him. He wasn't sure boys that were nearly ten tolerated being kissed, but he ran a hand over Radley's hair and kissed him anyway. "Thanks."

"You're welcome. See ya."

"Yeah." Mitch heard the door slam as he stared down at the little folded piece of construction paper.

"I didn't know he'd made it," Hester said quietly. "I guess he wanted to keep it a secret."

"He did a nice job." At the moment, he didn't have the capacity to explain what the paper and ribbon meant to him. Rising, he walked to the window with the card in his hands. "I'm crazy about him."

"I know." She moistened her lips. She did know it. If she'd

ever doubted the extent of Mitch's feelings for her son, she'd just seen full proof of it. It only made things more difficult. "In just a few weeks, you've done so much for him. I know neither one of us have the right to expect you to be there, but I want you to know it means a lot that you are."

He had to clamp down on a surge of fury. He didn't want her gratitude, but one hell of a lot more. Keep cool, Dempsey, he warned himself. "The best advice I can give you is to get used to it, Hester."

"That's exactly what I can't do." Driven, she went to him. "Mitch, I do care for you, but I'm not going to depend on you. I can't afford to expect or anticipate or rely."

"So you've said." He set the card down carefully on the table. "I'm not arguing."

"What were you saying before—"

"What did I say?"

"About when we were married."

"Did I say that?" He smiled at her as he wound her hair around his finger. "I don't know what I could have been thinking of."

"Mitch, I have a feeling you're trying to throw me off guard."

"Is it working?"

Treat it lightly, she told herself. If he wanted to make a game of it, she'd oblige him. "Only to the point that it confirms what I've always thought about you. You're a very strange man."

"In what context?"

"Okay, to begin with, you talk to your dog."

"He talks back, so that doesn't count. Try again." With her hair still wound around his finger, he tugged her a bit closer. Whether she realized it or not, they were talking about their relationship, and she was relaxed.

"You write comic books for a living. And you read them."

"Being a woman with banking experience, you should understand the importance of a good investment. Do you know what the double issue of my *Defenders of Perth* is worth to a collector? Modesty prevents me from naming figures."

"I bet it does."

He acknowledged this with a slight nod. "And, Mrs. Wallace, I'd be happy to debate the value of literature in any form with you. Did I mention that I was captain of the debating team in high school?"

"No." She had her hands on his chest, once again drawn to the tough, disciplined body beneath the tattered sweater. "There's also the fact that you haven't thrown out a newspaper or magazine in five years."

"I'm saving up for the big paper drive of the second millennium. Conservation is my middle name."

"You also have an answer for everything."

"There's only one I want from you. Did I mention that I fell for your eyes right after I fell for your legs?"

"No, you didn't." Her lips curved just a little. "I never told you that the first time I saw you, through the peephole, I stared at you for a long time."

"I know." He grinned back at her. "If you look in those things right, you can see a shadow."

"Oh," she said, and could think of nothing else to say.

"You know, Mrs. Wallace, those kids could come running back in here anytime. Do you mind if we stop talking for a few minutes?"

"No." She slipped her arms around him. "I don't mind at all."

She didn't want to admit even to herself that she felt safe, protected, with his arms around her. But she did. She didn't want to accept that she'd been afraid of losing him, terrified of the hole he would have left in her life. But the fear had been very real. It faded now as she lifted her lips to his.

She couldn't think about tomorrow or the future Mitch sketched so easily with talk of marriage and family. She'd been taught that marriage was forever, but she'd learned that it was a promise easily made and easily broken. There would be no more broken promises in her life, no more broken vows.

Feelings might rush through her, bringing with them longings and silver-dusted dreams. Her heart might be lost to him, but her will was still her own. Even as her hands gripped him tighter, pulled him closer, Hester told herself it was that will that would save them both unhappiness later.

"I love you, Hester." He murmured the words against her mouth, knowing she might not want to hear them but that it was something he had to say. If he said it enough, she might begin to believe the words and, more, the meaning behind them.

He wanted forever from her—forever for her—not just a moment like this, stolen in the sunlight that poured through the window, or other moments, taken in the shadows. Only once before had he wanted anything with something close to this intensity. That had been something abstract, something nebulous called art. The time had eventually come when he'd been forced to admit that dream would never be within reach.

But Hester was here in his arms. He could hold her like this and taste the sweet, warm longings that stirred in her. She wasn't a dream, but a woman he loved and wanted and would have. If keeping her meant playing games until the layers of her resistance were washed away, then he'd play.

He lifted his hands to her face, twining his fingers into her hair. "I guess the kids will be coming back."

"Probably." Her lips sought his again. Had she ever felt this sense of urgency before? "I wish we had more time."

"Do you?"

Her eyes were half closed as he drew away. "Yes."

"Let me come back tonight."

"Oh, Mitch." She stepped into his arms to rest her head on his shoulder. For the first time in a decade, she found the mother and the woman at war. "I want you. You know that, don't you?"

Her heart was still pumping hard and fast against his. "I think I figured it out."

"I wish we could be together tonight, but there's Rad."

"I know how you feel about me staying here with Rad in the next room. Hester . . ." He ran his hands up her arms to rest them on her shoulders. "Why not be honest with him, tell him we care about each other and want to be together?"

"Mitch, he's only a baby."

"No, he's not. No, wait," he continued before she could speak again. "I'm not saying we should make it seem casual or careless, but that we should let Radley know how we feel about each other, and when two grown people feel this strongly about each other, they need to show it."

It seemed so simple when he said it, so logical, so natural. Gathering her thoughts, she stepped back. "Mitch, Rad loves you, and he loves with the innocence and lack of restriction of a child."

"I love him, too."

She looked into his eyes and nodded. "Yes, I think you do, and if it's true, I hope you'll understand. I'm afraid that if I bring Radley into this at this point, he'll come to depend on you even more than he already does. He'd come to look at you as . . ."

"As a father," Mitch finished. "You don't want a father in his life, do you, Hester?"

"That's not fair." Her eyes, usually so calm and clear, turned to smoke.

"Maybe not, but if I were you, I'd give it some hard thought."

"There's no reason to say cruel things because I won't have sex with you when my son's sleeping in the next room."

He caught her by the shirt so fast she could only stare. She'd seen him annoyed, pushed close to the edge, but never furious. "Damn you, do you think that's all I'm talking about? If all I wanted was sex, I could go downstairs and pick up the phone. Sex is easy, Hester. All it takes is two people and a little spare time."

"I'm sorry." She closed her eyes, knowing she'd never said or done anything in her life she'd been more ashamed of. "That was stupid, Mitch; I just keep feeling as though my back's against the wall. I need some time, please."

"So do I. But the time I need is with you." He dropped his hands and stuck them in his pockets. "I'm pressuring you. I know it, and I'm not going to stop, because I believe in us."

"I wish I could, also, honestly I do, but there's too much at stake for me."

And for himself, Mitch thought, but was calm enough now to hold off. "We'll let it ride for a while. Are you and Rad up to hitting a few arcades in Times Square tonight?"

"Sure. He'd love it." She stepped toward him again. "So would I."

"You say that now, but you won't after I humiliate you with my superior skill."

"I love you."

He let out a long breath, fighting back the urge to grab her again and refuse to let go. "You going to let me know when you're comfortable with that?"

"You'll be the first."

He picked up the card Radley had made him. "Tell Rad I'll see him later."

"I will." He was halfway to the door when she started after him. "Mitch, why don't you come to dinner tomorrow? I'll fix a pot roast."

He tilted his head. "The kind with the little potatoes and carrots all around?"

"Sure."

"And biscuits?"

She smiled. "If you want."

"Sounds great, but I'm tied up."

"Oh." She struggled with the need to ask how but reminded herself she didn't have the right.

Mitch smiled, selfishly pleased to see her disappointment. "Can I have a rain check?"

"Sure." She tried to answer the smile. "I guess Radley told you about his birthday next week," she said when Mitch reached the door.

"Only five or six times." He paused, his hand on the knob.

"He's having a party next Saturday afternoon. I know he'd like you to come if you can."

"I'll be there. Look, why don't we take off about seven? I'll bring the quarters."

"We'll be ready." He wasn't going to kiss her goodbye, she thought. "Mitch, I—"

"I almost forgot." Casually he reached in his back pocket and pulled out a small box.

"What is it?"

"It's Valentine's Day, isn't it?" He put it in her hand. "So this is a Valentine's Day present."

"A Valentine's Day present," she repeated dumbly.

"Yeah, tradition, remember? I thought about candy, but I figured you'd spend a whole lot of time making sure Radley didn't eat too much of it. But look, if you'd rather have candy, I'll just take this back and—"

"No." She pulled the box out of his reach, then laughed. "I don't even know what it is."

"You'd probably find out if you open the box."

Flipping the lid, she saw the thin gold chain that held a heart no bigger than her thumbnail. It glittered with the diamonds that formed it. "Oh, Mitch, it's gorgeous."

"Something told me it'd be a bigger hit with you than candy. Candy would have made you think about oral hygiene."

"I'm not that bad," she countered, then lifted the heart out of the box. "Mitch, it's really beautiful, I love it, but it's too—"

"Conventional, I know," he interrupted as he took it from her. "But I'm just that kind of guy."

"You are?"

"Just turn around and let me hook it for you."

She obeyed, lifting one hand up under her hair. "I do love it, but I don't expect you to buy me expensive presents."

"Um-hmm." His brows were drawn together as he worked the clasp. "I didn't expect bacon and eggs, but you seemed to get a kick out of fixing them." The clasp secured, he turned her around to face him. "I get a kick out of seeing you wear my heart around your neck."

"Thank you." She touched a finger to the heart. "I didn't buy you any candy, either, but maybe I can give you something else."

She was smiling when she kissed him, gently, teasingly, with a power that surprised them both. It took only an instant, an instant to be lost, to need, to imagine. His back was to the door as he moved his hands from her face to her hair to her shoulders, then to her hips to mold her even more truly against him. The fire burned, hot and fast, so that even when she drew away he felt singed by it. With his eyes on hers, Mitch let out a very long, very slow breath.

"I guess those kids will be coming back."

"Any minute."

"Uh-huh." He kissed her lightly on the brow before he turned and opened the door. "See you later."

He would go down to get Taz, Mitch thought as he started down the hall. Then he was going for a walk. A long one.

* * *

True to his word Mitch's pockets were filled with quarters. The arcades were packed with people and echoed with the pings and whistles and machine-gun sound effects of the games. Hester stood to the side as Mitch and Radley used their combined talents to save the world from intergalactic wars.

"Nice shooting, Corporal." Mitch slapped the boy's shoulder as a Phaser II rocket disintegrated in a flash of colored light.

"It's your turn." Radley relinquished the controls to his superior officer. "Watch out for the sensor missiles."

"Don't worry. I'm a veteran."

"We're going to beat the high score." Radley tore his eyes away from the screen long enough to look at his mother. "Then we can put our initials up. Isn't this a neat place? It's got everything."

Everything, Hester thought, including some seamy-looking characters in leather and tattoos. The machine behind her let out a high-pitched scream. "Just stay close, okay?"

"Okay, Corporal, we're only seven hundred points away from the high score. Keep your eyes peeled for nuclear satellites."

"Aye, aye, sir." Radley clenched his jaw and took the controls.

"Good reflexes," Mitch said to Hester as he watched Radley control his ship with one hand and fire surface-to-air missiles with the other.

"Josh has one of those home video games. Rad loves to go over and play things like this." She caught her bottom lip between her teeth as Radley's ship barely missed annihilation. "I can never figure out how he can tell what's going on. Oh, look, he's passed the high score."

They continued to watch in tense silence as Radley fought bravely to the last man. As a finale, the screen exploded in brilliant fireworks of sound and light.

"A new record." Mitch hoisted Radley in the air. "This calls for a field promotion. Sergeant, inscribe your initials."

"But you got more points than I did."

"Who's counting? Go ahead."

Face flushed with pride, Radley clicked the button that ran through the alphabet. R.A.W. *A* for Allan, Mitch thought, and said nothing.

"My initials spell *raw*, and backward they spell *war*—pretty neat, huh?"

"Pretty neat," Mitch agreed. "Want to give it a shot, Hester?"

"No, thanks. I'll just watch."

"Mom doesn't like to play," Radley confided. "Her palms sweat."

"Your palms sweat?" Mitch repeated with a grin.

Hester sent a telling look in Radley's direction. "It's the pressure. I can't take being responsible for the fate of the world. I know it's a game," she said before Mitch could respond. "But I get, well, caught up."

"You're terrific, Mrs. Wallace." He kissed her as Radley looked on and considered.

It made him feel funny to see Mitch kiss his mother. He wasn't sure if it was a good funny or a bad funny. Then Mitch dropped a hand to his shoulder. It always made Radley feel nice when Mitch put his hand there.

"Okay, what'll it be next, the Amazon jungles, medieval times, a search for the killer shark?"

"I like the one with the ninja. I saw a ninja movie at Josh's

once—well, almost did. Josh's mom turned it off because one
of the women was taking her clothes off and stuff."

"Oh, yeah?" Mitch stifled a laugh as Hester's mouth
dropped open. "What was the name?"

"Never mind." Hester gripped Radley's hand. "I'm sure
Josh's parents just made a mistake."

"Josh's father thought it was about throwing stars and kung
fu. Josh's mom got mad and made him take it back to the
video place and get something else. But I still like ninjas."

"Let's see if we can find a free machine." Mitch fell into
step beside Hester. "I don't think he was marked for life."

"I'd still like to know what 'and stuff' means."

"Me, too." He swung an arm around her shoulders to steer
her through a clutch of teenagers. "Maybe we could rent it."

"I'll pass, thanks."

"You don't want to see *Naked Ninjas from Nagasaki?*"
When she turned around to stare at him, Mitch held out both
hands, palms up. "I made it up. I swear."

"Hmmm."

"Here's one. Can I play this one?"

Mitch continued to grin at Hester as he dug out quarters.

The time passed so that Hester almost stopped hearing
the noise from both machines and people. To placate Radley
she played a few of the less intense games, ones that didn't
deal with world domination or universal destruction. But for
the most part she watched him, pleased to see him enjoying
what was for him a real night on the town.

They must look like a family, she thought as Radley and
Mitch bent over the controls in a head-to-head duel. She
wished she still believed in such things. But to her, families
and lifetime commitments were as fanciful as the machines
that spewed out color and light around them.

Day to day, Hester thought with a little sigh. That was all

she could afford to believe in now. In a few hours she would tuck Radley in bed and go to her room alone. That was the only way to make sure they were both safe. She heard Mitch laugh and shout encouragement to Radley, and looked away. It was the only way, she told herself again. No matter how much she wanted or was tempted to believe again, she couldn't risk it.

"How about the pinball machines?" Mitch suggested.

"They're okay." Though they rang with wild colors and lights, Radley didn't find them terribly exciting. "Mom likes them though."

"Are you any good?"

Hester pushed aside her uneasy thoughts. "Not bad."

"Care to go one-on-one?" He jingled the quarters in his pockets.

Though she'd never considered herself highly competitive, she was swayed by his smug look. "All right."

She'd always had a touch for pinball, a light enough, quick enough touch to have beaten her brother nine times out of ten. Though these machines were electronic and more sophisticated than the ones she'd played in her youth, she didn't doubt she could make a good showing.

"I could give you a handicap," Mitch suggested as he pushed coins into the slot.

"Funny, I was just going to say the same thing to you." With a smile, Hester took the controls.

It had something to do with black magic and white knights. Hester tuned out the sounds and concentrated on keeping the ball in play. Her timing was sharp. Mitch stood behind her with his hands tucked in his back pockets and nodded as she sent the ball spinning.

He liked the way she leaned into the machine, her lips slightly parted, her eyes narrowed and alert. Now and then she would catch her tongue between her teeth and push her body forward as if to follow the ball on its quick, erratic course.

The little silver ball rammed into rubber, sending bells ringing and lights flashing. By the time her first ball dropped, she'd already racked up an impressive score.

"Not bad for an amateur," Mitch commented with a wink at Radley.

"I'm just warming up." With a smile, she stepped back.

Radley watched the progress of the ball as Mitch took control. But he had to stand on his toes to get the full effect. It was pretty neat when the ball got hung up in the top of the machine where the bumpers sent it vibrating back and forth in a blur. He glanced behind him at the rows of other machines and wished he' d thought to ask for another quarter before they'd started to play. But if he couldn't play, he could watch. He edged away to get a closer look at a nearby game.

"Looks like I'm ahead by a hundred," Mitch said as he stepped aside for Hester.

"I didn't want to blow you away with the first ball. It seemed rude." She pulled back the plunger and let the ball rip.

This time she had the feel and the rhythm down pat. She didn't let the ball rest as she set it right, then left, then up the middle where it streaked through a tunnel and crashed into a lighted dragon. It took her back to her childhood, when her wants had been simple and her dreams still gilt edged. As the machine rocked with noise, she laughed and threw herself into the competition.

Her score flashed higher and higher with enough fanfare to draw a small crowd. Before her second ball dropped, people were choosing up sides.

Mitch took position. Unlike Hester, he didn't block out the sounds and lights, but used them to pump the adrenaline. He nearly lost the ball, causing indrawn breaths behind him, but caught it on the tip of his flipper to shoot it hard into a corner. This time he finished fifty points behind her.

The third and final turn brought more people. Hester thought she heard someone placing bets before she tuned them out and put all her concentration on the ball and her timing. She was nearly exhausted before she backed away again.

"You're going to need a miracle, Mitch."

"Don't get cocky." He flicked his wrists like a concert pianist and earned a few hoots and cheers from the crowd.

Hester had to admit as she watched his technique that he played brilliantly. He took chances that could have cost him his last ball, but turned them into triumph. He stood spread-legged and relaxed, but she saw in his eyes that kind of deep concentration that she'd come to expect from him but had yet to become used to. His hair fell over his forehead, as careless as he was. There was a slight smile on his face that struck her as both pleased and reckless.

She found herself watching him rather than the ball as she toyed with the little diamond heart she'd worn over a plain black turtleneck.

This was the kind of man women dreamed about and made heroes of. This was the kind of man a woman could come to lean upon if she wasn't careful. With a man like him, a woman could have years of laughter. The defenses around her heart weakened a bit with her sigh.

The ball was lost in the dragon's cave with a series of roars.

"She got you by ten points," someone in the crowd pointed out. "Ten points, buddy."

"Got yourself a free game," someone else said, giving Hester a friendly slap on the back.

Mitch shook his head as he wiped his hands on the thighs of his jeans. "About that handicap—" he began.

"Too late." Ridiculously pleased with herself, Hester

hooked her thumbs in her belt loops and studied her score. "Superior reflexes. It's all in the wrist."

"How about a rematch?"

"I don't want to humiliate you again." She turned, intending to offer Radley the free game. "Rad, why don't you . . . Rad?" She nudged her way through the few lingering onlookers. "Radley?" A little splinter of panic shot straight up her spine. "He's not here."

"He was here a minute ago." Mitch put a hand on her arm and scanned what he could see of the room.

"I wasn't paying any attention." She brought a hand up to her throat, where the fear had already lodged, and began to walk quickly. "I know better than to take my eyes off him in a place like this."

"Stop." He kept his voice calm, but her fear had already transferred itself to him. He knew how easy it was to whisk one small boy away in a crowd. You couldn't pour your milk in the morning without being aware of it. "He's just wandering around the machines. We'll find him. I'll go around this way; you go down here."

She nodded and spun away without a word. They were six or seven deep at some of the machines. Hester stopped at each one, searching for a small blond boy in a blue sweater. She called for him over the noise and clatter of machines.

When she passed the big glass doors and looked outside to the lights and crowded sidewalks of Times Square, her heart turned over in her breast. He hadn't gone outside, she told herself. Radley would never do something so expressly forbidden. Unless someone had taken him, or . . .

Gripping her hands together tightly, she turned away. She wouldn't think like that. But the room was so big, filled with so many people, all strangers. And the noise, the noise was more deafening than she'd remembered. How could she have heard him if he'd called out for her?

She started down the next row, calling. Once she heard a young boy laugh and spun around. But it wasn't Radley. She'd covered half the room, and ten minutes were gone, when she thought she would have to call the police. She quickened her pace and tried to look everywhere at once as she went from row to row.

There was so much noise, and the lights were so bright. Maybe she should double back—she might have missed him. Maybe he was waiting for her now by that damn pinball machine, wondering where she'd gone. He might be afraid. He could be calling for her. He could be . . .

Then she saw him, hoisted in Mitch's arms. Hester shoved two people aside as she ran for them. "Radley!" She threw her arms around both of them and buried her face in his hair.

"He'd gone over to watch someone play," Mitch began as he stroked a hand up and down her back. "He ran into someone he knew from school."

"It was Ricky Nesbit, Mom. He was with his big brother, and they lent me a quarter. We went to play a game. I didn't know it was so far away."

"Radley." She struggled with the tears and kept her voice firm. "You know the rules about staying with me. This is a big place with a lot of people. I have to be able to trust you not to wander away."

"I didn't mean to. It was just that Ricky said it would just take a minute. I was coming right back."

"Rules have reasons, Radley, and we've been through them."

"But, Mom—"

"Rad." Mitch shifted the boy in his arms. "You scared your mother and me."

"I'm sorry," His eyes clouded up. "I didn't mean to make you scared."

"Don't do it again." Her voice softened as she kissed his

cheek. "Next time it's solitary confinement. You're all I've got, Rad." She hugged him again. Her eyes were closed so that she didn't see the change in Mitch's expression. "I can't let anything happen to you."

"I won't do it again."

All she had, Mitch thought as he set the boy down. Was she still so stubborn that she couldn't admit, even to herself, that she had someone else now too? He jammed his hands into his pockets and tried to force back both anger and hurt. She was going to have to make room in her life soon, very soon, or he'd damn well make it for her.

CHAPTER 11

He wasn't sure if he was doing more harm than good by staying out of Hester's way for a few days, but Mitch needed time himself. It wasn't his style to dissect and analyze, but to feel and act. However, he'd never felt quite this strongly before or acted quite so rashly.

When possible, he buried himself in work and in the fantasies he could control. When it wasn't, he stayed alone in his rooms, with old movies flickering on the television or music blaring through the stereo. He continued to work on the screenplay he didn't know if he could write, in the hope that the challenge of it would stop him from marching two floors up and demanding that Hester Wallace come to her senses.

She wanted him, yet she didn't want him. She opened to him, yet kept the most precious part of her closed. She trusted him, yet didn't believe in him enough to share her life with him.

You're all I've got, Rad. And all she wanted? Mitch was forced to ask himself the question. How could such a bright, giving woman base the rest of her life on a mistake she'd made over ten years before?

The helplessness of it infuriated him. Even when he'd hit bottom in New Orleans, he hadn't been helpless. He'd faced his limitations, accepted them, and had channeled his talents differently. Had the time come for him to face and accept his limitations with Hester?

He spent hours thinking about it, considering compromises and then rejecting them. Could he do as she asked and leave things as they were? They would be lovers, with no promises between them and no talk of a future. They could have a relationship as long as there was no hint of permanency or bonds. No, he couldn't do as she asked. Now that he had found the only woman he wanted in his life, he couldn't accept her either part-time or partway.

It was something of a shock to discover he was such an advocate of marriage. He couldn't say that he'd seen very many that had been made in heaven. His parents had been well suited—the same tastes, the same class, the same outlook—but he couldn't remember ever witnessing any passion between them. Affection and loyalty, yes, and a united front against their son's ambitions, but they lacked the spark and simmer that added excitement.

He asked himself if it was only passion he felt for Hester, but knew the answer already. Even as he sat alone, he could imagine them twenty years in the future, sitting on the porch swing she'd described. He could see them growing older together, filing away memories and traditions.

He wasn't going to lose that. However long it took, however many walls he had to scale, he wasn't going to lose that.

Mitch dragged a hand through his hair, then gathered up the boxes he needed to lug upstairs.

* * *

She was afraid he wasn't coming. There had been some subtle change in Mitch since the night they'd gone to Times Square. He'd been strangely distant on the phone, and though she'd invited him up more than once, he'd always made an excuse.

She was losing him. Hester poured punch into paper cups and reminded herself that she'd known it was only temporary. He had the right to live his own life, to go his own way. She could hardly expect him to tolerate the distance she felt she had to put between them or to understand the lack of time and attention she could give him because of Radley and her job. All she could hope was that he would remain a friend.

Oh, God, she missed him. She missed having him to talk to, to laugh with, even to lean on though she could only allow herself to lean a little. Hester set the pitcher on the counter and took a deep breath. It couldn't matter; she couldn't *let* it matter now. There were ten excited and noisy boys in the other room. Her responsibility, she reminded herself. She couldn't stand here listing her regrets when she had obligations.

As she carried the tray of drinks into the living room, two boys shot by her. Three more were wrestling on the floor, while the others shouted to be heard over the record player. Hester had already noted that one of Radley's newest friends wore a silver earring and spoke knowledgeably about girls. She set the tray down and glanced quickly at the ceiling.

Give me a few more years of comic books and Erector sets. Please, I'm just not ready for the rest of it yet.

"Drink break," she said out loud. "Michael, why don't you let Ernie out of that headlock now and have some punch? Rad, set down the kitten. They get cranky if they're handled too much."

With reluctance, Radley set the little bundle of black-and-white fur in a padded basket. "He's really neat. I like him the best." He snatched a drink off the tray as several other hands reached out. "I really like my watch, too." He held it out, pushing a button that sent it from time mode to the first in a series of miniature video games.

"Just make sure you don't play with it when you should be paying attention in school."

Several boys groaned and elbowed Radley. Hester had just about convinced them to settle down with one of Radley's board games when the knock sounded at the door.

"I'll get it!" Radley hopped up and raced for the door. He had one more birthday wish. When he opened the door, it came true. "Mitch! I knew you'd come. Mom said you'd probably gotten real busy, but I knew you'd come. I got a kitten. I named him Zark. Want to see?"

"As soon as I get rid of some of these boxes." Even arms as well toned as his were beginning to feel the strain. Mitch set them on the sofa and turned, only to have Zark's namesake shoved into his hands. The kitten purred and arched under a stroking finger. "Cute. We'll have to take him down and introduce him to Taz."

"Won't Taz eat him?"

"You've got to be kidding." Mitch tucked the kitten under his arm and looked at Hester. "Hi."

"Hi." He needed a shave, his sweater had a hole in the seam, and he looked wonderful. "We were afraid you wouldn't make it."

"I said I'd be here." Lazily he scratched between the kitten's ears. "I keep my promises."

"I got this watch, too." Radley held up his wrist. "It tells the time and the date and stuff, then you can play Dive Bomb and Scrimmage."

"Oh, yeah, Dive Bomb?" Mitch sat on the arm of the couch and watched Radley send the little dots spinning. "Never have to be bored on a long subway ride again, right?"

"Or at the dentist's office. You want to play?"

"Later. I'm sorry I'm late. I got hung up in the store."

"That's okay. We didn't have the cake yet 'cause I wanted to wait. It's chocolate."

"Great. Aren't you going to ask for your present?"

"I'm not supposed to." He sneaked a look at his mother, who was busy keeping some of his friends from wrestling again. "Did you really get me something?"

"Nah." Laughing at Radley's expression, he ruffled his hair. "Sure I did. It's right there on the couch."

"Which one?"

"All of them."

Radley's eyes grew big as saucers. "All of them?"

"They all sort of go together. Why don't you open that one first?"

Because of the lack of time and materials, Mitch hadn't wrapped the boxes. He'd barely had enough forethought to put tape over the name brand and model, but buying presents for young boys was a new experience, and one he'd enjoyed immensely. Radley began to pry open the heavy cardboard with assistance from his more curious friends.

"Wow, a PC." Josh craned his head over Radley's shoulder. "Robert Sawyer's got one just like it. You can play all kinds of things on it."

"A computer." Radley stared in amazement at the open box, then turned to Mitch. "Is it for me, really? To keep?"

"Sure you can keep it—it's a present. I was hoping you'd let me play with it sometime."

"You can play with it anytime, anytime you want." He threw his arms around Mitch's neck, forgetting to be embarrassed because his friends were watching. "Thanks. Can we hook it up right now?"

"I thought you'd never ask."

"Rad, you'll have to clear off the desk in your room. Hold it," Hester added when a flood of young bodies started by. "That doesn't mean shoving everything on the floor, okay? You take care of it properly, and Mitch and I will bring this in."

They streaked away with war whoops that warned her she'd be finding surprises under Radley's bed and under the rug for some time. She'd worry about that later. Now she crossed the room to stand beside Mitch.

"That was a terribly generous thing to do."

"He's bright. A kid that bright deserves one of these."

"Yes." She looked at the boxes yet to be opened. There'd be a monitor, disk drives, software. "I've wanted to get him one, but haven't been able to swing it."

"I didn't mean that as a criticism, Hester."

"I know you didn't." She gnawed at her lip in a gesture that told him her nerves were working at her. "I also know this isn't the time to talk, and that we have to. But before we take this in to Rad, I want to tell you how glad I am that you're here."

"It's where I want to be." He ran a thumb along her jawline. "You're going to have to start believing that."

She took his hand and turned her lips into his palm. "You might not feel the same way after you spend the next hour or so with ten fifth-graders." She smiled as the first minor crash sounded from Radley's bedroom. "'Once more unto the breach'?"

The crash was followed by several young voices raised in passionate argument. "How about, 'Lay on, MacDuff'?"

"Whatever." Drawing a deep breath, Hester lifted the first box.

*   *   *

It was over. The last birthday guest had been dragged away by his parents. A strange and wonderful silence lay over the living room. Hester sat in a chair, her eyes half closed, while Mitch lay sprawled on the couch with his closed completely. In the silence Hester could hear the occasional click of Radley's new computer and the mewing of Zark, who sat in his lap. With a contented sigh, she surveyed the living room.

It was in shambles. Paper cups and plates were strewn everywhere. The remains of potato chips and pretzels were in bowls, with a good portion of them crushed into the carpet. Scraps of wrapping paper were scattered among the toys the boys had decided worthy of attention. She didn't want to dwell on what the kitchen looked like.

Mitch opened one eye and looked at her. "Did we win?"

"Absolutely." Reluctantly, Hester dragged herself up. "It was a brilliant victory. Want a pillow?"

"No." Taking her hand, he flipped her down on top of him.

"Mitch, Radley is—"

"Playing with his computer," he finished, then nuzzled her bottom lip. "I'm betting he breaks down and puts some of the educational software in before it's over."

"It was pretty clever of you to mix those in."

"I'm a pretty clever kind of guy." He shifted her until she fit into the curve of his shoulder. "Besides, I figured I'd win you over with the machine's practicality, and Rad and I could play the games."

"I'm surprised you don't have one of your own."

"Actually . . . it seemed like such a good idea when I went in for Rad's that I picked up two. To balance my household accounts," he said when Hester looked up at him. "And modernize my filing system."

"You don't have a filing system."

"See?" He settled his cheek on her hair. "Hester, do you know what one of the ten greatest boons to civilization is?"

"The microwave oven?"

"The afternoon nap. This is a great sofa you've got here."

"It needs reupholstering."

"You can't see that when you're lying on it." He tucked his arm around her waist. "Sleep with me awhile."

"I really have to clean up." But she found it easy to close her eyes.

"Why? Expecting company?"

"No. But don't you have to go down and take Taz out?"

"I slipped Ernie a couple of bucks to walk him."

Hester snuggled into his shoulder. "You are clever."

"That's what I've been trying to tell you."

"I haven't even thought about dinner," she murmured as her mind began to drift.

"Let 'em eat cake."

With a quiet laugh, she slipped into sleep beside him.

Radley wandered in a few moments later, the kitten curled in his arms. He'd wanted to tell them about his latest score. Standing at the foot of the sofa, he scratched the kitten's ears and studied his mom and Mitch thoughtfully. Sometimes when he had a bad dream or wasn't feeling very good, his mom would sleep with him. It always made him feel better. Maybe sleeping with Mitch made his mom feel better.

He wondered if Mitch loved his mom. It made his stomach feel funny to think about it. He wanted Mitch to stay and be his friend. If they got married, did that mean Mitch would go away? He would have to ask, Radley decided. His mom always told him the truth. Shifting the kitten to one arm, he lifted the bowl of chips and carried it into his room.

* * *

It was nearly dark when she awoke. Hester opened her eyes and looked directly into Mitch's. She blinked, trying to orient herself. Then he kissed her, and she remembered everything.

"We must have slept for an hour," she murmured.

"Closer to two. How do you feel?"

"Groggy. I always feel groggy if I sleep during the day."

She stretched her shoulders and heard Radley giggling in his room. "He must still be at that computer. I don't think I've ever seen him happier."

"And you?"

"Yes." She traced his lips with her fingertip. "I'm happy."

"If you're groggy and happy, this might be the perfect time for me to ask you to marry me again."

"Mitch."

"No? Okay, I'll wait until I can get you drunk. Any more of that cake left?"

"A little. You're not angry?"

Mitch combed his fingers through his hair as he sat up. "About what?"

Hester put her hands on his shoulders, then rested her cheek on his. "I'm sorry I can't give you what you want."

He tightened his arms around her; then with an effort, he relaxed. "Good. That means you're close to changing your mind. I'd like a double-ring ceremony."

"Mitch!"

"What?"

She drew back and, because she didn't trust his smile, shook her head. "Nothing. I think it's best to say nothing. Go ahead and help yourself to the cake. I'm going to get started in here."

Mitch glanced around the room, which looked to be in pretty good shape by his standards. "You really want to clean this up tonight?"

"You don't expect me to leave this mess until the morning," she began, then stopped herself. "Forget I said that. I forgot who I was talking to."

Mitch narrowed his eyes suspiciously. "Are you accusing me of being sloppy?"

"Not at all. I'm sure there's a lot to be said for living in a 'junkyard' decor with a touch of 'paper drive' thrown in. It's uniquely you." She began to gather up paper plates. "It prob-ably comes from having maids as a child."

"Actually, it comes from never being able to mess up a room. My mother couldn't stand disorder." He'd always been fond of it, Mitch mused, but there was something to be said for watching Hester tidy up. "For my tenth birthday, she hired a magician. We sat in little folding chairs—the boys in suits, the girls in organdy dresses—and watched the performance. Then we were served a light lunch on the terrace. There were enough servants around so that when it was over there wasn't a crumb to be picked up. I guess I'm overcompensating."

"Maybe a little." She kissed both of his cheeks. What an odd man he was, she thought, so calm and easygoing on one hand, so driven by demons on the other. She strongly believed that childhood affected adulthood, even to old age. It was the strength of that belief that made her so fiercely determined to do the best she could by Radley. "You're entitled to your dust and clutter, Mitch. Don't let anyone take it away from you."

He kissed her cheek in return. "I guess you're entitled to your neat and tidy. Where's your vacuum?"

She drew back, brow lifted. "Do you know what one is?"

"Cute. Very cute." He pinched her, hard, just under the ribs. Hester jumped back with a squeal. "Ah, ticklish, huh?"

"Cut it out," she warned, holding out the stack of paper plates like a shield. "I wouldn't want to hurt you."

"Come on." He crouched like a wrestler. "Two falls out of three."

"I'm warning you." Wary of the gleam in his eye, she backed up as he advanced. "I'll get violent."

"Promise?" He lunged, gripping her under the waist. In re-flex, Hester lifted her arms. The plates, dripping with cake and ice cream, caught him full in the face. "Oh, God." Her own scream of laughter had her falling backward into a chair. She opened her mouth to speak but only doubled up again.

Very slowly Mitch wiped a hand over his cheek, then studied the smear of chocolate. Watching, Hester let out another peal of laughter and held her sides helplessly.

"What's going on?" Radley came into the living room staring at his mother, who could do nothing but point. Shifting his gaze, Radley stared in turn at Mitch. "Jeez." Radley rolled his eyes and began to giggle. "Mike's little sister gets food all over her face like that. She's almost two."

The control Hester had been scratching for slipped out of her grip. Choking with laughter, she pulled Radley against her. "It was—it was an accident," she managed, then collapsed again.

"It was a deliberate sneak attack," Mitch corrected. "And it calls for immediate retribution."

"Oh, please." Hester held out a hand, knowing she was too weak to defend herself. "I'm sorry. I swear. It was a reflex, that's all.".

"So's this." He came closer, and though she ducked behind Radley, Mitch merely sandwiched the giggling boy between them. And he kissed her, her mouth, her nose, her cheeks, while she squirmed and laughed and struggled. When he was finished, he'd transferred a satisfactory amount of chocolate to her face. Radley took one look at his mother and slipped, cackling, to the floor.

"Maniac," she accused as she wiped chocolate from her chin with the back of her hand.

"You look beautiful in chocolate, Hester."

* * *

It took more than an hour to put everything to rights again. By popular vote, they ended up sharing a pizza as they once had before, then spending the rest of the evening trying out

Radley's birthday treasures. When he began to nod over the keyboard, Hester nudged him into bed.

"Quite a day." Hester set the kitten in his basket at the foot of Radley's bed, then stepped out into the hall.

"I'd say it's a birthday he'll remember."

"So will I." She reached up to rub at a slight stiffness at the base of her neck. "Would you like some wine?"

"I'll get it." He turned her toward the living room. "Go sit down."

"Thanks." Hester sat on the couch, stretched out her legs and slipped off her shoes. It was definitely a day she would remember. Sometime during it, she'd come to realize that she could also have a night to remember.

"Here you go." Mitch handed her a glass of wine, then slipped onto the sofa beside her. Holding his own glass up, he shifted her so that she rested against him.

"This is nice." With a sigh, she brought the wine to her lips.

"Very nice." He bent to brush his lips over her neck. "I told you this was a great sofa."

"Sometimes I forget what it's like to relax like this. Everything's done, Radley's happy and tucked into bed, tomorrow's Sunday, and there's nothing urgent to think about."

"No restless urge to go out dancing or carousing?"

"No." She stretched her shoulders. "You?"

"I'm happy right here."

"Then stay." She pressed her lips together a moment. "Stay tonight."

He was silent. His hand stopped its easy massage of her neck, then began again, slowly. "Are you sure that's what you want?"

"Yes." She drew a deep breath before she turned to look at him. "I've missed you. I wish I knew what was right and what was wrong, what was best for all of us, but I know I've missed you. Will you stay?"

"I'm not going anywhere."

She settled back against him, content. For a long time they sat just as they were, half dreaming, in silence, with lamplight glowing behind them.

"Are you still working on the script?" she asked at length.

"Mmm-hmm." He could get used to this, he thought, very used to having Hester snuggled beside him in the late evening with the lamplight dim and the scent of her hair teasing his senses. "You were right. I'd have hated myself if I hadn't tried to write it. I guess I had to get past the nerves."

"Nerves?" She smiled over her shoulder. "You?"

"I've been known to have them, when something's either unfamiliar or important. They were stretched pretty thin the first time I made love with you."

Hearing it not only surprised her but made the memory of it all the sweeter. "They didn't show."

"Take my word for it." He stroked the outside of her thigh, lightly and with a casualness that was its own kind of seduction. "I was afraid that I'd make the wrong move and screw up something that was more important than anything else in my life."

"You didn't make any wrong moves, and you make me feel very special."

When she rose, it felt natural to hold out a hand to him, to have his close over hers. She switched off lights as they walked to the bedroom.

Mitch closed the door. Hester turned down the bed. He knew it could be like this every night, for all the years they had left. She was on the edge of believing it. He knew it; he could see it in her eyes when he crossed to her. Her eyes remained on his while she unbuttoned her blouse.

They undressed in silence, but the air had already started to hum. Though nerves had relaxed, anticipation was edgier than ever. Now they knew what they could bring to each other. They slipped into bed together and turned to each other.

It felt so right, just the way his arms slipped around her to bring her close. Just the way their bodies met, merging warmth to warmth. She knew the feel of him now, the firmness, the strength. She knew how easily hers fit against it. She tipped her head back and, with her eyes still on his, offered her mouth.

Kissing him was like sliding down a cool river toward churning white water.

The sound of pleasure came deep in his throat as she pressed against him. The shyness was still there, but without the reserve and hesitation. Now there was only sweetness and an offering.

It was like this each time they came together. Exhilarating, stunning and right. He cupped the back of her head in his hand as she leaned over him. The light zing of the wine hadn't completely faded from her tongue. He tasted it, and her, as she explored his mouth. He sensed a boldness growing in her that hadn't been there before, a new confidence that caused her to come to him with her own demands and needs.

Her heart was open, he thought as her lips raced over his throat. And Hester was free. He'd wanted this for her—for them. With something like a laugh, he rolled over her and began to drive her toward madness.

She couldn't get enough of him. She took her hands, her mouth, over him quickly, almost fiercely, but found it impossible to assuage the greed. How could she have known a man could feel so good, so exciting? How could she have known that the scent of his skin would make her head reel and her desires sharpen? Just her name murmured in his voice aroused her.

Locked together, they tumbled over the sheets, tangling in the blanket, shoving it aside because the need for its warmth was long past. He moved as quickly as she, discovering new secrets to delight and torment her. She heard him gasp out her name as she ranged kisses over his chest. She felt his body tense and arch as she moved her hands lower.

Perhaps the power had always been there inside her, but Hester was certain it had been born in her that night. The power to arouse a man past the civilized, and perhaps past the wise. Wise or not, she gloried in it when he trapped her beneath him and let desire rule.

His mouth was hot and hungry as it raced over her. Demands, promises, pleas swirled through her head, but she couldn't speak. Even her breath was trapped as he drove her up and up. She caught him close, as though he were a lifeline in a sea that raged.

Then they both went under.

CHAPTER 12

The sky was cloudy and threatening snow. Half dozing, Hester turned away from the window to reach for Mitch. The bed beside her was rumpled but empty.

Had he left her during the night? she wondered as she ran her hand over the sheets where he'd slept. Her first reaction was disappointment. It would have been so sweet to have had him there to turn to in the morning. Then she drew her hand back and cupped it under her cheek.

Perhaps it was best that he'd gone. She couldn't be sure how Radley would feel. If Mitch was there to reach out to, she knew it would only become more difficult to keep herself from doing so again and again. No one knew how hard and painfully she'd worked to stop herself from needing anyone. Now, after all the years of struggling, she'd just begun to see real progress. She'd made a good home for Radley in a good neighborhood and had a strong, well-paying job. Security, stability.

She couldn't risk those things again for the emotional morass that came with depending on someone else. But she was already beginning to depend on him, Hester thought as she pushed back the blankets. No matter how much her head told her it was best that he wasn't here, she was sorry he wasn't.

She *was* sorry, sorrier than he could ever know, that she was strong enough to stand apart from him.

Hester slipped on her robe and went to see if Radley wanted breakfast.

She found them together, hunched over the keyboard of Radley's computer while graphics exploded on the screen. "This thing's defective," Mitch insisted. "That was a dead-on shot."

"You missed by a mile."

"I'm going to tell your mother you need glasses. Look, this is definite interference. How am I supposed to concentrate when this stupid cat's chewing on my toes?"

"Poor sportsmanship," Radley said soberly as Mitch's last man was obliterated.

"Poor sportsmanship! I'll show you poor sportsmanship." With that he snatched Radley up and held him upside down. "Now is this machine defective, or what?"

"No." Giggling, Radley braced his hands on the floor. "Maybe *you* need glasses."

"I'm going to have to drop you on your head. You really leave me no choice. Oh, hi, Hester." With his arm hooked around Radley's legs, he smiled at her.

"Hi, Mom!" Though his cheeks were turning pink, Radley was delighted with his upside-down position. "I beat Mitch three times. But he's not really mad."

"Says who?" Mitch flipped the boy upright, then dropped him lightly on the bed. "I've been humiliated."

"I destroyed him," Radley said with satisfaction.

"I can't believe I slept through it." She offered them both a cautious smile. It didn't seem as though Radley was anything but delighted to find Mitch here. As for herself, she wasn't having an easy time keeping the pleasure down, either. "I suppose after three major battles you'd both like some breakfast."

"We already ate." Radley leaned over the bed to reach for the kitten. "I showed Mitch how to make French toast. He said it was real good."

"That was before you cheated."

"I did not." Radley rolled on his back and let the kitten creep up his stomach. "Mitch washed the pan, and I dried it. We were going to fix you some, but you just kept on sleeping."

The idea of the two men in her life fiddling in the kitchen while she slept left her flustered. "I guess I didn't expect anyone to be up so early."

"Hester," Mitch stepped closer to swing an arm over her shoulders. "I hate to break this to you, but it's after eleven."

"Eleven?"

"Yeah. How about lunch?"

"Well, I . . ."

"You think about it. I guess I should go down and take care of Taz."

"I'll do it." Radley was up and bouncing. "I can give him his food and take him for a walk and everything. I know how; you showed me."

"It's okay with me. Hester?"

She was having trouble just keeping up. "All right. But you'll have to bundle up."

"I will." He was already reaching for his coat. "Can I bring Taz back with me? He hasn't met Zark yet."

Hester glanced at the tiny ball of fur, thinking of Taz's big white teeth. "I don't know if Taz would care for Zark."

"He loves cats," Mitch assured her as he picked up Radley's ski cap off the floor. "In a purely nonthreatening way." He reached in his pocket for his keys.

"Be careful," she called as Radley rushed by, jingling Mitch's keys. The front door slammed with a vengeance.

"Good morning," Mitch said, and turned her into his arms.

"Good morning. You could have woken me up."

"It was tempting." He ran his hands up the back of her robe. "Actually, I was going to make some coffee and bring you in a cup. Then Radley came in. Before I knew it, I was up to my wrists in egg batter."

"He, ah, didn't wonder what you were doing here?"

"No." Knowing exactly how her mind was working, he kissed the tip of her nose. Then, shifting her to his side, he began to walk with her to the kitchen. "He came in while I was boiling water and asked if I was fixing breakfast. After a brief consultation, we decided he was the better qualified of the two. There's some coffee left, but I think you'd be better off pouring it out and starting again."

"I'm sure it's fine."

"I love an optimist."

She almost managed a smile as she reached in the refrigerator for the milk. "I thought you'd gone."

"Would you rather I had?"

She shook her head but didn't look at him. "Mitch, it's so hard. It just keeps getting harder."

"What does?"

"Trying not to want you here like this all the time."

"Say the word, and I'll move in, bag and dog."

"I wish I could. I really wish I could. Mitch, when I walked into Rad's bedroom this morning and saw the two of you together, something just clicked. I stood there thinking this is the way it could be for us."

"That's the way it *will* be for us, Hester."

"You're so sure." With a small laugh, she turned to lean her palms on the counter. "You're so absolutely sure and have been almost from the beginning. Maybe that's one of the things that frightens me."

"A light went on for me when I saw you, Hester." He came closer to put his hands on her shoulders. "I haven't gone through my life knowing exactly what I wanted, and I can't claim that everything always goes the way I'd planned, but with you I'm sure." He pressed his lips to her hair. "Do you love me, Hester?"

"Yes." With a long sigh, she shut her eyes. "Yes, I love you."

"Then marry me." Gently he turned her around to face him. "I won't ask you to change anything but your name."

She wanted to believe him, to believe it was possible to start a new life just once more. Her heart was thudding hard against her ribs as she wrapped her arms around him. *Take the chance*, it seemed to be telling her. *Don't throw love away.* Her fingers tensed against him. "Mitch, I—" When the phone rang, Hester let out a pent-up breath. "I'm sorry."

"So am I," he muttered, but released her.

Her legs were still unsteady as she picked up the receiver to the wall phone. "Hello." The giddiness fled and with it all the blossoming pleasure. "Allan."

Mitch looked around quickly. Her eyes were as flat as her voice. She'd already twisted the phone cord around her hand as if she wanted to anchor herself. "Fine," she said. "We're both fine. Florida? I thought you were in San Diego."

So he'd moved again, Hester thought as she listened to the familiar voice, restless as ever. She listened with the cold patience of experience as he told her how wonderful, how terrific, how incredibly he was doing.

"Rad isn't here at the moment," she told him, though Allan hadn't asked. "If you want to wish him a happy birthday, I can have him call you back." There was a pause, and Mitch saw her eyes change and the anger come. "Yesterday." She set her teeth, then took a long breath through them. "He's ten, Allan. Radley was ten yesterday. Yes, I'm sure it's difficult for you to imagine."

She fell silent again, listening. The dull anger lodged itself in her throat, and when she spoke again, her voice was hollow. "Congratulations. Hard feelings?" She didn't care for the sound of her own laugh. "No, Allan, there are no feelings whatsoever. All right, then, good luck. I'm sorry, that's as enthusiastic as it gets. I'll tell Radley you called."

She hung up, careful to bolt down the need to slam down the receiver. Slowly she unwound the cord which was biting into her hand.

"You okay?"

She nodded and walked to the stove to pour coffee she didn't want. "He called to tell me he's getting married again. He thought I'd be interested."

"Does it matter?"

"No." She sipped it black and welcomed the bitterness. "What he does stopped mattering years ago. He didn't know it was Radley's birthday." The anger came bubbling to the surface no matter how hard she tried to keep it submerged. "He didn't even know how old he was." She slammed the cup down so that coffee sloshed over the sides. "Radley stopped being real for him the minute he walked out the door. All he had to do was shut it behind him."

"What difference does it make now?"

"He's Radley's father."

"No." His own anger sprang out. "That's something you've got to work out of your system, something you've got to start accepting. The only part he played in Rad's life was biological. There's no trick to that, and no automatic bond of loyalty comes with it."

"He has a responsibility."

"He doesn't want it, Hester." Struggling for patience, he took her hands. "He's cut himself off from Rad completely. No one's going to call that admirable, and it's obvious it wasn't done for the boy's sake. But would you rather have him strolling in and out of Radley's life at his own whim, leaving the kid confused and hurting?"

"No, but I—"

"You want him to care, and he doesn't care." Though her hands remained in his, he felt the change. "You're pulling back from me."

It was true. She could regret it, but she couldn't stop it. "I don't want to."

"But you are." This time, it was he who pulled away. "It only took a phone call."

"Mitch, please try to understand."

"I've been trying to understand." There was an edge to his voice now that she hadn't heard before. "The man left you, and it hurt, but it's been over a long time."

"It's not the hurt," she began, then dragged a hand through her hair. "Or maybe it is, partly. I don't want to go through that ever again, the fear, the emptiness. I loved him. You have to understand that maybe I was young, maybe I was stupid, but I loved him."

"I've always understood that," he said, though he didn't like to hear it. "A woman like you doesn't make promises lightly."

"No, when I make them, I mean to keep them. I wanted to keep this one." She picked up the coffee again, wrapping both hands around the cup to keep them warm. "I can't tell you how badly I wanted to keep my marriage together, how hard I tried. I gave up part of myself when I married Allan. He told me we were going to move to New York, we were going to do things in a big way, and I went. Leaving my home, my family and friends was the most terrifying thing I'd ever done, but I went because he wanted it. Almost everything I did during our marriage I did because he wanted it. And because it was easier to go along than to refuse. I built my life around his. Then, at the age of twenty, I discovered I didn't have a life at all."

"So you made one, for yourself and for Radley. That's something to be proud of."

"I am. It's taken me eight years, eight years to feel I'm really on solid ground again. Now there's you."

"Now there's me," he said slowly, watching her. "And you just can't get past the idea that I'll pull the rug out from under you again."

"I don't want to be that woman again." She said the words desperately, searching for the answers even as she struggled to give them to him. "A woman who focuses all her needs and goals around someone else. If I found myself alone this time, I'm not sure I could stand up again."

"Listen to yourself. You'd rather be alone now than risk the fact that things might not work out for the next fifty years? Take a good look at me, Hester, I'm not Allan Wallace. I'm not asking you to bury yourself to make me happy. It's the woman you are today who I love, the woman you are today who I want to spend my life with."

"People change, Mitch."

"And they can change together." He drew a deep breath. "Or they can change separately. Why don't you let me know when you make up your mind what you want to do?"

She opened her mouth, then closed it again when he walked away. She didn't have the right to call him back.

* * *

He shouldn't complain, Mitch thought as he sat at his new keyboard and toyed with the next scene in his script. The work was going better than he'd expected—and faster. It was becoming easy for him to bury himself in Zark's problems and let his own stew.

At this point, Zark was waiting by Leilah's bedside, praying that she would survive the freak accident that had left her beauty intact but her brain damaged. Of course, when she awoke, she would be a stranger. His wife of two years would become his greatest enemy, her mind as brilliant as ever but warped and evil. All his plans and dreams would be shattered forever. Whole galaxies would be in peril.

"You think you've got problems?" Mitch muttered. "Things aren't exactly bouncing along for me, either."

Eyes narrowed, he studied the screen. The atmosphere was good, he thought as he tipped back. Mitch didn't have any problem imagining a twenty-third-century hospital room. He didn't have any trouble imagining Zark's distress or the madness brewing in Leilah's unconscious brain. What he did have trouble imagining was his life without Hester.

"Stupid." The dog at his feet yawned in agreement. "What I should do is go down to that damn bank and drag her out. She'd love that, wouldn't she?" he said with a laugh as he pushed away from the machine and stretched. "I could beg." Mitch rolled that around in his mind and found it uncomfortable. "I could, but we'd probably both be sorry. There's not much left after reasoning, and I've tried that. What would Zark do?"

Mitch rocked back on his heels and closed his eyes. Would Zark, hero and saint, back off? Would Zark, defender of right and justice, bow out gracefully? Nope, Mitch decided. When it came to love, Zark was a patsy. Leilah kept kicking astrodust in his face, but he was still determined to win her back.

At least Hester hadn't tried to poison him with nerve gas. Leilah had pulled that and more, but Zark was still nuts about her.

Mitch studied the poster of Zark he'd tacked to the wall for inspiration. We're in the same boat, buddy, but I'm not going to pull out the oars and start rowing, either. And Hester's going to find herself in some turbulent waters.

He glanced at the clock on his desk, but remembered it had stopped two days before. He was pretty sure he'd sent his watch to the laundry along with his socks. Because he wanted to see how much time he had before Hester was due home, he walked into the living room. There, on the table, was an old mantel clock that Mitch was fond enough of to remember to wind. Just as he glanced at it, he heard Radley at the door.

"Right on time," Mitch said when he swung the door open. "How cold is it?" He grazed his knuckles down Radley's cheek in a routine they'd developed. "Forty-three degrees."

"It's sunny," Radley said, dragging off his backpack.

"Shooting for the park, are you?" Mitch waited until Radley had folded his coat neatly over the arm of the sofa. "Maybe I can handle it after I fortify myself. Mrs. Jablanski next door made cookies. She feels sorry for me because no one's fixing me hot meals, so I copped a dozen."

"What kind?"

"Peanut butter."

"All right!" Radley was already streaking into the kitchen. He liked the ebony wood and smoked glass table Mitch had set by the wall. Mostly because Mitch didn't mind if the glass got smeared with fingerprints. He settled down, content with milk and cookies and Mitch's company. "We have to do a dumb state project," he said with his mouth full. "I got Rhode Island. It's the smallest state. I wanted Texas."

"Rhode Island." Mitch smiled and munched on a cookie. "Is that so bad?"

"Nobody cares about Rhode Island. I mean, they've got the Alamo and stuff in Texas."

"Well, maybe I can give you a hand with it. I was born there."

"In Rhode Island? Honest?" The tiny state took on a new interest.

"Yeah. How long do you have?"

"Six weeks," Radley said with a shrug as he reached for another cookie. "We've got to do illustrations, which is okay, but we've got to do junk like manufacturing and natural resources, too. How come you moved away?"

He started to make some easy remark, then decided to honor Hester's code of honesty. "I didn't get along with my parents very well. We're better friends now."

"Sometimes people go away and don't come back."

The boy spoke so matter-of-factly that Mitch found himself responding the same way. "I know."

"I used to worry that Mom would go away. She didn't."

"She loves you." Mitch ran a hand along the boy's hair.

"Are you going to marry her?"

Mitch paused in midstroke. "Well, I . . ." Just how did he handle this one? "I guess I've been thinking about it." Feeling ridiculously nervous, he rose to heat up his coffee. "Actually, I've been thinking about it a lot. How would you feel if I did?"

"Would you live with us all the time?"

"That's the idea." He poured the coffee, then sat down beside Radley again. "Would that bother you?"

Radley looked at him with dark and suddenly inscrutable eyes. "One of my friends' moms got married again. Kevin says since they did his stepfather isn't his friend anymore."

"Do you think if I married your mom, I'd stop being your friend?" He caught Radley's chin in his hand. "I'm not your friend because of your mom, but because of you. I can promise that won't change when I'm your stepfather."

"You wouldn't be my stepfather. I don't want one of those." Radley's chin trembled in Mitch's hand. "I want a real one. Real ones don't go away."

Mitch slipped his hands under Radley's arms and lifted him onto his lap. "You're right. Real ones don't." Out of the mouth of babes, he thought, and nuzzled Radley against him. "You know, I haven't had much practice being a father. Are you going to get mad at me if I mess up once in a while?"

Radley shook his head and burrowed closer. "Can we tell Mom?"

Mitch managed a laugh. "Yeah, good idea. Get your coat, Sergeant, we're going on a very important mission."

* * *

Hester was up to her elbows in numbers. For some reason, she was having a great deal of trouble adding two and two. It didn't seem terribly important anymore. That, she knew, was a sure sign of trouble. She went through files, calculated and assessed, then closed them again with no feeling at all.

His fault, she told herself. It was Mitch's fault that she was only going through the motions, and thinking about going through the same motions day after day for the next twenty years. He'd made her question herself. He'd made her deal with the pain and anger she'd tried to bury. He'd made her want what she'd once sworn never to want again.

And now what? She propped her elbows on the stack of files and stared into space. She was in love, more deeply and more richly in love than she'd ever been before. The man she was in love with was exciting, kind and committed, and he was offering her a new beginning.

That was what she was afraid of, Hester admitted. That was what she kept heading away from. She hadn't fully understood before that she had blamed herself, not Allan, all these years. She had looked on the breakup of her marriage as a personal mistake, a private failure. Rather than risk another failure, she was turning away her first true hope.

She said it was because of Radley, but that was only partly

true. Just as the divorce had been a private failure, making a full commitment to Mitch had been a private fear.

He'd been right, she told herself. He'd been right about so many things all along. She wasn't the same woman who had loved and married Allan Wallace. She wasn't even the same woman who had struggled for a handhold when she'd found herself alone with a small child.

When was she going to stop punishing herself? Now, Hester decided, picking up the phone. Right now. Her hand was steady as she dialed Mitch's number, but her heart wasn't. She caught her bottom lip between her teeth and listened to the phone ring—and ring.

"Oh, Mitch, won't we ever get the timing right?" She hung up the receiver and promised herself she wouldn't lose her courage. In an hour she would go home and tell him she was ready for that new beginning.

At Kay's buzz, Hester picked up the receiver again. "Yes, Kay."

"Mrs. Wallace, there's someone here to see you about a loan."

With a frown, Hester checked her calendar. "I don't have anything scheduled."

"I thought you could fit him in."

"All right, but buzz me in twenty minutes. I've got to clear some things up before I leave."

"Yes, ma'am."

Hester tidied her desk and was preparing to rise when Mitch walked in. "Mitch? I was just . . . What are you doing here? Rad?"

"He's waiting with Taz in the lobby."

"Kay said I had someone waiting to see me."

"That's me." He stepped up to the desk and set down a briefcase.

She started to reach for his hand, but his face seemed so

set. "Mitch, you didn't have to say you'd come to apply for a loan."

"That's just what I'm doing."

She smiled and settled back. "Don't be silly."

"Mrs. Wallace, you *are* the loan officer at this bank?"

"Mitch, really, this isn't necessary."

"I'd hate to tell Rosen you sent me to a competitor." He flipped open the briefcase. "I've brought the financial information usual in these cases. I assume you have the necessary forms for a mortgage application?"

"Of course, but—"

"Then why don't you get one out?"

"All right, then." If he wanted to play games, she'd oblige him. "So you're interested in securing a mortgage. Are you purchasing the property for investment purposes, for rental or for a business?"

"No, it's purely personal."

"I see. Do you have a contract of sale?"

"Right here." It pleased him to see her mouth drop open.

Taking the papers from him, Hester studied them. "This is real."

"Of course it's real. I put a bid on the place a couple of weeks ago." He scratched at his chin as if thinking back. "Let's see, that would have been the day I had to forgo pot roast. You haven't offered it again."

"You bought a house?" She scanned the papers again. "In Connecticut?"

"They accepted my offer. The papers just came through. I believe the bank will want to get its own appraisal. There is a fee for that, isn't there?"

"What? Oh, yes, I'll fill out the papers."

"Fine. In the meantime, I do have some snapshots and a blueprint." He slipped them out of the briefcase and placed them on her desk. "You might want to look them over."

"I don't understand."

"You might begin to if you look at the pictures."

She lifted them and stared at her fantasy house. It was big and sprawling, with porches all around and tall, wide windows. Snow mantled the evergreens beside the steps and lay stark and white on the roof.

"There are a couple of outbuildings you can't see. A barn, a henhouse—both unoccupied at the moment. The lot is about five acres, with woods and a stream. The real estate agent claims the fishing's good. The roof needs some work and the gutters have to be replaced, and inside it could use some paint or paper and a little help with the plumbing. But it's sound." He watched her as he spoke. She didn't look up at him, but continued to stare, mesmerized by the snapshots. "The house has been standing for a hundred and fifty years. I figure it'll hold up a while longer."

"It's lovely." Tears pricked the back of her eyes, but she blinked them away. "Really lovely."

"Is that from the bank's point of view?"

She shook her head. He wasn't going to make it easy. And he shouldn't, she admitted to herself. She'd already made it difficult enough for both of them. "I didn't know you were thinking of relocating. What about your work?"

"I can set up my drawing board in Connecticut just as easily as I can here. It's a reasonable commute, and I don't exactly spend a lot of time in the office."

"That's true." She picked up a pen, but rather than writing down the necessary information only ran it through her fingers.

"I'm told there's a bank in town. Nothing along the lines of National Trust, but a small independent bank. Seems to me someone with experience could get a good position there."

"I've always preferred small banks." There was a lump in her throat that had to be swallowed. "Small towns."

"They've got a couple of good schools. The elementary school is next to a farm. I'm told sometimes the cows get over the fence and into the playground."

"Looks like you've covered everything."

"I think so."

She stared down at the pictures, wondering how he could have found what she'd always wanted and how she could have been lucky enough that he would have cared. "Are you doing this for me?"

"No." He waited until she looked at him. "I'm doing it for us."

Her eyes filled again. "I don't deserve you."

"I know." Then he took both her hands and lifted her to her feet. "So you'd be pretty stupid to turn down such a good deal."

"I'd hate to think I was stupid." She drew her hands away to come around the desk to him. "I need to tell you something, but I'd like you to kiss me first."

"Is that the way you get loans around here?" Taking her by the lapels, he dragged her against him. "I'm going to have to report you, Mrs. Wallace. Later."

He closed his mouth over hers and felt the give, the strength and the acceptance. With a quiet sound of pleasure, he slipped his hands up to her face and felt the slow, lovely curve of her lips as she smiled.

"Does this mean I get the loan?"

"We'll talk business in a minute." She held on just a little longer, then drew away. "Before you came in, I'd been sitting here. Actually, I'd been sitting here for the last couple of days, not getting anything done because I was thinking of you."

"Go on, I think I'm going to like this story."

"When I wasn't thinking about you, I was thinking about myself and the last dozen years of my life. I've put a lot of energy into *not* thinking about it, so it wasn't easy."

She kept his hand in hers but took another step away. "I realize that what happened to me and Allan was destined to happen. If I'd been smarter or stronger, I would have been able to admit a long time ago that what we had could only be temporary. Maybe if he hadn't left the way he did . . ." She trailed off, shaking her head. "It doesn't matter now. That's the point I had to come to, that it just doesn't matter. Mitch, I don't want to live the rest of my life wondering if you and I could have made it work. I'd rather spend the rest of my life *trying* to make it work. Before you came in today with all of this, I'd decided to ask you if you still wanted to marry me."

"The answer to that is yes, with a couple of stipulations."

She'd already started to move into his arms, but drew back. "Stipulations?"

"Yeah, you're a banker, you know about stipulations, right?"

"Yes, but I don't look at this as a transaction."

"You better hear me out, because it's a big one." He ran his hands up her arms, then dropped them to his side. "I want to be Rad's father."

"If we were married, you would be."

"I believe stepfather's the term used in that case. Rad and I agreed we didn't go for it."

"Agreed?" She spoke carefully, on guard again. "You discussed this with Rad?"

"Yeah, I discussed it with Rad. He brought it up, but I'd have wanted to talk to him, anyway. He asked me this afternoon if I was going to marry you. Did you want me to lie to him?"

"No." She paused a moment, then shook her head. "No, of course not. What did he say?"

"Basically he wanted to know if I'd still be his friend, because he'd heard sometimes stepfathers change a bit once their foot's in the door. Once we'd gotten past that hurdle, he told me he didn't want me as a stepfather."

"Oh, Mitch." She sank down on the edge of the desk.

"He wants a real father, Hester, because real fathers don't go away." Her eyes darkened very slowly before she closed them.

"I see."

"The way I look at it, you've got another decision to make. Are you going to let me adopt him?" Her eyes shot open again with quick surprise. "You've decided to share yourself. I want to know if you're going to share Rad, all the way. I don't see a problem with me being his father emotionally. I just want you to know that I want it legally. I don't think there'd be a problem with your ex-husband."

"No, I'm sure there wouldn't be."

"And I don't think there'd be a problem with Rad. So is there a problem with you?"

Hester rose from the desk to pace a few steps away. "I don't know what to say to you. I can't come up with the right words."

"Pick some."

She turned back with a deep breath. "I guess the best I can come up with is that Radley's going to have a terrific father, in every way. And I love you very, very much."

"Those'll do." He caught her to him with relief. "Those'll do just fine." Then he was kissing her again, fast and desperate. With her arms around him, she laughed. "Does this mean you're going to approve the loan?"

"I'm sorry, I have to turn you down."

"What?"

"I would, however, approve a joint application from you and your wife." She caught his face in her hands. "Our house, our commitment."

"Those are terms I can live with"—he touched her lips

with his—"for the next hundred years or so." He swung her around in one quick circle. "Let's go tell Rad." With their hands linked, they started out. "Say, Hester, how do you feel about honeymooning in Disneyland?"

She laughed and walked through the door with him. "I'd love it. I'd absolutely love it."

From the *New York Times* bestselling author

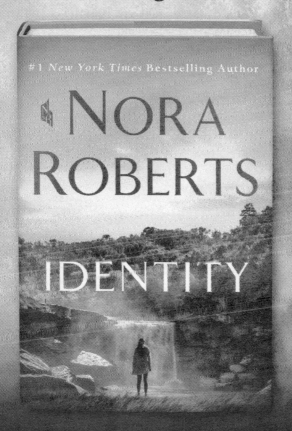

He stole her identity.
Now he wants her life.
How far will she go to take it back?

ST. MARTIN'S PRESS